The
PRICE of
MURDER

ALSO BY BRUCE ALEXANDER

Blind Justice

Murder in Grub Street

Watery Grave

Person or Persons Unknown

Jack, Knave and Fool

Death of a Colonial

The Color of Death

Smuggler's Moon

An Experiment in Treason

The
PRICE of
MURDER

※

B R U C E   A L E X A N D E R

G. P. PUTNAM'S SONS
NEW YORK

This is a work of fiction. Names, characters, places, and incidents either are the product of the author's imagination or are used fictitiously, and any resemblance to actual persons living or dead, business establishments, events, or locales is entirely coincidental.

ıllP

G. P. Putnam's Sons
Publishers Since 1838
a member of
Penguin Group (USA) Inc.
375 Hudson Street
New York, NY 10014

Library of Congress Cataloging-in-Publication Data

Alexander, Bruce, date.
The price of murder / Bruce Alexander.
p. cm.
ISBN 0-399-15078-1
1. Fielding, John, Sir, 1721–1780—Fiction. 2. London
(England)—Fiction.
3. Judges—Fiction. 4. Blind—Fiction. I. Title.

PS3553.O55314P75 2003   2003043224
813'.54—dc21

Printed in the United States of America
1   3   5   7   9   10   8   6   4   2

This book is printed on acid-free paper. ∞

For Merritt Moon

The
PRICE *of*
MURDER

ONE

*In which Sir John
is moved to fury at
the death of a child*

❧

I, who had recently become engaged to be engaged with Clarissa Roundtree, did walk with her on a Thursday morning in April 1774. We went hand in hand, as was her wish. Through the great market in Covent Garden we went. In the usual way of it, the "Garden," which it was most often called, was strong-smelling, crowded, and noisy. Greengrocers hawked the quality of their carrots and new potatoes. Ballad sellers sang their wares. All England, it seemed, had gathered there that they might make proper preparations for the coming Easter holiday.

As it happened, this year's Easter held special significance for Clarissa. She was quite determined that we publish our banns of marriage as soon as the Lenten season had passed.

"But Clarissa," said I, objecting, "what use is there publishing our banns when we cannot yet marry?"

"Oh Jeremy, you know far better than I that we *need* not be married after the banns are posted. It's simply that we *can* be married thereafter. We shall then be officially engaged."

"Yet what then is the use of being officially engaged when we shall not have money enough to marry for years to come?"

At that her face quite fell. "Years?" she echoed, as if having learned of this for the first time. It was always the same: she urging us forward, racing ahead, and I given the uncomfortable job of applying the brake. She knew the realities of our situation as well as I. Still, each time we discussed it, it seemed necessary to get her to admit that she knew what she knew.

I set about to do just that. Did I convince her? I doubted it. And she proved me right shortly thereafter by making me go through it all once again. Probably I did wrong by taking the same tack over and over. I did ever return to the matter of money. One could not marry if one had not enough of it to support a wife. That much seemed simple enough, did it not? Ah, but Clarissa was clever, for, each time she introduced the matter of marriage, she did so in some new way. This time, as an instance, she brought in the matter of the banns. What, I objected, was the use of posting banns if there could be no marriage for two years to come (when I should reach my majority and pass the bar)? Yet I understood her design well enough: she thought to marry me by degrees. Knowing full well that we could not be married till the banns first be posted, she meant to have that out of the way, so that she might then concentrate upon getting us before a priest. Much as I would have her—and have her at the soonest—I saw no way for it but to wait. I loved Clarissa dearly, yet I would not give up the career in the law that I dreamed of—no, not even for her.

Besides, what would Sir John and Lady Fielding say? They depended upon us now more than ever. We knew better than they that Molly Sarton, our cook, would soon be leaving them. She and Mr. Donnelly—surgeon, physician, and my great friend—would be married by the end of the year. Though Sir John and his lady were not privy to the information, as we were, they knew, or assumed, this was what lay in the near future for them. For this reason, Clarissa was being readied to take her place. Under Molly's cool supervision, she was learning her lessons well, yet in this week to come, she would be put to the test. Molly had agreed to hold a cooking class for the girls and women at Lady Fielding's Magdalene Home for Penitent Prostitutes. It had been agreed that Molly could not cook and teach simultaneous, and so it fell to Clarissa to do all that needed to be done at home, unsupervised and independent. Needless to say, this would include buying food for the family in the Garden. Thus had we set out together that morning—I to teach her where the best might be bought, and she to learn.

As for myself, it seemed that Sir John found more uses for me than ever before. First and most frequent, a magistrate, and most specially a *blind* magistrate (as he was), depended greatly upon his clerk, and Sir John's clerk, Mr. Marsden, was less and less dependable (and this through no fault of his own). Truth to tell, the clerk had never fully recovered himself following his bout with influenza late the year before. His lungs were the trouble, right enough. He wheezed and coughed and generally behaved as one not far from the grave. I did at first believe 'twas naught but a nasty catarrh which hung upon him all through the winter, and told myself that as spring approached he would improve. Yet he did not, and when I questioned Mr. Donnelly about it, he shook his head and said he thought it was something more serious, though he could not say exactly what it was. Then did he add: "If he would but give up that pipe of his, or at least cut down his smoking of it, he would be much improved." Yet, when I passed this on to Mr. Marsden, he laughed at me straightaway and said that life without the pipe would be no life at all. He must have missed a good quarter of his days beside Sir John, and who was there to take his place? None but your humble and obedient servant. In his absence, I discharged his duties as best I could and heard no complaint from Sir John Fielding. For myself, I quite enjoyed working in Mr. Marsden's stead. He knew something of the law, and I knew a great deal more. I specially liked interrogating the prisoners and the disputants before they were to have their time before the magistrate. It helped me ever after in the work of cross-examination.

Clarissa had been with me on earlier days during a number of my trips to the market. Yet there was then naught for her to learn upon such occasions, and she did simply hang on my arm and marvel at my ability to choose exactly the right vegetables for a stew. Today, of course, was different. She was here to discover all she might about how a potato got its "eyes" and what they, if sprouting, might portend; how to tell a tasty carrot from one that simply filled your belly; and what, if anything, a mushroom might tell you about its possibly poisonous nature. She was, in other words, learning all that she could from me in as short a time as possible. Thus did we spend the better part of an hour there in Covent Garden with no further talk of banns or marriage. 'Twas for me a blessed relief.

I believe we were at the stall of Mrs. Malter, who always seemed to have the best apples to be found in the Garden, when I happened to glance up and see before me a girl of sixteen or seventeen, who was staring quite intently at us. Who was she? She looked familiar to me, but in the course of the day, I saw so many in a city as large as London. Yet it was at Clarissa that she seemed to be staring and not at me. Then, as she began to move across the fifteen feet or so that separated us, I nudged Clarissa and nodded toward the unknown girl.

"Do you know her?" I asked. "She seems to know you."

Indeed she did. As Clarissa looked up, the girl saw her better, and, having her doubts thus removed, she fair flew at us, arms open wide.

"Elizabeth Hooker!" cried Clarissa. "Is it you, truly?"

"Clarissa!"

Then, arms wrapped so close round each other that they seemed as a single being, they danced before Mrs. Malter's stall, each talking at the other, neither able to hear for the noise she made.

It was quite unlike Clarissa to make such a spectacle of herself in a place so public. I knew not whether to attempt to pull them apart or to allow them simply to exhaust themselves then and there. At last, having run out of energy, they stopped, stared each at the other, and fell to laughing quite uproariously. The next few minutes were spent asking and answering questions. Both were from Lichfield. Each had come to London within months of the other (Elizabeth, I believe, had come later than Clarissa). Their fathers had died, and both girls had gone into service — Elizabeth as a kitchen slavey in the residence of Richard Turbott, silversmith, of Chandos Street; and Clarissa as a secretary and personal assistant (and, sometimes, maid and cook, as well) for Lady Fielding. The two made plans to visit the next day, since Miss Hooker had been given free the entire time from Friday to Monday, as the Turbotts would be out of town for Easter.

I listened as they reminisced, and I was interested enough in their two stories that I thought it merely amusing to note that in the excitement of their chance meeting they had quite forgotten me. Yet I was not to be long excluded from Clarissa's thoughts. Just as the two were about to part, she threw up her hands in dismay.

"Oh dear God," said she, "what could I have been thinking of? Elizabeth, you have not met Jeremy!"

"Jeremy?" Her friend turned to me with an amused smile upon her face. She saw the humor of it.

Clarissa, on the other hand, did not. "This is he," said she, grasping my arm and pulling me forward. "Jeremy Proctor, allow me to present you to my oldest and dearest friend, Elizabeth Hooker." This was accomplished with a great sense of dignity and brought to a conclusion with a most graceful gesture of the hand. Ah, well done, Clarissa!

So well done, in truth, that I thought to return her gallantry with a bit of my own. I bowed quite the grandest bow I have ever done. And Elizabeth, for her part, floated down into a curtsy which would have done honor to a duke. Then, of a sudden, applause burst forth on every side of us. We three looked round and saw we had attracted a crowd of onlookers—an audience, no less—and they showed their appreciation in the old-fashioned way. And why should they not? We had put on a bit of a show for them, had we not? We three had played at being gentle folk, as if upon the stage, and had had our efforts applauded. What fun! We felt so jolly that we did laugh as we bowed and curtsied our thanks to them (though not in a manner so grand as before). But already our audience had begun to drift away.

Clarissa and Elizabeth then said their goodbyes, and Clarissa promised faithfully to visit upon the afternoon of the next day. Yet then, as they parted, still waving as they backed away, Clarissa called after her friend, ran to her, and whispered in her ear. At that, Elizabeth's eyes widened; she looked at me and, giggling, ran off through the crowd.

"What was that all about?" I asked of Clarissa.

"What was what all about?"

"That last. What did you whisper to her?"

"Oh, *that*? Nothing much to it, really. I simply told her that we two are betrothed."

"That was a bit hasty, was it not?" said I. "It's *supposed* to be a secret."

"Well, it won't be after we have posted the banns."

You see, reader, what I had to contend with.

Having spent some time in Covent Garden, we had collected

two or three bags full of fruits and vegetables. Still, we had yet another stop to make, and probably the most important of all. Mr. Tolliver, our butcher and indeed the only one there in the Garden, was but two stalls down from Mrs. Malter's. He was busy that day, as he usually was, and, while waiting in line, I had the opportunity to enlighten and instruct Clarissa in his ways. He took care of each customer according to her needs (all were women), and so there was more than ample time to whisper to her of Mr. Tolliver's involvement with Lady Fielding before Sir John appeared and quite dazzled her with his knighthood. Since then, of course, things had gone well for the butcher. He had married, and married well—a widowed dressmaker from his home in Bristol, who earned money enough in her shop so that they might move from the two rooms in which they had begun their married life. They now lived in a modest house in the lower, respectable part of St. Martin's Lane.

"His only complaint today," I concluded, "is that his diligent and resourceful wife is apparently a bit too old to bear children. But then, if she were not, she would have the very devil of a time running her shop and cutting her copies of the latest in French fashions, with children all round."

I had spoken in such a quiet tone that I was reasonably certain that Mr. Tolliver had heard nothing. Indeed, I was certain of it when we stepped up before him.

He greeted me with a great smile and a wink. "Well, Jeremy," said he to me, "what shall I do for you today?" And then, before I could respond, he quietened me with this: "And who, pray tell, is that fine-looking young lady seekin' to hide herself behind you?"

With that, I introduced Clarissa to him, and told him that she would be coming round from time to time, doing the buying, when Molly or I were otherwise employed.

"And do you cook?" said he to her.

"I'm learning," said she.

"Well, that bein' the case, you'll wish to start with something simple. What about a nice stew—beef or mutton, either one."

"I've done both on a number of occasions, and it turned out well enough. So I thought, perhaps something a bit more demanding . . ."

"Something like a pot roast, you mean?"

"Something like that, yes. Have you the right meat for pot roast?"

"I do indeed," said he. "Here, let me show you."

And show her he did, hacking off a long corner of red from the side of beef that hung behind him. He then brought it over to show us.

"Now, what you want to do," he said, "is take this long piece here, roll it round and tie it so. Give it the better part of the afternoon in the oven with potatoes and carrots, and you'll have a fine pot roast for dinner."

"How will I tell when it's done?"

"I take it you'll be cooking this all by yourself? Molly won't be round to tell you how?"

She shook her head in the negative. "No," said she, "I'll be on my own this whole week or longer."

"Ah well, there's no problem that I can see. Just keep the heat up in the oven and sink a fork into it from time to time. When it goes in easy and comes up clean, you'll know it's right." Then he looked at her right sharp. "Now, what about tomorrow?" he asked.

"That's a question I can't now answer. I'll be back tomorrow, after I've given the matter some consideration."

"Fair enough," said he, "but just remember, the day after is a holiday, and you'll need to get here early—earlier than this."

She nodded solemnly and accepted the package he had wrapped for her.

To me, he said, "Shall I add it to your bill, or . . ."

"Put it on the bill," said I. Then did I take her arm and lead her away.

"Can we trust him?" Clarissa whispered to me. "I've heard tales of butchers adding half to a bill just for spite."

"You've naught to worry with Mr. Tolliver."

"Truly? He gave us no figure, after all. He could as well say that he sold us a pound's worth as a penny's."

"There's not a more honest man in Westminster."

Thus it was that we returned to Number 4 Bow Street. Entering by the door which led to that part behind Sir John's magistrate's court, we made our way to the stairs and were about to mount them when I heard Mr. Marsden's hoarse voice call my name. I urged Clarissa up the stairs and went to hear what he had to tell me. It was simply, as I supposed, that Sir John wished me to see him when I returned. Probably a letter to be taken in dictation, I told myself, or another to be picked up at the Post Coach House.

"Did he seem specially eager to see me? Worried? Angry? It's a question of whether I bring the groceries up before or after I report in to him."

"Well," said he, with a bit of a wheeze, "he didn't seem worried, exactly, but—" He coughed, then: "Not worried, exactly, but angry, I s'pose."

I sighed. "I'll go see him now."

Putting down the two bags of groceries which I had hauled back from Covent Garden, I trudged down the long hall to the magistrate's chambers. There I found him head bowed, pacing the floor before his desk. There was a space of no more than eight feet square, which he crossed and recrossed. He knew full well that if he were to venture farther in any direction, he would come crashing into a row of chairs. Though blind, he had memorized the room exactly. I held at the door, unwilling to interrupt his thoughts. I stood thus, waiting, for less than a minute. He stopped, turned, and faced the door.

"Well, what are you waiting for, Jeremy?" he demanded. "Come in, will you?"

I did as he bade and took a place upon one of the rear chairs, expecting him to retire to his desk. He did nothing of the kind but continued his pacing, saying nothing for some time. Then at last he did stop and turn in my direction.

"First of all, where were you? It's been near an hour since I put out the call for you."

"In Covent Garden, sir, showing Clarissa about and introducing her to one and another. She chose the makings of tonight's dinner."

"Oh . . . well, that's needful and necessary, I suppose, but dammit, lad, could you not have cut it short—or at least hurried things along just a bit?"

"Well, I—"

"Oh, never mind—but listen, 'twas near an hour ago that a little street urchin came running in, demanding to be heard. He'd been sent by a waterman at Billingsgate Stairs to report that he had pulled from the river the body of a child. A girl it was, of no more than six or seven years of age. I think it may be that one reported stolen by her mother a month ago. You recall, do you?"

"Oh, I recall," said I. "You pointed out to me that it was the second such disappearance that month. You said you suspected that they were being sold."

"Yes, but to what purpose? The earlier abduction was of a boy of about the same age. When kids are napped from the rich, they are held for a price. There was no demand for money in either case, nor would the parents be the sort you might hope to extort money from."

"Too poor?"

"By half." He sighed. "I recall my brother Henry talking of a series of kidnappings of adolescent children, yet they were shipped off to Jamaica and sold into slavery. But this was years ago, mind you, back in Jonathan Wild's time."

"The thief-taker general," said I.

"So he proclaimed himself."

"What will you have me do, Sir John?"

"I want you to collect the girl's corpus and bring it to Mr. Donnelly. You had better notify him before you go all the way to Billingsgate that we'll require his services as medical examiner this morning. If she died a violent death, I want to know about it—and quickly. Get on it, if you will, Jeremy."

"I will, sir." I rose from the chair which I had taken and started for the door.

"Oh, and Jeremy, do forgive my unhappy outburst when you did enter. I'd been awaiting you for a bit and had naught to listen to but Mr. Marsden's snuffling and coughing, and the woesome cries of drunks arrested the night before. In short, lad, I was impatient for your return. I could not, for the life of me, remember where you had gotten off to."

"Think nothing of it, sir," said I. "There can be no more said."

"Go then," said he. "Give me a report as soon as ever you can."

As I left him and started back down the long hall, it occurred to me for the first time ever that perhaps Sir John was, in some sense, growing old.

The Billingsgate Fish Market smelled, if it were possible, even worse than did the Smithfield Market. The offal of hoofed beasts gave off a thick and heavy smell, it's true. Nevertheless, the innards of sea creatures, most specially fish, stunk far worse. They were insidiously foul in a manner that can only be imagined as one might suppose hell might smell, and in the heat of the summertime could not even be imagined in such an approximation as that.

Billingsgate stands just off lower Thames Street, not far from London Bridge. 'Twas even before I reached the bridge that I smelled what lay ahead. Turning in at Billingsgate Dock, however, I found to my surprise that the deeper I penetrated the effluvium, the less I minded the odor. This may have been an actual, observable phenomenon, or it may have been because my attention was fully devoted to the closer handling required by the horses. (Yes, reader, I had, at last, learned from Mr. Patley, formerly of the King's Carabineers, the tricks of handling a wagon and team through the streets of London.) I had hardly got the two old nags turned round and properly placed when they began to balk and carry on. I could think of naught but the foul smell of death that would make them carry on so. At last I got them under control and safely hitched.

I made quickly for the stairs down to the river and descended to near water level. There were men grouped upon the platform, talking in low tones, discussing the bundle that lay at their feet. Undoubtedly, the child was wrapped within the blanket. I shouldered my way through them, begging their pardon as I went, until I came to the focus of their attention—a blanket-wrapped parcel of no particular shape and not much more than three feet in length.

"Is this the child found in the river?" I asked, looking round me at the glowering faces of the watermen.

"This be her," said one of them just opposite me. There came a chorus of "ayes" and affirmative grunts, giving confirmation.

"Who was it pulled her out?"

" 'Twas me," said the man who had answered my first query. He was in midlife, bearded, and wearing quite the most doleful expression that I had ever seen on the face of one in his work.

"Where did you pull her out?"

"Right here," said he. "I was first one round this morning, and I found her a-floatin' right here."

"Right here? I don't quite understand."

"Well, it's simple enough. She'd floated down near the mudbank and bumped into one of the boats — that one there. Her hair got tangled in the lines just enough to hold her till I got there."

"All right, now —"

"Just a minute," he interrupted. "Who are you, anyways?"

"Sir John Fielding sent me," said I. "You sent a boy to report this to the Bow Street Court, didn't you?"

"I did, right enough."

"Well, they sent me to pick up the body."

"You one of those Bow Street Runners I hear so much about?"

"No, I'm Sir John's assistant."

"Is that like a helper-outer?"

"That's close enough," said I. I noticed the rest of the men had stepped back and seemed to be regarding me with renewed respect. "Now, can we go on?"

"Yes, awright, I just wanted to know is all."

With that, I resumed my interrogation of the man. His name was Abel Bell, and he had been a waterman for better than fifteen years. He gave his address as one in Cheapside. He said that he reckoned every waterman had pulled at least one deader out of the Thames. This was his third. It had come about as he said: he was simply earliest upon the scene. I asked how long, in his estimation, she had been in the water. When he responded that he thought it was no more than a few hours — five or six at the most — I suggested that it was possible she had fallen off London Bridge.

"She didn't fall off no place," said the waterman.

"How can you be so certain?" I asked him.

"Well, one thing, she was nekkid when I found her. She wasn't walkin' London Bridge without no clothes on. You can be sure of that."

"I suppose not. Were there any marks of violence upon her? Wounds or bruises?"

"Nothing I could see."

"What about the blanket? Is it yours?"

"It's mine. Like I said, she was just plain nekkid in the water. I threw the bum blanket I had in the boat round her just to make her decent, poor child."

I sighed. "Well," I said, "perhaps you could give me a hand taking her up the stairs. I've a wagon up there."

"No, I'll carry her," said he. "It's the least I can do."

"Well, all right then. I'll thank you for it."

He picked her up carefully, keeping the blanket wrapped round her, as the group on the little pier made a path for us to the stairs. We climbed, but it was only when we reached the top that we met the stink of the dead fish, which were ranged in piles all the way to Thames Street. The wagon and team awaited us, the horses still restive but secure at the hitching post.

The waterman lifted the body carefully into the wagon bed and turned to me. "I said there wasn't no wounds nor nothin' upon her, but you'll find there's some raw places round her . . . well, down there in her privates. Maybe some fish fed upon her or maybe not. That's why I had her all wrapped up–like. I wanted to hide that."

"You want your blanket back? I could throw the tarpaulin over her."

"No, you keep it round her. My bum can go cold this day." He cleared his throat. "I'll leave you now."

With that, he turned and walked away, mumbling to himself. I'm sure that I heard the phrase "poor child" repeated. Nevertheless, it occurred to me that though the waterman and I had discussed the discovery of the body in all its aspects, I had not so much as taken a peek at the corpus itself. For all I knew, there could be a medium-sized dog bundled in the blanket. And so, once Abel Bell had disappeared down the steps, I unwrapped the head and took a look at the face of the dead girl. She was quite beautiful in death — though beautiful in the way of so many of her age: short-nosed, round-cheeked, and blond-haired. If you met her upon the street, you would not think her in any way unusual. Yet her early death conferred upon her a special quality, an air of pathos. Having taken but a brief look, I wrapped her face again and covered her over with the tarpaulin supplied by the livery stable. It bothered me a little that I could not remember the girl's name.

Once upon the table in Gabriel Donnelly's surgery, she had once again become no more than a thing—a dead thing, a body. As we did unwrap the bundle, I passed on to Mr. Donnelly the waterman's hesitant comments upon her condition.

"Where did he say?" asked the medico.

My embarrassed employment of euphemism had evidently communicated nothing to him. "I shall quote him exact," said I. "'There were raw places,' he called them, 'down there in her privates.'"

"Hmm, well, all right, let's have a look, shall we?"

That he proceeded to do—probing, inspecting, shaking his head, and, finally, letting forth a great groan of dismay.

"How old did you say this child was?"

"Six or seven seems to be the general consensus. Until her mother comes and claims the body, let that stand."

"From the look of her, she could be younger. But never mind that. Whether she's five, six, or seven, she'd had intercourse with a full-grown man—and probably far more often than once. That's hideous. The cause of death I'd give as an infection of the kidneys caused by the piercing of the walls of the vagina and the womb."

"Could you write that down, sir, so that I might present it to Sir John?"

"I certainly can and will," said he. "And you may tell him for me that I have never seen the like of it. Raw places indeed! The whole area was a mass of scabs. The water cleaned it off a bit and reveals it for the horror that it most certainly is."

He went straightaway to the wash stand and cleansed his hands well. Then did he sit down at the writing table and write his report to Sir John. I took it and ran down to the street. I jumped into the wagon, which I had hitched just outside Mr. Donnelly's surgery. In no more than a few minutes' time I was at Number 4 Bow Street.

There was this to say of Gabriel Donnelly's reports: He wrote them in plain, clear language. There was no mistaking the brutality which had been practiced upon the little girl. Poor child indeed! I had never known the magistrate to respond so violently or so immediately to any report which I had brought him. As soon as I had finished reading it to him, he jumped to his feet, stamped loud upon the floor, and shouted, full-voice: "But this is *monstrous*!"

Sir John raged on for minutes more—or so it seemed to me. I have found, as you may have also, reader, that it is difficult to judge time when the air about you is, of a sudden, filled with invective and fury. I could do little to persuade him to quieten his anger, for I felt also as he did. Still, I knew that we must get on with it now that it was to be a proper investigation. Perhaps, I thought, I might offer a suggestion. And so did I await the first gap in his tirading, cursing, and venting; and, finding it at last, I did jump in quickly to fill it.

"Sir John," said I, "would it not be opportune to search out the mother of the girl that you may question her further upon the details of her daughter's disappearance?"

He, now quite panting from his expense of anger, stood silent for a spell, red-faced and spent. Then, at last recovered, he turned toward me and nodded in the affirmative.

"Yes," said he, "that would be a good place to start. I quite agree, Jeremy. She must also identify the body. Get from Mr. Marsden her name and location, and bring her here to me. Do you recall who it was took the initial report?"

Though not entirely certain, I put forward the name of Mr. Patley, for I recalled discussing the matter with him. He had, as I remembered, certain doubts about the woman.

So it proved to be. Mr. Marsden took me to the small desk file of active cases which he kept, thumbed through it till he found the proper one, then pulled it from the drawer. He spread it out before us upon the desk.

"Here it is, as you see, Jeremy. Now, what was it you wished to know?"

"What her name might be, where she lives, that sort of thing. Sir John wants me to bring her in to ask some questions of her. The little girl died. They pulled her out of the river this morning."

"What a shame for the mother."

"What a shame for the little girl."

I copied down the necessary facts (Alice Plummer and daughter Margaret of Cucumber Alley), read quickly through the report, and noted that, indeed, it had been written by Mr. Patley. Then, with a stop at the livery stable that I might return the wagon and team, I made my way to the notorious Seven Dials area, just above Covent Garden. There she lived, somewhere in a rookery which faced onto the square—in Cucumber Alley, which was known to one and all as a place of ill fame.

It is well known and often said that Seven Dials is one of those parts of London which never close. Day or night are all the same to its denizens. Probably because most of them are so blindly drunk that they cannot tell the difference between sunshine and moonshine.

I knew I was getting closer to Cucumber Alley when I began to descry bottles in the gutter. Soon I spied the fellows who had dropped them there; slack-faced types they were, but sharp-eyed in spite of all. They looked to be the sort who, at night, would follow you into the alley or the rookery and knock you down for any valuables you might happen to have upon your person. My respect for Mr. Patley, who moved through these dark precincts quite fearlessly, grew greater with each step I took.

As I turned into the rookery, I held back before ever I stepped into the courtyard, lest I become the victim of some fellow awaiting me at the other end with a club in his hand. I stood for well over a minute in the short tunnel, listening for sounds of breathing, or the shifting of feet. There was nothing, and so I moved ahead. Coming out in the courtyard, I took a moment to count the doors behind which I must seek Alice Plummer who had, less than a month before, reported her daughter missing. A dozen, there was. There were neither names nor numbers upon the doors. It was evident that if I were to find the woman, it might be necessary to knock on each one.

'Twas a bootless task. Of the first half dozen I knocked upon, only two were answered. I wondered, would there be any point in knocking upon the rest? Well, putting my doubts behind me, I stepped up to door number seven and beat a harsh tattoo upon it. At first, I heard nothing at all, but then there were faint sounds stirring beyond the door, and a moment later, footsteps and a challenging shout.

"What do you want?"

It was a woman's voice, gruff and harsh, but, nonetheless, it was unmistakably that of a woman.

"I am come from the Bow Street Court in search of Alice Plummer," I shouted in return.

"Well, I ain't her."

"All right," said I, "but perhaps you could point out her door to me."

"Maybe I could do that."

"Well?"

There was a long moment's hesitation as the woman behind the door considered my proposal. Then did I hear her begin to throw off locks. Yet before she threw the last, she shouted at me once again.

"Now, you hear me now," said she, "before I throws this last lock, I want you to know I've a pistol here in my right hand. And if you're come to rob me, I'll shoot you down. I swear to God I will."

I knew not quite how to respond to that, and so I offered her the most pacific response I could imagine.

"If I misrepresented myself, you have my permission to shoot me."

At that the woman laughed—or rather, cackled—quite merrily. She pulled the last bolt, then opened the door a crack—just wide enough so that she might shove the barrel of the pistol through. Though I could not spy it, her eye must have been there, too; for, continuing to laugh, she threw the door open wide and we looked each the other up and down. She was plump and shy of forty, though not by much. Her hair was dyed a deep red, though what substance had been used to dye it I've no idea; it was, in any case, no natural color.

"Well," said she, "you look like a likely lad. Like to have your ashes hauled?"

I had no idea of what, exactly, was meant by that. Nevertheless, the look on her face made her general meaning clear.

"Uh, no," said I. "I am searching for Alice Plummer, as I said. She is the mother of the child who vanished near a month ago, a girl named Margaret, as I understand."

"She lived right next door of me, she and little Maggie. Alice ain't there anymore, though. She moved away just after Maggie disappeared, like."

That struck me as odd. "Moved away, you say? How would we know to make contact with her if the girl were found?"

"That ain't my problem, is it?"

"No, I suppose not."

This was most odd. Perhaps she had told Constable Patley of her intention to move and of her new location—and he had simply neglected to pass it on to Mr. Marsden. Yes, perhaps—but all the same, it was odd. I stood, pondering the matter there on the woman's doorstep, until I happened to note that she had become a bit restless: she wanted me gone.

"Just a question or two more," said I, hoping to hold her.

"Well, make it fast. I've not got all day."

"Fair enough. Who's living in her place now?"

"That's the peculiarest part," said she. "Ain't nobody living there, as near as I can judge. I've had my ear to the wall for near a month now, but I've not heard nothin' from next door. I saw her leave and gave her a wave goodbye. Last thing she said to me was, 'Katy, I'm goin' on a holiday, and I just might not ever come back.'"

"But then again, she might," I suggested.

"Might what?"

"Might come back."

"Oh. Well, maybe, I suppose. It's just, if I had all the money she's got, I wouldn't come back, and you can be sure of it."

All the money she's got? This was something new, wasn't it?

"When was this?" I asked.

"Well, it was the day after little Maggie disappeared. She didn't exactly *show* me all this money she had. She showed me her purse, though, and rattled it for me. I was just sure I heard guineas in there, along with bulls, neds, and bobsticks—all manner of His Majesty's coinage."

"Didn't that make you just a little suspicious?"

"Suspicious at what?"

"Suspicious that she may have . . . well, that she may have *sold* her daughter?"

"And what if she did? say I. Maggie was hers to sell, wasn't she?"

"That's not what the law says."

"Ah, well, the law," she sneered. "The law is for nobs and such."

"Well, you should know then, Mistress . . . Mistress . . . What *is* your name, anyway?"

She raised her chin and gave me a sharp look. "Katy Tiddle, if you will! Now, you tell me, what is this that I should know?"

And having made her demand, she raised the pistol she had pointed at me through the crack in the door and pointed it at me once again. And she did so most threateningly. Nevertheless, I noted that she had not pulled back the hammer on the pistol. I wondered if she could manage it; I wondered further if the pistol were loaded; and, finally, did I wonder if she had ever before fired such a weapon. If you judge from this that I was in no wise intimidated, then you judge the matter correctly.

"You should know," said I, "that young Maggie is dead. At least we think it's Maggie. I'd come here that I might collect Alice Plummer and bring her to the medico to identify the body there as Maggie's."

"Can't do that now, though," said she with a smirk, "can you?"

I noted that she had allowed the pistol barrel to droop, and she had not yet thought to draw back the hammer. And so, in one swift movement, I grasped the pistol and wrested it from her resisting hand.

"But you know her as a neighbor," said I, "so you'll do just as well. Come along."

Then did she not howl and yelp! She sounded as would a lowly cur in pain.

Indeed, she did carry on in this manner all the way to Drury Lane and Mr. Donnelly's surgery. Halfway to our destination, she did calm down sufficient to allow me to unhand her wrist and take her properly by the elbow. I would not release her completely, for I feared, with good cause, that she would dart into some dark warren at the earliest opportunity, and I might thus lose her altogether. Nevertheless, guiding her with a firm hand, I set a swift pace, and we were quickly cross the distance.

Somewhere along the way, it became evident that her objection had little to do with a loss of time, or some missed appointment. No, it was her mad fear of death—which is to say, her quite unreasoning revulsion from corpses in any condition. I assured her that Maggie Plummer's body and face had in no wise been ruined by her overnight sojourn in the Thames—all to no avail. It developed that it was not the condition of the body that disturbed her so mightily, but rather the mere fact of death. To be thus reminded of the fate that awaits us all was for her an experience utterly intolerable—or so she convinced me. Yet, tolerable or intolerable, she would nevertheless experience it when we did reach our destination, Mr. Donnelly's surgery.

When we did, we found the waiting room relatively empty. Only one, a woman of thirty or so, waited. Clearly a lady of quality, she sat high in her chair and attempted to take no notice of Katy Tiddle when we two came storming in from the hall. Yet she, on whom I kept my tight hold, was impossible to ignore. As near as I could tell, 'twas the peculiar red of Katy's hair which so fascinated the lady with whom we shared Mr. Donnelly's waiting room. Sitting across from her, it was quite impossible to miss the darting glances which she threw in our direction. Each one, it seemed, was aimed at the tangled mop of vermilion atop Katy's head. How had she managed such a color?

Without notice, the door to Mr. Donnelly's examination room opened, and out came a man of advanced age, wherewith the lady bounced quickly to her feet and stepped smartly to the hall door. Mr. Donnelly followed him out, murmuring something about the chemist's shop below. As the ill-matched couple left, the wife could not resist throwing one last look across the room. Katy Tiddle was waiting for her. She stuck out her tongue most impudently, surprising us all and propelling the gentleman and his lady out the door. Once they were safely gone, Mr. Donnelly could not withhold a chuckle or two.

"Who is she?" said he to me.

"Katy Tiddle is the name," said she before I could respond. "And if it was up to me, I'd be anywhere but here."

"She's come to identify the body," said I.

"Ah," said Mr. Donnelly, clearly a bit confused. "Not the mother, surely."

"The neighbor next door."

"Well, come along then."

He led the way back to the little apartment of rooms he kept behind the examination room. What we presumed to be the body of
Maggie Plummer lay upon a table in the first of the two. A sheet
covered her from head to toe. I glanced over at Katy Tiddle and saw
that she had her eyes tight shut.

"What will you, Katy?" said I, chastising. "You must open your
eyes for this."

"I've no wish to do it."

"Well, you must, my girl," said Mr. Donnelly. "And there'll be
no foolishness about it."

So saying, he threw back the sheet, exposing the face and shoulders of the child.

"There, Katy," said I, "open your eyes and take a look. Tell us if
the body upon the table is that of Maggie Plummer."

Still she held her eyes shut. Mr. Donnelly watched her with
increasing exasperation. Knowing that it could not continue thus
for much longer, I simply did what had to be done: I picked the
plumpest part of her upper arm, grasped near an inch of skin, and
pinched for all I was worth.

"OW!" said she, a loud cry that must have resounded through
every room. But her eyes popped open in surprise, and because she
had held her head down in an unconscious gesture of rejection, her
eyes fell quite immediately upon that which she had so diligently refused, till that moment, to see.

"Oh, my God, Maggie, it is you, ain't it? Forgive me!" She
screamed it, eyes wide open, wailing out great moans of sorrow. For
minutes, it seemed, she could not be quietened. Who would have
guessed that this was the sly creature who had declared that a
mother had the right to sell her child? Only after Mr. Donnelly had
covered over the face of the child did she at last begin to master her
emotions. Then did I lead her forth from the room. Gabriel Donnelly followed, closing doors after us.

"Well," said he, "I daresay we can now consider Margaret
Plummer properly identified."

"It was her, all right," said Katy Tiddle. "But one thing I want you to know, both of you." We stopped to listen to her in the empty waiting room, just at the door to the hall.

"And what is that, Miss Tiddle?"

"Alice thought she was doing Maggie a good turn, sending her off with that man. She may have sold her, right enough, but the way he told it to her, Maggie would be ever so much better off with these rich folks who couldn't have childrens of their own. But—"

"But what?" I asked.

"But I guess he lied."

It was not until into the evening that I recalled that I had been carrying about a pistol in my pocket for most of the afternoon. What was I to do with it? True, I'd taken it from Katy Tiddle; nevertheless, she'd doubtless stolen it from someone. I'd bring it to Mr. Baker, I decided, for he was the proper armorer for the Bow Street Runners. He could check the stolen property list and tell me what ought to be done with it. I'd abide by his decision.

Whilst attending to these matters, Constable Patley happened by, and we talked at some length of Alice Plummer, and little Maggie, as well as Katy Tiddle. I gave to Mr. Patley essentially the same report I had given earlier to Sir John.

"Well, I ain't surprised to hear it, any of it. There's a lot of kidnapping and child-buying goes on in this town of London," said he. "And it ain't for any good purpose."

"You said, didn't you, that you were suspicious of that woman Plummer right from the start."

"Something didn't seem right."

"Sir John's told me to bring in that Tiddle person. He thinks he might be able to get a bit more out of her."

"If anyone can, it's him."

'Twas just about then that Mr. Baker came over, and in a teasing way, he said to me, "Jeremy, you ought to tell a fellow when you're handing over a *loaded* pistol. You handle them a little different, you know."

"Why, I didn't think for a moment that it was loaded," said I, much embarrassed. "Sorry, Mr. Baker."

"I've not found it on the stolen property list, but I can tell you this—it's a fine and expensive piece of gunsmithing you lifted off that woman. Could be one of a set of two. It looks French to me."

That left me with something to think about, so it did. As I drifted away and up the stairs, I considered the matter further, wondering as I did, how and from whom Katy Tiddle had acquired that remarkable pistol.

And—let me see—just to bring things to a proper conclusion, I shall add one final note to this first chapter. The dinner of pot roast, which Clarissa prepared for the family that evening, was as good as any ever done for us by Molly—or, for that matter, by Annie, who preceded her. Clarissa would make a fine cook. There could be no question of it.

TWO

*In which a startling
discovery is made
by none but me*

⋙❈⋘

My arrival at Katy Tiddle's door was delayed until the middle of the next morning. Saturday it was, and the darkest day in the church's calendar. Yet one would not know it from the crowds upon the street. They were boisterous and jolly, most of them women out to buy for the great holiday next day. Mr. Tolliver's warning to Clarissa, that she had best do her buying early, was well given and taken to heart by her; she was out to Covent Garden and back, begging me to look upon the prizes she had made off with. True enough, she had done well for herself. Yet by that time, spurred to action by Sir John, I was pulling on my coat and making ready to go.

"Duty calls," said I, heading for the door.

"Can you not stay long enough to look upon this fine Easter ham?"

"I cannot," said I, "for I must fetch a witness that Sir John would interrogate."

"That proves it."

"Proves what?"

"That you would rather do Sir John's bidding than that of your very own stomach."

"Clarissa, you have but to cook that ham and I shall do it justice. You may count upon it."

With that, I was out the door, moving as swift as I was able through the many who seemed ever to move in the direction counter to mine. 'Twas only as I reached the Seven Dials and Cucumber Alley that I noted that it was no longer such a struggle to move ahead. The denizens of Seven Dials had little interest in the ecclesiastical calendar, nor in any other sort, for that matter. They kept their places at the bars and in the dives, sipping their gin and their rum.

I knew that it would be no easy matter persuading Katy Tiddle to open the door to me after her last experience; nevertheless, I had a plan. Having brought with me the pistol I had taken from her the day before, I had decided to use it as bait. She would certainly welcome me if it meant getting back the pistol. I had paid it little attention before handing it over to Mr. Baker. But when he gave it back and told me that he had not found it on the stolen property list, I took considerably more interest than before. It was indeed a beautiful piece, was it not? Engraved decoratively, perfectly balanced, it seemed more in the nature of a work of art than a lethal weapon. Mr. Baker had suggested there might be a twin of it somewhere about.

Still, how had Katy Tiddle come to own it? Such a pistol was not readily given away as a gift. Whether or not it had found its way onto the stolen property list, Katy had surely stolen it. Yet, until I knew that for certain, I had no choice but to return it to her. And now was the time to do just that.

I knocked politely upon her door. As it had been at my last visit, there was no immediate response — simply silence. I knocked again and waited. More silence. I listened, wondering if she might simply have gone out for food or an early gin. Perhaps I should walk around a bit and come back to try again. But no, I may have been a bit too timid in my first attempts. I would give her one last try and make it a good one. Having thus resolved, I beat hard upon the door, pounding upon it with my clenched fist and calling out her name. But then something quite remarkable happened: the door opened. Not only did it open, it flew open, banging against the wall behind from the force of my blows.

The room that was revealed was unlighted and dark. I examined the three locks upon the door, and I saw that not one of them had given way; all had been left unlocked. I stepped inside, drawing the unloaded pistol from my pocket and easing the door shut behind me. I stood for a moment at the door hoping to accustom my eyes to the dim, almost nonexistent, light. Then did I move forward, hold-

ing the pistol at the ready. (How I wished that it were now loaded!)
It was impossible, I found, to do this silently. The age of the building, the condition of the floors, made it quite impossible to take a
step without sounding forth a symphony of squeaks and creaks.
Anyone in wait to do me harm could chart my advance precisely.
So, seeing no harm in it, I called her name out softly—once and
then a second time.

In response, I heard something—a moan? a groan? an inarticu-
late complaint? Where did it come from? Was it Katy Tiddle had
made the sound? Or—

There it was again.

The single source of light in the room came from the far end,
where a poorly pinned curtain came together in an irregular strip,
admitting sunlight and blue sky. Between me and it was an empty
bed; all messed, untidy, and dirty, 'tis true, yet nevertheless a proper
bed. Katy must be in that narrow space between the bed and the
windows. To there I hastened and found that, indeed, she was—if
that poor, bloodied creature at my feet could be called by her name.

Saying nothing, I lifted her, with some difficulty, up to the bed.
I took but a moment to examine her, yet it was sufficient for me to
see that she had been stabbed repeatedly (afterward, Mr. Donnelly
counted no less than thirteen wounds in her trunk and two in her
throat), and she was not likely to live much longer.

"Katy," said I. "Who did this to you?"

Her mouth worked soundlessly. Something was then mumbled
and, at last, two syllables came, fairly clear: "Water."

Water, yes, of course. She must be quite unable to speak more
intelligibly without it. 'Twas a wonder she could speak at all with
those wounds in her neck. I found an empty cup on a table beside
her bed. That would do. It would have to. I remembered a pump out
in the middle of the courtyard. I would leave her just long enough
to fill the cup.

And that was what I did, rushing out the door and to the pump,
filling the cup, and then back to her room, spilling half its contents
on the way. In all, I could not have taken a great deal more than a
minute. Yet that was sufficient time for Katy Tiddle to die. I blamed
myself for leaving her. Had I not, she might have lived longer. Some
say that the human voice has life-giving qualities: to keep another

alive, you must talk to him, give him something on which to concentrate. Would it have helped in her case? Mr. Donnelly later said
it would not. True enough, the water would likely have killed her,
but so many of her vital organs had been punctured or cut that there
was no possibility that she could have lived. Better to let her talk, if
she had a mind to, for she had evidently stayed alive for many hours
by the power of her will alone, hoping to announce the name of her
killer. And so, to leave her at that crucial moment . . .

For that matter, if I wished to blame myself (as I seemed determined to do), perhaps it would have been more to the point had I
charged myself with depriving Katy of the only weapon she
owned—a pistol. Engraved and highlighted, it was; nevertheless, it
would have been one capable of ending the life of her assailant—or,
at the very least, of frightening him away. Why had I taken the pistol from her? Because I thought—nay, assumed—that she had
stolen it. And while I thought it still, it may well have been that her
practical needs for such a gun outweighed considerations of property. Yet, alas, it was far too late now to weigh these matters.

All recriminations such as these and others did I deal with during
the next few hours, whilst occupied with the dreary business of delivering Catherine Tiddle's body to Mr. Donnelly and reporting the
matter to Sir John. I recall that as I made my way down the long
hall to inform the magistrate, I felt oddly (and wrongly) to blame
for Katy Tiddle's death. As soon as ever I had finished, Sir John
commented upon this.

"The tale you tell seems punctuated by certain notes of guilt,
Jeremy. Why should this be?"

"Well," said I with a sigh, "if you look at the possibilities, you
must admit I could have done better."

"Oh? How so?"

Then did I unburden myself, making plain to him those doubts
and discomforts that I have thus far mentioned—and perhaps a few
that I have not. He listened with a patient lack of concern, and
when I had concluded, he gave a great shrug.

"Each of us can look back on such tests and decide we could
have done better," said he. "There are times that our feelings are jus-

tified. That is to say, yes, we could have done better. But just as often, the answer must be no—we could have done no better than we did. From all that you have told me thus far, I would judge the latter to be the case."

"Thank you, sir, I—"

"But," said he, interrupting, "I am far more concerned that you have given so little thought to *why* this deed was done. More often than not, you think as a constable, and all the while I urge you to think as a lawyer, *think as a lawyer.* Often you do just that, thus making me happy and saving us both considerable time and effort. I praise you for that, but now I urge you to put aside the question of how the poor woman was murdered and what you might have done to prevent it. Accept that it happened, and accept also that there is little you could have done for her. Get on now to the more important questions."

"Yes, sir," said I, properly chastised.

"For instance, have you considered the possibility that the murder of this Tiddle woman may have some connection to the matter which brought you to her in the first place?"

"The death of Maggie Plummer? No sir, I haven't, not really."

"Why not? She was most forthcoming regarding little Maggie's mother. She may have been spied in your company. It may well have been supposed that she knew even more than she told. After all, I thought as much. That is why I wished her brought to me— that I might question her further. If you wish to blame yourself for some aspect of this, then blame yourself for not taking her immediately to me after she had identified the body of the child, instead of then letting her go."

"Yes, I suppose that's what I should have done."

"There were hints that she held something back, were there not? What did she mean when she viewed the corpus and identified her, then asked the child's forgiveness?"

"Yes, of course, I see that now. She felt a degree of guilt."

"Perhaps a considerable degree," said Sir John. "And what did you tell me she had to say of the goodly price paid to Maggie's mother for the child?"

"Well, I don't recall the *exact* words, but Tiddle certainly left the impression that she was envious."

"Exactly! And she would only have been envious if she had played a larger role than mere observer, don't you think?"

"Well, yes, I see what you mean."

"No doubt you can come up with other examples, other hints, if you think back over what was said by her."

"No doubt I can. But sir?"

"Yes, Jeremy? What is it?"

"If such as these gave you pause for thought, then why did you not send me back immediately to bring Tiddle in for questioning? If you had done so, she might now still be alive."

"Why? *Why*?" He sputtered a bit, seeking a proper rejoinder. "Well, because I—that is, if—" Then did he pause and take a deep breath before proceeding: "Because, I confess that I am, as you, an imperfect investigator. My mind was on the nature of the crime, on the sins of our society, and, finally, like so many others because my hindsight exceeds my foresight. In short, I could have done better."

"Yes sir. I'm sorry, sir. I shouldn't have asked."

"No, you did well to put the question to me. But what I wish you to do now, Jeremy, is return to the room of Catherine Tiddle and find out all you can about her from the bits and pieces in her room. Can you do that, lad? Don't allow anything to slip through your fingers."

"I can, sir, of course. I'll give the afternoon to it."

With that and a quick goodbye, I started from the room.

"There was but one other matter," said he, calling after me.

"And what is that, sir?"

"Would you accompany Clarissa to her destination? It seems that she happened to run into a friend from Lichfield. She said that you knew about this?"

"That is correct, sir." He meant Elizabeth Hooker, of course. I recalled that they had arranged to meet that day that they might reminisce and do what other foolish things girls do at such an age.

"I understand that it's quite near your own destination—in one of those courts off St. Martin's Lane—the better part. Still, it *is* St. Martin's and quite near Seven Dials, so your company with her would be appreciated. You might make arrangements to walk back with her, too."

So it was decided for me. I mounted the stairs quickly and collected Clarissa from the kitchen. She had brought the leftover pot roast up to the point where it needed only to be popped into the oven. As I entered, she was sitting, her cloak over her arm, waiting for me. She took but a moment to throw the cloak round her shoulders and announce that she was ready to go.

Then, out in the street, we walked close together with barely a word between us for the length of Bow Street—or perhaps even farther. At last, Clarissa, who abhors silence, could endure it no longer. She turned to me of a sudden and demanded to know why I was not speaking.

"Why *I* was not?" said I in a most defensive manner. "I hear nothing from *you*, do I?"

"I was quiet because you were. Besides, I asked you first, didn't I?"

We could have gone round-about in such a way for an hour or more. And, a year or two before, we would have done just that. Yet now, as both of us attempted, with some success, to act in a more mature manner, such behavior hardly seemed appropriate.

"Oh, all right," said I, "to tell the truth, as we are now sworn to do, Sir John gave me a proper burning, then sent me off to accompany you to your friend's place. And by the way, where is it?"

"Dawson's Alley," said she, "number five."

"Should be easy to find."

"So you were—oh, how to put it? You were licking your wounds—mentally, that is."

I thought about that a moment. I understood the picture perfectly, but still . . .

"Not exactly the image I would use," said I. "Nevertheless, that sums it up pretty well."

"Well, forgive me," said she. "But is there nothing I can do to help?"

"No, not really. I deserved it, you see."

"Truly so? Wouldn't it help to talk about it?"

"Perhaps not as much as you think," said I uncertainly. Yet it was my uncertainty that led me to tell her all that had passed between Sir John and myself as she waited in the kitchen for me. Yes, I told her all and offered comments along the way regarding my responses and his own. To my surprise, it did indeed help to restore my equilibrium. The telling of it all, her comments as well as my own — all of this took a good deal longer than I expected. In fact, by the time the story was done, we had reached noisy St. Martin's Lane where the usual crowd of hawkers and barrow-sellers did congregate. 'Twas then just round the corner to Dawson's Alley and number five.

It was a larger, more imposing building than most of those there on the narrow little alley. Built of brick and three stories tall, number five was impressive by any measure.

"This is where her mother lives?" I asked. "Does she own this grand structure?"

"Ah, no, she rents out the rooms, fixes the meals, and does all that needs to be done. The owner collects the rents. I gather it's all quite respectable."

"It certainly *looks* respectable — more in the nature of a prison than a lodging house. You're expected, of course?"

"Oh yes."

"Well, do keep in confidence all that I told you on the way here, won't you?"

"Oh, I will," said Clarissa. "Let me repeat that I think you did right to remind Sir John that if he had suspicions earlier, he should have asked to see Mistress Tiddle most immediate."

"He admitted as much."

"We'll talk of it later, shall we?"

"Perhaps. In any case, I'll come by for you in about two hours, give or take a bit."

"Two hours it is."

With that, she left me, crossing to the door and banging upon it with the brass hand-knocker that had been there provided. No more than a minute later, Elizabeth appeared, threw her arms round her visitor, and pulled her inside. Clarissa barely had opportunity to wave goodbye to me. My duty then discharged, I set off in the direction of Seven Dials.

I had not been a great deal of time in Katy Tiddle's untidy room, not much more than an hour, when I received a considerable surprise. I had thrown open the curtains which covered the window, certain

that to do the sort of thorough search Sir John had asked of me, I
should need plenty of light. And, indeed, it was so. What the abundance of daylight revealed were bits and pieces of paper scattered
here and there round the place. Most of them were of no importance. Mistress Tiddle, it seemed, was in the habit of pulling the labels from all sorts of bottles—chemist's, whiskey bottles, even
French wine bottles (though how and where she had found that last
I have no idea). I collected them all, assuring myself that if they had
significance of any sort, I would more likely discover it through
careful study at Number 4 Bow Street. Yet it may well have been
that the labels had no significance at all.

The pile of numbered tickets and stubs I found in the single
drawer of her bedside table was another matter entirely. Could
Katy Tiddle read or write? Not likely. Did she know numbers beyond the ten digits she found upon her hands? These, I was sure,
were more interesting and of much greater significance—if I could
but determine what that significance might be.

Interesting as these might be—and they did, in the end, prove
so—they were not the "considerable surprise" to which I referred a
few lines back. That came, as I said, a little over an hour after my arrival. By that time, I had looked near everywhere—through her
clothes, under the bed, et cetera. As I remember, I was standing in
the middle of the room, checking the corners, looking about for new
places to search, when I heard a noise from the front of the room. I
had closed the door after me when I came in to search the place,
and, at first, I thought what I had heard was someone unknown to
me trying a key in the lock. But no, a moment later the tumbler
turned, and I understood that it was not the door to Tiddle's, but
rather the one to Alice Plummer's, that had just been unlocked.
When it swang open, creaking and complaining, I was sure of it.
Could it be Plummer come back?

There were firm steps upon the floor of the room just beyond
the south wall. The door had been left open. That meant, perhaps,
that whoever had entered had no intent to stay long. If I wished to
detain and question that person I had best act quickly and deci-
sively. I tiptoed quickly to Tiddle's door and opened it. Stepping out
into the daylight, I was immediately aware that all my efforts at
quiet had been quite unnecessary, for the person in the next room

was making a great racket on his own. It was a man. I was near certain of it. Only a man would throw things around and stamp about in such a way. I was in no wise prepared for this sort of interruption and would have liked the opportunity to think through my course of action, but, of course, there was no time for that. If I were to act, I should have to do so immediately.

I drew the pistol from my pocket and pulled back the hammer. Taking a deep breath, I counted to three and threw myself through the half-open door and then took a couple of running steps into the room. I came to a halt just as quickly when I saw who—or what— it was awaited me.

One could have called him a dwarf, I suppose, yet there was naught misshapen about him. Leave it that he was a small man, quite small, no more than child-size, yet fully a man. There could be no doubt of it, for, in defiance of custom, he wore a short beard, and, when he spoke, his words came out of him in a growling, rasping baritone.

"Who the Goddamned bloody hell are you?" he demanded.

He threw the bedclothes he had jerked from the bed down upon the floor. Then did he stand, hands upon hips, glaring up at me. Behind him, and to the right and left of him, was the chaos he had created in about two minutes' time. Drawers had been pulled from a bureau, and clothing was scattered across the floor. In one corner, there was a jumble of toys, crudely carved dolls and the like, all of them Maggie's, which, I was quite sure, had not been touched.

"Must I repeat myself?" he shouted out louder than before. "Who the Goddamned bloody hell are you?"

I fear that I stared at him, so far was he from what I had expected.

"I was about to ask you the same," said I at last.

"Well, I ain't afeared of giving my name, and I ain't ashamed of it, neither. Deuteronomy Plummer is what I'm called, and I am cursed with the burden of a sister."

"Alice Plummer?"

"Just so. And she is the sole excuse for my presence here—her and the daughter she don't deserve."

"You have a key," said I, bringing attention to the obvious.

"So I do," said he.

"How do you come by it?"

"How do I come by it?" He burst forth with a great booming laugh at that. "How indeed! I pay the rent on this hovel. Ain't I entitled to a key?" Pausing a moment, he looked me up and down and allowed his gaze to linger upon the pistol in my hand. "Now that I've accounted for myself, why don't you put that bloody big pistol away and return the favor."

Though I did not immediately dispose of the pistol, which did clearly make him uneasy, I complied with his request and introduced myself as Sir John Fielding's assistant at the Bow Street Court.

"What trouble has she got herself into now?" asked Mr. Plummer.

"Well, she may have got herself into a bit of it, but we won't be sure till we find her and have a chance to talk with her."

"What sort of trouble?" he repeated in a tone of quiet urgency.

I decided then and there that it would be best if he discussed that with Sir John. "I tell you what," said I, "it would be best, I'm sure, if you were to ask that of the magistrate himself. He will tell you all that need be known and no doubt he'll have some questions for you, as well. You see, it's all a bit too complicated for me, I fear."

He seemed to accept that: "Well, all right. Ain't that Sir John Fielding the one they call the Blind Beak?"

"Yes," said I, "that is how they call him—though not to his face."

"Oh, right you are. I'll not make *that* mistake. Just give me a little time to straighten up here. I'm afraid my temper got the best of me, and I threw things round a bit."

"Right," said I, "and I'll lock up next door."

I learned a bit more about him as we walked back to Bow Street. Indeed, I learned a great deal, for small though he be, Deuteronomy Plummer was a great talker.

"Now," said he to me as we trudged together along Cucumber Alley, "you might wonder how a fella such as I makes his money."

"Oh, well, I . . ."

"Let me tell you about it."

That he proceeded to do, telling from the beginning and at great length how he had come to London from some town in the north in pursuit of his sister. He found her in Seven Dials, pregnant and whoring and unwilling to return home with him. In the course of his searches for Alice Plummer, he had strayed as far as Shepherd's Bush. It being a Sunday, he happened to visit upon the day of the horse races at Shepherd's Bush Common. Now, Deuteronomy Plummer was no stranger to racing of that sort—the hell-for-leather, rough-and-tumble, dirty-tricks kind of racing.

"I growed up on it," he boasted. "From the time I was just a babe, I had me a way with horses, and when I started race-ridin', I found I was just small enough to duck most of the nastiness they'd put my way, and just smart enough to come up with nastiness all my own."

That Sunday in Shepherd's Bush he made a spot of cash, using his horse sense, and betting on sure winners. More important, he got acquainted with owners and saw that there were few riders in his class. And he proved it to the satisfaction of all when, just at the start of the last race of the day, a horse threw its rider, and, knowing full well it was allowed, he jumped into the saddle, gave his heels to the horse, and won the heat and the race. He won the heart of the crowd because of his daring and his diminutive size. And the fact that he had bet heavily on that same horse made him doubly a winner. Ever after, he rode for the owners at Shepherd's Bush, Blackheath, and all the rest of the major race meets round London. Betting on himself, and only on himself, he had made himself a small fortune.

"Racing, lad," said he to me, "'tis the only way a fellow small as me has the advantage."

I recall that we two were walking cross Covent Garden when he did speak these words, and it was there in the Garden, as well, that I took proper note of the reaction of the crowd to him. Early on, out in the street, I had seen the young, the ignorant, and the rude point at him and giggle at his size. He gave them no heed whatever, so well accustomed was he to such treatment by such ne'er-do-wells. Nevertheless, it was in Long Acre, or perhaps James Street, that I first noticed a different sort of reaction to my companion—and always from men. They noticed him most respectfully. A few did pass us with a smile and a nod; another, just at Mr. Tolliver's meat stall in the Garden, stepped aside and removed his hat; and indeed, he all but bowed to Deuteronomy Plummer. Previous to this fellow, little attention had been paid to them all by Mr. Plummer. We were not yet past him when the man beside me offered a dignified smile and touched his own hat in response. Then did he wink at me.

"Who are these people?" I asked. "They seem to know you."

"In a way, I suppose they do. That last fellow, the one who took his hat off to me, I see him at every race meet I run. He seems to follow me round, he does. Probably made a good deal of cash just betting on me."

"Then you're a sort of hero, a champion to him," I suggested.

"Something like that," said he pridefully yet modestly.

"Hmmm," said I, considering what he had just said. It was an odd idea to me, this notion of fame. In a sense, Sir John had fame, yet his face was so familiar here in Covent Garden that his appearance hereabouts was unlikely to cause the sort of notice that Deuteronomy had caused already. Deuteronomy? Indeed, I must ask him about that.

"Sir, may I put to you a question which may cause you some embarrassment?"

"Certainly you may. Though if I find it too embarrassing I might not answer."

"Your name is a rather singular one. How did you come by it?"

"Plummer?" He seemed to be toying with me.

"No, Deuteronomy."

He laughed at that. "Sooner or later they all get round to my name. I give you credit, lad. You held out longer than most," said he. "But, well, it's simple enough, you see. My father was, in his own way, a very pious man, a great reader of the Bible, in particular the Hebrew portion. He had five sons, of which I am the fifth. My brothers' names are Genesis, Exodus, Leviticus, and Numbers. You see? It makes perfect sense."

"All except Alice."

"Ah yes, our sister, our only sister."

"What of her? I should think a name such as Esther or Ruth would have been more consonant with your father's past practice."

"Perhaps, but it was never discussed within my hearing, nor was I bold enough to ask either of them about it. What I have ever assumed, though, is that my mother, who was also a strong-willed person, said that my father had had the pleasure of naming boys, for he was the father of them all. Yet, she said that since it was that the baby just born was a girl and she the mother, 'twas only proper she should do the naming of her."

"And the name she chose was Alice?"

"Just so."

"Why that name? Why Alice?"

"Oh, probably because it was her mother's name."

"Only that?" He had disappointed me. I felt almost cheated.

That was quite enough for Deuteronomy Plummer. He halted there, in the middle of the Garden, and where he halted, he fair exploded, stamping one foot and then the other as he shouted out his anger. All of those round us turned to look and wonder.

"How should I know how that silly cow of a sister got her name?" he cried. "What should I care?" Then, having seen the audience he had created for himself, he lowered his voice to little more than a whisper: "The only thing good Alice ever done was to have that daughter of hers. Have you seen her? Have you seen Maggie?"

"I have, yes." I could say neither more nor less than that.

"Well, then you know."

I feared he would begin to question me with regard to my "meeting," as it were, with Maggie. And so I urged him onward to Bow Street and Sir John. I was not the one to inform him of the death of his favorite niece. I knew not how much of the story Sir John would tell him, yet 'twas best for him to do the telling. In any case, I got him moving again. And while he would not say a word more about his sister, he spent the whole distance to the magistrate's court rhapsodizing about Maggie, praising her beauty, her sweetness, her every accomplishment.

Thus it was that we arrived. I showed him the way in and called out a greeting to Mr. Fuller, the day jailer, just to make sure that he was about. He answered in kind and stuck his head out to see what I might require, but then, when he caught sight of him who was beside me, his mouth twisted into a smirk, and his cheeks puffed in his effort to hold back laughter. (What a churl he was!)

"Is Sir John in his chambers?" I asked him.

He gave a hasty nod and retreated deep into his domain. Not a word was said in response—naught but an odd sound that may have been muffled sniggers.

"Down at the end of the hall," said I to my companion.

I did a fast pace down the hall, intending to distance us from Mr. Fuller as quickly as might be possible.

I paused at the door, allowing Deuteronomy Plummer to catch up, then introduced the two men without much ado. Sir John came forward, his hand outstretched in welcome.

"Deuteronomy Plummer?" he repeated. "Do I not know that name from the world of racing?"

Obviously flattered, Mr. Plummer hemmed and hawed a bit, unable to find words of sufficient graciousness, and, at last, mumbled that he rode "a little."

"Ah well, a good deal more than 'a little,' or so I've heard. What a pleasure to meet you."

"An *honor* to meet you, sir."

"Am I to assume from the coincidence of the two surnames that you are related by blood to the Alice Plummer whom we seek?" asked Sir John.

"I'm her brother, sir, and I seek her, too, as you might say. That's how me and the young man here met. I was searchin' her place in Seven Dials, just lookin' for some hint where she went to and along he comes."

"Young man?" Sir John repeated the phrase as if he could not suppose who might be meant. "Ah, you mean Jeremy, of course." Then, turning more or less in my direction, he said, "Jeremy, are you still here? Have you not other duties to occupy yourself?"

"None that I can think of, sir," said I.

"Come now. Are you forgetting Clarissa? She may need your protection. You cannot simply maroon her where you left her, now can you?"

"I suppose not," said I.

"Then on your way, lad."

On your way, said he. On my way, indeed! I was quite beside myself with indignation at Sir John's treatment of me, in particular before a witness I had brought to him. How could he have behaved in

such a way toward me? Was having Clarissa home to cook his dinner so important to him?

I stormed down Chandos Street in the general direction of
Dawson's Alley and the imposing building where I had left Clarissa
some time before. She was with her friend, was she not? She would
probably welcome an extra hour with her. But no, Sir John had instructed me to bring her back, and that is what I would do, no matter what her wishes in the matter. Thus was I prepared—oh, more
than prepared—to grasp her by the wrist and pull her bodily from
the house. I should then run with her at full speed for Bow Street
that I might return in time to hear at least a bit of Sir John's interrogation of Mr. Plummer.

I came quickly to Number 5 Dawson's Alley and pounded upon
the door with my fist. None could complain that I knocked too
weakly to be heard, as Sir John sometimes had done. Even if
Clarissa Roundtree and Elizabeth Hooker were chattering up on
the third floor, they would certainly hear my knock as a summons,
a demand for attention.

As it happened, however, they were not on the third floor, but
just round the corner in a little sitting room near the door. And so it
was that Elizabeth came to the door quite immediately. She curtsied
grandly, more or less duplicating that curtsy which she had offered
me to the delight of the crowd at Covent Garden. Ordinarily, I
would have greeted her similarly with a bow; but, wrapped up in
my own concerns, I offered nothing of the kind in return. As she
started to greet me, I spoke over her rather rudely.

"I've come for Clarissa," said I roughly, as if giving an order.

"I supposed you had."

Her face quite crumpled in response to my boorish manner. I
feared for a moment she might burst into tears, such a delicate child
was she. Immediately was I overcome by a sense of guilt.

"You must forgive me," said I to her. "What I said was in no
wise ill-intentioned. I am simply in a great hurry, and I—"

"Oh, Jeremy, you're always in a hurry." It was Clarissa's voice
rising above my own. Only then did she appear. "Indeed you are
late," said she, "though not so late as I expected. Nevertheless, as
you see, I am ready."

And true enough, she was. Wrapped in her cloak, she bussed Elizabeth upon the cheek and announced that she had had quite a wonderful time and that soon she would return that they might gab once again.

"I loved your story about the vicar," said she. "Caught out again, was he? That, I hope, has taught him a lesson."

And, so saying, they embraced hurriedly, and Clarissa slid by her friend and out the door. There were then further goodbyes called out, waves from both, and only then did the door close after her.

"Goodness," said she, "I'm so glad that's over."

I must have looked at her oddly then, for I was quite unsure that I had heard her correctly.

"Glad, oh yes, glad, Jeremy. I have never, I think, spent a more trying pair of hours in my life—not even in the Lichfield poorhouse."

"What passed between you two that you should be moved to such a complaint?"

"Nothing! That's just it, you see—nothing at all. After the first twenty or thirty minutes we had naught to say, one to the other. What an inert being she has become—utterly vapid, without purpose, quite useless, a kitchen slavey she is and she will always be."

"And yet you—"

"No, I take that back. Her great ambition, it seems, is to be a housekeeper, and she may indeed advance that far! She has not read a book in years—and seems proud of it. She . . . she . . ."

Whether from want of words or breath, her denunciation ceased at about this point, and Clarissa walked beside me quite panting, unable to go further.

"In short," said I, "you were bored."

She nodded. We went along in silence all the way up Chandos Street, at which time she resumed in a more moderate and less emotional tone.

"You've no idea how fortunate we are, you and I," said she to me. "When we sit at table, matters are discussed. We're encouraged to read books and to make plans for the future. I had never quite realized it until now."

"Sometimes I forget that myself."

"Just look at Annie—how she has risen—a leading actress in Mr. Garrick's theatre. Her story must be unique."

"Perhaps so. I see your point, in any case, and I agree." Again, I fell silent for a spell. "Nevertheless, Sir John can at times behave in the most confounding manner. Why, I brought to him today our best witness to date in the matter of Maggie Plummer."

"Who was that again?"

"Maggie Plummer. Oh, you remember—the dead girl who was yesterday pulled from the Thames. I told you all about her on our way over to Dawson's Alley."

"Oh—oh, yes."

Whereupon I told her about it once again, adding my encounter with Deuteronomy Plummer, and telling her of my frustrating dismissal by Sir John.

"Why did you so want to stay?" she asked when I had concluded.

"Well, I . . . I wished to listen in on the interrogation as, well, as part of my education in the law. And I . . . I . . . Hang it, Clarissa, I would know what this fellow had to say about his sister, his niece, about all of it."

"And why do you suppose Sir John wanted you away?"

I was silent for a moment, thinking through my response. I wished to be as truthful as I could be in this matter, yet at the same time I wished also to place myself in the best possible light.

"Well, he *said* he wanted me to fetch you and accompany you back to Bow Street."

"And I applaud him for that," said she. "But you seem to feel that he had another, ulterior motive in sending you away."

"I suppose I do."

"And that is . . . ?"

"To be more candid than I would wish to be, I must say that he probably supposed he could get more out of Mr. Plummer if I were not present."

I sighed, oddly glad to have come forth with it.

"You must have thought that yourself," said she.

"Why do you say that?" I sounded a bit tetchy, even to myself.

"You took Mr. Deuteronomy Plummer to Sir John without

telling him that his sister had sold her daughter, did you not? And neglecting also to mention to him that his niece was dead? And the only questions you put to him then were of a general nature, isn't that also correct?"

Again I sighed. "All true," said I. "You have made your point. Let us end the discussion right here and now."

And that we did, for, after all, we were quite near Number 4 Bow Street, were we not? And whatever had been discussed between us would now be set aside as we adopted our domestic personae.

As we entered into the "backstage" area of the Bow Street Court, and were just then about to mount the stairs, the footsteps we had heard loud in our ears brought to us Mr. Deuteronomy Plummer. They, the footsteps, were unsteady. He walked as a drunken man, unable to keep a steady forward rhythm—though I was certain that he was sober. He seemed to push past without seeing us; and, indeed, his sight may have been impaired by the tears in his eyes. He spoke not a word as he went out the door to Bow Street.

I did not discover the substance of Sir John's meeting with Mr. Plummer until after dinner that evening. He had invited me to come up and see him when I had finished the washing up. It took me a bit longer than I might have expected, for, as I washed pots, pans, and dishes, Clarissa took all the bits and pieces I had gathered from Katy Tiddle's room and spread them out upon the kitchen table. As I had, she went first to the labels and similar oddments of paper. She picked up each one and studied it, then placed it back upon the table. Eventually, there were two separate piles of these bits of paper—labels and all others.

"Jeremy," said she to me, "when you found all these, were they together, or in two separate groups, as I have them here?"

"Oh no, no, neither one," said I, wringing out the cloth I had used on the dishes. "They were scattered all over her room. Some were on the floor. Three or four I found in the folds of the blankets on her bed, and a few were under the bed."

"I see. Well, I fear I can't make any immediate sense of this

bunch, no matter how I divide them up." She shrugged quite eloquently. "Sorry."

"I hadn't expected much from them. But what about those others?"

"What others?"

"Those with the numbers scrawled upon them. They were all
together in a pile in the table next her bed."

"You know what those are, don't you? I certainly do."

"Not really, no."

"As near as I can tell," said Clarissa, "these stubs, tickets, et
cetera, are all from various pawn shops. Some of them are marked in
just such a way on the back. Come here and I'll show you, shall I?"

"No, Sir John has asked for me. Perhaps later."

With that, I left her and jog-trotted up the stairs and down the
hall to the little room he called his study. It was there that he went
to consider and suppose. Dark and light were one to him, and so he
sat most often in the dark as he thought. That, in any case, is how I
found him on the evening in question.

"Is that you, Jeremy? Come, sit down. Light a candle, if you like."

"No, I've no need," said I, as I took a chair across the desk
from him.

"I wanted to explain my dismissal of you earlier today."

"I understood it, Sir John."

"I hope you did. It was naught but my wish to get our friend
Deuteronomy alone and get him talking that moved me to send you
so roughly on your way."

"Well," said I, "you got him alone right enough. Did you get him
talking?"

"Yes, and I did not like the sound of all I heard from him. I truly
believe he would murder his sister if he were to come across her in
his present state. I gave him a stern warning, yet, in truth, I'm not
even sure he heard me, so overwhelmed was he by the news I had
given him. He was certainly attached to that niece of his, wasn't he?"

"He was indeed."

"He's claimed her body for burial at St. Paul's, Covent Garden.
I'd like you to attend the funeral service in case anything should
turn up there. Find out when it will be held from those at the
church, will you? Probably not until the day after tomorrow—tomorrow being Easter."

"I will, Sir John."

"You might even take Clarissa along to the funeral—with Lady Fielding's approval, of course. Women seem to know how to behave on such occasions." He sighed. "Let me see," said he, "what else? I'd also like you to find out from Mr. Baker if Mr. Plummer is riding to-morrow. Baker often attends these meets, I believe. If Deuteron-omy Plummer rides, I'd like you to attend and let yourself be seen by him. I want him to know that we are watching him, so that he does nothing foolish, nothing violent. You understand, I'm sure."

"Indeed I do, sir."

"And what, if anything, did you turn up in your search of that woman's place—the one who got herself murdered? Katy Tiddle? Was that her name?"

"I found odds and ends. There are labels of one kind or an-other—nothing of interest there. But more promising is a pile of tickets and stubs, each one numbered—that is, they would be promising if I could figure out just what they are and what the num-bers are for. Clarissa believes them to be pawn tickets."

"Oh? Then no doubt she's correct," said he, pleasing me little. "When handling a case like this, Jeremy, it is important to keep at it diligently. Do something on it each day. It is only thus that we shall ever manage to solve it. And I assure you, lad, that indeed we shall solve it." He hesitated, then added: "Why not proceed on the as-sumption that Clarissa is correct and see where that leads you?"

THREE

In which I view my
first horse race, and
the investigation begins

❧❧❧

And so it came about that I went next day to Shepherd's Bush in the company of Mr. Baker—or have I said that quite right? No, the way of it was that Mr. Baker—night jailer, armorer, and general keeper of quarters for the Bow Street Runners—told me the way there, even drew a rough map for me, and agreed to meet me there in midafternoon. Thus might he have the opportunity to take a few hours sleep before the first heat of the first race. He told me he had often done it so, for as I learned, he was quite passionately devoted to what was even then called by some "the sport of kings." In all truth, I know not how George III, nor the late Louis of France, felt about the racing of horses round a specified course. I do know, however, that any man who gave to it the dedication and enthusiasm that Mr. Baker offered would surely have felt in his heart that he was king, if only for a day. Which day? Why, racing day, of course.

Because it was Easter, I felt obliged to renew my acquaintance with the faith in which I had been baptized. That done—the Easter anthems heard and the cries of "He is risen!" raised on high—I set forth on the long journey from Bow Street to Uxbridge Road, Shepherd's Bush, with naught to sustain me but two of Molly's hot cross buns.

When first I broached the matter of the race meet to our Mr. Baker, he was curious as to why I, having shown no previous interest in the sport, should of a sudden wish to give it my full interest.

But then, I told him of Mr. Plummer and his relation to the mother of the girl who had been pulled from the Thames the day before.

"So Deuteronomy Plummer is her brother," said he. "Is that the way it is?"

"That's indeed the way it is. Will he be racing at any of the courses Sunday?"

"At Shepherd's Bush Common, as I've heard. I was intending to go myself. I'd invited Mr. Patley to accompany me."

"Could I come along?" I asked.

And that, reader, is when we worked it out so that I might meet him there. When we had done, I put another question to him.

"Do such race meets always start so late of a Sunday?"

"Naw," said he, "it's 'cause it's Easter. I believe Shepherd's Bush is the only one going, and that's 'cause it's pretty far outside London."

"How far?"

"Well, you'll be afoot, so it's going to take you the better part of the morning to get there, probably."

And it did. In general, taking Mr. Baker's advice, I followed the river. Though, in its way westward, it took bends and twists, it was nevertheless the safest route. To go off roaming through Tothill Fields might save some time if the right way were known, yet if you were as ignorant of this piece of territory as I certainly was, you would no doubt become hopelessly lost. And so I went my way, curious at the volume and nature of the river traffic, and seeing that most of it was vegetables for Covent Garden and pleasure boats for those rich enough to have them. 'Twas not till I approached near to Hammersmith that, following Mr. Baker's directions, I turned north for Shepherd's Bush. From that point on, it was naught but a matter of holding to the map he had sketched for me.

The town of Shepherd's Bush was a bit disappointing. What there was of it was stretched out along Uxbridge Road. Why had such a place been chosen for race meets? Ah, but then, as I advanced a bit, I spied a bit more of the town far over on the other side of what I had taken to be green fields. Yet I saw the gathering crowd at the most distant part of the field and noted horses which had been unloaded from specially built carts of a kind seldom seen in London. Having seen thus much, I realized that this large open field was nothing more or less than Shepherd's Bush Common: I had come to my destination.

From mixing with the men and the few women who had thus far arrived, I soon came to the conclusion that their number did not include either Mr. Baker or Deuteronomy Plummer. I cannot say that I was surprised by this. Though I knew not the exact time, I had the feeling that it was still quite early. Looking round, I noticed a man who, like me, was simply standing about, observing the work of the rest. He also appeared prosperous enough to be the possessor of a timepiece. I approached him diffidently and made to him a polite inquiry.

"I wonder, sir," said I. "Have you the correct time?"

"I do," said he. "I most certainly do."

Yet he made no move to produce the timepiece, neither did he inform me of the hour and minute. He simply turned away from me and stared off rather pointedly in another direction. Had he misunderstood me? Was this his notion of a joke?

Still most politely I put the question to him in a manner which could not be misunderstood.

"Would you *tell* me the time, sir, if you please?"

He continued to look away as he said, "No, boy, I do not please, and I shall not tell you the time." Then did he add: "Go away."

I looked upon that face of his—arrogant, fat, cold, and utterly unsympathetic—and willed myself ever to remember it. And, indeed, I did remember it always. It became for me the face of all that I knew to be wrong with England.

Then, my face quite burning with embarrassment and unexpressed anger, I turned away from him. I left them all to their preparations for the race meet and walked cross Uxbridge Road to an inn, the Elephant and Castle. They, I was sure, would have a clock ticking away upon the wall; and there I might quench the thirst that had come upon me in the course of my long walk.

True enough, they had both. I took a place at the long bar where most had gathered, ordered a tankard of bitter, and found a clock just above me which told me that there was just over an hour to the start of the first heat of the first race. It should not be long, I assured myself, till Mr. Baker arrived.

Thus it was that I sat sipping my ale, listening to the talk swirl round me. And all the talk was of horses and jockeys, of which might last through all four heats to the final race, and who might then be in the saddle. Numbers were quoted back and forth. At first, I was near certain that these would be the numbers worn by the horses, and then I thought that perhaps those would be the jockeys' numbers. Then I understood at last that these were odds which they were reciting. Who were these men at the bar? The odds-makers? the touts? I'd no idea, really.

One of them looked familiar to me. Who was he? Where had I seen him before? It was recently, and of that I was sure. I remembered that round face, smiling. The curious thing was that he seemed to know me, too. That more or less confirmed that we had met recently, did it not? He seemed even more certain of it than I, for as I kept an eye upon him—not staring, you understand—he separated himself from the group at the end of the bar and came straight over to me.

"Beg pardon, young sir," said he, "but though we an't personal acquaint, I reco'nized you right off."

"Then you have the advantage on me, sir," said I, "for though you appeared most familiar to me, I have not, for the life of me, been able to settle upon the specific occasion of our meeting."

" 'Twas but yesterday. I was in Covent Garden on a matter of little importance, and here you come, arm-in-arm, so to speak, with Mr. Deuteronomy. That's what they call him, you know."

"Of course," said I. "I remember very well now. You removed your hat to him, did you not?"

"I did and will again when the opportunity arises. Have you seen him ride?"

"I must confess that I—"

"That's as I s'posed," said he, interrupting, "for I an't seen you at none of his other races."

Speaking thus, he altered his manner ever so slightly, allowing it to become a bit heavier. There was perhaps an element of accusation in his observation of my absence at Deuteronomy Plummer's earlier meets. I attempted, perhaps a little too hard, to justify myself to this stranger.

"Ah well," said I, " 'tis no easy matter for a young fellow such as myself to travel so far out of town to attend a race such as this. And what's more," I added, "being a humble apprentice, I've no money of my own to wager."

"Ah, but I meant no offense," said he, all smiles once again. "Here, let's have us another ale, shall we? Innkeeper!"

He called out and waved to him behind the bar. Then, over my protests, he ordered two more ales. By the time they arrived, he had introduced himself to me as Walter Hogg and fetched from me my own name. We talked idly of one thing and another. I recall having told him that Mr. Plummer commented upon his presence, and said that he believed Mr. Hogg attended all his races."

"He recognized me then, did he?" said Walter Hogg. He seemed as pleased as could be to hear it. "Let me tell you, I've won a good bit, putting my money on him."

At that I could not but laugh. When asked why, I told him that indeed, Mr. Plummer had also said something of the sort.

Mr. Hogg let out a whoop of delight and then cackled. "He said that, did he? Imagine it, would you!" Then, rather inappropriately, he asked, "You said you was an apprentice. What line of work you apprenticing to?"

I thought it an odd question, coming from him, but I saw no reason to lie or evade. "I'm for the law," said I.

He seemed to be quite impressed by that. "The law, is it? A young fella like you?"

"I won't always be so young," said I, quite reasonably.

"Well, that's true. Who're you 'prenticing to?"

"I'm reading law with Sir John Fielding."

"The Beak? The Blind Beak in Bow Street?"

"The very same."

"Well, what did he want with Mr. Deuteronomy? He ain't committed no crime, has he?"

It was then, or perhaps just a little earlier, that it occurred to me that this man Hogg was asking too many questions. "I really couldn't say," said I to him. "He must have some interest in a case of Sir John's, but I couldn't suppose what it was."

He nodded and fell silent for a moment—which gave me time enough to glance up at the clock and let out a yelp of dismay.

"Dear God," said I, "Just look at that clock, will you?"

"Look at it? What's wrong with it?"

"It's the time. Why, I was to meet my chums ten minutes ago. They'll be quite angry with me, I fear. Sorry, Mr. Hogg, but I fear I must be going." I slid off the stool and began backing off toward the door.

"Oh, oh yes. I understand. I'll be looking for you when the races begin."

"Awfully good talking to you, but I must go find them now."

Calling to me that he understood, he waved a goodbye to me as I escaped through the door. And there I was, ready to rush cross Uxbridge whether Mr. Baker be there or not.

Preparations for the race were much further along. Riders were on their mounts, circling them about as they warmed them for the first heat. Those horses scheduled for later heats were walked round by their grooms. There were horses, touts, jockeys, oddsmen, bettors, and watchers quite everywhere. The level of shouting and talking had risen to a level I would not earlier have supposed to be possible. The number congregating in this corner of the Common had tripled, perhaps quadrupled, in the hour or so during which I had been inside the Elephant and Castle. How was I to find Mr. Baker in such a crowd of people? or, for that matter, Deuteronomy Plummer?

I plunged into this great, milling mob of people and crisscrossed it a couple of times, looking for a familiar face, hoping to find one before more strangers came and added to my difficulty. Yet, as it happened, 'twas not I who was the finder, but another who found me. I recall discovering myself trapped in an unyielding knot of bettors surrounding an oddsman who shouted his numbers louder than all the rest. Since I could not move, I remained in place, listening to him chant in the manner of an auctioneer as he went down the listings on his slate. In this sense, I was reminded by him of the arcane activities of the patrons of Lloyd's Coffee Shop in the City of London.

I felt a hand upon my shoulder and a squeeze, at which I turned to find—not Mr. Baker, as I half-expected, but rather Constable Patley.

"If you're thinkin' of putting down a wager, Jeremy," said he to me in a voice strong enough to be heard by one and all, "you'd do well to do it with another who gives better odds. This fella just shouts the loudest."

There was a round of laughter at that. I joined in, but the odds-man certainly did not. As his audience fell away and began drifting off in every direction, he looked darkly at Mr. Patley and snarled some quite incomprehensible malediction at him.

"And right back at you, sir," responded Mr. Patley to him. And then, to me, he said: "Come along, Jeremy. We've got us a good place to watch from."

And he then guided me along the course to one of the horse carts placed there as a marker on the way. He was right. The cart provided an excellent view of the race course, and the two Bow Street Runners, my companions, were incomparably well-informed guides to the sport. Nor was I surprised by their knowledge, for Mr. Baker was well known in Bow Street for his love of the turf; and it did but stand to reason that Mr. Patley, who had done army service in the King's Carabineers, a mounted regiment, would bring with him his equine interests into civilian life. The two men carried on long-running debates on the virtues of this horse or that, or one jockey or another. In sum, I could not have found two better teach-ers in all of London.

My education began with a question.

"Tell me, Jeremy," said Mr. Baker, "is this your first time out to a race?"

I admitted that it was so, and, in my defense, offered about the same excuses I'd given to Mr. Hogg when he asked me if I had ever seen Deuteronomy Plummer race. All that I had said was true, of course, yet what was also true was that I simply had not had the right sort of occasion to do so.

"Well, you come to the right place to start," said Mr. Patley.

"Why? Is this one expected to be a specially good one?"

"Oh, it'll be good enough," he assured me. "There's a lot of good horses and a lot of good riders. But that ain't really what I had in mind."

"What then?"

"Well, this right here—the Shepherd's Bush Common—is about the best, and cert'ny the longest course round London."

"Just look at it," put in Mr. Baker as he gestured toward the large expanse before us. "There's a full eight acres here the way it's laid out. And when horses make it four times round carrying their riders, that's quite a stretch for them."

"I can see that," I assured him.

"Only thing wrong with it," said Patley, "is that it's laid out kind of peculiar."

"Peculiar in what way?"

"Take a look at it. See? It goes from the start, to there, to up here where we are, and then back to the start again. In other words, it's a triangular course."

"They laid it out that way to make it long as they could," said Mr. Baker, "but it makes for an awful big scramble and pileup here."

"Where?" I asked, not quite understanding.

"Right here, where we are in this horse cart. See, Jeremy, this cart where we've taken our places to watch all, this serves as the 'Distance Post.' They've all got to go round it and sometimes it gets kind of crowded. If they fail to circle it, or haven't circled it by the time the leader has made one full tour of the course, then they must drop out of all the following heats. You understand now, don't you?"

"Oh, well, yes—yes, of course." Or so I said. In truth, I had understood only a portion of it. Yet, it seemed to me that I should understand quite all after I had watched a heat of the race run.

"Good lad," said both together in what seemed a single voice.

I hung over the side of the cart and studied the final preparations for the race at some distance. Two drummer boys beat a rat-tat-tat upon their drums, signaling that the horses were to come forward to the starting line.

As they came up, I asked, "Which of the riders is Deuteronomy Plummer?"

"Aw, I heard you met him and came to watch him particular," said Mr. Patley. "Well, that's the man, third along the line. See?"

Yes, I did see. There was little to distinguish him from the rest of the jockeys—only the colors that he wore, which were green and white. They were indeed a colorful lot. Every color of the rainbow and all mixtures thereof were there at the starting line. As I studied them, a thought occurred to me, and I thought it might be wise to frame it in a question to my tutors.

"Both of you seem to agree that this corner of the course can get quite crowded as the horses round the cart. Is that right?"

"Oh, it is indeed."

"Right as ever can be."

"Then this must be a dangerous spot from which to watch."

"Well," said Mr. Baker, "you might say so, but it's a great place to see the action, ain't it, Patley?"

"Oh, none better, not in all Shepherd's Bush Common."

"But dangerous," said I.

"Well, I'll tell you what. If the cart starts to go over—and it's been known to happen—just get over to the other side and jump clear, far as you can," said Mr. Baker.

"Good advice," said Mr. Patley.

Not in the least comforted by what I had heard, I returned to my study of the horses and riders at the starting line. I concentrated my gaze upon Mr. Deuteronomy and the beautiful red mount beneath him. Did beauty, in this case, mean quality, I asked them.

"Aw, he's a beauty, in truth, ain't he?" said Patley. "Name is Pegasus, and from what I hear he deserves it. Ain't he the horse with wings in the storybooks?"

"Onliest thing to be afraid of," said Mr. Baker, "is that he looks headstrong, and might not run the race Deuteronomy tells him to. This is his first race, y'see."

A bugler on horseback appeared, put his horn to his lips, and blew a call. The horses at the starting line didn't care for that at all—and Pegasus least of all. He broke ranks with the rest, and it was all that his bearded rider could do to bring him back into place.

"Oh, he's a good horse, all right. He's ready to go," said Patley.

"That call was just to the stragglers, but there ain't no stragglers, so in just a minute, or maybe less . . ."

Quite without warning, a shot was fired. I looked about me, half-expecting one of the crowd to fall wounded. But no, 'twas rather the signal for the heat to begin. Yet not all the horses, or their riders, seemed to know that. Horses reared. Riders fell. Nearly half were left at the starting line. The rest, who had got off to a good start, thundered toward us. There must have been a dozen or more on the long straightaway, and to see a small army of large animals coming direct at our horse cart at full gallop made me most uneasy.

Without quite willing it so, I found myself pulling to the far side of the cart, from which Mr. Baker had advised me to jump if—

"Easy there, Jeremy," Mr. Patley shouted to me above the noise of the crowd and the horses. "No need to jump yet."

At that I nodded my understanding, though I reserved my agreement for a bit later.

The pack was upon us. I was surprised to see that Pegasus— and Mr. Deuteronomy—were not in the lead. No, nothing of the kind. Horse and rider were comfortably in the middle. They circled wide round us as the rest jammed in tight at the apex of the triangle. Whips flashed. Jockeys pushed back and forth, one at the other. Horses were thrown against our cart. They bit. Riders howled and threatened. Then, fast as they had come, they were gone, down the far leg of the triangle to its base, where all but Pegasus were involved in the same sort of close combat as we had witnessed here, near at hand; again, Pegasus gave it a wide berth and fought to keep his place, which was comfortably in the middle of the pack. Then did they come up at us again, and they fought ever harder to make it round us at the apex.

So was it with each successive tour of the course—until, at the end of the fourth, a gray won the heat. Pegasus, ridden by Mr. Deuteronomy, came in a modest third. I was quite disappointed by the performance, and I said as much to my companions.

"Aw, not so, not a bit of it," said Mr. Baker to me. "Remember, Jeremy, what we just seen was no more than the first of four heats. Ain't that so?"

I allowed that it was. "Nevertheless," said I, "would it not be a matter of honor to at least *try* to win *every* heat?"

"No, listen, Jeremy. This is the way Deuteronomy does it with every horse he rides. The only honor involved here is winning the race."

"Just look at Pegasus," said Patley. "He ain't even properly worked up a sweat." And it was true. As his rider started him round the course to cool him off, the big red seemed not to glisten, as did the rest.

It appeared that the winning gray—named Storm Cloud, as I recall—looked as if he had fought a great battle to win the heat— and indeed, he had. He was applauded by those who had bet the heat and won. (Nevertheless, he was one of three eliminated in the next heat.)

When Mr. Deuteronomy passed us by, leading Pegasus, we applauded him warmly. And for his part, he accepted it in good spirit, removing his jaunty little cap and waving it in response. Yet I noted something odd: though he waved, he did not smile. The features of his face, seen close, were cold and unmoving as any statue's.

"Now, you just wait, Jeremy," said Mr. Baker. "Next two heats will go just like this one. Pegasus won't win, but he'll finish close enough that he'll have a spot for himself in the final heat."

"And what will happen in that one?" I asked, though I'd guessed the answer, of course.

"Why, he'll win, bless you lad, he'll win."

"And he'll collect the prize of fifty pounds for his owner," said Mr. Patley. "But I wonder if it ain't your friend, Deuteronomy, deserves it more than the horse."

"Remember what I said just before the heat started?" said Baker. "About the horse? I said, he's got the stuff to win, but he's headstrong. If he just runs the kind of race his jockey tells him to run, he'll do just fine. Well, he proved he can follow orders, so it's a good bet he'll win the final heat."

And that, reader, is just how it went. The only real test offered Pegasus and Mr. Deuteronomy that afternoon was in the last heat at the "Distance Post"—in other words, just beyond the cover afforded us by the cart. Horse and rider had then to establish their primacy, nor did they shrink from the task. They rode into the tight turn at near top speed. Deuteronomy fought his way forward by flailing left and right with his whip. And Pegasus did his part well by biting the leader that crowded him on the inside, causing the horse to shy into our cart and sending us into a frightening tip. Yet, thank God, we righted and saw Pegasus speed away from the tight turn. After that, they gave him space aplenty.

Indeed, as predicted, Pegasus did win and this, I found out, was the first time ever he had raced. He received a drum-and-fife salute. His owner stepped forward to accept his fifty pounds, all of it in a jingling bag. When I spied the face of him who claimed the prize, my eyes widened and my face gave expression to my dismayed surprise.

"What's got into you, Jeremy?" Mr. Baker asked. "You look like you just bit into a sour apple."

"I feel like it, too. That man up there, the one who just collected the fifty pounds, he was damned rude to me when I asked him the time of day."

"Well," said Mr. Patley, "there's rude and there's damned rude. Now, what was it qualified Lord Lamford for felony rudeness?"

"*Lord* Lamford, is it? Wouldn't it be so?" said I. Then did I proceed to tell them of the incident. And in truth, told so, it amounted to little. I could tell that neither man was greatly impressed by my anecdote. Yet had they been there and received his verbal slap in the face, I was certain that each would have reacted as I did.

"Yes, well, Jeremy, these lords and ladies, they get pretty tetchy when you approach them just as you might anyone," said Mr. Baker.

"Oh, I know that, and I was polite as could be. It's just . . . Oh, let's end it right there, shall we?"

"Perhaps we'd best," said Patley. "We got to collect our winnings before the oddsman does a scarper on us. We'll meet you right here, and we'll all ride back to town together. Suit you, Jeremy?" Then, as an afterthought: "Deuteronomy, by the bye, rides mostly for Lamford."

With that, they left me where I stood, and I moved a few steps closer to Lord Lamford—close enough, in any case, that I might hear him boast to his fellows in his self-assured drawl of how *he* had won the race: ". . . told my man to hold him back till the last heat, and then—*then* did you see him go?" And did they not all crowd round him to listen to his braggadocio! One would think that Deuteronomy Plummer had just sat astride Pegasus all afternoon because the rules required it: all two-year-olds must be accompanied by an adult—something of that sort.

As my mind went to Deuteronomy, so also did my eyes. He stood, saying naught, holding loosely onto the reins of the horse. I studied him at a distance of forty or fifty feet. He talked to no one and looked neither right nor left until, of a sudden, he turned in my direction and looked straight at me. It was as though he had known all along that I was there. Then, staring at me in the expressionless manner he had looked at us when we applauded him, he handed the reins to a nearby groom and came straight over to me. When he arrived, he looked me up and down and said naught for a good long bit. When at last he did speak, he expressed doubt.

"Are you really the Beak's assistant?"

"Yes," said I, "yes I am. If you want to hear that confirmed, you can wait for those two men I was with to come back. They're both constables at the Bow Street Court."

"No, if you say so, then I'll believe you. Just keep that in mind, though, 'cause if you lie to me, I'll find out, and then I'll never believe you again. Even if you told me today was Easter Sunday, I'd say it wasn't."

"All right, what do you want to know?"

"I want to know if he's going to do something about all this that has to do with Alice and—you know—my niece. Is he going to do something, or just shake his head and go on to the next thing?"

"That's not his way. If you'd seen him when I brought him word, then you'd know that."

"Did he shed a tear? I wept for that child all night long."

"No, that's not his way, either. He can't cry. It's to do with his blindness."

"All right, put it like this: Has he got anybody working on it?"

I hesitated but a moment. "I'm working on it right now."

He sniggered in spite of himself. "You? What're you doing here? Investigating the horses?"

"No, Sir John sent me here because he believed you were capable of killing your sister when you left him yester evening. He thought it would be good if I showed up here, so you'd see me and know that we were keeping an eye on you."

"I b'lieve I could have done her in if I'd come across her *then*."

"But not now?"

"No, not now. Whilst I was busy shedding tears, I did some thinking. And it seemed to me that he—and prob'ly you, too—are better at investigating than I'll ever be. So the best thing would be if we was to investigate together. You help me, and I'll help you."

"After all," said I, "whatever you think of your sister, it wasn't she who killed her daughter. We'll need her to find the one who did."

"That's where I come in," said he. "I've got some ideas where she might be. And I thought we might go together, that is, if you . . ."

"I'll need all the help you can give me, Mr. Deuteronomy."

"All right then, what say we get us together and meet at the coffee house that faces onto Haymarket Square—say about eleven o'clock."

"I know the place. I'll be there at eleven."

With that, he nodded, turned, and walked away. Well, I thought, there'll be a lot to talk about with Sir John when I get back to Bow Street.

On the contrary, my report to Sir John was given to him quickly in his study. He listened carefully to all that I had to say, nodding thoughtfully but making no comment. Even when I came at last to the offer made by Deuteronomy Plummer to join in the search for his sister, Sir John's immediate response was simply a grunt. 'Twas only as I completed my recital and rose to return to the kitchen that the magistrate commented upon the information I had given him.

"I take it you accepted Deuteronomy's offer of help?"

"Why, yes I did," said I. "Is that not as you would have it?"

"Oh yes, certainly it is. But let me give you a bit of advice."

"Please, sir."

"Simply put, it is this: Though he may have said that you know more than he about how to conduct an investigation, he will nevertheless try to wrest control of the investigation from you. Don't allow him to do that. Remember that you have something specific that you had intended to attend to. One way or another, with him or without him, you must attend to it. You will, won't you?"

"I will, sir," said I, yet still I hung on, unwilling to leave.

"You may go, Jeremy. Your dinner may be cold, yet I think you will deem it one of the best you've eaten."

"I'm indeed looking forward to it, sir, but . . . well, may I ask, is there perhaps something wrong?"

"Wrong? How do you mean that, Jeremy?"

"You seemed so silent, so removed."

"Oh, I heard you well enough, but my mind was, I admit, upon

other matters. It being Easter, I found myself thinking upon this
Plummer case—the little girl pulled dead from the Thames, perhaps
sold by her mother to a fate so hideous it cannot, should not, even
be mentioned. I wondered what, if anything, God thinks of all
this—if He may wonder from time to time if it was all worth the
trouble." He sighed a deep—oh, a profound sigh. And only then did
he add, "I received Mr. Donnelly's final autopsy report today. Mr.
Marsden read it to me. It seems then that in spite of all that was
done to her, Margaret Plummer died of asphyxiation. She was
smothered."

With that, I bade him goodnight and went down to claim my
dinner. A considerable slice of that glorious ham, of which Clarissa
was so proud, had been warmed for me upon the fire in a pan. The
potatoes and carrots, more difficult to warm, were served to me cold
by her.

Ah, but Clarissa was afterward anything but cold. We did hug
and kiss, squeeze and fondle, for now that we were engaged to be
engaged, she allowed me liberties (indeed, took a few herself)
which were never before offered, nor even requested. Such was our
situation: we carried on a courtship under the very noses of Sir
John and Lady Fielding, altogether certain that they guessed
naught of the change in our relations. But perhaps they knew more,
and knew it earlier, than we had supposed.

Next day, when I met with Deuteronomy Plummer at the Haymarket Coffee House, I spread out before him on the table all the numbered stubs and tickets which I had found in Katy Tiddle's room.

He glanced at them indifferently, shrugged, and said, "What
about them?"

"Well, what are they? I've studied them, and all I can tell you is
that the numbers were written by diverse hands, and that, no matter
how they are arranged and rearranged, they make no sense. That is
to say, there was no code discernible. But how could there be, with
so many numbers in so many different hands? After all—?"

"Leave off, leave off," said Mr. Deuteronomy in a way somewhat gruff. "You mean to tell me that you've no proper notion of
what these here bits of paper might be?"

"None at all." I hesitated. "It's been suggested to me that these may be pawn tickets, though somehow I doubt it."

"Well, that tells me more about you than it does about this Katy Tiddle woman. Of course they're pawn tickets. Did you never pawn?"

I was annoyed at the lordly manner he had, of a sudden, taken on. "What does that tell you about me?" I demanded.

"It tells me you was brought up as a child of privilege, for one thing," said he.

"If it tells you that, it tells you false, for I am an orphan and nothing more. I work as I do for Sir John to pay my keep. I am the servant, and he my master."

That, reader, was by no means a fair summary of where I stood with regard to Sir John, nor he with me. If you have read thus far, then you know that he was to me far more in the nature of a teacher. And the things he taught did often exceed lessons in the law. It would not have been too much to claim him as my stepfather, yet I would not do so to Deuteronomy Plummer, for his remark had irritated me beyond telling. Child of privilege, indeed! I had all manner of household duties to perform. I served as Sir John's amanuensis, writing the letters he dictated to me and often delivering them, as well. I served as the magistrate's eyes during investigations of every sort, and, upon occasion, also as his bodyguard. And, finally, I had lately played substitute for Mr. Marsden, Sir John's court clerk, during his recent bouts with influenza. And so on.

Yet I told Mr. Deuteronomy none of this, for he gave me little opportunity to speak out, blurting forth so swiftly that I doubt he heard my voiced reply at all.

"And what it tells me of Katy Tiddle is that she is a woman made poor by her drinking, as is my sister. I've met the woman upon occasion, she livin' next door to my sister, and that is the opinion of her I have formed. Those numbered stubs and tickets—call them what you will—is from pawn shops hereabouts. It took two days time, and you still hadn't figured out what they were, nor where they was from. Anybody don't know what pawn tickets look like is a proper child of privilege, as far as I'm concerned. And anyways, why should we be chasing after what this woman pawned? Why ain't we out chasing after Alice herself?"

"Just how much did Sir John tell you about Katy Tiddle and how she fits into this case?"

"Well, I . . ." He hesitated, unable for a moment to express himself. Then did he begin again: "Truth of it is, after I heard about little Maggie, how she died and all, I didn't get much after that. I remember he said something about Tiddle, but I'm afraid I didn't take in what it was."

"I can understand that. But listen, we've good reason to think that Katy Tiddle brought the man who took Maggie away to your sister. She served as a sort of go-between. It seemed to me that he came back and killed her to keep her from naming him."

"How do you know this?"

"From things she said when she identified the body. I thought we might go out to the pawn shops, at least a few of them, there around Seven Dials and take a look at the things she pawned to see if they give us any hints."

"Hints of what?"

"Hints of just who this man was."

"Well, all right," said he. "There's a couple of places, taverns and inns thereabouts, places Alice drank, where we can stop and ask after her. But, well, she's been gone awhile, ain't she?"

"She has," said I with a sigh, "but drink up, and we'll get started."

Having thus compromised, we set off for Cucumber Alley. It seemed best to work out in a sort of circle from there down into the heart of Seven Dials. And so we did. In a manner of speaking, there was little difference between the territory we explored and Bedford Street, which I knew far better. Yet there was this about Seven Dials: it attracted a lower class of inebriate. After observing the puffed faces and bleary eyes of passersby and of those sitting about on doorsteps, I asked him quite direct why he had chosen such a place as this to install his sister and niece. (This was a question, reader, which had plagued me ever since I had heard he paid the rent.)

"That is a question easily answered," said he, "for truth to tell, I did not choose it. She did. When at last I come to find her, she'd had Maggie and was sharing a room with a whore. I tempted her out of that situation, but she would not leave Seven Dials—oh no, young sir, she would *not*. So I got her into that room you saw and gave her a little each week so she wouldn't have to whore."

"But what about Maggie?"

"What about her?"

"Well, such circumstances could not have been good for the child."

"No, they wasn't, but Maggie never seemed to mind much — just so long as she had her dollies to play with. Truth to tell, Maggie wasn't quite right in the head. I suspicion that Alice dropped her once or twice whilst she was carryin' her about — but she said she never."

Though I have since heard worse, I recall thinking at the time that in the bare facts just given me by Mr. Deuteronomy, I had the saddest, squalidest, most wretched story I had ever heard. I recalled, too, something told us by Katy Tiddle when she went unwillingly with me to Mr. Donnelly's surgery to identify the body of Maggie Plummer.

"I am reminded," said I to Deuteronomy, "of what was said by Katy Tiddle of the man who took your niece away."

"Oh?" said he, now quickly on guard. "And what was that?"

"She told us that while it was true that your sister had probably taken money for little Maggie, it was also true that she was told that he would be bringing her to wealthy parents who would bring her up as one of their own. He told her Maggie would be happy with them, and Alice believed him."

"And what did Maggie say?"

"That we were not told. But see here, Mr. Deuteronomy, why not give your errant sister the benefit of the doubt? Perhaps she was aware of her shortcomings as a mother. Perhaps she did truly believe that Maggie would be better off with others. Perhaps —"

He cut me off: "Perhaps, perhaps, perhaps. Say whatever you like, but the child is still dead, ain't she?"

"Yes, but not at her mother's hand."

To that he had no response.

There were but three pawn shops in the vicinity of Seven Dials, yet by the time we had visited all three, we had disposed of all but one of the numbered bits of paper; there must have been about thirty in all. Though, as we learned, some (a very few) of the items pawned by Katy Tiddle had been sold to buyers off the street, the greater number were still available and in the shops. By invoking the name and authority of Sir John Fielding, I forced them to bring forth the items the woman had pawned. We examined them and found them to be, with only a few exceptions, the sort of treasures that might be fetched forth from a gentleman's pocket—watches, watch chains, kerchiefs of silk, cameos, et cetera. So, it seemed that Katy Tiddle was more skilled as a pickpocket than as a prostitute. The exceptions—items too large to be carried about in a pocket—clocks, a looking glass in a gilt picture frame, a jade chess set, et cetera, left me wondering if Tiddle were not perhaps a burglar, as well. But perhaps not, for the few clocks were quite heavy—at least a stone each. She may have bargained her quim with a proper burglar for such as that.

I learned much about the economics of the place. Seven Dials, it seemed, was supported by petty theft, for the most part. Bedford Street, by contrast, lived off grand theft, gambling, prostitution, and pimpery, and a hundred other more sophisticated and less legal enterprises; theirs was the more diverse economy.

Then, by earlier agreement, we moved on to what Mr. Deuteronomy assured me were his sister's favorite drinking spots; each, it turned out, was more dreary than the last. When I called this to his attention, he puffed his cheeks and blew air dismissively.

"They all seem the same to me," said he. "But then I ain't no gin-drinker, and gin is what them in such places crave."

And they craved little else, it seemed, for when we began our canvass of Alice's haunts we were struck most immediate by the quiet which pervaded them. There was little talk or laughter to be heard—a few mumbles from the tables, perhaps—but nothing so demanding as a conversation. That awful silence is what I recall most vividly. And again, how different this was from those rowdy dives in Bedford Street. There one could barely hear his own voice from the roar of the crowd, day or night. A few even offered music of a sort.

Why, I recall the last such place we called at in Seven Dials— and well into the afternoon it was. The place had no name, or at least none that I can remember—and no sign or decoration of any sort; all that I can recall is the single word, GIN, painted in bold letters upon the door.

We entered, and for a moment we were blinded by what at first seemed a total absence of light within the place. Yet the absence was not complete; a few candles burned inside, and as our eyes customed to the dimness, we did at least perceive the size and shape of the world we had entered. And yes, a "world" was just what it seemed, so distant and different was it from that we had just left. There must have been twenty-five or more seated at tables and standing at the bar. A few of them looked our way, staring at two who plainly did not belong. We were intruders, no question of it. Slowly, still surveying the dark interior as best we could, we made our way to the bar. (I noted, by the bye, that none made comment upon Mr. Deuteronomy's size at that location, nor had they in such places as we had visited earlier.)

The innkeeper climbed down from the stool upon which he was perched and came over to us.

"Which will it be?" he asked us. Then did he point to a sign up above his head. The sign did read: DRUNK FOR A PENNY/DEAD DRUNK FOR TUPPENCE.

"Neither one," said I. "Sir John Fielding did send me here to Seven Dials to ask a few questions of you. We're curious what's the last time you might have seen Alice Plummer?"

"Who's she?"

"Well, you *ought* to know her," said Mr. Deuteronomy to the innkeeper quite sharply. "She would come round here for her first glass of the day."

"That so? Well, we ain't too good on names round here. You take all what's in here now, about half of them couldn't tell you their *own* names, much less anyone else's. What's she look like?"

I, who had never seen the woman for whom we searched, could only shrug and gesture toward her brother. Yet, he provided quite satisfactorily.

"She's taller than me by near a foot," said Deuteronomy. "She's got kind of mousy-colored hair, blue eyes, and wears a blue cape which I gave to her."

"That ain't much of a description."

"Well, it's the best I can do."

"What about this?" said I. "She had a daughter about seven years old—but small for her age—name of Maggie."

"We don't serve them that young around here," said the innkeeper sternly. "You got to draw a line somewheres."

"I didn't say you did serve the little girl," said I. "I meant only that she might have been along."

"Oh, well, let's see." He concentrated visibly, a hand to his forehead, a pained look upon his face. "Wasn't there a Beak Runner come around a couple of times, asking after her? I mean the little girl, of course. He said she'd been stole. Now I recollect her and the woman who used to bring her in."

"That's her, all right," cried out Mr. Deuteronomy as loud and jubilant as if she had thus been brought back to life. "That's the both of them!"

"Well, I'll tell you what I told that Beak Runner. I ain't seen either one of them for near a month."

FOUR

*In which Maggie is
buried, and her uncle
continues the search*

❄️

Had there been mourners in attendance, the funeral of Margaret Plummer would have been grand as any. Strange it was to hear choir and organ in the nearly empty nave of St. Paul's, Covent Garden. They thundered forth in that early morning hour, yet only Deuteronomy Plummer, Clarissa, and I were present to hear. Mr. Deuteronomy sat front and center in the first row, and we two but a few rows behind him. The vicar said a proper funeral mass, at the end of which he ascended to the pulpit and preached a brief sermon.

Sermon, did I say? It was hardly that. There was little could be said as eloquently as was stated by the mere presence of that sad, small coffin before the altar. Yet it was, I suppose, a sermon right enough, for the vicar quoted St. Matthew, chapter 18, verse 6.

"But who so shall offend one of these little ones which believe," said he in a voice that rang forth strongly and filled the great church, "it were better for him that a millstone were hanged about his neck, and that he were drowned in the depth of the sea."

Then, pausing but a moment to look each of us in the eye, he continued, signaling by some lightening of his tone that he no longer quoted scripture but spoke now as himself: "It should be understood that this is the most frightening passage of any in the gospels. I know of no harsher words to come from the lips of our Lord than these. Why then did he save them for those who commit crimes against children? The answer should be plain to us all. Because such as they are quite unable to defend themselves. They must depend upon the generosity of others for their defense. I am told that this child, Margaret Mary Plummer, had no chance at all—that she was sold into a life no better than a form of slavery, which quickly ended her, and . . ."

The vicar, a man of sixty or more, went on in this vein for a bit longer, but my notice was just then diverted to Mr. Deuteronomy. 'Twas Clarissa who called my attention to him. She gave me a sharp nudge with her elbow in my side. Having thus signaled, she pointed across the rows which separated us and showed me how the vicar's words had affected our friend. His head was bowed, and the line of his shoulders was irregularly visible only just above the pew, for those little shoulders of his heaved up and down quite uncontrollably. He was weeping forlorn and bitter tears.

Even the vicar seemed to notice. He hurried his remarks through to the end and called for the pallbearers. Two men—no more—appeared from some spot secluded from our sight. Placing themselves one on each side the small coffin, they lifted it, and, to some stirring anthem sung by the choir, followed the vicar to the side door of the church, which, as I knew, led out to the churchyard. Mr. Deuteronomy fell in behind the coffin, and we behind him.

One of the pallbearers looked remarkably familiar. Though I could not immediately place him, I was inescapably certain that I had not only seen but also talked with him most recent. Now, who was he? Then, soon as I had put the question to myself, I had the answer. 'Twas Walter Hogg, the fellow I had talked with before the race in Shepherd's Bush. He it was had also removed his hat to the jockey the day before the race when we met by chance in Covent Garden. I'd no idea why he served as pallbearer. How strange that he should have popped up again this way. Had he volunteered for such duty? I resolved to speak with him at the earliest opportunity and find out.

The grave, newly dug beneath an oak tree, was easily detected as soon as we made our way through the entrance into the church-yard. It was a choice location. Deuteronomy Plummer must have paid a pretty penny for it, I reflected, for there's naught that comes cheap in such a funeral as this one. And of course Mr. Deuteronomy would spare little or nothing in providing his niece with the finest for her final resting place. By and by we came to the spot. The pall-bearers rested the coffin upon the cross bars above the grave and stepped aside. Then did the vicar begin his prayers at the graveside as Deuteronomy wept on ceaselessly. At the prayer ("Man, thou art dust") the vicar indicated that Mr. Deuteronomy might toss a handful of dirt upon the coffin, but the offer was declined. At another signal, the two pallbearers picked up the ropes with which the coffin would be lowered into the open grave. Yet there was something still to be done. The vicar seemed to be looking at me and pointing down. At first, I had no notion of what he wished from me, yet a bit of gesturing made it all clear: I was to pull out the cross bars which supported the coffin. I scrambled to it, and as the pallbearers supported the box with the ropes, I whisked the wooden bars out from under it. And then slowly, little by little, it disappeared down into the darkness of the earth. "Ashes to ashes, dust to dust . . ."

Oddly, Mr. Deuteronomy seemed to regain his composure immediately after the graveside service. He went straight to the vicar and, after blowing his nose loudly into a silk kerchief and dabbing at his eyes to dry the tears, he pulled from his coat pocket a purse filled with coin and opened negotiations with the clergyman.

And, for my part, I sought out Walter Hogg that I might discover how he came to participate in these proceedings. As it happened, he was on the far side of the grave, working free one of the ropes on which the coffin had rested. He wound it swiftly and expertly round his arm. He seemed eager to be away. Clarissa followed me out of curiosity and listened in.

"May I have a word with you, Mr. Hogg?"

"Well, I haven't much time now, have I? Must be on to another funeral," said he.

"Have you something to do with the church here?"

"Naw, naw, 'tain't like that at all."

"But you're not a friend of Mr. Plummer, are you? I seem to recall from our conversation that you . . ."

"No, I told you I never had sand enough to walk up to him and meet myself up to him. Arthur and me"—he nodded at his companion—"we work for the embalmer. Learning the secrets of the trade, as you might say."

"Surely not as an apprentice? You're a good deal too old for that."

"No, we just works for him. That's all. Part of workin' for him is we fill in as pallbearers when it's necessary, as so it was today."

"Well, all right," said I, "but wouldn't you like to meet Deuteronomy Plummer? I'd be happy to introduce you."

"No time for that. Like I say, another funeral."

With that, he turned his back on me and, having concluded his winding of the rope, he called quietly to his companion: "Arthur, you ready, are you?"

Arthur nodded, shouldered his coil of rope, and shuffled about, indicating his readiness to depart. Walter Hogg turned back to me.

"Now, if I understood a-right," said he, "that little girl in the coffin, she was some relation to Mr. Deuteronomy, ain't that so?"

"That's so," said I.

"Well, I wonder, will he be riding at Newmarket this Sunday? It's a King's Plate race—all the best from all the counties will be there. Didn't mention anything about that to you, did he?"

"Not a thing."

"Just as I feared. Well, I'll go there and take me chances. Good-bye to you, young sir"—with a nod to Clarissa—"and to you, young lady."

Then did he leave with Arthur in tow. The two men headed for the gate which led to Bedford Street. Their wagon was there in the alley, no doubt, and indeed, I vaguely recalled an embalmer's shop in King Street, if I were not mistaken. But it was not the sort of thing that would stay in your head, was it?

"What was that all about?" Clarissa whispered.

"I'm not sure," said I quite honestly. "Just someone popping up where he wasn't expected. Probably just a coincidence."

"Writers of romances know there is no such thing as 'just a coincidence,'" said she smugly. "For what it's worth, I didn't like the looks of the fellow at all."

"I'll tell you all that I know about him later on."

"See that you do."

Having come at last to a figure that suited them both, Mr. Deuteronomy and the vicar clasped hands. Then did the jockey count out the sum into the clergyman's hand. Though I had not a good view, judging from the time it took to count it out, it must have been a considerable amount. He turned round then and came toward us, casting not a downward glance as he passed beside the open grave. Looking from one of us to the other, he made it plain that he wished to be introduced to Clarissa. I did the formalities with dispatch and (I thought) a bit of style, as well.

"I wish to thank you both for coming to the service," said Mr. Deuteronomy. "She got a proper sendoff, don't you think?"

Clarissa seemed puzzled. "She?"

"Maggie, Margaret Mary—my niece."

"Oh," said she. "Oh, yes of course—the funeral. It was all quite grand. I . . . I shall always remember it. The sermon!"

"The choir," said I.

"Anyways," said he, "it seemed like the least I could do for her."

"You . . ." I hesitated, not knowing quite how I might best frame the question. "You may not wish to go out today in search of your sister. I can well understand if you do not. Just say the word and—"

"Oh no! No indeed," said he, interrupting. "I would not think of deserting the hunt. Not now, not ever! Just give me time to duck back to me ken to change me duds, and I'll meet you at that same coffee house we met at yestermorn. That suit you?"

I nodded. "It suits me well."

"Good. Then it's agreed, ain't it? Oh, but one more thing. When we first met, you had a pistol you was carryin' about. You recall, you took it from that Tiddle woman."

"I recall right enough."

"Bring it along again, would you?"

"Why? Are the places we'll visit today so dangerous that we must enter them armed?"

"No, not so. I've got a notion about that pistol, so bring it along. I'll tell you about it when I see you in the Haymarket. And bring along that last pawn ticket, will you? That's part of my notion."

I spent the length of our walk to Number 4 Bow Street bringing Clarissa to date on aspects of the case. She wanted first to know all I could tell her about Walter Hogg—which, in truth, was not much.

"What is most interesting about him," said I to her, "is that he has appeared quite unexpectedly twice since he first doffed his hat to Deuteronomy Plummer here in Covent Garden."

"But, as I said earlier, Jeremy, there are no coincidences."

"Well, no doubt they are rare, but surely this is one."

"Perhaps—but I doubt it. Do you think he and Mr. Deuteronomy are acquainted?"

"I doubt that very strongly. You recall I offered to introduce him to Mr. Deuteronomy? Well, it seemed to me then that the fellow was truly in awe of the jockey. Look upon it so, Clarissa. We may see Deuteronomy as no more than one who rides upon racing horses—though having seen him at it, I can well believe that he is the very best there is—nevertheless, Mr. Hogg sees him as something more, a source of money, dependable income. I doubt not that Hogg makes more by betting upon Mr. Deuteronomy each Sunday than he does from laboring the rest of the week for his embalmer."

Clarissa gave that some thought. "Do you mean, Jeremy, that there is so much to be made from wagering upon horses?"

"I'd say there was no question of it. Why, I saw near as much cash changing hands at Shepherd's Bush a day past as I saw of an evening at Black Jack Bilbo's Gaming Club."

"Really? I'd no idea."

"And bear in mind," I continued, "that the meet in Shepherd's Bush was by no means one of the grand races—nothing, that is, compared to what's held at Newmarket out on the heath. You heard what Hogg had to say about that, didn't you?"

"That all the best from all the counties would be there—horses, presumably."

"Horses indeed! And they'll be there to run because the prize money is grandest there—though Mr. Patley insists that for the owners and breeders it's the honor of winning that means most."

'Twas when this was said that we left the Garden and struck off down Russell Street on our way to Bow Street, just round the corner—that much I recall exact, though I am not near so certain of the precise words of Clarissa which followed. I believe, however, that they went something like this:

"Jeremy?"

"Yes, Clarissa, what is it?"

"That King's Plate race in Newmarket—that's next Sunday, is it not?"

"So it is."

"Will you be going to it, as you did to Shepherd's Bush, in order to keep an eye on our Mr. Deuteronomy?"

"I doubt it," said I. "First of all, Newmarket is quite some distance north—near Cambridge it is. And then, too, Deuteronomy has been so cooperative the last day or two that I, personally, think there's no need to keep a close watch on the fellow."

"But say you were to go up there," said she. "Since this is an all-England event, might it not be that there would be an even greater number of bettors, and consequently greater sums wagered?"

What was she getting at, I wondered. "That would be a probable result," said I.

"Well then, Newmarket offers a great opportunity."

"An opportunity of what sort?"

"Just think of it. If we were to combine your money with mine—we each have a little, after all—the combined amount would be, well, no longer just a little, but more than that."

"Yet still not a lot!"

"Nevertheless," she declared, "it could be enough to win us our fortune, given favorable odds."

"*Favorable odds?* Dear God, Clarissa, are you seriously proposing that we gamble away the little money we have in pursuit of making a fortune for ourselves? Why, that's . . . that's laughable."

"Not with favorable odds and the right attitude."

Though what she said was silly, somehow she did not appear silly saying it. No, the expression she wore on her face was one of quiet conviction. She believed profoundly in what she said.

"And what, pray tell, is the right attitude?"

"Prayerful and submissive."

At that I threw up my hands in dismay. "Oh, Clarissa, be serious, won't you?"

"I *am* being serious—and never more so. This is our future we're discussing, is it not? Don't you see? We could be married!"

Arriving as I did in the Haymarket Coffee House only minutes after my departure from Number 4 Bow Street, I expected to pass a quarter of an hour or more sipping my favorite Jamaica brew be-

fore the arrival of Mr. Deuteronomy. Had I not hurried the distance
that I might enjoy myself thus? Some men can spend a day drinking
their good English bitter, others will consume gin or rum as long
as they are upright. Yet my passion had been and always would be
to drink coffee. It is in every way superior to those alcoholic bev-
erages, for while they stupefy him who partakes of them, coffee
quickens and sharpens the senses and improves the function of the
brain. Let all who doubt me note that coffee is the favored refresh-
ment in all such places as Lloyd's and the Old Bailey, in which the
leaders of commerce, business, and the law do gather. Now, the
Haymarket's patrons, while in no wise leaders in such fields, were in
no wise in the same class as the louts, criminals, and drunkards,
who frequented the dives and grog shops in Bedford Street and
Seven Dials. It was, however, as one might suppose, just the sort
of place that might be frequented by one such as Deuteronomy
Plummer.

And he was here already, having preceded me by half-a-mug of
Jamaica brew. He was all for leaving at the moment of my arrival
that we might continue our search for his sister. But pleading an
early rising time and the need to discuss his new notion regarding
the pistol taken from Katy Tiddle, I managed to convince him that
it would be best to discuss the next step to be taken before taking it.
I ordered a coffee for myself.

"Did you bring that pistol along?" he demanded. "The one I
asked you to?"

"Certainly I did," said I, and, having said that, lifted it carefully
out of my pocket and placed it on the table between us. The server
came just then with my mug of coffee, and his eyes widened as he
beheld the thing on the table—yet he said not a word. Indeed, it was
a rather lethal-looking piece, was it not? Yet, it had a certain beauty
to it, too—the engraving upon the hammer, the butt, even the barrel; and, of course, the evident signs of skill and craftsmanship that
were to be seen in every detail of its construction.

"And what about the pawn ticket? Have you brought that,
too?" he asked in a manner most insistent.

"Yes, of course."

I produced it and laid it down beside the pistol.

"Good, that's very good indeed. See here," said he, looking about the coffee house and lowering his voice, "what I got in mind is this: The pawn ticket here ain't no real pawn ticket at all."

"Then what is it?"

"Why, it's the sort of ticket you're given in any sort of shop that serves the gentry when you bring in something that needs repair — to a tailor, a dressmaker — or to a gunsmith."

"I don't understand," said I. "What is it put you in mind of this?"

"Well, the paper it's on, for one thing. When we was passing it back and forth a day past, I happened to give it a careful look, and I noticed that it was printed upon substantial stuff and not the flimsy sort of the rest. Another thing — the numbers are just jotted down in pen and ink on the pawn tickets."

"Whereas on this one here . . ." I held up the small rectangle of stiff paper.

"The number — what is it? twenty-nine? — is printed, well, stamped upon it, really. Now, it would take a very fancy shop to use such a device as one to make a stamp with different numbers, now wouldn't it?"

"I suppose it would, but how do you know that it's a gunsmith's shop?"

"I don't — not truly. 'Tis just a maggot that's fixed itself within my head, but there's good reason to think it, ain't there? You said a while back that you took it away from that Tiddle woman. And just look at it. How would the likes of her come by such? That we don't know, but we do know that she had naught in her possession of greater value, nothing that even came close. Why, if you added up the true value of all the items we looked at yesterday — I mean the things she pawned with no intention of redeeming — we'd probably find that all together they weren't equal in worth to this pistol. So . . ."

"So? What are you suggesting?"

"That we try our luck at some of the gunsmith shops nearby. I know of a few. You probably do, too."

Since I could think of nothing better to suggest, I agreed to follow his suggestion, though not without some misgivings. What about Sir John's warning against allowing Mr. Deuteronomy to take the investigation out of my hands? Why had I not planned for the next step in this peculiar search? It seemed that I could do little more than ride the coattails of him I had earlier permitted merely to help.

I found Deuteronomy Plummer surprisingly knowledgeable in all matters pertaining to firearms, spouting information wherever we did go. The thought came to me, as we set off on what seemed to me a bootless effort, that my companion may simply have planned it all this way that he might escape the burden of what may have been for him simply another boring day.

We thought it best to proceed on the same general principle as we had established the day before: that Katy Tiddle was too lazy and too besotted with booze to wander far from Seven Dials. So we would try those gunsmiths who were nearest first. I admit that I found the bits of gun lore I learned along the way quite anything but boring. I recall that in the first shop we visited — Wogdon's, I believe, right there in the Haymarket — the clerk admired the pistol we showed him but said they had nothing like it in the shop. The clerk also said that the ticket we showed him was not one of theirs. But then, just as we were leaving, he asked if we might not like to see something "a little special." Before I could decline, Mr. Deuteronomy had accepted the invitation and had us looking over an early-sixteenth-century hand cannon. When I said quite innocently that I'd no idea there were firearms quite so early, I was set a-right by both men who, together, lectured me at great length on the history of firearms in Europe. At the next, which was Nock's, I received the word on firing devices — matchlocks, wheel locks, and flintlocks, and had to listen as Nock's clerk puffed Henry Nock's contribution to the history of firearms (his patented lock), which he called a "great step forward." It slips my mind just now what it was I learned at Manton's, but at the shop of Joseph Griffin in Bond Street I learned nothing at all.

That was because when the clerk emerged from the rear of the shop, presenting himself all spruce and dapper, he took up the ticket I had placed upon the counter and smiled in recognition.

"Ah," said he, "I'd been wondering when someone might drop by for this. A pistol, isn't it?"

"No doubt it is, sir. It should be a mate for this."

And so saying, I hauled out the pistol which I had taken from Katy Tiddle and placed it on the counter.

"Ah yes, of course. I shall be but a moment." He then did turn and disappear behind the curtain into the rear of the shop.

Saying nothing, yet wearing an I-told-you-so expression, Mr. Deuteronomy offered me a wink. We had not long to wait, for quick as Bob's your uncle, the fellow was back, carrying a box about a foot square and half-a-foot deep.

"Here we are," said he, "a bent hammer, or so it says on the repair slip. I'll not ask how it came to need fixing," said he, chuckling as if he had made a great joke. "Perhaps you would like to check it over." And having said that, he laid down the box before us and opened it. The thing did fairly gleam at us from its bed of plush. "If you like, I shall polish up the one you brought in whilst you inspect this one."

As I smiled and handed over the pistol I had pulled from my pocket, I happened to glance at my companion and, expecting him to be smiling in triumph, found him looking troubled instead. No, more than merely "troubled," Mr. Deuteronomy seemed absolutely thunderstruck. He was reading the repair bill, and I wanted to ask him just what it was had so taken him aback, yet I thought it unwise to do so within the hearing of the clerk.

When the latter returned from the buffer, the pistol in his hand seemed to sparkle and gleam like the one from the case that now rested in the right hand of Mr. Deuteronomy. Snap-snap-snap, it went — just as it should.

"You see?" said the clerk. "It now works as well as its mate. Not much of a job, really."

"Well yes, I understand," said I, "but how much will that be? You see, this is evidence — important evidence — in an important investigation conducted by the magistrate of the Bow Street Court."

An uneasy look appeared upon the face of the clerk. Clearly he did fear that I would simply claim the pistol, the case, and all, in the name of Sir John Fielding.

"Never mind that, lad," said Mr. Deuteronomy. "Let's hear the cost of it, shall we?"

"Just half a pound," said the clerk. "Ten shillings."

"I've not got much with me," I muttered sotto voce to Mr. Deuteronomy.

"I have," said he, wherewith he dug from his pocket and counted out the amount demanded by the clerk. "And well worth what you ask, I'm sure."

"We guaranty all our work," said the other fellow smugly.

As Mr. Deuteronomy began packing up the gun case, I realized that we were leaving a bit too quickly. I had a number of questions that should be answered. I informed the clerk of that and noted gratefully that he seemed eager to cooperate, if only to be rid of us the more quickly.

"Not quite so fast, if you please. There are some things I wish you to tell me. First of all, a remark you made when we came in did imply that the pistol has been here in the shop for quite some time. How long has it been here?"

"Well, that's easily answered," said he, picking up the repair bill. "Right after the first of the year it was—January sixth. So we've had it here about four months."

"All right, fair enough. Who brought it in?"

Again he looked at the repair bill. "A Mr. Bennett—or so it says here."

"Not good enough," said I. "You must have some memory of the fellow. Or was it a fellow? Could it have been a woman brought it in?"

"Not likely."

"Oh? And why not?"

"Well, because ninety-nine out of a hundred who come in here are men."

"Then you have no memory of the fellow at all?"

"None . . . Well, give me a moment. Let me think about that." He did just that, covering his eyes, concentrating. "It seems to me," said he, "that the man who brought it in was not the owner of the pistol—but a servant—something of that sort."

"What was he physically? Fat? thin? tall? short?"

Again, hand over eyes, he went into a brief trance from which

he emerged to say: "Of medium height, robust though not fat. I recall nothing of his face at all."

"Nothing of his nose? his eyes?"

"No, nothing."

"But there—you see? You've remembered more than you
thought you did."

He smiled at that as if surprised at himself. "So I have," said he.

"About the pistol itself," said I, "is it of Joseph Griffin's manu-
facture?"

"Oh no, certainly not. This, as is its mate, is of French making."

"How can you tell?"

"Well, first of all, look into the barrel—not when it is loaded,
certainly—and you will see that it is rifled. It's not done with English pistols—very rarely, in any case. And the bore is a good deal
larger than what might be found in an English dueling pistol. From
the look of them, I'd suspect that LePage was the maker, though for
the life of me I can't suppose why his name is not engraved upon the
pistols or at least stamped someplace upon the case."

"These are specifically intended for dueling, then?"

"Oh yes."

"One last question. Why were the pistols separated? That is,
why did I carry one of them into your shop looking for its mate?"

"That is our policy here at Griffin. We do not take into our
charge any pistol or rifle on which we are not doing repair work of
some sort. And we do not sell consignment. In that way our liability
is lessened greatly."

"Thank you then, Mr. . . . Mr. . . . ."

"Blythe."

Having all that from him, I turned to find that Mr. Deuteronomy had packed up the pistols in the case and was waiting with it
for me by the door. We left the shop together, and I cheered considerably when he did turn to me and declare:

"I must say, young sir, that you got more from that fellow Blythe
than I would have thought possible. How you will fit it all together,
however, I've no idea."

"Nor have I!" said I, laughing. "I simply do as Sir John does: I
ask questions until a pattern begins to emerge."

He joined his laughter with mine (which I thought a bit excessive) and kept it up a bit longer than necessary. Then did I notice that he seemed to be drawing away from me. Slightly alarmed at this, I put the matter to him quite directly:

"Where are you going, sir," said I to him, "with those dueling pistols?"

"Why, I . . . I thought to show them round a bit that we might find us out who these belong to, *really*. To do this right I'll need to borrow the pistols for a day or two." He hesitated, and then he added more aggressively: "Besides, 'twas me put up the money so as we could get them out of the shop, was it not? I ought to be able to take them anyplace that I want."

"Your logic is faulty," said I.

"My . . . what?"

"It's true that you put up the money to claim the repaired pistol, but you took both of them. If, by keeping it overnight, you honestly believe that you can find your way to this Bennett, or to whomever it was sent him there to Griffin's to get that pistol repaired, then I'll let you try. But I'll thank you to give back to me the one I brought to the gunsmith. Do you accept those terms, for otherwise I'll claim them for the Bow Street Court in the name of Sir John Fielding — and you'll either give them up, or face a charge of impeding an investigation and have a year for yourself in Newgate."

I said it all as coldly as ever I could. Mr. Deuteronomy had better believe me, for I believed myself. And indeed I could tell that I had made quite an impression upon him, for he had said naught during my speech, neither did he attempt to respond immediately. He simply stared at me, shocked and dumbfounded.

"You'd do that to me, would you?" said he at last.

"Without another thought," said I. "Do you accept my terms?"

Saying nothing, he went down on his hands and knees right there in Bond Street at the doorstep of the shop of Joseph Griffin, gunsmith; and there, as a crowd gathered, he opened the case, took from it one of the pistols, and handed it up to me. I pocketed it. The crowd, behaving as crowds will, laughed at what they had seen. Muttering and buzzing about it, they began to drift away. I offered Mr. Deuteronomy a hand up. He was slow to accept it.

" 'Twas not my intention to shame you," said I. "Simply to show you that I was serious in the matter." Yet that, too, was said in a tone of seriousness that may have sounded cold to any listener.

Nevertheless, he took my hand, and I helped him to his feet.

"You made your point," he replied.

"I've a question for you. Since I'm trusting you with court materials, I must know where you live."

"In the Haymarket," said he, "just above the coffee house."

No wonder he had arrived there so quickly!

"And another," said I. "What are your plans regarding the Newmarket race next Sunday?"

"Ah, you heard about that, did you? Well, I'll be there to ride Pegasus, and we'll win—damn me if we don't!" He hesitated, then blurted out. "And you can tell your Sir John another thing. Tell him that I expect to find my sister there."

That did little more than confuse me. How would he find her so far away? And why should he find her in Newmarket, of all places?

"Explain that, if you please," said I.

"And if I don't?"

"Do it anyway."

He came close and lowered his voice. "Once, whilst in her cups, she told me that she had met Maggie's father in Newmarket at the races. Maybe she thinks she'll find him there again. Maybe she already has."

With that, he wheeled about and bolted off in the direction of the Haymarket. In a sense, he seemed to be daring me to catch him if I could. I did not accept his challenge, but turned and started back to Bow Street. I had much to tell Sir John, as I well knew. I was certain, too, that he would be most interested in that last bit of intelligence that Mr. Plummer had given us.

So much had happened through the morning that I thought the day near done by the time I reached Bow Street. There was no telling from the gray sky above just what time it might be; I had not seen the sun the whole day through. Yet as I approached Number 4, I heard a commingling of sounds which told me that it was not near so late in the afternoon as I had supposed. There was, first of all, the rumble of many voices together, and then a beating of wood upon wood and one loud, low voice (unmistakably that of Sir John) which stilled the rest. It could not be much after one o'clock. Then came the sound of another voice—high, sharp, and hectoring in tone. Good God! It was Clarissa! What had been threatened once or twice had come to pass. When I was unavailable to take the place of Mr. Marsden, Sir John found that Clarissa had not as yet left for the Magdalene Home, and so did draft her for duty as his clerk. She, of course, would have been delighted. I wondered how she had done—and managed to wonder it without feeling that sense of anxiety which heretofore had always come in those situations in which I imagined us in competition, each with the other. I no longer supposed that, though just what our true relationship might be, I would have been at a loss to say. Engaged to be engaged? What, in all truth, could that mean?

I slipped into the last row of the courtroom, attracting no notice at all. If I were recognized, it would only have been by those whores and layabouts who saw me doing the day's buying in Covent Garden. I had become as one easily passed over by then, unnoticed in the background. That pleased me somehow, though I should be at a loss to explain why it did.

The case before Sir John was one of those disputes between merchants in Covent Garden which he was known to settle so even-handedly. The disputants were a man and a woman, as more often than not was the way of it. The man had a choice plot just at the entrance to the Garden through Russell Street, and he meant to hold on to it—in spite of the challenge put to him by the woman. (A Mrs. Penney, as I recall.) It seems that she approached the vendor (whose name I cannot now for the life of me remember), and offered to buy the space from him. Her offer of cash suited him, and he gave his consent orally. She presented him with a bill of sale which her solicitor had drawn up and asked him to sign. Reading the document carefully, he saw that there was no provision for him to have a space from which to sell his fruits; he had assumed they would trade spaces, and he, having the more desirable one, would get the cash amount in addition. By no means, said she. A place for him to sell his goods had not been under discussion. What he did after selling his place to her was up to him, but he had agreed to sell, she said, and now he must do that. He refused, and hence the two disputants wound up in magistrate's court before Sir John Fielding.

Sir John asked a few questions in order to get some feeling for the two disputants. She, needless to say, was the more aggressive of the two. Her plan, it seemed, was to sell raw produce from both locations. When it came time to interrogate the second disputant, Sir John asked the man if he contested any of the facts which Mrs. Penney had presented; he did not. He asked him then how he had come by the plot in question, and was told that it had been in his family for years. How many years? Fifty, at least—his grandfather had bought it from a widower without children. And why had the greengrocer agreed to sell it now? Sickness in the family, said he. At that, Sir John nodded and asked to have the bill of sale which was in contention. Mrs. Penney handed it up to Clarissa, who, at Sir John's request, read it carefully.

To her, he said, "Is it just as has been presented?"

"It is, Sir John."

"Then give it me, please."

She complied, and the magistrate took the bill of sale and ripped it into as many pieces as was convenient.

"There," said he, "that is what your bill of sale is worth, Mrs. Penney. You may have another made up, which includes a trade of the two properties as well as a sum of money, for his property is unquestionably more valuable than your own."

His decision threw the courtroom into mutters and mumbles. There came male laughter and strident female objections. All was in turmoil until one voice broke through and dominated all the rest.

"I do not think that altogether fair, Sir John. After all, a solicitor's time costs money, does it not? Could the original bill of sale not have been amended to include those stipulations you demand? Of course it could. Yet now—*now* of course it could not. And another thing . . ."

That voice, reader, you may suppose was that of a dissatisfied Mrs. Penney. Nevertheless, if you supposed such, then you would be wrong, for it was none other than our Clarissa who spoke out so boldly against Sir John.

Even I, who knew her so well, was surprised at this intemperate outburst. Yet if I was surprised, the rest in the courtroom were quite stunned. Of a sudden, a pall of silence fell over the seated crowd. Nothing like this had ever happened before. Oh, they themselves had often misbehaved — indeed they had done so just now — like children in school. Occasionally, though very rarely, one of their number was so rowdy that he (or she) would be expelled from the courtroom, but the usual thing was simply to quiet down when Sir John banged with his gavel and called for order. All this, certainly — but never, never anything like what all had just witnessed: criticism of the magistrate by the very clerk who sat beside him. This was outright rebellion and must be put down. But how? Not only had the crowd fallen quite still, but also those in my row shifted forward in their seats and seemed to hold their breath. I felt it was done so in every row and corner of the place.

Clarissa, too, had noticed the sudden silence and the sense of anticipation all around her. She was made uneasy by it but bravely (if a bit foolishly) attempted to continue.

"And another thing . . . Sir John . . . we know not the financial circumstances of the woman in the case, do we? She may be . . . that is . . . she may be a widow . . . She may be . . ."

And there, having noted the reaction of the crowd and feeling greatly oppressed by it, she, at last, sputtered to a halt. For the better part of a minute, she said nothing — nor, for that matter, did anyone else speak up. But then, addressing Sir John, she spoke up in a much smaller and less confident sort of voice.

"I'm making a fool of myself," said she, "am I not?"

He sighed and nodded. "I fear so."

Even from my place in the last row I could see tears glistening in her eyes.

I do believe that at that moment she might have jumped up and run from the place had Sir John not restrained her with his hand upon her own.

"Please forgive me," said she.

"You are forgiven."

Then, once again, the unexpected: quite spontaneously, the entire court burst into applause. Sir John, certain that he wanted such demonstrations never again repeated, simply ignored this one. He picked up his gavel and beat thrice upon the tabletop.

"The court is dismissed," said he.

And so they waited, he and Clarissa, until their audience had filed out in ones, twos, and threes, and at their own pace. Once again, Sir John restrained her with a hand upon hers. But once the crowd had gone, and he removed the restraint, she was up and away in a matter of seconds. She quite flew through the door which led to the "backstage" area, and, through it, to the stairs to our kitchen above. Indeed, even before she was out the large room and into the hall, she had a kerchief in hand and had begun weeping.

"Come ahead, Jeremy," Sir John called out, rising. "Let's go to my back room and talk of your morning."

"How did you know I was here?" I responded.

"I not only knew you were here, I knew also when you arrived. Just at the beginning of that sorrowful mess with Mrs. Penney, was it not?"

"It was, but how could you tell?"

"A certain step you have—a certain squeak in the shoes perhaps. I know not what it is, but it is enough to tell me when you enter a room."

We left the courtroom by way of the door through which Clarissa had exited a minute or two before. I knew not quite what to do with regard to her. I was, first of all, quite proud of her for admitting her mistake and asking Sir John's forgiveness before all, as she had done; and a good part of me wished to go, find her, and comfort her. Yet I did naught, for, on the other hand, I owed a greater debt to Sir John; and he had, with little difficulty, convinced me that all our efforts must be concentrated upon finding the killer of Margaret Plummer.

"I'm sure you perceived what had happened," said Sir John as we entered his chambers. "Mr. Marsden fell ill not long after you left to meet that Plummer fellow. A coughing fit it was, yet I have never known one quite so violent and long-lasting. I fear for the man, in truth I do. I was about to send Clarissa to bring you back. But then she prevailed upon me to allow her to fill in for the clerk. It is not a demanding job, certainly. The real work of it is in the record-keeping and filing done afterward, so I thought, why not? I gave her a bit of instruction and sent Marsden home. The poor fellow had no voice left, or next to none. But it was a light day. There were two cases of public drunkenness and another of pissing in the street, and one other dispute besides the one to which you were witness—just the sort of easy day to try her out. What could have possessed the girl? Ordinarily, she is quite polite—but strong-headed and willful, there can be no doubt. What could have possessed her?"

What indeed? I decided that Sir John's question should be answered.

"Perhaps, sir," said I, "she supposed herself at table with us in the kitchen where all speak their minds and give their opinions as they will."

"Perhaps . . . but how could she be taken in by that Magdalene Penney? That woman has boasted she will own all of Covent Garden in five years."

"Does Clarissa know that?"

"Well . . . no . . . I suppose she doesn't. Still, that's no justification for arguing one of my decisions with me."

"No, certainly not, Sir John."

"I must talk to her about that." He sighed—unhappily, as it seemed to me; perhaps he was thinking of what he might say to her. But then did he rouse himself to say: "Do tell me what you accomplished this morning. I've a feeling you did well. Now, don't tell me that I'm wrong."

And I certainly did not: I told him all, and he seemed well satisfied by my report. He applauded my threat to Mr. Deuteronomy, saying that a year in Newgate seemed justified in such a case as this one. He also thought it justifiable to allow Deuteronomy to "borrow" the pistol in its case, so long as we knew where to find him and get it back. Yet Sir John became most excited when he learned that Deuteronomy would be riding at Newmarket on Sunday and that he thought there was some chance his sister would also be there.

"He said that, did he?" asked Sir John. "Do you feel that he was serious about this?"

"Oh, I do," I assured him, "for he told me that once when she had been drinking she told him that she had met Maggie's father there at Newmarket. She's a simple soul, sir. She probably believes it will all happen again just as before."

"Perhaps," said he, "yes indeed, perhaps." He seemed troubled; nevertheless, I knew not what seemed wrong with what I had just told him. Yet he explained: "The trouble is with the magistrate of Newmarket, you see. It could be difficult to arrest Alice Plummer, or even to remove her to London for questioning. The magistrate seems to feel that unless a crime be committed in Newmarket, it is no true crime at all. I have had dealings with him before, but each time matters had to be negotiated. Oh, he can be —"

Sir John halted at that point, for a voice, a very familiar one, intruded. From the sound of Clarissa's voice and her hastening footsteps, I could tell she was most agitated.

"Sir John! Jeremy! I've news for you!"

The magistrate, now risen from his chair, seemed perturbed, unhappy with the interruption. "What is it, child?"

"Elizabeth is missing."

FIVE

*In which Sir John
seeks a thread tying
Maggie to Elizabeth*

⁂

It became clear, after a few moments of awkward sputtering, that Sir John had no notion of just who Elizabeth might be. Clarissa and I set about to explain it to him, yet, between us, I feared that we may only have made things a bit worse.

"Now, please, both of you," said he, "let me see if I have this properly now. Elizabeth is a girl whom you knew back in Lichfield," now addressing Clarissa. "Yet about the time you came here, so did she. Is that correct?"

Of course, it was. Nevertheless, he took us painstakingly through all the information that we had heaped upon him, getting confirmation for each bit and fact until it became evident to me that he had used this as a device to slow things down a bit.

"And you say that she has now gone missing?"

"Indeed she has," answered Clarissa. "Her mother brought this distressing news just now."

"Is she here?"

"Oh, indeed sir—and terribly distressed."

"Well, bring her here, child, bring her here."

Needing no further encouragement, she set off down the hall at a dizzying clip. When she returned, she had with her a woman of no great age, yet one who bore a face that was lined and careworn; it was plain that the woman had been crying.

Sir John rose, bidding her to sit down. Once he had resettled himself behind his desk, he leaned forward and asked her name.

"Jenny Hooker," said she.

"And you are the mother of Elizabeth?"

"I am, sir, and she don't have nobody but me. Her father died a few years past. I'm a widow now."

"I see. Well, could you tell me how long she's been gone? All the circumstances of her disappearance as you've been able to discover them?"

The tale that she told must have been common enough in London at that time, when such disappearances were reported almost monthly. Nevertheless, Elizabeth was not some faceless name, but rather someone I had met, someone you might say that I knew. As Mrs. Hooker told the details, she began to snivel till Clarissa hastened to her and supplied a kerchief that she might blow her nose.

It seemed that both mother and daughter had been invited to Mrs. Hooker's sister's home in Wapping for Easter dinner. Mrs. Hooker's duties at the lodging house made it impossible for her to attend, but she encouraged Elizabeth to take the walk there and spend the day with her uncle and aunt. This was what she did, enjoying herself greatly, eating her fill—and then some. She did, in fact, stay so late that her aunt feared that it would be dark before she reached home. Why not stay the night? Yet Elizabeth insisted that she go, for she was certain that the long walk would greatly help her digestion, and so she started out. That was the last anyone had seen of Elizabeth Hooker.

Sir John listened patiently to Mrs. Hooker and allowed her to tell everything at her own pace. He waited until he was sure that she had done with all. Only then did he lean forward and ask a few questions which he deemed necessary.

"Now, Mrs. Hooker," said he, "how do you account for your delay in notifying me of your daughter's disappearance?"

"Well," said she, "I waited all through Easter Monday, expecting her to come along just anytime, for I'd assumed, you see, that she'd stayed the night with her aunt and uncle. But the day passed, dark came, and at last I made up my mind that I must go out to Wapping early next day and find out what had happened to her."

"And did you do that?"

"I did, sir, and what I found was that they were as puzzled as I was and had no better idea than me just where she might be. Because they had not heard from me, they thought she had got home without a problem."

"And then you came here to me, did you?"

"Not direct, sir, no, I didn't. I went first to Elizabeth's employer, Richard Turbott, a silversmith, who had just returned from an Easter holiday with his family."

"And explained the situation to him?"

"Just so, sir."

At that, Sir John fell silent, as if he had, for a brief moment, fallen asleep. I had often seen him in such a state, and Clarissa, too, had witnessed this strange behavior of his. So neither she nor I was concerned overmuch when, of a sudden, he seemed to have vacated consciousness. Mrs. Hooker, however, fell back with her hand to her heart, obviously unsure of what might happen next. Clarissa leaned forward and gave a reassuring pat to the woman's hand.

What happened next was simply that Sir John then roused himself and put a question to the woman; one of a more indirect sort.

"What sort of complaints has your daughter?"

"Complaints?" Mrs. Hooker echoed, puzzled. "Do you mean illness, sir? What *do* you mean?"

"Not physical complaints, no. But as you say, she has no one but you. Does she confide in you? Is she satisfied? If not, why not? What are her dissatisfactions with life?"

"Oh, she has none." She seemed quite taken aback with the suggestion that Elizabeth might indeed be in some way unhappy with her lot in life.

"Let me put it another way. How old is your daughter?"

"Fifteen, sir. She'll be sixteen in October."

"Fifteen and she has no dissatisfactions? no complaints? What sort of girl is she?"

"A very good girl, sir."

"I've no doubt of it, but has she no dreams? no . . ." He ended in a shrug, hands uplifted.

"Oh, no sir. Her father and I, we knocked all that sort of foolishness out of her long ago. We used Clarissa here as an example of what happens to a girl when she . . . well . . . You understand, I'm sure. You *did* rescue her from the poorhouse, as I've heard."

I glanced over at Clarissa and rolled my eyes in despair. The woman was quite impossible, was she not? Clarissa's description of Elizabeth—utterly vapid and without purpose—rang once again in my mind. What I had supposed to have been said in a mere fit of pique might well have been accurate, if Mrs. Hooker was to be credited.

For his part, Sir John could do little more than sigh unhappily.

Mrs. Hooker gave him a moment, then did she ask: "Will that be all, sir?"

"I shall require some addresses from you," said Sir John, "and that, then, my good woman, will be all."

One of those addresses was that in Wapping, of Elizabeth's uncle and aunt, the last to see her on that fateful Sunday. It fell to me to take the hike along Wapping Dock to find their place in Green Dragon Alley, tucked in between a brewery and one of the many timber yards of that district.

Sir John had counseled me to seek from them any hints that their niece might have had some sort of escape planned for her late departure. Precious little was said by Jenny Hooker about certain aspects of Elizabeth's visit. Sir John wished me to find all I could from the two of them. Thus it was that as I tramped along the Thames, I planned, insofar as I was able, just what I should ask and of whom I should ask it.

Yet when I knocked upon the door of the little cottage in Green Dragon Alley, I found, unexpectedly, that both were out—or so I was to hear. First did I knock, then did I beat upon the door. Then, at last, did I attempt to rouse those within the little house by shouting. It brought no response from inside, but a neighbor opened her window, stuck out her head, and inquired just what my business with them next door might be. I told her direct as I could, adding that I was Sir John Fielding's assistant. That usually brought me an extra dash of respect, but from this gray-haired old harridan at the window it brought me naught but a sneer of derision.

"What sort of help might you be able to give at your age?"

I went over to her. "Why, I ask questions—and I usually get answers."

"Do you now? What's your secret?"

"I have a wonderful smile."

"Have you? Well, let's see it, shall we?"

She leaned far out the window and waited. At last, I understood: She was flirting.

"Oh no," said I. "That's not how it's done, not at all."

"How then?"

"First I ask a question, and then you answer it. If I like your answer, then you receive a smile."

"Oh, it's that way, is it? All right, let's get on with it."

"Where are your neighbors, the Chesleys?"

"Well, the mister is where he always is during the day—and that's at the brewery across the way. He works there, you see. And the missus, I trust, is doing the buying for dinner about now. Could be she's buying a few of them spring potatoes she might've forgot first time she was out. Oh, she's *always* gadding about, that one."

At that, I gave her a smile.

"Is that the best you can do?" she demanded, showing me a bit of a pout.

"Oh no," said I. "I can do much better. I should have mentioned, I suppose, that the more important the question and the better the answer, the bigger the smile. Ready for another?"

She seemed a little less eager to play than before. Nevertheless, she nodded, and I began to frame the next question.

"If I may take you back to Easter Sunday," said I after a moment's delay, "what do you remember of the visit of the Chesleys' niece, Elizabeth Hooker? You know who she is, I'm sure?"

"Cert'ny I do. What do I remember? Well, I remember that her and her friend come to the house next door early in the afternoon. I would say it was about—"

Only then did I realize what had just been said. I interrupted her forthwith: "Stop where you are there. You said her and her *friend*?"

"Didn't I? 'Course I did. Didn't I see the two of them coming up Green Dragon Alley whilst I was coming in from the outhouse? Course I did. What's a poor widow to do 'cept spy on her neighbors?"

"So you saw Elizabeth with someone else, did you?"

"Didn't I just say so?"

"Well, was that someone else male or female?"

"Oh, female—meaning girl, I suppose—one just like her, anyways. I swear, they looked enough alike to be sisters—or cousins, at least. They come prancing up the alley, giggling and carrying on like they were having the time of their young lives."

"This other girl, the one with Elizabeth, she couldn't have been a daughter of the Chesleys', could she?"

She dismissed the notion out of hand. "Oh no," said she. "They ain't got but two children, both of them grown-up men. Live up around Lichfield, somewheres like that."

"Just one more question," said I, quite excited to have learned what I had. "Their departure—the two girls—when was it?"

She shrugged. "I ain't got a proper clock here, but I would say that it was gettin' on toward dark. Not dark yet, understand, but it would have been in another hour."

"And the two girls left together?"

"Indeed they did, for I had this very window open, and I watched it all, right from where I'm standin' now."

I was by that time quite eager to get back to Bow Street and tell Sir John what I had learned, yet I knew that since I had been sent to Wapping to interview the uncle and aunt, I had better make a greater effort to do so than I had thus far done. Thus, I made ready to depart from my informant.

"Could you tell me your name, madam?"

"Hetty Duncan," said she. "But I must say I'm proper let down by that smile of yours. Not much to it, if you ask me. As you said yourself, you could do better. And you seemed properly carried away by what I told you about Elizabeth's little friend."

"Not another word," said I, and, so saying, I grasped her grizzled head and planted a buss square upon her lips.

She giggled at that, and I grinned the widest grin ever. "There it is," said she. "That's the smile I was hoping to win from you."

I waved and ran for the brewery. I knocked loud upon the door, as was necessary, for there was a great deal of competing noise from beyond it. 'Twas not long before I heard the lock turn and the door swung open; a man, sweating and disheveled, stood and asked my business.

"I wish to speak to Mr. George Chesley," said I.

"Better be important. He's the brewmaster here."

"Tell him then 'tis to do with his niece, and I am come from the Bow Street Court to ask him a few questions."

"I'll tell him that," said he and slammed the door and turned the lock.

I waited a proper length of time—and then some. At last, I heard heavy footsteps on the other side—again the lock—and the door came open. The man revealed seemed quite as wide as he was tall, though not as fat as that might suggest. He was well into his sixth decade, and what I saw of the hair beneath his hat told me that there was near as much gray as dark in it. His face was lined, yet in such a way that said he wore a smile a fair part of the day.

"You the lad from the Bow Street Court?" he asked.

I acknowledged that this was so.

"I've no doubt this is about the disappearance of our niece," said he, closing the door behind him. "What have you to ask?"

I then put to him a series of routine questions that had to do with time of arrival and departure, and that sort of thing. They were intended to put him at his ease. He answered them readily enough but hesitated a bit when I put to him the question which I had been leading up to.

"Mr. Chesley," said I, "having spoken with your neighbor Hetty Duncan, I learned that there were two guests at your home, yet as it was reported to us by Elizabeth's mother, Jenny Hooker, her daughter was alone in her visit to you. Now, which am I to believe? Your neighbor, or Mrs. Hooker?"

"Well," said he—and there he stopped for a considerable time, less than a minute, no doubt, but such an interruption can seem considerable whilst one is waiting for an answer.

"Well," he repeated. "It's Hetty has it right," said he at last. "It was my wife was the cause of it all. You see, Jenny's her sister, though you'd never know it to look at them. For one thing, Mary, my wife, was the oldest in the family and Jenny the youngest. There was three brothers came betwixt oldest and youngest. Even so, the two of them were pretty close. And when Mary and me got married, there wasn't anything going to stand in Jenny's way on her way to the altar. She wasn't but sixteen or so, and Mary was near ten years older, but once Jenny got asked that was it—all she needed. She was just at that age, you know. The babies just kept comin'. Jenny had three sons—but only two of them lived. Then, when she had Elizabeth, her husband got the idea of going up to London. We'd been here a good five years or more by then. People in London liked the taste of that bitter ale we had up in Lichfield, so they just up and hired me and brought me down to London. My two boys stayed up in Lichfield, though.

"Now, this fellow Jenny married—Thomas Hooker was his name—he was a strange sort. Back in Lichfield he ran a stable for a man who owned two of them. But Tom was one of the pious sort, who thought he was better than everybody else just because he prayed harder than they did. He was sure he was better than me because I was involved in the making of 'the devil's own concoction'— which of course was ale—according to him. To tell the truth, I've no way of proving this, but still I've always suspected that he got it in his head to come to London just because I come down here— wanted to prove that because he was one of the Lord's own he could make a greater success than an old sinner like me. So he just up and moved the whole family down here without having even the prospect of a job—said he put his trust in the Lord. Well, the Lord kind of let him down, because after he found out there weren't any jobs in the line he had worked all his life. So what did he do? He came to me and asked for work. And what did I do? I hired him. My wife wouldn't have it any other way."

There he paused, and I, who had waited for just such an opening, intruded myself into the small space he had given me.

"But Mr. Chesley, please," said I, "you were going to tell me about that other girl, the one who came with Elizabeth Hooker."

"Oh, I'm comin' to that, but I just wanted you to know how all this fits together."

"Well . . . go on."

"I'll make it quick, so I will." He took a deep breath and then continued: "He died right here, he did, he did. He was always taking chances here in the brewery—though I warned him oft to be more careful—he said he was safe in the Lord. But whilst the Lord was looking the other way, Tom Hooker drowned in a vat of ale."

"And now to the girl Elizabeth brought along to dinner."

"What? Oh . . . oh yes." He resumed: "Well, you can imagine what sort of girl Elizabeth was with parents like these—because Jenny was just like Tom in the way she handled her daughter. One of Elizabeth's brothers had run away, and they lost touch. Anyway, my Mary kept contact with Jenny, even helped get her the job she's got. But Jenny keeps such a tight hand on Elizabeth, it's a wonder she lets her out of her sight long enough to do her work at the silversmith's. She lives quite close to him, you know."

"No, I didn't know," said I. "But I'd like to hear something about that girl who came with her."

"Oh yes, that. Well, as you may have heard we invited both Jenny and Elizabeth. Jenny decided she had too much cooking to do, but since it was family and Easter, it would be all right if Elizabeth came alone in her stead. Well, Elizabeth figured that if her mother wasn't coming, there'd be plenty to eat and room for one more at the table. She was certainly right about that."

"But who was the girl she brought with her?" I asked.

"Oh, let's see, it was Katherine, or Kathy, or some such name. I can't quite recall exact, but it's the girl she works with at the silversmith's. A nice youngster she is. You'd like her, I'm sure. Anybody would."

"But why did your wife not tell her sister that Katherine, or whatever her name, came here in her stead?"

"Well, I should think that would be obvious."

"Not to me."

"Well, because if she had done, then it would be none but Elizabeth would take the blame for it. Indeed, Elizabeth made my Mary promise she would not tell. She meant that, of course, *specially* to her mother, so Mary was just keeping her word, was all."

"She shouldn't have," I declared, all sure and certain.

"That, indeed, is what I told her. But you will now set things straight, will you not?"

"Certainly! But I have one last question. Did the two girls leave together?"

"Did I not say so?" said he, a bit indignant.

"No, earlier you said that Elizabeth had left in good time to make it back before dark."

"Did I? Well, Kathleen—that was her name—she left with her, just like she came."

"Thank you, sir," said I to him. "That is all I needed to know." With that, I tipped my hat and set off at a run for Bow Street.

Not that I ran all the way. Nevertheless, so elated was I to have discovered a new witness, one who could potentially tell us much more about Elizabeth Hooker's disappearance, that I must have run near a mile before slowing to a walk. I am of an age and profession today when such youthful exhibitions of energy would be considered undignified. Yet how I do miss the feeling of the cobblestones beneath my quick feet. Perhaps what I miss most of all is youth itself. I look back on those days with Sir John and Lady Fielding, and all the Bow Street Runners, as the happiest in my life. Having often discussed this with Clarissa in the preparation of these books, I know that she feels as I do in this.

'Twixt running, jog-trotting, and fast walking, I must have made it back to Bow Street in half the time it had taken me to travel on to Green Dragon Alley. Even so, when I went to tell Sir John of my discovery, I found that he had left with Clarissa for the residence of Richard Turbott, the silversmith. My informant, Mr. Fuller, said that both had been gone for over an hour.

"Did they leave an address?" I asked him. "I've no idea where to go."

"Oh, now, just wait," said he. "That girl of yours did pass something on to me for you. Now, what did I do with it?"

He began patting his pockets, searching through his clothes. He emptied one pocket, examined its contents, and then dug into another. He found nothing.

"Perhaps you laid it down somewhere? Where were you when they left?" said I, trying to be helpful.

"Well, I don't see how that could . . ." He wandered over to Mr. Marsden's area behind the strongroom. The files were there, as well as the paperwork in which the clerk had been engaged when the coughing fit came upon him. "Well, what do you know? Here it is." Mr. Fuller reached out and plucked a much-folded note from the top of the clerk's writing table. "Here's your billy-doo, Master Proctor."

(That last bit he delivered in a fluting falsetto. He was ever making sport of my relations with Clarissa—in fact, long before there were truly any relations to be made sport of.)

On it was written an address in Chandos Street—that and nothing more. She well knew that it was likely that I should wish to follow them to the silversmith's—and follow them I would. Was I not told that Kathleen was "the girl she works with at the silversmith's"? Indeed I was. She would have something to tell—if Sir John had not got it all out of her by now.

"Well, I thank you, Mr. Fuller. This was indeed what I had hoped for from her."

"Lots of exes and hearts, I'll bet."

"It would be dishonorable for me to tell." And, at that, he laughed a dirty laugh indeed.

The sound of it followed me all the way to the street.

Though I was tempted, it would not do for me to have run the short distance to Chandos Street, for I knew I must keep an eye upon the far side of the street for Sir John and Clarissa.

The street was crowded, for Chandos is at the very heart of London. Its shops and stores—dressmakers, drapers, et cetera— are among the finest in the city. And all are just a single street distant from the clamor and indecency of Bedford Street. Whilst on my way, I stole a glance at the note in my hand left by Clarissa, just to make certain that the address matched the one in my head. It did. Simple enough, yet it made me marvel somewhat: I must have passed the silversmith's shop a hundred times—no, more, far more than that—and yet I had never noticed that there was such an establishment in Chandos Street. Which proved, I suppose, that I had little interest in silver and those things made from it. Sir John was right: I must improve my powers of observation. He "sees" more with his blind eyes when he enters a room, I told myself, than I or any ordinary man could ever do. As I entered the shop, I took a quick look in the window and reassured myself that it did, at least, look familiar. I took some comfort in that.

"Yes sir, how may I serve you, sir?"

He who had spoken those words to me I took to be no older than myself—indeed, he proved to be somewhat younger. Quite rightly I supposed him to be an apprentice; he was one of three in the shop.

"If I am correct," said I to him, "Sir John Fielding, magistrate of the Bow Street Court, is here in an investigation into the disappearance of one Elizabeth Hooker, an employee of Mr. Turbott."

"Oh, right you are," said he, "and with a rather nice-looking young lady, is he not?"

"Well . . . yes . . . I expect he would be."

I may have grumbled a bit at that. Though I thought it instructive to learn how the rest of the world viewed her, I didn't like it in the least to hear her described in such a manner.

"You'd like to see him then, of course."

"I would, yes."

"Just a moment then, till I get someone to take over the shop. I believe I know just where he is."

He went to a corner, away from the showcase, and tugged upon a line, and far back in the shop I heard a bell jingle. It was not long till, through the curtained doorway, another lad emerged of about the same age and general description.

"Harry," said my young fellow. "Will you keep an eye on things in front whilst I show this gentleman to Sir John? I take it that he's still downstairs?"

"Last time I looked," said Harry.

The first fellow then said to me: "Right this way, if you'll just follow me."

The moment I stepped behind the curtain I found myself in quite another world. It was the one in which the pretty little items in the window were manufactured. It was a large area, of about the size and shape of the rear of one of the booksellers and publishers' shops—though not near so crowded with bits and pieces of the process. Against the walls on either side were candelabra and bowls and such. In the far rear, there was a kind of miniature blacksmith's forge, round which three men had gathered and at which they concentrated with remarkable intensity. My first impulse was to rush forward to discover the object of their concentration, yet my guide through Vulcan's domain held me back with a discreet pressure upon my arm. We stood and waited. It was not long till, at a signal from one of the three, another picked up a long-handled ladle, and a third positioned himself behind him, checking the bolts on a mold. What followed was like steps in an intricately conceived ballet. At a second signal, the movement began: the man with the ladle backed away from the forge and, holding tight to the long handle, he turned round and poured the ladle's hot metal into the mold; the other two fell back as the ladle was replaced, and then came forward to inspect the mold. I had, without quite willing it so, been holding my breath for I know not how long. It was only then, when the action had ceased, that I resumed.

"That was silver they were pouring, was it not?" I asked my guide.

"It was," said he, "and it's a specially difficult metal to work with, for it must be poured steady and even, not too fast and not too slow."

"The fellow who did the pouring—he's not an apprentice, surely." He seemed older and more experienced.

"Oh no, that's Mr. Tarkington. He's a journeyman. But Joe, who handled the mold, he's an apprentice in his last year."

"I see," said I, "and the third man is Mr. Turbott?"

"Just so," said he, "and his part is as important as any, for it is he who must decide just when the silver is ready to be poured."

"This, then, is all there is to it?"

"Oh no. It's just the first step in the process. Those things you see in the wall shelves are, most of them, waiting to be taken through the next steps. But—"

"Yes?"

"Sir John awaits. Down these stairs, if you please, to our kitchen."

There, where I was left by my guide, did I find Sir John and Clarissa engaged in an interrogation of an older woman, obviously the cook. He asked the questions, and Clarissa watched her answers (a bit obtrusively, it seemed to me) for evidence of prevarication and subterfuge. She gave a curt nod to me; Sir John gave no sign of recognition, yet I was sure he was aware of my arrival.

"And you say that the last you saw of her was Easter Sunday?" Sir John was saying.

"That was the last of it," said she. "Easter morning it was. And

Lizzie was all dressed up for church, or Easter dinner, or whatever it was. I don't know which for I did not ask her."

"And she was not expected back until . . ."

"Well, maybe that night or next morning. Monday noon at the latest."

"And that was because . . ."

"That was because the master and the mistress would be back by one, and they said to me they didn't care how we came and went just so there was someone in the house at all times and when they got back the place was clean."

"Those sound like reasonable requirements," said Sir John. "But tell me, you have rather a small household staff here, do you not?"

"Just kitchen help—me and the two girls. Now just one."

"How does that work—I mean normally. For instance, who does the cleaning?"

"The 'prentices."

"And makes the beds and so on?"

"The two girls."

"And you all eat down here?"

"Well no, not quite," said she. "The master and mistress take their meals on the first floor. The girls serve them there."

"And the apprentices?"

"They eat with us down here."

"And they sleep . . . where?"

"Up on the top floor."

"Including the journeyman?"

"No, he lives off somewhere. You'll have to ask him where."

"With so many doing extra work, it makes things busier for the staff, doesn't it? Is this a happy staff?"

"Well," said she, "Mr. Turbott, he sets a good table, and he treats everyone pretty well, so I'd say yes, on the whole, and on the average, day in and day out, it's a happy staff."

"What about Elizabeth Hooker?"

"What about her?"

"Was she happy?"

She hesitated at that, leaning back, stroking her jowls as she considered the matter.

"Well now, that's pretty hard to say, ain't it?" said she. If you mean *really* happy it's hard, anyways—not like Kathleen over there. She just whistles her way through the day here in the kitchen. Ain't that so, Kathleen?"

The girl, not much older than sixteen, smiled shyly and nodded in response.

"But Lizzie—that's as we called her—she was something different. Half the time she had her mind somewhere else, so that more often than not you had to tell her things two or three times before they'd get done. Not lazy, you understand, just sort of dreamy. But she's a great favorite with the Turbotts—specially the master. He's forever teasing her and carrying on."

That was where the cook (whose name I later learned was Aggie Liston) ended her description of Elizabeth Hooker. What surprised me was that Sir John allowed her to end it there. In truth, she had said very little. I was sure that he could have gotten more out of her. "I should like to have a moment to talk with my young assistant, Jeremy Proctor, who has just arrived. Then perhaps you might take me to where Miss Hooker sleeps. Has she a room of her own?"

"No, no she ain't. She shares one with Kathleen."

"I thought so. Well, perhaps you might take Clarissa and show her the room—that is, if Kathleen has no objection."

"No, I've none," said the girl.

"Good," said Sir John. "Now, if there is somewhere he and I might talk with some degree of privacy?"

"What about the pantry?" said Aggie.

"Sounds ideal. If you would not mind waiting, Kathleen?"

"I'll be right here," said she.

"Very good."

With that, we were shown into the pantry, where a single candle burned. Sir John waited till the door was shut, then turned in my direction with a scowl upon his face.

"Now, what *is* it, lad? You must have something grand to tell me, for ever since you came down the stairs you've been hopping from one foot to the other in your eagerness to tell me this great something."

"But—but—how did you know?" said I, flummoxed and flabbergasted. "How could you tell?"

"Why, for the very reason I've said. You smell of sweat. You must have run a good part of the distance from Wapping. Everything about you bespeaks a bursting desire to have my attention. Well, now you have it. Speak your piece, if you must."

And so, quick as ever I could, I gave my report to Sir John on what I had learned from Hetty Duncan, the neighbor next door, as well as a few of the supporting details from George Chesley. It was a pleasure to see that scowl of annoyance turn to an expression of keen interest as my tale unfolded. By the time I had done, he was all but rubbing his hands in delighted anticipation of the next development.

"This is very interesting indeed," said he. "Mrs. Chesley, the very sister of Jenny Hooker, was so reluctant to let her know that another had attended the dinner in her place that she failed to mention it to her. You'll notice, too, Jeremy, that we are beginning to get a much different picture of Elizabeth as we learn more about her — as we probe deeper — a girl who indeed has dreams of her own."

"Yes, the cook had some very interesting observations, did she not? I can hardly wait till Kathleen has her say. You realize, don't you sir, that she and not Elizabeth's uncle and aunt was the last to see her."

"Hmm. Yes. Quite." Sir John seemed to be far ahead of me. "Let me make you an offer, Jeremy," said he at last. "Since it was you came up with this interesting bit of information, you may interrogate Kathleen, if you like."

"I welcome the chance, sir," said I.

"Very well, the burden is upon you then. But do keep in mind that even though she has not stepped forward with this information, she *need not* have done so. Do not accuse her. Simply draw her out and let her tell her story."

"Yes sir."

And so saying, I opened the door, and we two stepped out into the kitchen. Kathleen stood where she had when we entered the pantry. I pulled out a chair for Sir John, and I invited her to sit down there at the large kitchen table. She accepted, smiled, and dropped into a chair nearby. I sat down opposite her.

"Kathleen is your name?" I asked.

"It is, sir."

"What is your surname, Kathleen?"

"Surname, sir?" She did not know the word. Could she read, I wondered.

"Yes, surname—your family name."

"Ah!" said she. "Kathleen Quigley is my full name, sir."

"What sort of name is that? North of England, perhaps Scottish?"

"Irish, sir."

Kathleen Quigley was a pretty girl who, had she been asked, might have agreed that she was pretty but would have argued that it meant little in London in such times. Which is to say, she was a realist—as Clarissa perhaps was not.

"I want you to know, Miss Quigley, that you made a great success on Sunday."

"Sir?"

"With the Chesleys—Elizabeth's aunt and uncle."

"Ah, you saw them, did you?"

"Why yes, and their neighbor, too—Hetty Duncan."

"Oh that funny old woman who lives next door? I saw her peeking out her window at us. What did she have to say?"

"She thought you and Elizabeth looked enough alike to be sisters."

"And what did you think of that?"

"Well," said I, "when she said that, I didn't know *what* to think, for I hadn't met you then, had I?"

"All right, now what do you think?"

She raised her chin and looked away slightly, as if she were posing for a portrait.

"Oh, there's no question in my mind. You're much the prettier."

"Kind of you to say so. We was wearing frocks that was similar. I ain't sure how well she could see us at that distance, though."

"Obviously not too well." I let that hang between us for a long moment. Then: "Why did you not tell us? Or tell Mrs. Hooker when she was about asking after her daughter? Or tell Mr. Turbott?"

"Well . . ."

I saw that she was reluctant to answer. Why? But then did I notice that the cook had reentered with Clarissa close behind—and I understood.

"What was the difficulty? What was the problem?" I asked. "Surely it's quite a commonplace sort of thing—Mrs. Hooker is unable to go, and so Elizabeth invites you to come along in her mother's place. What could be more natural? You were her work-mate in the day and her bedmate at night, were you not? And after all, that walk to Wapping is a terribly long one — much too long to take alone, surely."

"Well . . . yes . . ." She hesitated, then, after fighting a brief skirmish with herself, she plunged on: "What you just said was the way I thought about it when Lizzie put it up to me — especially that part about the long walk to Wapping. But it wasn't the walk *to* Wapping frightened me, 'twas the walk back."

I could tell that she was truly disturbed by something — the memory of that evening, no doubt — and I must now do or say some-thing that would assure her that all was well, that she had only to tell her story and all would be well. I reached across the table and patted her hand.

"Whatever you are holding back," said I, "can only help bring her back."

She nodded, sniffled, and dabbed at her eyes with a dirty kerchief.

"All right," said she, "I'm sure you're right." Then, lowering her voice, she told her tale.

Just as Mrs. Chesley had told her sister, she had warned Eliza-beth against leaving so late, and had gone so far as to invite the two girls to spend the night in the spare room. Otherwise, she said, they would find themselves on central London's wildest and most dan-gerous streets toward the end of their journey.

But Elizabeth was adamant: "Not if we leave now and hurry along. We shall run if we have to, won't we, Kathleen?"

And that is just what they did — though their running was more in the manner of skipping. (I may say that with some authority, reader, for Kathleen arose from her chair and demonstrated their step.) They skipped and giggled their way across London until at last, when they came upon Drury Lane, that wicked thoroughfare which cuts so close to Bow Street, it was fair dark.

Now, Drury Lane is an exceptional street in a number of ways, yet foremost is this: at no other place in the city do those who have plenty and those who have naught, move in such proximity. There is, of course, Mr. Garrick's Drury Lane Theatre, as there is also the

Theatre Royal, popularly known as the Covent Garden Theatre, just off that thoroughfare and touching the north corner of Covent Garden; these, as well as an eating place or two, provided the attraction for the rich, and the rich attracted the poor. There is a good deal of pickpocketry and petty thieving along the way, but, most of all, prostitution and pimpery do there abound. Elizabeth and Kathleen were quite uncomfortable walking there.

It was Elizabeth Hooker's harebrained notion that they might cut across Covent Garden and save a good deal of time, even though it be dark. And so, over Kathleen's objections, they left Drury Lane and came down Long Acre. Then, with the Theatre Royal in sight, they made their way toward it along Phoenix Alley. They were not long on this leg of the journey before they were made aware that much went on in this alley that neither would have guessed at. First of all, what had been thought to be deserted was actually peopled by a considerable number of prostitutes. They hissed at the pair from every dark corner along the way. Elizabeth and Kathleen fair flew down the alley, driven by cries of "Git out!" "This is our spot!" "You've no right to be here!" And so on. They had no wish to stay and make the acquaintance of any of these dark ghostly figures.

When they reached the arcade wherein the theater was located, they were out of breath and frighted, and only too happy to see a couple of nice-looking young fellows who came out into the light, looking concerned and asking how they might aid the two girls. They explained that they had become bored with that evening's presentation at the Covent Garden and had left early. And now they had been standing about wondering how they might fill the rest of the evening.

"And what better way than to aid two young ladies of obvious good character," said one.

"How may we help you?" said the other. "You look as if you could use a pair of protectors. Will we do? I've a stout stick, as you can see. And Robert has with him a pistol. Have you not, Bobby?"

Though they were properly dressed, these two did not quite seem to be proper gentlemen — not to Kathleen Quigley, at least.

For her part, Elizabeth Hooker seemed convinced of the good intentions of the two young men and immediately revealed to them her plan to cut across Covent Garden. They agreed with her that much time would thus be saved.

Kathleen pulled her friend aside and argued against accepting their protection. "We don't know them. They could be the greatest villains in London, and we would be none the wiser. Come with me. Bow Street Court is just round the corner here. A constable will see us home."

Elizabeth laughed at her friend and declared she would go with these two fellows, no matter what Kathleen chose to do. "The fact is," said she, "I fancy one of them, the one named Robert."

And so it was that Kathleen then left Elizabeth and headed for Bow Street. She looked back but once and saw that her friend and coworker had disappeared into the darkness.

That, Kathleen told me, was why she had held back her story; she felt she had betrayed her friend in allowing her to go off by herself in the company of the two young men.

Sir John cleared his throat, turned to me, and asked if I had further questions for her.

"Only if she went through with her plan to go to Bow Street to find a constable to accompany her here." I looked to her then. "Did you?" I asked.

"I did," said she, "and indeed one of the constables did take me here. He was a strange sort of man, he was. He spoke bare a word to me on our walk."

"Sounds like Mr. Brede," said I to Sir John.

"It does. We shall check with him, of course."

The three of us argued our positions all the way to Bow Street. Clarissa's was, simply put, that the girl described by Kathleen and the cook simply could *not* be the one she had spent two or three hours with the other day. Sir John believed that we must accept Kathleen's testimony only with considerable amount of salt, which is to say, each part of it must be tested. And my own position? I put my faith in Kathleen Quigley. If she said that it was Elizabeth's nature that led her to go off with her two "protectors," then that more or less settled it, insofar as I was concerned.

Thus we argued in the hackney coach until we arrived at Number 4 Bow Street. It was still light enough that Clarissa might hurry upstairs and begin preparations for dinner. Sir John could go to his chambers and wait for Constable Brede to make his appearance. And I could follow him there and provide a surfeit of details from Mr. Chesley's testimony. It seemed a shame and altogether wrong that a day so rich in revelations should end in such a way. Yet, it turned out, there was still a single surprise left for me. Mr. Fuller called me back as I followed Sir John.

"What then, Constable Fuller?"

"A fellow came by and left something for you, a box it was."

I took it from him and saw immediately what it was. The size and shape of it gave it away. I opened the box and saw that it was the dueling pistol, which Mr. Deuteronomy had taken with him. I had its mate in my pocket. There was a note inside, addressed to me. I fumbled it open. Mr. Fuller, ever curious, watched me with interest. I read:

Mr. Proctor:
     I am returning this early, for I have no further use for it. I'm fair sure that my sister will be at Newmarket, therefore I am booking you a room there at the Good Queen Bess on Commerce Street. See you at the races.
                                        — Deuteronomy Plummer

"The fella who brought it was that one who's uncommon short, just the size of a child is all," said Mr. Fuller.

"It's all right," said I. "I know who he was."

SIX

*In which I am sent
to the Newmarket
meet by Sir John*

⛧

We did not get round to discussing Mr. Deuteronomy Plummer and
Newmarket until that evening after dinner. Mr. Brede came by and
confirmed that indeed he had accompanied a young lady from Bow
Street to some house or other in Chandos Street. He hadn't thought
it of sufficient importance to include in his report, he said, but he remembered her well. Irish, wasn't she?

Then did Mr. Bailey come in and bring with him a whole calen-
darful of problems having to do with scheduling.

Then—oh well, one thing after another until it was time to eat
dinner upstairs. Clarissa's dinner wasn't quite up to what she had
offered us earlier in Molly's absence, so that I, for one, was secretly
glad that our regular cook was returning. Stew it was again—and
she had done it better two nights before. Talk flew round the table.
Most of it had to do with the "girls" at the Magdalene Home for
Penitent Prostitutes and how well they had taken to Molly's cooking course.

"There are two or three who could take Molly's place," said
Lady Fielding, "if it ever came to that."

"Thank God it has not," said Sir John. Then, lest that be taken
amiss by Clarissa he complimented her on the stew, and of course
all the table joined in, praising the meal as though it were some culi-
nary masterpiece. Clarissa smiled graciously and acknowledged our
thanks with a nod. However, once the meal was done, and we had
the kitchen to ourselves, she did not hesitate to say what she truly
believed. I recall that she had been sitting quietly at the table whilst

I rubbed and scrubbed at the pot in which she had cooked our stew. Of a sudden she did speak. It was more than a remark; it was, rather, a pronouncement, a declaration.

"False praise is worse than no praise at all," said she.

"What do you mean by that?" I asked her.

"Just what I say! I was quite disappointed in you, Jeremy—the way you added your voice to the rest, lauding that mediocre meal when you knew as well as I just how good it was *not*." She had me there, all right.

"Well," I replied, "I would admit that it was not up to your very best, but after all, Clarissa—"

With a wave of her hand she silenced me. "Oh, never mind," said she. "This has not been a good day for me, but you're certainly not the cause of it."

"Then . . . who is?"

"*I* am, of course. I've no one to blame but myself. How *could* I have spoken up to Sir John and challenged him in his very own courtroom? What right had I? What sort of clerk was I to do such a thing?"

"Oh, you mean that matter to do with the woman who's buying up all of Covent Garden."

"But of course I didn't *know* that, did I? Yet even so, I should not have spoken out as I did. Why must I always . . . always . . . be me?"

My heart went out to her. Sitting there at the kitchen table she had wound herself round her chair in such a way that she seemed smaller than she truly was. She hung her head, avoiding my gaze. Still, I suspected that there were tears in her eyes once more. Women are such emotional creatures, are they not?

I was about to say something to her—something of a comforting nature, I suppose, though I cannot now imagine what it might have been. That was when Sir John's voice rang out from the floor above, summoning me to him.

"Just finishing up here," I called back to him. "I'll be with you in a moment, sir."

That seemed to satisfy him, for I heard nothing more. Having scrubbed the pot well, I put it aside and made ready to go.

"I'll finish up for you," said she to me, rising from her chair and dabbing at her eyes.

"Well, all right," said I. "Shall I tell Sir John how . . . how you feel about all this?"

She looked, of a sudden, quite horror-stricken at my suggestion. "Oh no," said she, "say nothing of the kind. Whatever he wishes to say should be said—to me. Please, Jeremy, don't play the peacemaker, not this time."

"All right," said I. And, having said that, I saw there was nothing else to say. With a nod, I turned and hastened up the stairs.

He was, as I expected, sitting in the darkened room he called his study. And, also as I expected, he urged me to light the candles on his desk if I'd a wish for more light. Naturally, I declined. I do not think those candles had been lit for a year or more. As soon as I had settled in the visitor's chair, he put a question to me.

"Where were we?"

"Sir?"

"As I recall, you had just told me that Deuteronomy Plummer had dropped off the pistol in its case a bit earlier than expected. And that was when Mr. Brede came in, confirming Kathleen Quigley's story . . . or part of it," said Sir John with a proper harrumph.

"Indeed, Sir John," I agreed.

"Then there were a number of other interruptions, followed by dinner, followed by me asking you where we were."

"Ah, of course. Well, there was a note to me in the case."

"A good place to start. What did he say in the note?"

"I can fetch it for you and read it, if you like."

"Quite unnecessary. Please, just summarize."

"He simply said that he was returning the pistol early, as he had no further use for it. Then did he repeat that he was fair certain that his sister would make an appearance at Newmarket. Indeed so certain was he that he had taken the liberty of booking a room for me at an inn in the town—had rather an odd name, so it did."

"The Good Queen Bess, was it?"

"How did you know, sir?"

"Ah well, I've been to Newmarket a time or two, and I've stayed there."

"Is it the only place in town?"

"Far from it. Nevertheless, it's the only place for the racing crowd. You'll no doubt enjoy your stay."

"Then I'm going?"

"Oh yes. Had you not supposed that you would?"

"When do we leave?" I asked rather excitedly. Indeed, I was rather excited by the prospect of such a trip.

"Not 'we,'" said he. "You'll go alone—or not quite so, for a constable must accompany you, should you have the opportunity to make an arrest. It seems to me that we are working not so much on two separate cases but upon a single one, as will eventually be revealed when we are a bit further along with each of them. The way to solve this single big case, it seems to me, is to work hard to push both the two smaller ones along. Therefore, I shall remain in London and work upon the disappearance of Elizabeth Hooker, and you, it seems, would best pursue the mother of little Maggie Plummer up in Newmarket."

"Supposing I find Alice Plummer," said I to him, "on what charge is she to be arrested?"

"Ah, now Jeremy, you really are starting to think as a lawyer." He speculated: "What charge indeed? Certainly not murder. We cannot even say with certainty that the child was murdered—and, in any case, she was not when under her mother's supervision. My feeling is that she can only be arrested and held on a charge of slavery—specifically child-selling. The important thing is to get her back here so she may be questioned. But of course all this supposes that you and your constable can get round the matter of jurisdiction. You'll do that as best you can, working in concert with the constable. Whom will you take with you?"

"Constable Patley," said I, "for he is the only one of the Runners who knows Alice Plummer by sight. As for the rest of it, Patley may not know much law, but he is resourceful."

"Then he is your man. You two will leave soon as Mr. Marsden returns."

Thinking the matter settled, I rose from my chair, only to be told most emphatically to sit down once again. I obeyed.

He waited a moment, then leaned forward and lowered his voice. "What do you think of this Hooker girl?"

"How do you mean, sir?"

"Well, you must concede, surely, that two distinctly different versions of the girl have emerged."

I responded hesitantly: "I would say . . . that much . . . is evident. Clarissa's Elizabeth is much different from Kathleen Quigley's."

"Yes, quite. And Mistress Quigley has already passed the first test with Constable Brede."

"As I did say earlier in the coach, I am inclined to accept Mistress Quigley's version of events and of Elizabeth's character. She would have little to gain by lying."

"True," said Sir John, "but Clarissa knew the girl longer and, presumably, better. And she said that the girl is naught but a bore — no ambitions, no dreams." He held back a moment, but then came forth with it: "Tell me, Jeremy, what do you think of Clarissa as a judge of character?"

I took a moment to glance behind me and make sure that the door to the hall was shut tight: it was. Nevertheless, I lowered my voice to address Sir John.

"I think highly of her ability to judge people," said I. "There have been a few times, I suppose, when she was off the mark, but in general I would say that she is far better than most at that sort of thing."

"I would have said the same," said he. "But there is such a disparity between her view of Elizabeth and the girl who emerges from Mistress Quigley's testimony that it is necessary to accept one or the other."

"Bear in mind though, sir, that the girls had not seen each other for near five years, or perhaps more. It could be that Clarissa was, without intending it, passing judgment upon the ten-year-old girl she had known then. Most of us, I think, are bored by ten-year-olds."

"Hmmm," said he, "an interesting theory. Let me put it to her. Ask her to come in here, will you?"

"That is all then, sir?"

"I should think that quite a lot. 'Tis not every lad who gets himself sent off to Newmarket for a race meet."

"For which you may be certain that I am indeed grateful," said I with a properly impudent grin upon my face.

I was then up and out of the room before he could change his mind.

Clarissa was in the kitchen, sitting at the table where I had left her. She looked up as I descended the stairs and entered the kitchen, relieved at my careless manner. It was only as she pointed to the chair beside hers with the pen in her hand that I noted that she had been writing in what she called her "journal-book." After I had presented it to her the Christmas before, I had only glimpsed it two or three times as she carried it about. Not that she was secretive about it: nevertheless, there was a certain sense of privacy about it to which, in my mind, she was well entitled. I took the chair she had indicated and sat down. She was, I think about to speak.

"He wants to see you," said I.

"Oh dear," said she. "Is it . . ." She left the sentence unfinished, just as she did the next: "You didn't . . ."

"No, no, no," said I. "Nothing like that. I think what he really wishes is to talk to you about Elizabeth Hooker."

"Oh, really?" She seemed let down somewhat, almost disappointed. "Well, all right"—laying her pen aside, closing the journal-book, and marking her place with a blotter—"That's not so frightening."

She stood and, with a forced smile, she marched away and up the stairs. I watched her go.

After the first few minutes of sitting and waiting for her to return, my eyes fastened upon Clarissa's journal-book. Now, ordinarily, I would not think of invading her privacy by reading such a document. Nevertheless, there were other factors involved. First of all, when I face a period of waiting, I become quite desperate for something—anything!—to read. I recall having said something about this some months before. In any case, she knew of this; she had been forewarned. Secondly, she had left the journal-book out upon the kitchen table within my easy grasp. It was there before me as a temptation—nay, more, as a provocation. It was almost as though she *wanted* me to open it up and read. What was I to do? My eyes played over the book for some minutes (well, two or three, anyway), and, at last, I found that there was naught to do to solve the problem, but to reach out for it and open it up.

What greeted me, at first, surprised me, for I found pictures—

an abundance of them in nearly every corner and margin of every page. Pictures of what? Oh, flowers of one kind or another, buildings and trees. And faces — faces of all sorts, men, women, and children, some of them quite skillfully done. She was not without talent, certainly — yet she had quite successfully hidden it from all of us — or so I supposed.

As for what she had written therein, the text wound about her drawings, in some instances taking on the shape of the object with which it shared the page. A number of them seemed to be books in synopsis, mere ideas for books, or the beginnings of books. And some of the faces that surrounded these entries might well have been the faces of the characters as she visualized them. Could the faces have come first? An interesting supposition, that.

Thus entranced, I paged through more than half the journal-book, which is to say, near all that she had written in it. Yet 'twas not her text that stopped me and held me there: again, it was the drawings, the sketches, the pictures. One of them, that one of a bearded man, that could be none other than Black Jack Bilbo — and the face beside his, a woman, there was something about it — Marie-Helene? Of course! Then did I find on the overleaf a rather good sketch of Tom Durham, and below it, another male face, which I could not quite recognize. There was something familiar about it, yet . . .

I turned back to the beginning of this section and began to read:

"Why not [she wrote] a book about Jeremy and me? It would be great fun and a considerable relief to write of events just as they happened. I would be relieved of the need to plot, which I find so difficult. And after all, the events of our lives, arranged in order, and perhaps tightened up a bit are just as exciting as any can be read in a romance, and the sentiments presented in it would be real as can be. I could include, perhaps even begin with, the capture of Marie-Helene by Black Jack Bilbo and their eventual escape. In a sense, that happened to Jeremy and to me as well as to them. But no, to begin there would be to lose too much of our story, Jeremy's and mine — individually and in concert. Ah, how romantic it will be to trace our early history—the squabbles and the wrangles which persisted intolerably long until they end—as they will—in wedded bliss. Should I use real names? I'm not sure. In a way, it matters little what names I give them if they are well-described. To speak of a certain blind magistrate would surely bring only one man to mind. And if I were to describe another as a lexicographer from Lichfield, he would—

There did her projections end, for at that point I must have appeared with the invitation from Sir John that she come and join him for a talk. And by a strange coincidence of events, I did hear her step upon the stairs at just that moment. Hurriedly I replaced her journal-book, making every effort to fix it in the exact angle in relation to the ink bottle. Afterward, I wondered why I was so careful to put the book back in place just as it had been, for I would have words with her about it, or know the reason why I should not.

She appeared, stepping sprightly with a smile upon her face. "Well," said she, "that was not so bad. No, not bad at all."

"I thought it would not be," said I rather coolly.

'Twas not what I said, but the manner in which I said it that seemed to disturb her. She looked at me closely as if to find the reason for the slightly sullen expression written upon my face.

"What ails you?" said she.

I said naught but looked her straight in the eye.

She settled down in the chair at the table wherein she sat before her interview with Sir John. Looking about her, she suddenly understood and started to laugh.

"You've been looking at my journal-book, have you not?"

"Well . . . I . . ."

"Admit it," said she with a proper chuckle. "I was half-hoping you would read through it in any case. What did you think of it?"

"Well . . . I . . . that is . . . I thought your drawings were very good," said I, thinking it better to begin upon a positive note. "I'm amazed that you've kept your light under a bushel for so long. Have you no wish to study? To learn to paint?"

"No, not a bit of it. Women publish books. They don't paint portraits. I draw pictures to amuse myself and to help me in my writing." With that, she leaned back and looked upon me with curiosity. "But that's not what has set you going, now is it?"

"Well, no," I admitted.

"What then? It was what I'd written, of course."

"I suppose it was."

"Were you surprised to find that I'd not made a diary of it—the kind all girls keep when they're eleven or twelve?"

"Perhaps a little."

"Disappointed?"

"No!"

"But what was it upset you so to find I'd made of it a repository for all my ideas for writing?" (But the question was rhetorical and not truly directed at me.) "I know! It was the last thing in the book, was it not? That upon which I was working when you brought to me Sir John's summons. You object to having our life put before the world, do you? Well, does it mean naught to you that I hold our lives to be as truly exciting and adventurous as any in a romance— or a book of any sort? Real life is grand, Jeremy. Don't you—"

"Still, Clarissa," I said, interrupting her, "'a certain blind magistrate,' 'a noted lexicographer from Lichfield?' How could you?"

"Oh pish-posh," said she, "I was but having a bit of fun there."

"Well, your fun may be another's misery."

"None of that now. Sir John and Samuel Johnson can defend themselves."

I was about to reply to that when she spoke up once more and uttered words that proved prophetic.

"Sometime in the future, Jeremy, you yourself may write books about Sir John. And why not? What better memorial could he have? Until then, let us consider that he can and should be written about by one of us. Does that not seem reasonable?"

I had to admit that it did. Perhaps, reader, I had already, at that early date, begun to think about writing this series of books. There we left the matter. I, for one, was quite exhausted by our quarrel— if quarrel it was. But, as Clarissa gathered up her things, I added what, for a while, I later came to regret.

"It's been decided," said I to her, "that I shall be going up to Newmarket for the big race, as we discussed."

"I know," said she. "Sir John told me."

. . .

What I later came to regret for a little while was that Clarissa had not given up that daft idea of hers of combining our savings and betting all upon the longest shot on the boards. She made that plain when, just as I was waiting to leave with Mr. Patley next day, she suddenly appeared and, from her large apron pocket, drew a great, jingling pile of coins tied up neatly in a kerchief.

"Here," said she, "you'll find a pound and eleven shillings. You don't need to count it, for I've done that over and over again. You've probably twice that amount. Just put it together with mine and wager it where it will do the most good."

"But Clarissa—"

"Not a word, Jeremy! Just remember what I said: favorable odds and the right attitude. That will do it."

And, having spoken thus, she planted a kiss upon my cheek and ran for the door. There she waved and disappeared inside.

So there I stood in Bow Street, awaiting the arrival of Mr. Patley, so that we two might leave together for the Post Coach House and catch the evening mail coach to Newmarket. I knew that there was time to spare till it departed; nevertheless, I was eager to be under way.

Mr. Marsden had come to work early that day as if to assure Sir John and the rest of us that he was fit to do all that was asked of him. Even so, his voice was thin and wheezy, and he seemed to speak only when it was absolutely necessary. I was worried about him; and Sir John, though he voiced no doubts, did not demand much from him.

The magistrate took me aside and told me that I might continue with my packing, for he accepted Mr. Marsden's assurances that he was well enough to finish the week out. I was to alert Mr. Patley that all would be proceeding as planned.

Before leaving, I sat down in Sir John's chambers and took down a letter from him to the magistrate of Newmarket, explaining who Mr. Patley and I were and what purpose we had there in the town. He asked the cooperation of the magistrate in our efforts and assured him that we would respect his jurisdiction in all matters.

When he had signed the letter, and it was sealed with his official seal, he handed it over to me and told me to tuck it away someplace safe.

"Between us I will advise you only to make use of this if you get into trouble with his constables. You will then have to explain why you did not present the letter the moment you arrived."

"And what shall I tell him?" I asked.

"Anything you like," said he with a sly smile. "Lie, prevaricate, give him the best sort of story that you can make up quickly. But at such a distance, I warn you, I cannot help you much."

"I noticed that you said nothing in the letter about firearms. Am I to take it that that means we are to take none with us?"

"You have taken it correctly," said he. "Mr. Patley may take his club, and you, I suppose, that God-awful weapon you secretly carry with you wherever you go."

"The cosh?"

"That's it. But you may make use of them only in the *most* extreme situation. You understand that, do you?"

I assured him I did.

"And you will pass it on to Mr. Patley?"

"I will, sir."

"Then Godspeed to you, Jeremy. Come back with Alice Plummer, and we'll be much closer to solving this case. I believe that to be true with all my heart."

With such a leavetaking as that, you may well suppose that I was determined to do my very best, and I took the hand he offered me in both of my own and gave his a proper squeeze.

"Good lad," said he.

I left his presence and took my place just outside the door to Number 4 Bow Street, my new portmanteau at my feet, and there I awaited the arrival of Mr. Patley.

After bouncing along for the entire night, we came at dawn to Cambridge. Though not so grand as Oxford, the towers of the university there gave it the appearance of some fairy-tale city of a past that never was. Then, as we approached, the rays of the rising sun caught them so that for a minute or two they shone quite brilliantly. The early morning sun can make even London look thus enchanted.

There we stopped, and, as the great bags of mail were tossed down, I myself descended to the cobblestones and helped down two of the passengers—an elderly man and his much younger wife. The couple had grumbled all the way from London at the roughness of the road and the speed of the horses. I was glad to be rid of them. I walked about then in the early morning cold, glad to have the chance to stretch my legs a bit. In the distance, I could see what I took to be the university buildings, yet I was not to get much closer to them than the coachyard, on that trip. Then came a call from the driver, and I hopped up into the coach and closed the door after me.

Through it all, Constable Patley had slept. I, on the other hand, had dozed only fitfully, and that during those brief periods wherein the horses were walked that they might rest a bit. Yet we were not long beyond the outskirts of London when the constable had fallen into a dreamless sleep—no mumbling, no tossing nor turning; he was simply dead to the world for the duration of the journey. Later, I asked him how he had accustomed himself to sleeping so soundly under such conditions. He told me that it was a skill (if that be the word) he had developed whilst serving in the army. "Oftentimes," said he, "'tis necessary to take your sleep whenever you have the opportunity—and such times come more often in the army than you might suppose." Mr. Perkins, who had the same sort of ability, told me much the same thing: he developed it in the army.

Not far out of town, we came upon the river Cam and followed it alongside until Newmarket was visible in the distance. It is no match for the Thames, as you may suppose; by comparison, it is hardly more than a stream. Nevertheless, the river and the bankside greenery are as pretty as any could wish. Indeed, some of the scenes I saw along the way were quite beautiful in the quiet way of the English countryside.

As it grew brighter, Mr. Patley began to stir. He stretched, flailing round him slowly in ever-widening circles. He blinked his eyes open, saw that we were alone there in the coach, and let out a moan.

"Ohhh, Jeremy, I've a terrible piss must be taken."

I banged upon the ceiling of the coach and felt the conveyance grinding to a halt most immediately. Yet Patley did not wait for a complete stop. He jumped out the door as soon as it was safe and ran to the side of the road.

"Why didn't your friend do his business back in Cambridge like the rest of us?" the driver called down to me.

"He was asleep," was my reply.

"Asleep, was he? Well, I've half a notion to leave him where he's now standin'."

"You do that," said I, "and you'll have Sir John Fielding to answer to back in London."

"What's he to do with you two?"

"You'd find out soon enough."

I would go no further with my threat. Truth to tell, I thought perhaps I'd gone too far already. We were headed into territory in which Sir John's name had not quite the weight that it carried round Covent Garden. From this point on, I promised myself that I would use his name much more sparingly. But now was Constable Patley returned, and there was no need to wrangle further with the driver. He hopped inside and closed the door after him.

"Ah, I'm a new man," said he.

"I hope not," said I, "for I liked the old one pretty well."

"Let me tell you something, Jeremy, old lad. There's few in this world who I owe anything to—but you're one of them."

"Oh? How's that?"

"I can write as well as any of the constables now, which ain't to say I can write perfect. And I can even read a bit now. It's a great time-passer, it is."

I, who had no difficulty passing the time, had never thought of reading in quite that way before. What he had said struck me as funny—and so I did what may have struck him as rude: I laughed. Yet he took no offense.

"No, it's true," said he. "You take a fellow like me, he gets out of the army, and all he knows to do when he ain't workin' is go out and drink as he used to do in the army. And y'see that ain't right, for it's too easy to fall in with the same element you're keepin' an eye on whilst you're on the job—the whores and the robbers and such—if you get my meaning, and that ain't right."

"Oh, I understand," said I—and indeed I did. 'Twas the first time I had considered the matters he spoke of.

"Now I know for fact that readin' ain't *just* to pass the time. You got all your learning, which is considerable, out of books, didn't you?"

"Well, not quite all. A lot that isn't facts and some that is I got from Sir John."

"And *him*," he laughed. "He was just born with it, I reckon."

"Indeed," said I, "he must have been."

"But whenever I come to a word I don't know, I just take a look into that Johnson dictionary you gave me—and there it is. I know what it means, and I know how to spell it proper. I want you to know, Jeremy, that giving me that dictionary is about the most considerate thing anybody ever did for me. And I've read that *Robinson Crusoe* book twice through, I have!"

"Well, it's about time then that you got another, don't you think so?"

"You just tell me what to get, and I'll get it."

"Well," said I, "let me give some thought to that."

"You do that."

Then did Constable Patley sit back, blushing with excitement at having said his piece. He nodded a good, firm, manly nod.

"I just wanted you to know."

"Thank you, Mr. Patley."

We finished the rest of the trip to Newmarket in complete silence—or near it.

Yet, as we entered the town of Newmarket, Mr. Patley pointed off to the left and called my attention to the heath just beyond us.

"It's there they run the race," said he. "It's the longest and the fastest, and the only one that's run on a permanent course."

Of the events that followed—our arrival and search for the Good Queen Bess, and our disappointment at learning Mr. Deuteronomy and his party had not yet arrived—I shall have nothing to say. Such mundane details have little place in such a report as this, for they seem only to clutter the narrative. Let me begin this section, rather, with our first survey of the race site. We were, I suppose, searching for Alice Plummer, yet neither Mr. Patley nor I expected to find her quite so immediate. And, truth be known, I do believe that both of us would have been disappointed if we had found her quite so soon, for we must then have turned round and taken her back to London without ever having viewed the great race for the King's Plate. I had told Patley of Mr. Deuteronomy's bold boast that he would win, riding Pegasus, and we were both greatly impressed by that. We would see him win—sister or no.

In my case, after we had rested ourselves a bit in the room provided us, we went out to get a proper view of the race course and a sense of the town. Newmarket itself was not much—nor is it today, if what I have heard of it still pertains. The surrounding countryside is pretty enough, but the buildings in the town have to them a rather decrepit air, as if a good, strong wind might blow them all down. The main street in town is the same road we took from Cambridge. It is withal, as its name implies, a market town—and probably has been such for near a thousand years. There is a central square, and in it, foodstuffs—fruit and vegetable—are sold. Though not so grand as Covent Garden, I do believe a greater variety of growing things are sold there. Yet what the town of Newmarket may or may not be matters little, for it is known not so much as a town (there must be half a hundred or more like it) as it is a location for the greatest horse-racing to be found in all of England. Without its race course, it would be simply another market town.

The King's Plate race was still a few days into the future, yet there seemed to be more people in the area surrounding the course than in the town proper. Was it always so? Their number would doubtless increase on race day. Where had they all come from? Where did they sleep? These visitors must have surely doubled the population of the town already.

As we merged with the crowd, Mr. Patley and I noticed a number of familiar faces from Bedford Street and Seven Dials in London: whores and pickpockets they were, and in such number as I had not seen before. The whores flirted one with another. The pickpockets dipped their hands each in the other's coats and waistcoats. It was a carnival for thieves. We came at last to a rail fence which marked one of the limits of the course. Coaches and carriages were parked there, hard by, and the dukes and earls stood atop them, observing the activity out on the track through telescopes and spyglasses. Each seemed to boast a surrounding retinue of a sizable number. There was a good deal of teasing comment which passed back and forth between them. It was for the nobles, as I saw, that this pageant was played out. But what was it they watched so intently out there on the course? I put the question to Mr. Patley.

"I don't rightly know," said he. "I reckon, though, that they're studying their horses out there—not so much for speed as for gait and behavior on the course and whatnot. There's a lot to learning a course like this one."

"Why this one, especially?"

"Well, because of its length and the many rough places out there on the heath."

"Not an easy course then, eh?"

"Oh, no. Ain't a bit of it easy."

We had a good view of the horses on the track—though not so good as the nobles and aristocrats atop their vehicles. We had found a spot between two coaches, somewhat protected from the crowd. From it, I watched and took in all that Mr. Patley had to say about the racing of horses in general, and the racing of them at Newmarket in particular. In the course of my days in Newmarket, he passed on to me a wealth of information. It all began, as I recall, with a question I asked about the number of horses out on the track. There was a great swarm of them following those on which the owners had their spy-glasses trained. They were moving along at a ragged pace and with no style whatever. It was almost as if this second line of riders were hoping that some reflected glory might be cast back upon them from the first.

"They can't *all* be running in the King's Plate race, can they?" I asked Mr. Patley.

"No, not at all. But it's one of the faults of this race that there's far too many in it."

"They put no limit on the number?"

"Well, in a practical way I s'pose they do. They put the entry fee up so high, there's not so many can afford it. But those who can are free to get out on the course and ride round it as often as they like." He smiled and shook his head. "It makes for a pretty crowded field, don't it?"

"It does indeed."

We watched on as the leaders and the pursuing line of stragglers reached the farthest point from us. Then did Patley lose interest (or so it seemed to me) and began looking up and down the rail fence, as if for something he knew had to be there. Having found it, he pointed down to our right.

"There, Jeremy, just take a look." There was a line of horses, with overweight riders perched on top awaiting the arrival of the mob of horsemen so that they might join them.

"What about them?"

"Well, just look. They're waiting to take their trip round the course, and there's none checking to see if they got any right to be here at all, much less to tour the track."

"So right now anybody could get on the course?"

"As long as he's got a horse to ride."

I looked them over, those waiting impatiently for the mounted mob to make the circle complete. I had one more question, the last for a while.

"Who are those people waiting their turn on the track?"

"Local gentry." He spat it out as if it were an oath or an obscenity.

As near as I could tell, the entire event was staged simply for the entertainment of the local gentry. The nobility—that is, those who owned the horses running the race—seemed to take it all quite earnestly.

When Mr. Patley announced his hunger to me, I realized that I, too, was hungry, and suggested we return to the Good Queen Bess where we might find us something in the tap-room. And so we started back, pushing our way through the crowd, which had grown a bit during our time at the rail. We pressed on, hands in our pockets, holding tight to our money bags. Just then did we spy the early odds posted at a turf-accountant's stall. 'Twas Patley saw it first; he gave me a proper nudge in the ribs and pointed out the slate to me.

"There," said he, "that might be of some interest to you, Jeremy."

And, indeed, it was of interest—though not so much for the entries it carried as for the one it did not. I studied the list, then, having noted an omission, I studied it again.

"Mr. Patley," said I. "Pegasus is not here on the slate."

"I see he ain't," said he, attaching little importance to the fact.

"But why should Mr. Deuteronomy tell us he would be here, and then fail to arrive?"

"Oh, if he said he'd come, I for one believe he'll be here. You see, Jeremy, they can't post odds on a horse unless he's present and officially entered."

I nodded, accepting Mr. Patley's explanation, yet not quite put at ease by it. I wondered what it was had held them up.

The turf accountant's stall was at the very fringe of the area surrounding the race course. We went from it quickly through town and arrived at the Good Queen Bess in less time than it would take to tell.

"I believe I'll inquire at the desk and find out if Mr. Deuteronomy has yet arrived to claim his room," said I.

"Do as you like."

Thus did we companions separate — I to make my inquiry, and he to the tap-room. Having no luck at the desk, I turned away, and who should I then spy entering the front door of the inn but Deuteronomy Plummer himself.

We greeted warmly with much hand-slapping and back-slapping. He asked me if all was right with my room, and I assured him that it was. Then did I inquire after his trip to Newmarket.

"We took it nice and slow," said he. "Arrived just as intended."

"And Pegasus is in good fettle?"

"Ah, ain't he though! Every morning I give him a good talking-to, telling him just how he's going to win this one."

The idea of a conversation with a horse struck me as rather funny: I laughed, again in spite of myself. For his part, Mr. Deuteronomy was somewhat taken aback at my response.

"You think he don't understand me? Well then, sir, you think wrong. Ain't a smarter horse in the world than Pegasus!"

"Well, I'm sure that's true, but . . ." I left the sentence unended and hanging in the air. "Mr. Plummer, could you wait just a moment? I've a companion in the tap-room. He's a Bow Street Runner, and a great enthusiast of your riding. Let me get him, and —"

"No, I've got to get these horses stabled," said he, interrupting, "and watered and fed. Bring him to the track real early tomorrow. We'll be out there at dawn, or close to it, learning the course."

He then called to the clerk behind the desk, claiming his room, and ran out to tend to his horses. Well then, thought I, dawn it would be then for me—though Mr. Patley will no doubt be disappointed.

Yet he wasn't, not in the least: "Oh no, I'm not surprised—and therefore I ain't disappointed. He's a real horseman, he is. Most of your lords and your gentry and whatnot, they have no sense of how to treat a horse. First rule we learned in the army was, take care of your horse's needs, and after he's been looked after, then—and only then—you take care of yourself."

I had entered the tap-room to find him at a table near a window. There were two dark ales upon the table, a small loaf, and a big chunk of Stilton cheese. He looked as pleased and contented as I had ever seen him. He beckoned me over to him and gestured grandly at the bread and cheese, as if to say that that should hold us till dinner time. 'Twas then I told him of my meeting with Mr. Deuteronomy, expecting a howl of frustration in response and getting instead the well-reasoned lecture on the necessity of caring first for the horses.

That I have quoted to you already, reader, yet what I have not told is that, having said his piece, he became, of a sudden, most interested in something or someone just beyond the window. He stared. Then did he rub his chin and stare once again.

"By God," said he aloud yet to himself, "I believe it's her. I really do believe it's her."

Then did my own eyes turn most immediate to the crowd outside the window. "Where?" said I. "Which one? You mean Alice Plummer, don't you?"

Yet Constable Patley was already on his feet and running out the door. I pursued him, hesitating just long enough to tell the serving woman to leave all upon the table, for we would be back.

But when?

SEVEN

*In which our luck
goes down and up in
the next few days*

❦

I rushed out the inn expecting to find Mr. Patley in hot pursuit of Alice Plummer, yet found him just beyond the door, standing, looking about, scratching his head. He'd been flummoxed, confused utterly by the great number of women he saw. They were all, it seemed, heading off in three or four different directions, but in general, most moved toward the race course, whence we had just come. Oh, there were men, as well, as many or more than the women. But just at that moment, since it was a woman we searched for, there seemed to be a superabundance of them about. I approached Mr. Patley warily, for he seemed at that moment to be reasoning out in which direction she might have gone. I stood beside him, hesitating. At last, feeling I could wait no longer, I spoke up.

"Constable Patley," said I, "was it Alice Plummer you spied through the window?"

"What? Oh yes, indeed it was. I seen her a number of times round Seven Dials. I'm just sure it was her. And of course when she reported her little girl missing, too."

"How was she dressed? What was she wearing?"

"Oh, I don't know. I'll have to think about that." And that he proceeded to do, placing a hand over his eyes that he might better concentrate. "Truth of it is, I was looking at her face and not at her clothes, but it *seems* to me that her dress was a sort of dark red going into blue. Plum-colored, you might call it."

"That's a pretty rare color for a dress. Why don't you go off in one way, and I'll take another, and let's see if we can't find her."

"But you don't even know what she looks like," he objected.

"That may be," said I, "but I know what color her dress is. I'll just stop every woman in a plum-colored dress and ask if her name is Alice Plummer. There couldn't be too many in such a color."

"I s'pose not."

And so it was agreed. He would follow the crowd moving off toward the right, and I the column moving along to the left. We would mix all through and keep our eyes open for the dress of the right color. We would keep going in such a manner until we met at the place where we had viewed the horses out upon the track. If, after a few minutes' wait, we failed to meet there, then we would go back the way we had come and meet again at the tap-room of the Good Queen Bess. We started upon our separate ways.

Like so many things in life, this plan, so simple in the telling, proved much more difficult in its execution. The chief problem lay in the number of individuals to be struggled through, around, and, ultimately, past. The inertia of the crowd resisted and dominated my every push and squeeze, so that I could finally do little more than find a place and move my feet along at the same rate as the rest. In this way, I reached the rail fence at approximately the same point that we had left earlier. There I waited, quite exhausted by my struggles against the multitude.

Needless to say, I saw no woman in a plum-colored dress.

Whilst resting against the fence, I became aware that, when I left it, I would have to struggle up the hill against the tide, which would be even more difficult. I decided to wait a bit longer for Constable Patley—at least as long as it took for the sweat to dry upon my brow.

I gave my attention to the horses out upon the course. They were still out there, learning the ups and downs, the jumps and full-out gallops. And of course the second-rank was there still, following at a respectful trot; and if anything, its number had grown.

Of the owners there was little more to say. They were yet standing, spy-glasses in hand; their number had also grown—or so it seemed. One of them looked quite familiar, a newcomer, I was sure. He was as well-dressed as any in that line of observers, but fat enough that he had wisely avoided the roof of his coach; if he had managed to climb up upon it, the weight of him might indeed have collapsed it. And so, he stood at the rail not much more than ten feet away. Who was he? I knew that I had seen him before my arrival at Newmarket. As I studied him, I even recalled the sound of his voice—a sort of whining drawl that perfectly matched his rude manner. Then I had it! He was the owner of Pegasus and the employer of Deuteronomy Plummer. I knew him not by name but by title—Lord Lamford he was, and a less likeable man I had never met. I looked round him and saw no sign of Mr. Deuteronomy about, and that was just as well, it seemed to me, for if he were, I'd feel obliged to speak to him, and that seemed wrong here and now.

Ah well, said I to myself, there's naught for me to do but return to the Good Queen Bess and the tankard of flat ale which awaited me there. Taking one last look about for Mr. Patley and failing to see him, I plunged ahead into the great crowd and kept an eye open for any color that might be judged plum. Thus did I reach the inn at the top of the hill.

Entering the tap-room, I found the constable sitting where he had formerly sat, a new tankard of ale before him, and deep in talk with the serving woman. As I took my place at the table, he ended his conversation and asked for a fresh ale "for my young friend." Then did he push the plate of bread and cheese toward me.

"I fear I've had more than my share," said he. "We can order some more, if you want it."

I could not but notice that Patley seemed far more rested and relaxed than I. How long could he have sat here talking with the serving woman? Could he really have made the same arduous journey that I had just made? Yet, just as I was searching for the right words with which to express my doubts to him, the serving woman returned with my dark ale. After I sweated the way to the race course and back, I confess, my thirst was so great that I quaffed off half the tankard in a few gulps. Then did I dig into the Stilton, slicing off a generous chunk and piling it upon the bread. That took some chewing, and as I chewed, I thought, and by the time I finished it, I had devised my approach.

"Mr. Patley," said I, "you must have reached the rail fence round the race course long before I did—been there and gone.

Sorry to have missed you, but I was wondering: did you happen to notice Lord Lamford there?"

"Uh, no, I can't say as I did," he replied uneasily.

"I was going to ask if you'd seen Mr. Deuteronomy with him. But of course, if you didn't see Lord Lamford, then you couldn't have seen Deuteronomy with him, now could you?"

"Well . . . yes, that's good thinking on your part, Jeremy."

I gave him a look of a certain kind. I tucked in my chin and gave him a frown. I'd meant it to seem dubious, suspicious, and it must have, for it wrung from him this confession:

"I suppose I really ought to tell you, Jeremy, old friend, that I never really made it down as far as the rail fence."

"Oh? And how did that come about, Mr. Patley?"

"Well, you see, it's like this," said he, "here I was, pushing and shoving my way through this great bunch of people, and I wasn't getting nowhere at all. But I kep' going and looking for that woman in the plum-colored dress. Oh, I looked and looked, but I never did see anyone in a dress of such a color—and then it did come to me. Alice Plummer wasn't in such a dress when I glimpsed her from this very chair I'm sittin' in now. Oh no, it wasn't plum-colored, it was blue—teal blue is what it was. Of a sudden, I was just sure of it. And it wouldn't have done any good at all to start looking for her, for I must have let pass about a dozen or more just the little ways I'd gone."

"Oh," said I, "I must have let twice that number go by."

"Well, there you are," said he. "It's an altogether common sort of dress in a common sort of color."

"But I went all the way down there for no purpose at all, didn't I, Mr. Patley?"

He hesitated for a long moment. "I wouldn't say it was for no purpose at all," said he.

"Oh? And how is that, sir?"

"At least we know she's here in Newmarket, don't we?"

When the knock came upon the door, I bounded out of bed, ready to greet the day, even though a glance out the window gave proof that it must still be night. I had asked that I be knocked up at five.

Had they made it four just to give me an early start? No matter, though, whatever the hour, I was well awake and ready for the day. I gave Patley a shake and received only groaning mumbles for my trouble. Ah well, let him sleep, if sleep he must. Then did I empty my bladder and begin my morning ritual—taking care to wash well and to dress warmly. Yet I'd a feeling that I must leave a reminder of some sort for Mr. Patley. I gave him another shake.

"Mr. Patley," said I, "can you hear me?"

Again the groans and the mumbles; there was, nevertheless, a sort of affirmative sound to them.

"I'm going down to the track now. If you wish to meet Mr. Deuteronomy, come down there quickly as you can. I can't say when I'll return. But I'll look for you in the tap-room when I come back."

Was all that clear to him? I hoped it was. Yet that single grunt I received in response was anything but encouraging. And so, having no better thought, I hurriedly wrote a brief note in which I said much the same thing as I had just spoken in his ear. I propped it against the candle and blew the candle out. I recall my surprise that at that moment the room was not, of a sudden, plunged into complete darkness; the dawning of a new day had begun.

Downstairs in the lobby the standing clock in the corner said that it was near half past five. Had I taken so long to wash and dress?

"Can I get a cup of coffee in the tap-room?" I asked the fellow behind the desk.

At that he barked a laugh. "At this hour? Not the least chance, I fear. The tap-room opens at seven."

I nodded and headed for the door. There I paused and turned back to him.

"Has Mr. Deuteronomy Plummer left yet?"

"You mean the small fellow? Oh, you may be sure of it. 'Twas near an hour ago, I should say."

Again I nodded as I threw open the door and left.

It was cold out there. I pulled up the collar of my coat and thrust my hands deep into my pockets. Starting off along the same route I had walked the day before, I thanked God for all the threats and pleas that Clarissa had used to force me to bring along the waistcoat which now kept my chest properly warm. Then did she press her entreaties on the matter of the wager, as she repeated to me her formula—"favorable odds and the right attitude"—as a sort of incantation.

Yesterday evening, as Constable Patley and I ate dinner in the tap-room, I described to him in general terms (not mentioning Clarissa) the nature of my problem. He listened, nodding, rubbing his unshaven chin, as I explained all as best I could, even repeating to him her magic formula.

"'Favorable odds and the right attitude,' is it?" said he, "and what might the right attitude be?"

"Prayerful," said I.

He laughed at that, but then said that it was as good as many he had heard of.

"Do you mean I should do just as this person has asked?"

"Well now I didn't say that, did I?" He paused, taking a moment to consider the matter. Then: "Here's how an experienced bettor would handle the problem. First of all, if the person you describe entrusted you with money and those instructions, I'd say you had an obligation to do it just that way—with that person's money."

"But Mr. Patley!"

"No, hear me out, Jeremy. What an experienced bettor would do is use his own money to hedge the bet he'd made for the other person."

"*Hedge* the bet?" said I. "What do you mean?"

"Well, you put the money on the safest bet you can make—a sure win, if there is such a thing. That way you've more or less insured the loss of the money bet at favorable odds. Of course, the safe bet you make to hedge the other one won't pay near as well because everybody else will be betting him, too. But it'll probably pay off just enough. You'll be covered against the loss, you see?"

Indeed I did see. "It sounds to me like the only sensible way to bet."

Patley let that stand for a moment or two, though it was clear that he was made a bit uncomfortable by it. But then did he come out with this. "Sensible it may be, but if a body was sensible, he wouldn't be betting in the first place. Betting is, well, it's having an inspiration. It's having a thunderbolt hit you so that you know *this is the one!* You don't look at the odds. You don't worry about how the horse has done in past races. You just *know* this is the horse that's going to win *today*!" It sounded almost like poetry the way he said it then—and perhaps it was a kind of poetry to him. But he did add: "Most of the time it's just money thrown away when you bet like that. Ah, but once in a while it happens just the way your vision said it would—and what you've won is not just a bet, it's letting you believe your life's going to get better, that maybe you'll win all in the end."

I knew not quite how to take that, and so I did no more than nod and say rather timidly, "Thank you for telling me about hedging bets. That should solve the problem nicely."

"Think nothing of it."

We parted shortly afterward—I to our room, where I read myself to sleep, and he to join the group at the bar, men who, like us, had come up from London. I marveled at his endurance, yet then reminded myself that he had slept the distance from just outside London all the way to Cambridge—and I, of course, had not.

It was still quite gray by the time I reached the race course. Indeed, I wondered, from the look of the sky, if it might not rain that day. (It did not.) There was one man alone who stood hunched over the rail. Even from behind—perhaps specially so—I could tell that the onlooker was *not* Lord Lamford. It was not, however, till he turned round and I saw his face that I recognized him from Shepherd's Bush on Easter Sunday, one of those who tended Pegasus following the race. I gave him a greeting and received one in return; then did I settle myself relatively near the fellow but made no attempt to question him nor start a conversation with him. We simply watched at some distance, one from the other.

What we saw surprised me somewhat, for, though at a considerable remove, Mr. Deuteronomy and Pegasus were nevertheless visible in the still-dim light. Yet the surprise was that, though the horse was saddled, the jockey led him by the reins at a slow pace that was comfortable to them both. I watched, fascinated, for he seemed to be communicating as they walked. Were his lips moving? They seemed to be; if so, he was communicating directly with Pegasus, for there was no one about at his end of the track to whom he might be speaking. Here and there he took the trouble to point things out along the way. I cannot say that the horse understood, but he certainly gave Mr. Deuteronomy his full attention. I watched them so for some minutes; then, unable to contain myself further, I put to my companion at the rail a question.

"Do my eyes deceive me," said I, "or is Mr. Deuteronomy actually talking to Pegasus?

"Yes, that's what he's doing, pointing things to watch out for along the way, and where they might speed up, and so on."

"And does the horse . . ."

"Does he understand? Yes, I'd say he does. Deuteronomy, he's got a special talent with them animals. I never seen nothin' like it in my life before."

Nor had I. The question that came to me, however, was whether the "special talent" was Mr. Deuteronomy's or the horse's. It would be difficult to say.

"Pegasus won't let nobody but him on his back," said my companion. "He'll let me lead him, saddle him, rub him down to dry him off, all of that, but I dare not sit on his back."

"That is indeed interesting," said I, "Mr. . . . . Mr. . . . ."

"Bennett. And you'd be young Mr. Proctor, I s'pose. Deuteronomy said you'd be coming by early."

So this was the Bennett who had brought the pistol to the gunsmith Joseph Griffin. I would know what Deuteronomy had asked him. Later.

He pulled from his pocket a collapsed spy-glass and offered it to me.

"Here," said he. "It's getting lighter. You might want to take a look through this."

I accepted it with thanks, opened it up, and peered through it. It only tended to confirm what my unaided eyes had suggested. Mr. Deuteronomy kept up a fairly constant chatter with Pegasus at his side. Indeed, through the spyglass, the image of the jockey came through so plain that, were I a lip-reader, I am sure that I could have caught every word he spoke, all at a distance of a furlong or more. I wondered what he spoke. Which is to say, did Pegasus understand the King's English, or did the two have a separate lan-

guage between them? I entertained that thought, and others no less
fanciful, whilst I studied the horse and the man approaching. I returned the spy-glass to Mr. Bennett just as the two arrived at our
vantage point. He ducked under the rail and gave Mr. Deuteronomy a leg up that he might mount Pegasus. The jockey spoke his
thanks politely to Bennett; to me, he gave only a nod. Then did the
two, horse and man, start off on a tour of the course.

The first time round, and the second, they did no more than go
at a trot. Then, at a signal from Mr. Deuteronomy, Pegasus sped up
to a canter. It was twice round so—and then a walk, a trot, and a
walk round again, this time Pegasus led round by his rider. Never
once did they take the course, or any part of it, at a full gallop. But
by this time, too, other horses, and their riders and trainers, had
arrived. Deuteronomy signaled Bennett that it was time to go.
Halfway up the hill there seemed so many horses marching down to
the track that I was certain there would be a repetition of yesterday's mob-scene in that part we had just left.

I fell in beside Mr. Deuteronomy, eager to talk, yet I saw that he
was occupied by thoughts of the race, which was by then but two
days hence. He signed his readiness to talk by opening the discussion himself.

"You see from this crowd of horseflesh why we got down here
so early," said he to me.

"Oh, I do indeed. Yesterday there were so many horses on the
course, there was scarce any room for those entered in the race. That
was in the late morning or early afternoon—sometime in there."

"Oh, I know how it can be. I hope it clears out a bit this
evening, for Pegasus needs a light workout. If it's as bad as you say,
I'll take him out on the country roads. We have to bring him up to a
peak in a couple of days, though. Not easy."

"Still think you'll win?" I asked.

"I haven't seen any yet who could likely take him."

We trudged along in silence for a fair distance, but then did I recall one of the reasons that had brought me down to the track so
early in the morning. I had news for him.

"Yesterday, just after I saw you in the Good Queen Bess, we
saw your sister."

"Alice? I wasn't just a-leading you on, now was I? Did you catch her?"

"No, she got away from us—or not that exactly. Constable Patley, who knows her by sight, saw her through the tap-room window. But by the time we got outside, she was nowhere in sight."

"But you're sure it was her?"

"Oh, I'm sure as long as Mr. Patley is—and he is truly sure."

"I'd like to meet him."

"And he'd like to meet you. There's not much about horse racing he doesn't know."

"That so?"

"He was a horse soldier, he was. I hope to find him there in the tap-room, eating breakfast."

"Hope" was the operative word in that statement, for while it was true that I hoped to find him there, I had no certainty of it. Thus was I surprised and gratified to see him there in the tap-room, just beginning what looked to be a considerable breakfast, eggs and all. I pointed him out to Mr. Deuteronomy, then ushered him over that I might introduce the two men. When Mr. Patley saw us approaching through the crowd, his mouth dropped open in surprise, and he rose in awe to accept the honor that was about to be bestowed upon him.

"Mr. Patley," said I to him, "I have the pleasure to present to you Mr. Deuteronomy Plummer."

He was quite speechless, so overcome that when the jockey offered him his hand, all he could do was stare down at it for an embarrassing length of time until he realized at last that Mr. Deuteronomy wished to shake hands with him. Then did he grasp it and pump the hand so hard I feared he might do it damage. Mr. Patley urged us to sit down and waved over the serving woman.

What passed during the next hour or so was a fascinating discussion of Mr. Deuteronomy's career as a race rider, of which I understood only about half, at most. I simply hadn't the background in racing to comprehend many of the questions asked and the answers given. Nor could I be so bold as to attempt to reproduce any part of it here. What I can offer the reader, however (and which may be somewhat more germane to the matter at hand), is the comparatively brief conversation which the two had regarding Deuteron-omy's sister, Alice.

This postscript to the main body of their talk occurred after the last bite of breakfast had been eaten and the final cup of coffee had been downed. I recall that a lull came, and, in the course of it, Mr. Deuteronomy leaned back and fixed the constable with a most piercing look.

"I understand, Mr. Patley," said he, "that you met my sister a day or two after her daughter, Maggie, was taken away."

"That's correct, Mr. Plummer, sir."

"And she claimed that Maggie had been stolen?"

"True, sir."

"Why do you suppose she did that?"

"Ah, well. I wondered that m'self. And the best I could come up with is this: If she said that her daughter had been stolen, then whatever happened to the girl, she would be free of blame. Children are bought, sold, and stolen every day in London, but still, buying and selling them *is* against the law."

"I recall," said I, "that Sir John once said that it is considered as slavery in the sense that it is commerce in human beings."

"And if someone should just happen to notice that Maggie was no longer about and that your sister was somewhat richer, they might point the finger at her, but nothing could be proved, for, after all, she'd reported that her child had been stolen from her."

"But that was what happened, was it not?" said Mr. Deuteron-omy. "Someone did envy her that she had become richer of a sudden, didn't they?"

"Yes," said I, "'twas her neighbor next door, Katy Tiddle, the day before she was murdered. Yet she herself was in on it in some way, and that, I'm sure, was what got her killed."

Deuteronomy Plummer nodded at that, and he did keep his silence for what seemed a very long time. At last he turned to me and said, "What do you think about this?"

"First of all, from what I've heard from you and from others about your sister, I'd say she was not bright enough to think of that matter of reporting Maggie stolen."

"Oh, I agree with you there," said he. "What sense she had, left her with all that gin she drank. Must've been that Katy Tiddle, or someone a bit higher up the ladder."

"And it was Katy Tiddle from whom I took the pistol, the one which must be a mate to that one brought in to the shop of Joseph Griffin, Gunsmith, by *your* Mr. Bennett."

"Yes, well, I've spoken to him about that, and he doesn't know a thing about it, so he says. Can't imagine how that pistol came into her possession."

"And you accept that, do you?"

"Oh yes."

He was, it seemed to me, a bit too quick with his assurances.

"I've a question for you," said Mr. Patley to Deuteronomy.

"And what is that?"

"How did it come that you were so certain that your sister would be here in Newmarket around race day? I was glad when Jeremy here invited me along, but I didn't expect for a minute that we would find her in this great mob of people—the main reason being I didn't think that she'd be here, didn't think there was a chance of it. But here we come, Jeremy and me, and we catch sight of her first day."

"So I hear. But truth to tell, I was sure she'd be here because she told me she would be."

"Told you she'd be here?" Patley repeated, somewhat amazed.

"Yes, it was two or three years ago, maybe three or four. Anyways, I'd located her at last, and I'd been riding in races round London for about a year. We was on better terms then, mostly because of little Maggie. She was the sweetest little thing you ever did see back then—small for her age and she couldn't talk much, but *so* pretty and just as affectionate as she could be. Took my heart away, she did.

"Anyways, as I said, we was on better terms then, and I took them both to the Crown and Anchor in the Strand, celebrating something or other. Alice kept Maggie quiet giving her little sips of gin—watered down o'course. So the two of them was both gettin' pretty tipsy, and we hadn't had a thing to eat yet. Alice was actin' more silly and sentimental by the minute. Pretty soon she started talkin' about Maggie's father. Seems that when she ran off from the farm—the family farm—she wandered round for a while, then come upon Newmarket just as they were gettin' ready for the races here. Well, for a country girl run away from home there couldn't be anything more exciting than this here—most particularly when she met a young fella about her age, so tall and fair she'd never seen nothin' like him ever before. She was just carried away by him, she was.

"'Oh, Deuteronomy,' she says to me. 'He took my maidenhead, yet never was one so freely given. We was together a month or so, then we had our first quarrel—just a little lover's tiff was all it was, but I got all carried away and left for London right off.'

"But she promised me right then that if ever she got a little money ahead she would go right back up to Newmarket and make another baby with her tall, straw-haired young fellow. That was how she put it. She *promised* me."

The rest of that day went much like the one before. We searched for Alice Plummer—without result. There was but this alteration in our plan. Whereas we had spent the morning looking for her between our inn and the track below, we spent the afternoon exploring the area *above* the Good Queen Bess; for after all, was she not coming *down* the hill when Constable Patley spied her through the tap-room window? So she was—and so there was naught to do but go higher and search more industriously. Yet how large or small the town of Newmarket was had to play some part in all this. It was not a place of immense size, after all. True, its population had been swollen many times over, but we could cover the space of it in not much more than a couple of hours. And so we wandered through that area upon the hill above and saw that it was much like the area that surrounded the inn. There were inns, stables, houses, no shops to speak of, but many tents, lean-tos, and other temporary shelters. It appeared to me as if the good burghers of Newmarket were making a pretty penny from this notable event, now a feature of the racing calendar.

I recall remarking on this to Mr. Patley in the midst of our searches, and he responded, "Well, it ain't bad as London for stealing a poor man's coppers, but you put a lot of money into any town in England, and this is what you're likely to get."

"I think if we were to make this tour at nightfall," said I, "we would find that the residents of the makeshift dwellings are holding their own insofar as separating a poor man from his coppers."

"P'rhaps so," said he. "Are you truly proposing that we make such a tour?"

"No, not really. I believe we can spend our time better in another manner. Mr. Deuteronomy said to me earlier that he would be taking Pegasus out for a run in the early evening if the course is not too crowded. I thought you might like to see him put through his paces."

"Would I, though! Indeed! Just as soon as the sun goes low in the sky."

Thus was it agreed. We had by that time looked so long and hard for Alice that I felt not the slightest guilt in temporarily deserting our search.

So it was that at the time suggested by Mr. Patley we made our way down the hill to watch Pegasus's second run of the day. It would not be long until sundown and, again, not long after that before night fell. All the many against whom I had struggled to return to the Good Queen Bess yesterday in the early afternoon were now returning; and so it was a bit of a battle making our way down to the track whereon I had watched Pegasus through his morning workout.

Yet we arrived in ample time, for, just as we approached, I spied Mr. Bennett aiding Mr. Deuteronomy with a leg up into the saddle.

"Look how well he sits up there!" Mr. Patley exclaimed admiringly.

And it was true. I have not done justice to the rider's seat upon his mount. Though a small man, as I have described him, one had no doubt that he was in command once he took his place upon Pegasus. It was there in his erect posture, even in the set of his features. A few words to the horse—I would have given anything to know what he said—and they were away. The horse went at a trot and only later increased his pace to a canter—and how beautifully the two of them did move together. The way ahead was clear.

Meanwhile did Bennett retire, ducking beneath the rail, then leaning over it, that he might study horse and man better. He, too, in his way, knew horses as well as Mr. Deuteronomy. He stood some distance away from us, so that I was certain that I would not be overheard if I were to voice to Mr. Patley my opinion of him.

"That man there," said I, nodding toward Bennett.

"The trainer?"

"I suppose that's what he is, yes. I like him well enough, but I don't accept his disavowal of all knowledge of how that pistol came into the hands of Katy Tiddle."

"Disavowal?"

"Denial. Nor do I accept Mr. Deuteronomy's ready acceptance of that denial."

"Seemed a little hasty to me, too," said Mr. Patley. "What do you plan to do about it?"

"Nothing, for the moment," said I, "but I just wanted you to know how I felt about them — and find out how you felt, too."

"Much as I like our Mr. Deuteronomy, that's how I feel."

We left it at that and turned our attention to the track. This was indeed the time to watch Pegasus at exercise. The light held good for far longer than I expected, and it was not long until the two of them, horse and rider, were the only such pair upon the course. It was then that the rider urged the horse to a canter. And only when all the rail-birds (as they are known) had departed, he allowed Pegasus to break into a full gallop, as the horse had been straining to do for many minutes. 'Twas not, by any means, the horse's fastest, or so I was informed by Constable Patley. But fast enough it was, and both jockey and mount gloried in it. Nevertheless, it was growing dark — too dark to circle round at such speed. Or so Deuteronomy judged it, for he reined in to a halt just as a most impressive coach and four pulled up at the rail.

Who could it have been but Lord Lamford?

He hopped down from the coach quick as his considerable bulk would allow and was followed by a sharp-featured man of uncertain age.

"Hi, you there, Deuteronomy! Give us another lap on Pegasus, will you?"

"Can't do it, Lord Lamford. It's a bit too dark for it now."

"Do as I say, fellow. I want the Duke of Queensberry to see what he can do."

"Well, all right. Will a trot round the course do for you?"

"Certainly *not*. Do it at full gallop."

"He could break a leg, my lord."

"Then I'll buy another like him. *Do as I say!*"

With a sigh and a shrug, Mr. Deuteronomy took the leg up offered him by Mr. Bennett.

"Your jockey's right, you know. It is a bit too dark for this track," said the Duke of Queensberry. (Whatever his reputation otherwise, he knew his horses.)

"I just want you to see what he can do," said Lord Lamford.

"Well, let's see, by all means."

Mr. Deuteronomy leaned forward and whispered something in the horse's ear. Mr. Bennett backed away, and, seconds later, the horse was off at a gallop.

Ah, but was it a full gallop? Of that I was unsure. I thought I had seen Pegasus run faster but a few minutes before, and I was sure I had done so last Sunday in Shepherd's Bush. A horse like Pegasus (I was later told by Mr. Patley) can often appear to run at his utmost and still hold back a bit to be called from him by the right jockey. There could be no doubt that Mr. Deuteronomy was the right jockey, but he chose not to call from him that something extra.

Mr. Patley looked my way and gave me a wink.

Once Pegasus had cleared the brook that ran cross the race course, it was evident that he would not break his leg—at least not that evening. He drew up just opposite us. Deuteronomy halted him so sudden that the horse reared, and just as soon as four hooves were firm upon the turf, the rider slid off and handed him over to Mr. Bennett.

"Ah, well, Lord Lamford," said the Duke of Queensberry, "you've got a good little horse there. He'll win a few races for you. I've heard of your jockey, though. What's his name?"

"Er . . . Deuteronomy something. I'm not sure."

"I'd like to meet him."

"Certainly, certainly."

And having said that, he called out for Mr. Deuteronomy. As the jockey marched past us, he muttered out the corner of his mouth that he would meet us for dinner in the tap-room.

"I've something to tell," said he.

Once he was past and presented to the Duke of Queensberry, I turned to Mr. Patley and suggested that we be on our way. He was more than willing—eager, in fact, to be quit of Lord Lamford. We wasted no time.

When we had started up the hill, Patley turned to me and said, "Now, Jeremy, I understand why you have so little use for that fellow Lamford—or whatever his family name might be."

But I hardly heard him at all, for I was just at that moment looking at something so astonishing that it did fair amaze me. 'Twas the slate which hung high above the stall of the turf accountant, giving the odds on each horse. I had looked at it the day before and complained that Pegasus was not even listed, and the constable had explained that it was because he had not yet been officially entered. Well, now he was entered and was listed at the very bottom.

"Mr. Patley," said I, "just look at the odds on Pegasus!"

"Well, it don't matter what they be," said he. "The place is closed for now, and . . . and—oh, dear God in heaven, I never did see such odds as that!"

Yet there it was, posted plain upon the slate: "Pegasus, 33 to 1." We stopped, stared, repeated it each to himself, over and over again.

"Well," said I, recalling Clarissa's instructions, "those are certainly favorable odds."

"They are indeed."

By the time we found our way to the tap-room, we could only hope that Mr. Deuteronomy would still be present, for we two together had caught bettor's fever. Mr. Patley spun great fantasies of just what he might do if he were to put all his money on Pegasus or perhaps kept a modest hedge bet or two upon the favorites, Charade and Red Devil. In any case, any bet at 33 to 1 would bring him wealth he had never hoped for in a lump sun. The difficulty was, said he, that deep down, he was a practical man, and even to dream of such wealth made him a bit uneasy. Still, said he, what might he do with a large sum? buy land? build a house? perhaps get married? It was all too much for a man of modest ambitions such as himself even to consider. (All of which was nonsense, of course. He was a betting man and a dreamer.)

All this went on as I washed myself, brushed the dust from my clothes, and generally prepared myself for dinner below. For myself, my case of bettor's fever, though not so virulent as Patley's, came upon me quietly and in the form of a question: To talk of hedging bets was one thing, but to do that was to bet *against* Mr. Deuteronomy, and, knowing him as well as I did, how could I then do such a thing? When I was a mere boy in the service of Sir John, I used to be certain that, as I grew a bit older, matters would become more certain and less complicated. Yet I have found that the truth of it is just the opposite.

In any case, as I have said, what with Mr. Patley's fantasies of great wealth and the problems it would bring, and my own moral difficulties considering friendship along with the thrill of wagering all or none, we two were late enough that I feared we might have missed Deuteronomy altogether. But no, he was there at a table within sight of the door, waving us over, bidding us to our places.

"We're late," said I as I sat down.

"Think nothin' of it," said he. "Until a short time past there was a great long line awaiting tables. I've sat just long enough for a glass of wine."

"We was stunned to see the odds posted on Pegasus," said Mr. Patley.

"What does that mean—thirty-three to one?" I asked.

"What that means," said Mr. Deuteronomy, "is that the gamblers don't think we got a chance in hell to win. And that suits me just fine."

"But aren't you insulted?"

"Not a bit. How could they think anything else? Pegasus has got no racing history, and I've taken care to exercise him too early or too late for them to get much of a look at him. I'm still confident."

"You are . . . truly?" I asked in a manner most naive.

"Oh yes. I spend a good part of the day at the rail looking over the rest of the field. I ain't impressed. But I'll tell you how confident I am," said he, lowering his voice. "I've got a hundred pounds with me that I intend to bet on Pegasus on race day if I can just drive the odds up a little higher."

"Maybe the Duke of Queensberry will have something to say about that," said Mr. Patley. "He knows his horses—or so they say.

He might risk a few thousand on Pegasus. God knows he could afford it."

"He owns Charade. He wouldn't bet against his own. But
enough of this, eh? I, for one, am quite starvin'. The beef here is
good, and the mutton ain't bad, neither."

We ordered, we ate, we drank, and, at last, I did remember why
it was we had gathered at Mr. Deuteronomy's invitation. The tap-
room had by then emptied out considerably. There were but three
or four other tables at which diners and drinkers sat, though the bar
was yet well-filled and noisy. But as our purpose there came to me,
I thought it important enough to interrupt the discussion of horses
and horse-racing between the jockey and the constable, which
never seemed to end, and to ask of him a question.

"Mr. Deuteronomy, sir, you said that you had something to tell.
What might that be?"

"Ah yes, so I did," said he. "It may not be specially significant,
but I hear tell that it's the details that people sometimes pass over
that turn out to be most important."

"That's the way it is more often than not," said Constable Patley, pretending to an authority he did not really possess.

"Just as I thought. Well, it was today it came to me whilst Bennett and me were visiting Pegasus in the stable. My sister told me
something—actually two things that I thought might help you find
him—and through him, her. She gave a name to Maggie's father,
and I believe it was Stephen. Now, as I said, she described him as
tall and fair. I b'lieve she said, he had straw-colored hair. Did I tell
you that?"

"I'm not sure," said I, quite honestly.

"Well, that's a description of a sort, ain't it? And there's this, too.
She made some remark about waking up beside him with hay in her
hair. Now that, to me, says that she was sleeping in a hayloft. Where
do they have haylofts?"

"Well, all over—in farms for one."

"Where else?"

"In stables," said I, "right here in town. So if we find a young
fellow, tall and fair, named Stephen, working in a stable here, then
we're also likely to find her?"

"That's as I see it," said Mr. Deuteronomy.

"Well, I be damned," said Constable Patley.

When we ended, we two thanked Mr. Deuteronomy most effusively and respectfully as our host settled the bill with the serving woman. We began drifting away. But our host summoned me back by name. Mr. Patley, eager to get himself to the jakes, hurried on.

"What will you, sir?" said I, returning.

"A couple of matters," said he, "that I'd like to discuss with you. The first is none of my affair. I'm simply Lord Lamford's errand boy in this. Last thing he said to me was he didn't want me talking to you anymore. You can see by the way we spent the last hour or so, just how much I respect that."

"But why?" said I. "Why should he object to me?"

"I be damned if I know—except somehow or other he's gotten wind that you work for the Blind Beak. He said something about you having no right to nose about where you're not wanted for Sir John. So I was going to ask you not to come to Pegasus's evening workout. You're welcome to come to the one in the morning. He never gets up till noon, anyways. If his lordship ain't around, we can talk. Suit you?"

I sighed. "Suits me well enough."

"Well and good. Now, the second matter is from me and me alone, and it concerns me and me alone, and I'd like it to be confidential between us two. Agreed?"

"Agreed."

"I'd like you to place that hundred-pound bet for me, the one I mentioned I was going to put down on Pegasus, put it in your name and not mine."

"Would I be doing anything illegal if I did?"

"No, I would never ask you to do anything like that. They get nervous when they see a jockey wearing racing colors placing a bet on any horse."

"I can understand that."

"And I want you to wait until just before the race, because there's just a chance that the odds may be even more favorable then. We'll see. I'll get the money to you on race day. But that's the day after tomorrow, ain't it?"

Then did we part with a clap and shake of the hands.

EIGHT

*In which we capture
our quarry and
the race is run*

Next morning, Mr. Patley and I were up and out very early. In point of fact, we arrived only minutes after Deuteronomy, Bennett, and Pegasus. There was but a suggestion of gray dawn in the east as we took our places at the rail end. Yet it grew lighter and lighter most swiftly, and by the time Pegasus was saddled and the jockey was atop the horse, it was not long till sunrise. All this was done in near-complete silence. There seems to be something in the early morning air that enforces quiet. Mr. Deuteronomy made no effort whatever to attempt to communicate with me.

He took two laps at a trot, then a canter, and back to a trot, then, for the first time that morning, at a full gallop, and only then was Pegasus allowed a walk. The important thing, as Mr. Patley explained it, was to keep the horse moving. Yet there was never any sign from Pegasus that he wished to rest. He seemed always to be ready to go round again at full gallop—and not only to be ready, but eager to do so.

Mr. Patley shook his head and whispered to me, "I never saw a horse so willing."

At the first sign of another horse and rider, Deuteronomy pulled him in and ended Pegasus's sport. No more gallops, though he might be permitted to prance a bit.

"What say you to a bit of breakfast?" asked Mr. Patley. "My turn to buy."

"Well," said I, "that suits me well, but let's return by way of the market."

"Why? You so hungry that you can't wait?"

"No, it's just that I was figuring that if we're hungry, then Stephen and Alice must be, too. I think it's a good time of the day to look for her there."

"How is it you always got an answer for me that makes good sense?"

"I guess I'm just a sensible young fellow," said I.

"There you go," said Patley. "You did it again."

The market area was even larger than I had at first realized. There was a whole street of fruit and vegetables that led off from the market square, which I had not noticed previously. The sun was well up now, and the crowd from the hill poured down from above. I dawdled my way through the market that the constable might have a chance to peer into the face of each and every woman we passed, whether she be dressed in a teal-blue or a plum-colored frock, or whatever. Alas, he looked in vain, for she was nowhere to be seen. I rewarded him for his effort with an apple—from the barrel, of course, but unbruised and unspotted. It cost me a pretty penny.

Up at the inn, eating a breakfast of johnny-cakes and coffee, we discussed how we might go about seeking Alice Plummer, and what we might do with her if and when she be captured.

"'Twould be an awful pity to leave Newmarket before the race is run," said he to me.

"Well," said I, "that's true enough. I've even agreed to do a favor for someone. I'd have to back out of my promise if we headed right back to London."

Mr. Patley put on a gloomy face and let go a great sigh. "It ain't good to back out of a promise. That someone you're doing the favor for wouldn't happen to be Mr. Deuteronomy, would it?"

"It might be just anyone, but I'm not free to say who it is."

"I'll take that to mean that I'm right."

"Just as you choose," said I with a smile.

And why the smile? Not merely to bedevil Mr. Patley, for there were simpler ways of doing that. I'd had an idea, one that would make it unnecessary to tie our prisoner to the bed in our room at the Good Queen Bess; to bind and gag her; or to do anything that might ultimately prove embarrassing to us and reflect badly upon Sir

John; one, in short, that would work to the satisfaction of all except Alice Plummer.

Though I now had an idea of just where Alice might be, and Mr. Deuteronomy had told us enough about Stephen so that we might recognize him in a small crowd, it was still no easy matter to find them. We must have visited near a dozen stables, asking for Stephen, telling our lies and half-truths about our need to find him, lies which sounded merely specious even to me. Then, let us say, at the thirteenth stable (it may have been at a greater or lesser number, but that is what we shall call it), we found our Stephen.

Mr. Deuteronomy's description had done him fair justice: he was tall (about six feet) and certainly fair (his hair was so blond that it appeared at first look to be white), and he could not deny his name was Stephen, for he answered to it when Mr. Patley bellowed out the name. He came from the rear of the stable, a pail of water in his hand. I allowed Mr. Patley to take the lead at this place, as he had at each one thus far.

"Your name is Stephen, then?" Mr. Patley asked.

"Supposing it is," he said, "what was it you wanted?"

"We're looking for a woman named Alice — Alice Plummer. Do you know her?"

He gave it some thought, then pouched his lower lip and shook his head in a firm denial. "No, I can't say I do." Then he surprised us by adding, "But I used to know a woman by that same name, I think it was. What was the last name again?"

"Plummer."

"Yes, I knew an Alice Plummer, all right, but that was seven or so years ago."

"Oh, well, have you seen her about in the last few days?"

"Why no. Is she here?"

"She's been seen. If you happen to run into her, or if she comes by for a visit, ask her to get in touch with us, will you? That's Mr. Proctor and Mr. Patley at the Good Queen Bess. We're up here from London, and we've a message for her about her daughter."

"Well, what is the message? I'll pass it on to her if I see her."

For some reason, Mr. Patley looked at me in an inquiring man-

ner, as if wondering what now he might say and asking me for a suggestion. I was ready for him.

"We've been told to give the message to none but her," said I.
"Sorry."

He hesitated, and then, certain there was no other way out, he
promised to pass the message on to Alice, should he happen to run
into her. We left him, staring after us and looking a bit confused.

We were no more than a few steps away and just out of earshot
when, in quiet tones, I called the constable's attention to a wall just
round the corner where we might wait for Alice.

"I give her five minutes at the most," said I.

"Closer to two, I vow."

If we'd had a wager riding on it, Mr. Patley would have won.
There was no mistaking her voice: first, a mildly acrimonious overture as she and Stephen wrangled over whether or not she should
go to the inn and discover the nature of the message about Maggie.

"Alice, dear Alice, don't you understand? 'Tis only a device to
force you out, to get you to show yourself."

"And don't *you* understand?" came the muffled reply (for they
were still inside the stable). I've little choice — none at all! If Maggie
needs me, then I must go to her."

Then did they quite explode into view — she running out the
door of the stable, and he pursuing her, catching her up, grasping
her arm to pull her back. The two nearly collided with another couple, older and ill-tempered, who abused them with harsh words and
curses. Then, as Alice struggled to free herself from Stephen's grip,
they gathered a crowd round them, which was not at all to our lik-
ing. Yet those in the crowd were mostly women, and they set up a
great din in her favor; whores and pickpockets were they by the
look of them; they were her jury, and they found in her favor.

"Leave her be!"

"Unhand her, you bully!"

"She did naught to deserve such treatment, I wager."

Her friend Stephen found it impossible to withstand such force.
In spite of myself, I pitied him, though had he prevailed, our immediate problem might have been greatly complicated. Yet his last
words could have been, and should have been, much gentler.

As he released her, he snarled, "Awright then, you drunken

cow, you're goin' into a trap. I'll do what I can for you, but I'll have to wait till my relief comes on." He turned away and headed back to the stable.

Alice, now free to go, stumbled about for a moment, looking round her wildly. Then, without a word to her rescuers, she set off down the hill at an awkward run.

I had then to restrain Constable Patley. He was all for catching her up and detaining her soon as ever we could—chasing her down, if need be.

"No," said I, "all we need do is keep her within sight. And even if we should lose her, there is little doubt that she will be there awaiting us."

We trampled along a good many yards behind her. No longer attempting to run, she now walked, staggering a bit, balancing with some effort. Years of gin-drinking had plainly taken a toll upon her.

In spite of all, I felt troubled—though I could not at first fathom the reason. It came to me then that I felt guilty. In spite of the fact that we had found Alice Plummer and would soon have her safely in custody, the means we had used to do this preyed upon my conscience somewhat. Had we not used Alice's own maternal feelings against her? Indeed we had. But had she not also acted against these same feelings when she sent her daughter off to be the paramour of one whose notions of carnal love were utterly perverted? Yet had she known that of him? What Katy Tiddle had said suggested she had not. But reporting Maggie as a stolen child to Mr. Patley indicated that she suspicioned that something was not right about the unnamed recipient of her child. And why, if she truly believed she were bettering Maggie's life, had she accepted money for her child?

Such questions always seemed to be clouded over with moral considerations of this sort, so why, indeed, should I feel guilty? And why, for a final why, must all be so damnably complicated?

In point of fact, we did lose her just as she came to the Good Queen Bess, yet that was because she had circled round it that she might enter respectably by the front door of the place.

She was leaning forward over the desk, speaking in a rather distraught manner to him in charge. Indeed, she was repeating our names over and over again. Then did he glimpse us with obvious relief as we entered.

"Ah, but here they are now. What a happy coincidence!"

She whirled round and, seeing us, ran to us.

"I heard you had a message from my daughter," said she, wheezing slightly from her trip downhill.

"No," said I, "that's not quite right."

She turned from me in disappointment and looked hopefully at Constable Patley. "It was you who said it, wasn't it? But—but I know you from before, don't I?"

"That's right, Alice. You and me talked together."

"About Maggie, wasn't it?"

"Maybe we could step inside the tap-room. We could sit in there and talk," I suggested.

She frowned at me in a somewhat befuddled way.

"Would you like something to drink?"

"A glass of gin would be nice."

"Well, then." I gestured toward the door to the tap-room, and she nodded and followed. I noticed the deskman continuing to look at us with considerable curiosity.

We must have made a strange-looking trio as we entered the room. And though I cared little what the many who gaped might think of us, I did wish to keep our conversation with this poor woman as private as might be possible. I directed the other two over to that same table in the corner, where Mr. Patley had seen her first. Then did I hasten to the serving woman and order two coffees and a glass of gin.

"Who's the gin for?" she asked suspiciously.

"For her," said I.

"This ain't that kind of place. They won't let you upstairs with her."

"I'll keep that in mind. Now, if you permit, we'll have two coffees and a glass of gin."

Without another word, she turned away from me and made for the bar.

I went to the table and found Alice and Mr. Patley engaged in the sort of talk that I can only call neighborly. Though I should have, I'd never really noticed what a personable manner he had. He seemed to get people to do what he wished them to do simply by being agreeable, kind, or what they had taken lately to calling "nice." What was it they were discussing as I sat down with them? As I recall, it was something to do with how and when he had happened to see her out the window.

"When was that, yesterday? or the day before? I ain't sure about that, but I am sure I looked right out the window, and there you were." He tapped it. "This very window," said he.

"Is that how it was?" said she. "Just imagine!" She managed a smile.

It was strange to see him so. I realized that there were things that I could learn from him.

"I think," said she, "that must have been day before yesterday."

"Is that so? You've got a pretty good memory. You know that?"

"Better'n some people think."

He chuckled at that. "How long have you been up here?"

"A long time, but I ain't sure just how long."

"Well, take a guess at it, why don't you?"

"It was right after I talked to you about . . . about Maggie. That's when I left London and come here—near a month ago."

"But you didn't tell anybody where you'd gone. If we'd found Maggie, how could we let you know?"

"Well, I knew you wouldn't find her, because she got adopted."

The serving woman came then with what I had ordered. She insisted on immediate payment, an interruption in the flow of the interrogation which could cost us dear. But at last she accepted payment and was away. Alice drank greedily from the glass of gin, and Mr. Patley judged her ready to begin again.

"Who told you about this practice of adopting, Alice?" he asked.

"Well, first it was Katy next door, and then it was Walter."

"Walter? Who's he?"

"He was the one took my Maggie away to the good couple who couldn't have a child all by themselves. Never did find out his last name. But I told Maggie all about how her new family would love her and have money enough to take good care of her, like I never could. And so when Walter took her away she didn't make no fuss nor nothin'. Just kissed me goodbye and waved."

"Did Walter give you the name of this couple he took Maggie to?"

"No, not hardly. He said it had to be a secret because if it weren't, sometime when I got to missin' her bad, I might go and try to steal her back. Oh, and I might, because even now I get to missing her so bad I can't hardly stand it." There she paused and looked up winningly at Mr. Patley. "Could I have another gin?"

He glanced over at me, and I, feeling that the interrogation had gone well thus far with a glass of gin to loosen her tongue, decided that a second glass might make it go even better. I signaled for another gin to the serving woman who pulled a sour face but passed it on to the man behind the bar. It was most quickly forthcoming. Alice took it from the serving woman with polite thanks and treated herself to a hasty sip. Then, with a smile, she returned her attention to the constable.

"There is only a couple more questions we got to ask you," said he to her. "You're doin' fine so far, Alice."

She smiled foolishly at that. "All the right answers?"

"No mistakes yet. I'd like you to tell me, though, just how it was you came into all that money?"

"All what money?"

"Well you came up here from London on the mail coach, didn't you?"

"Certain'y. It was the onliest way I could get here, 'cept walk." She remained silent for a moment, then said playfully, "Oh, *that* money!"

"Yes, Alice, *that* money."

"Well," said she, "I never asked for a penny—truly I never. But the day that Walter came for Maggie he brought me a proper bag of coins and said that the couple wanted me to have this money, 'cause they were so grateful. I never did get a proper count on it in pounds and pence, but it's a lot, and it's lasted me a long time. Course I knew where I'd go just as soon as ever I got that much money in hand."

"And where was that?"

"Why, right here—right in Newmarket—to see my sweetheart, Stephen. He's been my sweetheart for years and years."

"Did you two write letters to each other? Did he invite you to come?"

"Stephen? Oh no, he didn't know where I was, and I couldn't write to tell him, because I never had any learning. But I just came to him, and we picked up just where we left off. It was beautiful. Course he's angry—now, maybe a mite jealous, because I came down here to see you two." She said nothing more for a moment, but thrust out her lower lip in a pout. "When are you two going to give me that message from Maggie I been waiting to hear?"

"In a while, Alice. It won't be long," said the constable. "Just one more question."

"All right, what is it?"

"Whose idea was it to report Maggie as missing? Was it yours?"

"Oh no, nothing of the kind. Katy Tiddle thought it up. It was all her idea. She said it would keep people from asking a lot of questions when they noticed that Maggie was gone. I could just say she was stolen and I'd reported it to the constable."

She waited, frowning. "Well," said she, "I answered your last question. Ain't I goin' to hear now what Maggie has to say?"

Mr. Patley looked at me with great uncertainty. Clearly, he wished me now to assume the burden.

"Alice," said I, "we didn't say we had a message *from* Maggie. We said we had a message *about* her."

"Well, all right, what's the message *about* her then?"

The difficulty I was having putting the information that I had into words must have shown in my face. No doubt I looked terribly distressed, for that was indeed how I felt.

She read my face. For, of a sudden, the expression upon her own altered to one of alarm, then went beyond that to horror, utter horror.

"Oh, dear God in heaven," said she, "Maggie's dead, ain't she?"

"I fear it's true, Alice. You were deceived by Katy Tiddle and Walter."

"What do you mean? Say it!"

"Uh . . . well, it's . . ." I temporized, glancing at Mr. Patley and finding no help there, unable to find the right words, unwilling to say it plain. I sighed, then plunged on: "Alice, there was no nice couple waiting for Walter to deliver your daughter to them. Walter may have kept Maggie for his own use, or sold her on to someone quite rich. We think—I think—that the latter is the way of it."

"Can you help us find Walter? He made a whore of her, Alice," said the constable. "If he delivered her to someone else, then he can tell us who, so we can get to that someone else."

"How do I know you're telling the truth? How do I know she's really dead? Maybe this is just another trick to get me back to London."

"A waterman pulled her body out of the Thames. I took it to the doctor who pronounced her dead, and then your brother had her buried in the churchyard at St. Paul's, Covent Garden."

"My brother? Deuteronomy?"

"That's right. He's right here in Newmarket. He'll tell you everything we said is true."

"No, keep him out of it. He's always tellin' me what to do."

Having heard all that we had to say, she sat quietly, as if devising a plan of action. Neither Patley nor I spoke. We simply waited. I know not quite what we expected from her, yet certainly not what she gave us; in fact, she quite astounded us.

She began to scream.

I know not quite how to describe her cries, for there was naught of surprise nor fear in them. Call them, rather, screams of outrage: protests against the cruelty of fortune, the unfairness of fate.

In any case, they had an immediate and electrifying effect upon all there in the tap-room. Those at the tables and bar—thank God the place was not then greatly crowded—turned immediately, open-mouthed in shocked surprise. The innkeeper and the serving woman came running. And as for Patley and me, we had leapt to our feet and were making helpless gestures with our hands. Yet what more could we do?

"You must get her out of here!" shouted the serving woman at a volume that seemed to match that of the screams.

"Yes, but how?"

"I don't care how you do it. Just *do* it!"

There was a rhythm to Alice's cries, and they were of a predictable duration, so that as she halted to take a breath, Mr. Patley, a man of fair proportions, was able to clap a hand over her mouth and pull her to her feet.

He quick-marched her out. There was little for me to do but run ahead and get from the innkeeper the location of the magistrate's court. This was a situation that called for desperate measures.

"I knew you was bringin' trouble the moment you came through that door," the serving woman shouted after us.

Luckily, I had with me the letter dictated by Sir John to the magistrate of Newmarket, Malachi Simmons. I had carried it round with me in the inside pocket of my coat since we had left London. I recalled well that there was a problem in using it, and that had to do with when it was presented to the local magistrate. It was best to use it only in an emergency, Sir John had said, but if it were offered too late, it had best be given with a good excuse as to why it had not been presented earlier. I believed I had just such an excuse.

Alice Plummer had quietened down a bit by the time we arrived at the magistrate's court. Not that she had reconciled herself to the shocking news we had given her. No, indeed. I believe, rather, that the strain put upon her throat by her repeated screams had overtaxed it to the point that she could scarce speak above a whisper. Yet that was not immediately apparent to us, for at some point shortly after we three had left the Good Queen Bess she silenced herself altogether: she spoke not a word, nor did she scream again. And I thanked God for it.

The magistrate's court stood upon that very street off Market Square which I had latterly overlooked; the name of that street, if indeed it ever had one, I have completely forgotten. We found the house quite easily, a couple of hundred years old it was, but large and imposing. I banged loudly upon the door, and as we waited for a response, I muttered to Mr. Patley that he was to let me do the talking. He nodded his understanding and agreement. We heard steps behind the door, and a brief moment later, it flew open to reveal one who was at least as tall and wide as Bow Street's Constable Bailey.

"What's your business here?" he demanded.

"We wish to have some words with the magistrate, Mr. Malachi Simmons."

"And what about?"

I stifled the urge I felt to tell him that it was no business of his, whatever it was. Rather, did I smile sweetly and inform him that I had a letter to deliver.

"Must be a pretty long letter if it takes three of you to deliver it," said he, then added, "From London, are ye?"

I said that we were.

"Well then, stay where you are, all three of you. What's your name?" He pointed at me.

"Jeremy Proctor," said I, "but I doubt he'll know me. But say, we're come from the Bow Street Court."

"Stay here."

Then did the fellow close the door, as one might upon a beggar, in our very faces. Patley and I exchanged looks, shrugs, and sighs of resignation. After a long wait, we heard footsteps once more and the door came open again.

"He'll see you," said the fellow. "Right this way."

He led us down a long hall and another, so that we were at the farthest corner of the house from the door through which we had entered. Our guide moved at a swift pace, indeed so swift that Alice had some difficulty in keeping up. He was a strange sort of butler, was he not? Probably butler cum constable cum turnkey, and who could say what more? He knocked upon the door at the end of the second hall, waited a moment till he heard something beyond it, then opened the door, and nodded us inside.

These were the magistrate's chambers. Malachi Simmons sat hunched at a table—or could it properly be called a desk? He was, in any case, a man of sour countenance. He looked at all three of us in a suspicious manner, as if trying to determine which among us were the criminals and which were not. 'Twas upon me that he settled.

"With what are you charged?" he asked in an unpleasant, nasal voice.

"Well . . . well, I'm not charged," said I most emphatic.

He thrust his head forward and squinted at me. "Not charged? Then why are you here?"

Why indeed? "I've a letter for you, sir."

"What? a letter? Oh yes, now I remember. Well, hand it over, lad." As I was fishing it out of my inside pocket, he added: "Who's it from?"

"Sir John Fielding of the Bow Street Court in London. I am his assistant, Jeremy Proctor. This gentleman at my left, sir, is—"

"You're exceeding your brief, young sir. I asked for the letter, not an introduction to each of your company. Now, give me the damned letter, would you?"

I hastened forward and dropped the letter before him upon his desk. He broke the seal, opened the letter, then threw it down in disgust.

"How am I to read that?" said he. "I've not got my spectacles. You—yes, you young man. You read it to me, will you?"

I did as he asked, laying special emphasis on our respect for his jurisdiction in all matters and the collegial appeal Sir John made to Malachi Simmons for his assistance in these matters. As I read, I glanced up at the magistrate more than once and found him nodding with what I assumed to be satisfaction. Yet when I finished, I found him to be anything but satisfied.

"That's a very good sort of letter, very well phrased—and you read it well—but I find it just a bit heavy in the generalities and light in the particularities."

"How do you mean, sir?" I asked.

"Just what I say. About all I get from what you've just read me is that you've come here to Newmarket to search for a woman named Alice Plummer, and to apprehend her, and return her to London. Mistress Plummer, I take it, is the young woman between the two of you. Is that correct?"

"Yes sir, she is."

"Tell me why then she has been so energetically pursued by you two—all the way from London, after all. What is the charge that she faces back in Bow Street?"

"Child-selling, sir."

"Ah, well, that *is* serious. And what do you wish me to do with her?"

"If you could hold her overnight, we would be greatly in your debt."

"Hold her? You mean in our strongroom? I should need a bit of proof for that, something in the way of evidence. Have you the child here? Where is the child?"

"Dead and buried," said I.

"Sounds worse and worse," said he. "But surely your Sir John had a lesser charge that he might employ to hold her. Are you familiar with the term 'holding charge'?"

"I am, and we have such: Giving false report of a crime."

"But that can't be proven, either, I suppose."

"On the contrary, sir. Constable Patley, to my left, was given the false report by Mistress Plummer."

The magistrate, Mr. Simmons, turned his attention to Mr. Patley.

"What about it, sir? Are you willing to swear to that?"

"I am, sir," said Mr. Patley. "And she's confessed all to us."

"Well, it may not be necessary. But what's she got to say for herself?"

"Not much," said Patley. "I fear she's passed out on her feet, sir. If I wasn't holding her up, she'd fall over on the floor."

"You're sure of that?"

"Sure as I can be, sir."

"Unhand her then. Let's see if she manages to keep her feet."

Mr. Patley shrugged, removed his hands from her waist and her arm. Alice promptly crumpled to the floor, bumping her head rather nastily. She, however, seemed quite oblivious of the hurt.

"Well!" said the magistrate, "just as you said. I'd say she was drunk, wouldn't you?" This he directed to me. I nodded, not knowing quite what he hoped to prove by this.

"Indeed I would say she is quite drunk," said I.

"Well then we three are enough together to comprise a bit of the public, and so I fine her a shilling for public drunkenness."

"A shilling?" said I. "That's a pretty light fine. Sir John fixes it at a pound."

"Those are city prices. We get a lot of drunks out here and not a one of them could afford a pound." Then did he call out loud and clear: "Mr. Yates, come here. I've a need for you."

And so, without delay, came the big, hulking fellow who had led the way to the magistrate's chambers. I recall that I decided that he must have waited just outside the door, expecting the call.

"Yes sir," said he who had answered the call. "What will you?"

"Take her away and lock her up in one of the cells, will you?"

Needing no more detailed instruction than that, Yates bent down and swept her off the floor. He threw her over his shoulder as carelessly as one might toss a rag doll.

"Let her sleep it off."

Yates gave a kind of mock salute and marched out with his prisoner. I must say that I was impressed.

"All right," said Malachi Simmons to us. "I'm little pleased to have those from other jurisdictions coming round and waving their warrants and what-not at me. In short, I don't like it. Me and your Sir John have clashed more than once on just such matters. Come back in the morning no later than seven, pay her fine, and you can have your prisoner. That satisfy you?"

We fair danced out the door, Mr. Patley and I. Though we had been careful not to parade our feelings of triumph before the magistrate (for he was a tetchy old bird), once out of earshot, we surrendered completely to them. We giggled and capered our way downhill. Mr. Patley, who had a talent for mimicry, did a fair imitation of the magistrate's nasal whining and managed to attract a bit of attention from the crowd.

"Hi, Jeremy," said he, "what say we wet our whistles at the next tavern we come to? I could sure do with an ale. Now that we got our prisoner taken care of till morning, I'm for a bit of a celebration. What say you to that?"

I was, indeed, eager to join him, but somehow I was certain that this was not the time for me to relax my efforts. As it was, I felt a bit guilty about arranging things so that I might be present for the big race the next day. There were too many loose ends, matters still to be arranged before our departure, and now was the time to attend to them.

"No, Mr. Patley," said I to him, "I've a few things to do yet. But go and have an ale on me, and I'll join you soon."

"But not too soon."

And so, as good as his word, he left me at the next inn we came to, the Green Man (one of a hundred such scattered round rural England). I promised to come by for him there in an hour, or not too much more. Then did I proceed to the track where I began my search for Mr. Deuteronomy.

I found him without too much difficulty, exactly where I supposed he might be: poised over the rail, the spy-glass to his eye, evaluating the horses upon the track. There were not as many of them as before, and all of them seemed to be genuine entries. Mr. Bennett was beside him, making notes as Mr. Deuteronomy called off orders to him.

"The black is good. Find out his name, who's riding him, and where he stands in the betting. He ain't Charade, but he looks good. Oh, and the big red, too. Get the same information on him, too." Bennett then departed.

Then, at last, did Deuteronomy take down the spy-glass. 'Twas then that he saw me there, awaiting his attention.

"Jeremy," said he, "just the man I've been searching for."

"And I've news for you," said I.

I told him hurriedly of the successful search for his sister, of her near blameless confession, and of her present whereabouts.

"You can visit her there right up to seven in the morning."

"I think I'll decline that pleasure," said he. "I get sick enough as it is before a race. No need to go stirring up more trouble. But now, let me tell you where we are on the matter of the wager."

He then explained that the odds on Pegasus had gone down rather than up, that it now stood at 30 to 1. "Still favorable," he said, "still marvelous, but this is as long as I care to wait. So here, Jeremy. I'd like you to put this on Pegasus to win."

And so saying, he brought forth from his coat an envelope fat with bank notes and handed it to me.

"It's a hundred, no more nor less. And for my own reasons, I'd still like you to place the bet for me."

I took the envelope from him and agreed to do as he directed.

"There may be a bit of difficulty getting your winnings to you right after the race, though," said I. "I may even have to take it with me to London. That is, assuming there *are* winnings. We'll have to run for the mail coach as soon as ever we can. Your sister will be with us, you know."

"I know. Take it with you to London. And don't worry about whether or not there'll be winnings. That's my responsibility, as you'll see."

I left him then with a firm clasp of the hands and a whispered "Good luck to you then."

Though tempted, I avoided those strolling turf accountants with their fast-changing slates and their line of chatter, for Mr.

Patley had warned me that all too often they stroll out of sight when it came time to pay off winners. Rather, did I go to the turf-accountant's stall where first I saw the odds against Pegasus posted. There I placed two separate wagers, both of them in my name: one for a hundred pounds, and another, much smaller one, for five pounds, eleven shillings, both at the posted odds of thirty to one. The accountant looked at me queerly when I made it clear that both bets were to be put upon Pegasus; then did he call me an optimist. Nevertheless, he wrote me out two chits with all the relevant matter upon them. I tucked them away, glad to be relieved of the awful responsibility put upon me by carrying about a great sum of money belonging to another. I remember that I mused on my way to the post house that I had given no thought whatever to hedging my own bet, nor would Clarissa have had me do so. Thanks to her, and thanks, as well, to Mr. Deuteronomy, I had become less cautious and more willing to take chances—in short, a proper betting man.

As it happened, I was stopping by at the post to present my letter of preference for places on the first post coach following the conclusion of tomorrow's race. In effect, I had, with the letter of preference, reserved three places (one each for me, for Patley, and for Alice Plummer) on the five-o'clock post coach to London. This was, as I discovered, one of the prerogatives of traveling on official business for the Bow Street Court. Three coach passengers could even be thrown off to make room for us. This, however, was unlikely to be necessary, according to him I talked to at the Newmarket post house.

Then, at last, a return to the Green Man, where I had agreed to meet Mr. Patley. I'd no idea of the time, though surely I had made the one-hour time limit I had set for myself. I would have been most uneasy if he had wandered away. But no, there he was, sitting at the bar, flirting with the barmaid, holding forth as one might at an ale house in the Strand. He spied me entering the place and threw open his arms in welcome.

"Jeremy, old friend," said he, "come sit beside me and have an ale with me. I've had three."

Three, was it? Perhaps I'd been gone considerably longer than an hour.

"I'll gladly have an ale, Mr. Patley. But tell me, are you not getting a bit hungry?"

"Well, now that you mention it . . ."

As if by magic, an ale in a pewter tankard appeared before me. I took a deep draught and understood at once how Patley might have consumed three such in the space of an hour. It was a bit bitter, but properly so, and not the sort to put a pucker upon your face. In short, I liked it.

He turned to the barmaid and asked about dinner.

"Well," said she, "it's not yet six, and there ain't many eat quite so early, but I always thought it best to eat when you're hungry." She must have thought that a great joke, for she laughed long and loud at it. Mr. Patley joined in.

In any case, we ordered alike, a beef chop apiece, and we did eat at the bar, because, as Patley explained to the barmaid, "We wouldn't want to get too far away from that good ale." This, too, was thought to be quite funny.

I would not wish to present myself as above all this foolery, reader, for it was not long till I was acting near as silly as Mr. Patley. Ah well, I assured myself, this was to be something of a celebration, was it not?

Oh, indeed it was to be just that, yet both Patley and I felt that there were other things at stake. Oddly enough, it was my companion who brought that home to me when, without overture or opening, he peered at me and said, "Well, did you find him?"

"Find who?" said I, though I'm certain, looking back, that I must have known just who he meant.

"Deuteronomy, of course. When you're not with me, you're with him." (This was said without malice.)

"Well, yes I did see him. I felt that he should have a chance to see his sister. I told him where she was."

"Did he go to see her?"

"I doubt it. He said he would not. He got sick enough before a race as it was without adding more to it—that's what he said, anyway."

We had eaten well. Each of us had had another ale to top off what we had already had. The place had become more crowded, and consequently noisier. There was no reason to stay. We settled up with the barmaid and made our way through the crowd to the outside.

"Well," said Mr. Patley, "we might as well walk up the hill to the Good Queen Bess."

"Might just as well."

We hiked the distance to the inn in silence. As for myself, each step I took told me that I should make an early night of it. But, after all, why not? I knew I must rouse early to collect Alice Plummer from the magistrate's court. Early to bed and early to rise, et cetera.

Patley, on the other hand, seemed to take on new vitality with each step. I quite marveled at the fellow. Had he not eaten the same heavy meal that I had? Had he not drunk four ales to my two? Or was it five to my two?

And so, of course, I was not surprised when, as we entered the inn, he proposed that we go into the tap-room "for a little something to make us sleepy." He took it in good stead when I told him that I needed nothing to make me sleepy, for I was quite tired already. I would go up to our room, I told him, and read myself to sleep. It shouldn't take very long.

I shall get through the second episode at the magistrate's court as quickly as possible. It was a bitter disappointment, and every barrister will tell you that there is no sense in dwelling upon disappointments.

I banged upon the door of the magistrate's court a bit before seven in the morning. It was answered by another, just as large and just as ugly as he who had answered the door the afternoon before. He looked at me sourly and asked my business. When I told him that I had come to collect Alice Plummer, he said that I'd come too late, that her fine had been paid and that she had been taken forth by a townsman—all this on the day before. Was he sure of this? Certainly he was, he assured me, for he was the constable delegated by the magistrate to fetch her out of her cell.

I insisted on hearing this from Malachi Simmons himself, and the constable shrugged. It was a matter of indifference to him. He said that the magistrate would be down soon, and he pointed to a bench next to the door and said I might sit there, if I chose.

Only minutes later I heard footsteps upon stairs somewhere deep in the house, and a few minutes after that the constable came and told me that the magistrate would see me. Then: down the two long halls once again and into the chambers of Malachi Simmons. This time, of course, I was much disturbed and not in the least given to accommodating his feelings. In short, I fear I was rather rude.

What I heard from the magistrate was this: About an hour after Mr. Patley and I left him, he was visited by one Stephen Applegate, who described himself as "a friend of Alice Plummer." He wished to know if she were being held here. The magistrate acknowledged this and acquainted the young man with the charges which awaited her in London. These Stephen brushed aside as lies and half-truths. He dealt, for example, with the matter of child-selling by telling him (as he had no doubt been told by her) that in truth she had believed that she had been giving the child out for adoption. She had not solicited any amount of money in payment for her daughter but had been given it as a reward.

"And I have heard, young man," said the magistrate, "that your methods of questioning her were highly suspect." I demanded to know what was wrong with our questioning of Alice Plummer, and he explained what I myself should have realized: One does not fill a witness with gin whilst interrogating him or her. At best, you would be drawing from her unconsidered responses, and, at worst, she would tend to agree with all that was said to her.

Where could he have heard that? Why, of course! Stephen would have remembered that Mr. Patley and I had announced ourselves as guests at the Good Queen Bess. He must have headed there as soon as he was free to leave the stable—and then into the tap-room, where he would have heard the serving woman on the matter of the two glasses of gin, and the innkeeper, of course, must have tipped young Applegate on just where he might find his Alice.

I attempted to defend my methods, telling the magistrate that she was drunk before ever we asked a question of her.

"And so you attempted to make her drunker, did you? No, young sir, I fear that won't do at all. Not only did Stephen Applegate present a good case against you and your methods, he is also from a very old family here in Newmarket. They've owned and run that stable for as long as anyone can remember. Of course I would take his word over yours. He paid her fine, and he took her out of here. That was about an hour or two after you left last evening."

"But—"

"No buts! Out of here now, or I'll throw you into the same cell she had."

I had no choice but to leave. But, I believe, I ran all the way up to the Good Queen Bess without stopping. Indeed, I'm sure I did, for I remember that when I attempted to explain the situation to Mr. Patley in our room, I was so out of breath that I could do naught but begin again after I had properly caught my breath. I ended with a shout: "We must find her again!"

"Well, the first place to look," said the ever-practical Mr. Patley, "would be where we found her in the first place."

And so, as soon as Patley had dressed and made himself otherwise presentable, we started up the hill to Applegate's stable. Stephen seemed to be waiting for us, so sure that we would be coming round to see him that he had not even sought the darkness at the rear of the place. He was leaning upon the door as we approached, his pitchfork within easy reach (just the thing for driving away the unwanted). He had a proper smirk upon his face.

"Good morning to you," said he. "I'm sure I know who you're looking for and why you're here."

"Well," said I, "where is she?"

"She ought to be in London by now."

"You sure about that?"

"Just about as sure as I can be at this distance."

"You have any objection to us taking a look around?"

"No, go ahead, but you'd do better to check the list of passengers on the post coach that left last evening around nine. But go ahead, suit yourself. I'll wait right here."

We looked, of course. If we had not, we would not have seemed to be searching seriously for her. We even climbed the ladder in the rear and tramped through the hay in the loft—without success, of course. Nor was I surprised at that, for Stephen's indifference was not feigned. It was plain that he was confident we would find no trace of her. Mr. Patley was of the same mind.

"It don't look like she's here, does it?" said he.

I shook my head. "No, it doesn't. We should go and check the passenger list as he dared us to do, but I'm sure she'll be on it."

We climbed down from the loft and headed out of the place.

Stephen silently watched us go. But then, thinking better of it, he called after us as we started down the hill.

"I tried to get her to stay. Told her I could hide her so you'd never find her. But she said no. There was something she had to do in London."

I turned and nodded, yet I certainly would not thank him.

"No reason not to go to the big race now," said Mr. Patley. "Come to think of it, I'd better go and place my bet whilst I still can."

I didn't ask him how much he was betting, nor on which horse, yet I was greatly curious about one thing: "Mr. Patley, are you hedging your bet?"

He looked at me a bit sheepishly. "No, I'm not. The little fellow's got me convinced that the two of them can really do it. I've got ten pounds, the last of my mustering out pay, on Pegasus to win. But what about you?"

'Twas then my time to look embarrassed. "No, he's convinced me, too — and those odds!"

"I know," said he. "They're just irresistible."

Again, just as at Shepherd's Bush, there were so many horses entered that it was necessary to run the race in heats. Pegasus was in the first heat of the day, which meant that he was running against a field of horses which, the odds said, had no chance in the final race of the day. Still, Mr. Deuteronomy held him so in check that Pegasus did not win outright but rather placed second. (Three from each heat would compete for the King's Plate in the last race.) Yet Pegasus had qualified, and that was all that had been asked of him, and the horse had more than two hours in which to recover himself.

The course was oval and about a mile in length. It was proper to walk a horse once round it after he had run. Deuteronomy walked Pegasus thus much at least, then trotted him round a time or two. It seemed that in the next couple of hours the horse was never completely still except when Mr. Bennett was massaging his legs.

"You see what they're doing, don't you?" said Mr. Patley, as always my guide in this new world.

"I think so," said I. "Deuteronomy seems to be running exactly the same sort of race that they ran last week at Shepherd's Bush."

"That's right. And he's keeping Pegasus warm and loose without tiring him."

No one else had seemed to notice the technique they employed, yet once it was explained to me, it appeared to be both sensible and necessary.

As Mr. Patley amplified his earlier comments, he pointed out that the favored horses raced in the last heat before the final run, so they were warmed up and ready to go when the last race of the day came. If Pegasus were to have a chance at the King's Plate, he would have to be as properly warmed up as any that had run in the previous heat; and it appeared that he was. Yet he would also have to achieve this racing peak without having tired himself out. Mr. Deuteronomy, in his green and white racing colors, was proving — to us, at least — that there was more to jockeying than sitting on a horse.

Charade, the Duke of Queensberry's entry, was the favorite in every way — not only the favorite of the bettors, but also with the rail-birds who crowded around us at the first pole. The reason for this was quite evident: there was probably never before or after a more beautiful horse than Charade. Big, strong-looking, and generally handsome — if races were beauty competitions, he would have won every time.

Pegasus, on the other hand, was simply smarter than the rest. He and his rider, Mr. Deuteronomy, demonstrated that very early on. Of the nine horses at the line, three reared, and two otherwise shied at the starting gun, and so Pegasus, taking off as smoothly as a ship launched into the sea, had an immediate advantage over half the field. He kept it up to the brook, which flowed across the course at that point. All four of the leaders cleared it without difficulty, yet Deuteronomy was finding it hard to find a path through the leaders. He shouted something and somehow seemed to relax his grip on the reins, giving Pegasus his head. The horse broke to the outside, and, in this way, worked past the others, one by one, up to second place — behind Charade. Both those fine animals were galloping apparently for all they were worth. The crowd, many more than five thousand in number, cheered loudly at the sight of them beating their way down the stretch. And again, Deuteronomy shouted at Pegasus, and then, little by little, Pegasus began to move up and away from Charade.

Pegasus won by a full length. There could be no disputing it. As that single, stunning fact was communicated to the vast assemblage of people all round us, they fell silent. To my ears, it seemed that Mr. Patley and I were the only two who rejoiced. And why should we not? We had suddenly become rich men.

NINE

*In which we go back
to London and find
Elizabeth returned*

※

We narrowly made the post coach to London. What with collecting
our winnings and storing banknotes in our luggage that we might
travel with them without calling undue attention to ourselves, it was
just on five in the afternoon when we came running up to the coach.

"Here," said the footman, reaching for my portmanteau, "you'll
want your bags up top, I'm sure."

Mr. Patley and I exchanged glances and thus found ourselves in
agreement. I jerked it back from his grasp and politely declined.

"I'll hold it upon my lap, thank you."

He gave me a queer look, then turned to Mr. Patley. "And you?"

"I'll keep mine, too."

"All right, then. Into the coach with you both. We've got a
schedule to keep."

Jumping inside, we arranged ourselves as best we could among
the four other passengers (all of them quite respectable-looking)
and made ready to go. After the footman had climbed up to his
place beside the driver, there was no delay. A rowdy call, a crack of
the whip, and we were off through the streets of Newmarket. It
took only a few minutes for us to be out in the country on the road
to Cambridge.

Unlike the trip up to Newmarket, the return journey to London
was spent by us in a state of intense wakefulness. I, for one, learned
in the course of that one night alone what a remarkable burden a
large amount of money can be. Yet no matter how heavy, we pre-
ferred to keep our baggage right there in our hands. I'll not pretend

that supporting the weight of our good fortune, as we were, ours was—or could have been—a comfortable trip. Nevertheless, that is how we made the trip, and no complaint was heard from either of us.

We arrived at the Post Coach House in London well before sunrise, our legs so stiff and our backsides so battered that we could scarce walk. Yet as our muscles loosened a bit, we were able to pick up the pace, and it was not long till we found ourselves crossing Covent Garden. It occurred to me then that we might be on the very path taken by Elizabeth Hooker in the riskful company of her two young gallants. I wondered then—alas, for the first time!—what Sir John had turned up in his investigation of that odd situation. What had the girl at heart? Would we ever know? I realized then how glad I was to be back in London, working once again with Sir John. A life in the law was a life I had never dreamed of till I came here, to the city—and now I could imagine none other for me. Such thoughts never failed to put a smile upon my face. Yet then I thought of the report that I brought back with me—how we had found Alice Plummer and then lost her. In all truth, I was properly ashamed of how little we could claim for all the time we had spent there.

Even in the dim dawn light, Bow Street appeared the same, and as we entered through the door of Number 4, I noted that the place even smelled the same—rock oil and strong soap. Catching first glimpse of us, Mr. Baker called out a greeting.

"Which horse won at Newmarket?" he asked.

"Ah well," answered Mr. Patley, "we've a story 'twill shock you and delight you."

But I begged off: "Mr. Patley knows the story well as I. He'll tell it better. I'm for a bit of a nap."

With that, I staggered up the stairs, hauling my portmanteau behind. I did not knock upon the door, which would have admitted me to our kitchen; rather, did I throw it open and, unintended, send Clarissa jumping from her chair in surprise.

"Jeremy," said she, "it's you!"

"Who else but me? And I sat up the entire night long on the bumpiest mail coach that I might see you a few hours earlier."

"Really?" She ran to me, threw her arms about my neck and quite covered my face with kisses. I confess that I rather liked it.

"Sit down, sit down," said she. "You must be quite perishing with hunger. The breakfast tea is still hot, and I've just cut into a pan of Molly's soda bread. Do sit down, Jeremy, and I'll serve you."

I did as she urged and watched her whiz round the kitchen, throwing together my breakfast. Only moments before, she had been writing in her journal. There, indeed, it was, open, with quill and ink pot beside it. I wondered what she had written in my absence, though I suspected that she would never again be quite so free in allowing me opportunity to view its contents as she had been before, so that I might never know.

Though hastily improvised, my breakfast was in no wise inferior: the tea was warm and tasty; Molly's soda bread was beyond compare; and the butter I daubed upon it was as fine as could be. She took her place at the table just opposite me, and, with a hand propped beneath her chin, she stared at me for an interminable length of time. I felt embarrassed to be studied so. At last she spoke.

"You're back," said she. "I've missed you even more than I expected."

"Things seem much as they were when I left, though. Not much changed?"

"Oh no, on the contrary. Much has changed."

My first thought was to the case at hand: "Has Sir John got to the bottom of this perplexing matter with your friend Elizabeth?"

"No, no, nothing of that. So far as I know, it remains unchanged. The news is much closer to us." She looked up and about the room, as if seeking a place to start. Then, beginning again, she said, "Molly and Mr. Donnelly have made plain their intentions. They've announced to all their wish to marry. This was, I hasten to add, after he and Sir John had discussed the matter thoroughly — not exactly asking Sir John's permission, but . . . well, you understand."

"Not entirely, no, but I certainly catch the drift of it."

"Well, she's a widow, this would be her second marriage, and all that Sir John could or would say is that he had no objection to it at all. He congratulated Mr. Donnelly and offered her a kiss upon the cheek and his best wishes for a long and fruitful union. It's rather a delicate matter, after all."

"Oh? How so?"

"The religion matter, of course. They must be married by a Roman Catholic priest — but of course officially there are none here in England. So they must either marry in secret or go off to Ireland to have it done. They favor having it done in Dublin, so that his family may meet her and all. But to me, marrying in a secret ceremony seems so much better — more romantic, literary, poetical."

"Oh," said I, "you would view it so, I'm sure, but just imagine all of the complications, having to prove time after time that you are truly married."

Clarissa's mouth flew open, as if she were about to argue the point with me. But then her expression softened, and she smiled a little smile.

"Oh, Jeremy," said she, "must you always be so practical?" Then did she sigh. "You're right, of course."

"How did Lady Fielding take all this?"

She lowered her voice to a whisper: "Not so well at first. She seemed to feel that Molly is somehow beneath him. She talked around all this just yesterday whilst we were at the Magdalene Home. Oh, but what does it matter? Mr. Goldsmith thinks it to be a fine idea. So does Benjamin Bailey. There seems to be some family relation there that I don't quite understand . . ."

"Oh well, no matter," said I.

There discussion ended rather abruptly. Yet, the frown upon her face told me that there was a good deal more that she wished to say. It seemed to me that she was merely trying to decide if now were the right time for it to be said. Still, when had she ever shown herself to be faint of heart?

"You realize, don't you, Jeremy, what this means?"

"It means a good many things, doesn't it? We shall be getting a new cook, I suppose, and —"

"Oh, Jeremy, you're often just impossible! Do you not realize that an obstacle to our own wedding plans has just been removed?"

I was teasing her, of course. "*An* obstacle," said I, "but there are others."

I rose from my chair, hauled up my bag, and placed it upon the table.

"Better move that inkpot," said I to her as I unbuckled the straps to the portmanteau. Then, holding it together, I added, "As I recall, you were so deeply concerned about our financial situation that you entrusted your own paltry savings to me and urged me to bet them where the odds were most favorable. Isn't that correct?"

"Oh yes—*that*." She seemed embarrassed that I had remembered. "Not one of my more reasonable ideas, I fear. I sometimes have these harebrained notions that Divine Intervention will rescue us. I hope that you did not put your money with mine, as I asked you to do."

"Truth to tell, I did," said I. "And this, dear Clarissa, was the result."

I then threw open the portmanteau and revealed to her a profusion of banknotes, as impressive an array as I myself had ever seen. "Would you not say that Divine Intervention has struck?"

She was open-mouthed with awe, speechless, breathless. At last, she did manage to say, "Dear God, Jeremy, is all of this ours?"

"Unfortunately, no," said I, "but one hundred fifty-one pounds and thirteen shillings of it is, which is more than you or I ever expected. I thought I would give you a glimpse of the full swack just to dazzle you proper before Mr. Deuteronomy takes his larger share."

"How much larger?" she asked in a small voice. "How much is here exactly?"

"Well, there's our hundred fifty-one pounds and Deuteronomy's three thousand."

"Three *thousand*? But that's a fortune!"

"That's right. He won on Pegasus, the horse he rode Easter at Shepherd's Bush. He asked me to place a hundred-pound bet on Pegasus."

"And what were the odds?"

"Thirty to one."

"I've never heard of such odds."

"Well, that's what they were, and that's what they paid."

I then asked a question which had been at the back of my mind ever since she first gave voice to her plan for making us rich.

"Clarissa," said I, "how did you learn about racing, and odds, and betting, all of that?"

"I learned about it from my father, of course. How else might I have done?"

Her reprobate father, the cause of so much misery for her, had, in this way, compensated in part for his mischief.

"He was a confirmed bettor," said she. "He kept promising to take me to all the race meets round London when first I arrived here. Yet in the end he never did."

I slapped the portmanteau together and buckled it up tight. "I doubt that I shall bet again," said I, "unless I am well advised by Mr. Deuteronomy himself."

'Twas not long afterward that Molly came down, rubbing her eyes and yawning. I made my excuses and, wishing to put off my report to Sir John as long as I might, I declared that I would sleep until summoned.

The summons came from Sir John and was brought to me by Clarissa, who was most agitated by the message she carried.

"Jeremy, come at once, oh do!"

I'd heard her footsteps upon the stairs and was sitting up in bed when she came a-rushing into my garret room.

"What? What is it?"

"Elizabeth is returned!"

"Who? Elizabeth? Who is — oh yes, Elizabeth Hooker."

"Sir John wants us both with him. She's evidently much the worse for her ordeal."

"What ordeal? Tell me."

"No, get dressed. You'll hear about it on the way."

I did as I was told. I could not have slept long — an hour or two perhaps — for my mind was foggy and my tongue was thick. There was little for me to say in such a state, and so I did the wise thing and simply listened as we sped across town to Number 5 Dawson's Alley, where her mother kept a lodging house. She had sent a neighbor boy with the news of her daughter's return. Sir John had got little from him, but that little he repeated to Clarissa and me as we rocked along over the cobblestones in our hackney coach.

"From what I gather," said he, "she was in a rather bad state when she appeared at her mother's door. She was not fully dressed, though in no wise naked—in her shift, as I gather. She was altogether gaunt—lost weight noticeably in less than a week—again, according to the boy. The mother is understandably upset but seems to know little more than we do. If we can just keep the girl away from others, and more or less a 'clean' witness, then we may learn a good deal from her."

Clearly, this was his hope. He had often stressed to me the importance of seeing witnesses as quickly as possible and getting their story fresh from their lips. When many have talked to a witness before the investigator has his chance, then the story may have been edited in any number of ways to flatter the witness or to please the investigator. Or, worse still, the unauthorized questioner may suggest many things to the witness, which she, in turn, passes on to the investigator as having truly been seen or heard by her. Thus Sir John did continue to search for such a "clean" witness, though rarely did he find one.

Though I had not asked the time of anyone, from the position of the sun in the sky I judged it to be not much after eight in the morning when we arrived at Number 5 Dawson's Alley. The streets were crowded with pedestrians, as I had observed through the hackney window: the residents of London were hurrying off to their day's employment. My two companions went to the door as I settled with the driver of the coach and then hurried after them. Just as I reached the step, the door to the lodging house swung open and a man of large proportions presented himself.

"You must be Sir John of Bow Street," he blurted out, "the Blind Beak, as they say."

"Why? Is there but one blind man in all of London?" Sir John asked belligerently. He was not at all fond of the epithet.

The man who had loomed so large in the doorway now seemed to shrink before our eyes. "I didn't mean no offense by it," said he, stepping aside and opening the door wide.

Clarissa and I exchanged glances. I noted that she had pursed her lips that she might not break into snickers. I winked; she winked back.

"Jeremy?"

With that Sir John called me into action. In a trice, I was by his side, my arm extended that he might grasp it as we followed the man up the stairs to the first and then to the second floor. All during our climb, our guide talked ceaselessly.

"Aw, it's a terrible thing, ain't it?" said he, throwing the words back over his shoulder to us. "She come back in the middle of the night just weepin' and cryin' something terrible, and wakin' up half the house. For myself—my room is right there next to where Mrs. Hooker dosses—I heard her right off. I was up and on my feet and sticking my head out my door even before she opened up to find out who was there."

"What time of the night was this?" asked Sir John.

"Oh, I don't know, round three, four o'clock at night, I reckon."

"Could you be a bit more exact than that?"

"Oh I s'pose I could. It must have been closer to four than three, 'cause it wasn't long till I heard the church bells strike four."

We kept climbing. It was not long till we heard something of a buzz above us. There was little to say between us: Each had his own notion of the number of people who waited above. Yet none, I think, was prepared for the many we saw crowded round the Hooker door. And there must indeed have been more inside, for the attention of those in the hall was directed past the threshold and into the apartment. I will say for them, however, that, for such a group, they were reasonably quiet—listening.

". . . and then did I at last admit to myself," came a familiar voice, "that I could do naught but jump." (It was Elizabeth, the heroine of her own story.)

"Brave girl!" responded one of the audience in the hall.

"You showed good English pluck, dearie. Didn't she, all?"

And to that there sounded a great affirmative chorus, even a scattering of applause from her listeners.

"So I did what had to be done—and I *jumped*!"

Then did the scattering swell to an ovation, the like of which I had heard exceeded only at Mr. Garrick's Drury Lane Theatre.

We were not at their level, and though the crowd of people at the door, male and female, was even larger than I had expected, they were remarkably well behaved.

"How many would you say there are?" Sir John whispered.

"There are a good many, surely more than twenty," I replied sotto voce. "Twenty-five at least."

"I shall count on you to make a path for me."

This was a task which so often came to me that I had developed a method for clearing the way for the magistrate. I did, first of all, speak in a voice much louder than was my wont. I kept in sight (though, naturally, I never used) the cosh which Mr. Marsden had given me; and, in general, I chose my words carefully.

"Make way, one and all," I shouted, "for Sir John Fielding, magistrate of the Bow Street Court. All who dare impede him in the discharge of his duties by thought, word, or deed, do so at their own risk. All here are answerable to him and punishable by jail terms of up to ninety days to be served in Newgate."

Having thus said my piece, I felt a little like the crier for some Oriental potentate. And, indeed, that could not have been far from the impression I created, for all fell silent and opened the way before us three to the Hooker rooms. Did I say that *all* fell silent? Not quite, I fear, for, behind me, I heard a few ill-suppressed giggles and knew they could only have come from Mistress Clarissa Roundtree.

Even Elizabeth seemed to hang upon my words. She half-lay upon a love seat, ensconced beneath a comforter. Her mouth was half-open as she regarded the three of us.

"Clarissa," said she, "how nice of you to come and bring . . . your . . . your employer."

"Jeremy," said Sir John, "close the door that we may have some modicum of privacy as we question Mistress Hooker."

As I turned to do as he bade me, Elizabeth jumped up from the little nest she had made for herself upon the love seat and waved dramatically at the crowd outside the door.

"Friends," said she, "I ask you to remain, and I shall finish the story. You will hear all!"

There were unhappy groans as I shut the door.

"Mother," Elizabeth called out, "do you think they will stay?"

Mrs. Hooker came forth from a dark corner of the room. " 'Twould be better, daughter, if they did not. Your worry should be naught but making sure all is told to Sir John."

"Thank you for that bit of advice, Mrs. Hooker. Your daughter would be well-advised to follow it." He turned left and right as if he were looking round the room. "I have the sense that the room is in disorder. Has the furniture been moved?"

"It has, Sir John," said I. (I was long past wondering how he managed such feats.)

"Then move things back again, will you?"

With a little help from Clarissa, and Elizabeth pointing the way, we managed to do just that.

"Now bring me a chair."

I placed one under him and indicated to Elizabeth that she was to resume her place upon the love seat just opposite Sir John.

"Are we ready to proceed?" he asked. Then, hearing our assent, he began. "Elizabeth, we are aware that you attended Easter dinner with Mistress Quigley at the home of your aunt and uncle in Wapping. Is that correct?"

She hesitated, then said, "Yes sir."

I glanced over at Clarissa. She, in turn, nodded toward Elizabeth's mother. The woman was visibly shocked. Nothing of this was known to her.

Sir John took the girl through all that we had learned of her actions up to and including the moment that she departed from Kathleen Quigley at the Theatre Royal and took off across Covent Garden in the company of the two young gallants.

When she acknowledged that this, too, was true, it was altogether too much for the Widow Hooker. She had suffered in silence up to then. Now she cried out her daughter's name as you might wail the name of one who was lost, near dead, or drowning.

Sir John turned to her. "I must caution you against making such a disturbance again. If you do, you must suffer the consequences. Is that clear?"

She said that it was, yet even so, she whimpered and sniffled all through the interrogation. Afterward, he conceded to me that his threat to her was but so much bluffing, and that the mother's presence was probably a good thing, for she served as a balance to the stern manner he had adopted.

"My question to you, Mistress Hooker—and I charge you to speak only the truth in answering—is this: What happened to you after you left your friend, Mistress Quigley?"

"The two young men, as I should have known, were blackguards, plain and simple," said she. "No sooner was I separated from Kathleen than the two of them fell to arguing between themselves about me."

"About you? In what way?"

"Well, the whole question seemed to be whether or not I would do.'"

"Do? Again, in what way?"

"Whether I would—how shall I put it?—make the grade. Whether I should, well, qualify."

"Qualify for what?"

"That is what I earnestly sought to discover. They talked of me as if I were not present, as if I were an animal of some sort."

"I don't quite understand," said Sir John.

"Well, Dick—he was the one on my left—kept repeating that my bosom was not of sufficient size to be interesting. Bobby—it was him on my right—he insisted it was. Or, what he said in all truth was that it didn't make much difference. Dick said I wasn't pretty enough. Pretty enough for what, I wanted to know."

"And you did ask them?"

"Well no, not directly. I wanted to know where they were taking me, for I have a fair sense of direction, and I could tell they weren't taking me the right way."

"Which direction were they taking you?"

"Well, north, it seemed to me—which was just opposite of the way I wanted to go."

"And did you inform them of this?"

"Oh, I did! I told them they were making a great mistake if they thought they could take me some other place but home. They laughed at me. I dug in my heels and told them I would go no further. They did not then laugh, but they dragged me along for thirty or forty feet until I started to scream."

"And then what?"

"They became quite cross with me. Dick went so far as to shake his walking stick at me and threaten me, telling me what he would do to me if I did not cooperate. But I laughed at him and screamed again. That was when he belabored me about the head, and I fell unconscious."

"You actually fell upon the ground?"

"Well, not quite, I suppose. They held me up, one each side, and I s'pose I was making my feet go. But I was dazed, unable to know where we were headed. Oh, I was in a terrible state!"

"No doubt you were, but—"

At that moment, a knock sounded upon the door to the hall. Had I not made it sufficiently plain with my threats that we were not to be disturbed?

"Jeremy, see what that's about, will you?"

"Certainly, Sir John. Shall I send them away?"

"Let's see who it is first, and then decide, shall we?"

(It was on such occasions as this that he often made me feel an utter fool.)

I went to the door, opened it, and found a small woman of a size not much larger than Mr. Deuteronomy. She was old, about sixty, and swarthy of complexion.

"Tell her that Goody Moss is here," said she to me.

"Tell who?"

"The Widow Hooker. 'Twas she who sent for me."

"Remain here, please," said I and closed the door.

I went back and announced the woman. Elizabeth's mother caught her breath. "Oh, the midwife, of course! I completely forgot that I had sent for her—to examine Elizabeth. I thought you would want that, Sir John. It should not take long for her to be pronounced intact. You do want that, I assume?"

He sighed a great sigh and rose from his chair. "Yes, all right," said he. "Jeremy, come along. We'll wait out in the hall. Clarissa, I'd like you to remain to serve as witness to these proceedings."

And so I opened the door once again and beckoned Goody Moss into the room. Then did I see Sir John out and into a corner some distance from the door. About half of those who listened with such sympathy to Elizabeth's account of her escape had stayed on to hear the tale told complete; they stared at us timidly. I commented upon this to Sir John.

"Indeed they seem quite fascinated by her," he commented. "But why not? She is quite the actress." He hesitated, then: "And I hoped for a 'clean' witness!"

We waited impatiently. In particular, Sir John seemed most unhappy with the interruption and the consequent delay. He tapped his foot and sighed. At one point he did speculate: "I wonder what reason that woman, Mrs. Hooker, could have had to summon the midwife." And then, a moment later, he answered his own question: "She must have been so certain of her daughter's virtue that she wished to demonstrate it to me."

And that was how we passed our brief exile in the hall—whistling, tapping our feet, asking questions of ourselves. Yet, as I say, it was but a *brief* exile: It was not long before the door was opened to us and Goody Moss came forth and made her way to us.

"You, sir," said she to Sir John, "would want to know, and so I shall tell you."

"Please do."

"Though her maidenhead is long gone, there is no sign of entry . . . recently."

"When you say recently, what does that mean?"

A knowing smile. "Oh, a day or two perhaps—or a night and a day."

"Is that what you told Mrs. Hooker?"

"I told her what she wished to hear. To you I tell the truth. I whispered to the girl—what is her name? Clarissa?—all the details. She's a good girl, very smart. She can tell you all you need to know—if you need to know more." She gave us a wink. "Goodbye, then, eh?"

She started for the stairway, but stopped, turned, and came back to us.

"You did know that she was pregnant, eh?"

"We knew nothing of the kind," said Sir John.

"Indeed she is—about a month or two gone, I would say. Not so she would show. She may not even know. But we have ways of knowing."

And then she left us. I watched her go, wondering what those ways of knowing were. From her dark face to her bright garb, she seemed an altogether mysterious sort. Her name did not fit her, nor did her slightly odd manner of speech.

"Who is she, sir? What is she? Her accent of speech was something new to me."

"Goodwife Moss is a Gypsy, my lad. I do know that mode of speech, for a number have appeared before me in Bow Street, though not many are to be found in the cities. They are, for the most part, country people, traveling people. And did you notice the striking odor of the scent which she wore?"

"Now that you mention it, yes."

"All Romany females seem to wear it—from the youngest to the very oldest. But let's go inside, shall we? I cannot say how this bit of knowledge she gave to us will change anything, or if it will at all, but it is certainly of considerable interest, is it not?"

Without awaiting my agreement, he started to the room we had left. I offered him my arm, and in we went. Sir John entered with a question, thus beginning precisely at the point at which he had earlier been interrupted.

"As I recall, in response to your screams, you were beaten upon the head with a heavy walking stick by one of the two young men who had promised to see you home. Is that correct?"

"Yes sir."

I know not why, but just at that moment I happened to glance over at Clarissa, and noticed that she was sending me a message. Emphatically was she shaking her head in the negative. I noted that neither of the Hooker women could see her in the place she had chosen. Answering with a single affirmative nod, I resolved to discuss the entire matter of Elizabeth's abduction with Clarissa at the earliest opportunity.

"Then, as you said, you were in a dazed state, not quite fully conscious, yet still moving your feet and stumbling along between the two men. And you were moving in a northerly direction. Is that correct?"

"All of it, yes."

"How long do you reckon you were going in that way?"

"Well, that's not easy to say, is it?"

"Perhaps we can work it out. For instance, you must soon have passed out of Covent Garden and onto the surrounding streets. Think back. Do you remember walking upon the streets?"

She gave the matter some thought. "Yes, oh yes, we walked some ways upon the street."

"You say 'some ways,' by which you must also mean some time. Did you hear church bells chiming the hour? St. Paul's, I believe, strikes every quarter hour. Did you hear it strike once?

twice? three times?" Again, she concentrated, pulling a suitably fierce face.

Then, nodding, smiling. "Why yes," said she, "I believe I heard it strike three times."

"Good! Then that means that, even considering that there are no straight streets in London, if you had been proceeding in a general northerly direction, you would have been somewhere between Holborn and Clerkenwell—that is, with at least a half hour's walking time. Is that correct?"

"Well, I suppose so."

"But now, what I would know from you is how you managed to travel so far in such a state and cause no notice among those you met along the way? Though it was after dark, it was not late. The area north of Covent Garden is one of the most populous in the city. You must have passed dozens along the way. Even Clerkenwell and Holborn have many afoot that time of the evening. What must it have been? Somewhere round eight, would you say? And here are two young men conveying a girl of your years between them. She is disoriented—dazed, by her own admission—so that she can hardly walk. Would you not challenge them? Would you not raise the hue and cry?"

He had hit home. He had upset her. He had penetrated the bravado that had heretofore supported her so well. Her lower lip began to tremble as her eyes began to tear. She was about to lose that edge of containment that had sustained her and made it possible to resist him thus far. Yet she found it in her to strike back.

"How should I know why no one stopped those two and challenged them?" she cried out, holding back the tears. "Ask them, all those people who paraded by me and did nothing to help."

"But of course you ask the impossi—"

"Wait! Wait!" She shouted it out, interrupting, insisting, attempting to regain control. "Now I remember. There was a man who stopped us and asked to know what was wrong with me. I didn't get much of a look at him, for I was in that half-conscious way, but I had the idea that he was a watchman or a constable."

"Oh? And do you recall how your condition was explained?"

"Certainly I do. They said I was drunk." At that she forced a laugh.

Her mother came to her defense: "Ne'er a drop of the devil's drink has ever touched Elizabeth's lips," said she.

"And never will!" her daughter declared.

"Admirable," said Sir John. "But let us get back to that constable, or whatever he might have been. Did he give his name?"

"No, he did not."

Then did a loud, insistent knocking come upon the door. Who could that be? I hurried to open it, and I had barely accomplished that when the door flew out of my hand, and, for a moment, I found myself pushed against the wall.

That moment was just enough to admit three men I recognized from the silversmith's shop in Chandos Street. They were Mr. Turbott, the proprietor; Mr. Tarkington, the journeyman; and the apprentice who was in his last year, named Joe; these were the three I saw pouring silver at the back of Turbott's shop. They rushed forward as if to rescue Elizabeth.

"Who is here?" shouted Sir John as he jumped to his feet, ready to do battle, if need be.

Mr. Turbott gave him little attention but rushed to Elizabeth's side that he might comfort her. It should not be necessary to quote him here, for the words he used were not particularly well chosen. I will say, however, that watching them together gave me a good idea of just who the father of the child growing within her might be. Nevertheless, he managed, after some moments, to tear himself away and identified himself to Sir John as "Elizabeth's employer."

"And, I assume," said Sir John, "that having just heard of her return, you rushed here from your shop to learn as much as you can of all this. Is that correct?"

"Quite right," said he.

"Well, I, sir, am Sir John Fielding, magistrate of the Bow Street Court, and I am conducting this investigation. I have no intention of going back over what we have heard from her already. It would be unnecessary for me, and, no doubt, quite painful for her."

"Oh, no doubt you're right."

"I will, however, briefly summarize what has already been established."

And this he proceeded to do in his impressive and inimitable fashion. None but Lord Mansfield, the Lord Chief Justice himself, could even begin to approach Sir John's powers of summary. His, I do honestly believe, was the more logical mind. When he had concluded with that, he made an offer to Mr. Turbott.

"Sir," said he, "I shall allow you and those who have come with you to remain and hear the rest of this sad tale. But I do so only on the condition that all three of you will keep silent and allow me and only me to conduct the interrogation. There will be no additions, interruptions, or comments. Do you agree to this?"

"Oh, certainly! And without reservation. I speak for myself and my employees," said the silversmith.

"All right then, I believe that Mistress Hooker was about to tell us that she was taken to a house in . . . Would you say Holborn or Clerkenwell?"

"I think that Clerkenwell is the more likely," said she.

"Why do you say that?"

"Well, I've visited there once or twice on errands for Mr. Turbott." She turned to him and offered him a smile. "And I was less dazed than before. I took note of my surroundings, you see, and it was all quite familiar—the fields and that."

"I understand," said Sir John.

"But there was a house at a crossroads—I can't say where any better than that—and that turned out to be the place we were headed."

"And what did it look like? What was its appearance?"

"Its appearance was ordinary. It was just a house."

"Come now. You can do better than that, surely. Was it a house of one story or two? Had it been painted? What color had it? What of the yard—large or small? Please, Elizabeth, you must make a blind man *see* that house."

Quite inappropriately, she giggled at that last request of his. Yet she soon brought herself under control and gave a fair description of the place. It was, she said, a house of two stories and a garret. ("How well I remember that garret!") One would not call it a house in good condition, for it was unpainted—or if indeed the house had once been painted, any trace of color had long ago disappeared from it. There were trees in the yard, though none of them of any real size, and a great pile of leaves, left over from last autumn. And one final detail: As she had declared earlier, it was a house at a crossroads; there was another, a proper farm house, at the opposite corner. It was well built and well maintained—all that the house she described was not.

(So fixed was my attention upon Sir John and Elizabeth that I had not noticed until she began her description that Clarissa was taking down all that was said by her with paper and pencil. This was something new.)

"Now," said Sir John to Elizabeth, "you have given a fair and complete description of the place to which you were taken, but I note that much of it, perhaps most, could only have been noted by you from a distance. You seemed to have known in advance to which house you were headed."

"Well, I didn't!" said she rather hotly. "Whilst I was prisoner in that house I had much opportunity to study the details which you eagerly sought. But for that matter, my two captors talked of it in such a way that I knew we were close."

"Saying . . . what?"

"Oh, they wondered what sort of price I might fetch. The one called Dick seemed to doubt whether I would be taken at all, kept insisting that I was not pretty enough, nor was my bosom sufficient."

"All right. I'll accept that," said Sir John. "Let's get on with it, shall we. You entered this old house in the company of the two men, and then what?"

"We went round the back and entered through the kitchen. I remember they knocked upon the door and said who they were. Bobby and Dick, they said, and the door was opened to us. Waiting for us there in the kitchen were three people—a man about forty, a young girl who was fair pretty, and a woman with the ugliest face I did ever see. It was her, the ugly one, that the two men who brought me bowed and scraped to. She looked me over proper, pinched my arm and my bosom and just all over. And finally she says to me, 'What about it, dearie? Will you join us?' Which I took to mean, will you follow the Devil's path? And then—"

At this point, Mr. Tarkington, unable to contain himself further, interrupted, calling to his chief, the silversmith Turbott: "Sir, that sounds like Mother Jeffers's house to me—from the look of the house, the way she describes the old harridan herself."

"You've been there?" Turbott demanded.

"A time or two."

"What about it, Elizabeth?" cried Turbott. "Was that the woman's name?"

"I . . . I think so. Yes, perhaps it was. When I said no and declared I would have no part of her life she slapped my face, took my dress from me, and said I should be thrown into the garret. Then did the two men say, 'Yes, Mother Jeffers.' That was it! *Mother Jeffers!*"

The room then fell into complete turmoil. Mrs. Hooker was shouting out in praise of her daughter for resisting the Devil and his minions. Mr. Tarkington shouted, "Well, let's go out and get the old witch." Joe the apprentice urged that they bring a rope. And Mr. Turbott cried, "Let's see if some of those people out in the hall might wish to come along." But Sir John, alone of them all, resisted these calls for swift justice and sought to restore some order.

"Listen to me," said he who could outshout them all. "I warned you, gentlemen, that you must leave if you did not keep silent—and you agreed to my terms. Now you have violated your side of the agreement, so I must ask you to leave this room most immediate."

"Oh, we shall leave right enough," called out Mr. Turbott, "and we shall head for Clerkenwell. You may command in this room, sir, but once outside it, we shall command, as you will see."

"I put you on warning, sir, that all who defy the law will be punished severely, and that includes yourself. I will not allow rule by mob in my precincts."

The difficulty—as Sir John well knew—was that he could not confidently speak of "my precincts," for, truth to tell, though there was no strict division of territories, as a matter of custom, it would generally have fallen to Mr. Saunders Welch, as magistrate of Holborn to deal with this matter; Clerkenwell, after all, was near to Holborn. All this and more we discussed once we had returned from that memorable visit. Yet as we four—Elizabeth, Clarissa, Sir John, and I—rocked back and forth along the way to the house at the four corners in Clerkenwell, we spoke little amongst ourselves. The reason for this, of course, was the presence of Elizabeth, whom we had come to regard in a different light from before. No longer a hapless victim, she now seemed to be hiding more than she had disclosed, altering facts to suit her, and generally providing unreliable information. There was but a brief period at the beginning of our journey when we, the Bow Street contingent, felt free to speak our minds, and that was when Mrs. Hooker was preparing Elizabeth for the trip as we awaited the putative victim in the hackney coach. 'Twas then that Clarissa opened the discussion with a confession.

"Never, I believe, have I been so mistaken about a person," said she, "as I have been about my old friend Elizabeth."

"Oh?" said Sir John. "Mistaken in what way?"

"In every way. I thought her dull and commonplace, unimaginative and without ambition — oh, specially without any sort of intellectual ambition."

"And now what do you think of her?" I asked. "You were signaling something to me from across the room of her consistency."

"Oh yes, that! Yes, of course, it proves my point."

"What do you mean by saying that it proves your point?" asked Sir John.

"Simple enough," said she. "You remember when she claimed to have been beaten about the head by one of the two who had abducted her? She said she was in a daze for quite some time afterward."

"Yes, naturally I remember."

"Well, the midwife — what was her name? Goody Moss, I believe — she wanted me to stand close and observe all that she did. It was all *most* interesting."

"Yes?" said I. "Go on."

"Oh, of course. I was also near enough that I might look down upon her head, and I can assure you that there was no sign that she had been beaten in the way that she said."

"No scabs? No scars?"

"Nothing of the kind. In truth, her hair had been washed, so that indeed I would have seen such, had there been anything to see."

"Interesting, yes, very interesting indeed."

"And another thing — though I hesitate even to mention it. I went with the midwife to the door, so that she might explain all that she had done and seen. And what she whispered to me was the most remarkable thing of all. She said that Elizabeth was pregnant. I don't think I could ever have supposed such a thing of her."

"She told us the same," said Sir John. "And I—"

"Caution, sir," said I. "They are on their way now."

Mother and daughter approached the hackney, but only the daughter entered the door, which I held for them. Sir John inquired of the mother if she were not also coming. She declared that she was not.

"'Twould be worth my immortal soul to step inside such a place," said she with a great shudder. "I think it a great shame that Elizabeth should have to return." Then did she depart.

Then, only minutes later, the caravan pulled out of Dawson's Alley. It was a rather strange array, which moved forth on the way to Clerkenwell. There were two coaches—our own hackney and another, which I understood Mr. Turbott rented more or less regularly from a nearby stable. In a trailing line were five or six on ponies and nags that had been rented or borrowed for the occasion.

As we traveled, Sir John took the opportunity to question Elizabeth further. There was not much left for her to tell. For, once she was locked in the garret, she stayed there, a prisoner, for over a week. She had naught but a pile of straw to sleep upon and a thin blanket to keep her warm. She was fed thin gruel and water once a day and visited by the one she now called Mother Jeffers. Elizabeth was asked by her again each day if she would join their company, and each day she refused. This continued so until the night before, when she at last managed to loose the window which overlooked the great pile of leaves in the yard. Then, waiting till all was silent within the house, she perched upon the window sill and leapt down into the leaves. With only the blanket to wrap round her and her shift beneath it, she started south and found her way home to her mother's place in Dawson's Alley.

"How many do you reckon were in the house?" Sir John asked.

"Well," said she, "I saw four, but there were probably a couple more."

"So, six in all? And how did they divide between men and women?"

"Probably four women and two men. Something like that." She seemed curiously indifferent of a sudden.

"But you could only identify four?"

"If that."

Sir John accepted that and put no more questions to her. And in no more than a few minutes' time she was asleep in the corner of the seat. It seemed to me strange that she could sleep so peacefully as we bounced about so wildly. Clarissa evidently wished to resume our conversation regarding Elizabeth. Sir John must have sensed this, for when she began to address him, he shook his head in the negative and put a finger to his lips, thus calling for quiet. With that gesture, he communicated his suspicion that her sound sleep was feigned.

After near half an hour of backtracking and wending our way in a general northerly direction, we came to open country and picked up our pace. It was then but a short time on a swift road that we drew to a halt behind Mr. Turbott's coach. I threw open the door and hopped down to the road at about the same moment Mr. Tarkington descended from his perch next to the driver. He opened the door like a proper footman and out came a whole squad of men. Those trailing on horses rode up. As all formed round him, Turbott raised his voice so loud that I wondered, could he not be heard inside the house just ahead.

"We know not what awaits us there"—pointing ahead as if aiming at a target—"so I must ask, how many of you have weapons with you?"

In response, a number of hands shot up—and in those hands were deadly weapons of every sort, pistols, knives, and fowling pieces. Turbott himself brandished a ceremonial sword of some sort.

"Good God, Jeremy," said Sir John, "this is as bad as I feared. Help me down from here, and I shall accompany you. We cannot allow these men to attack this house on such flimsy evidence."

I did as he asked, whilst Turbott divided his men into two groups—those with and those without weapons. He then gave his troop of irregulars a proper harangue. And, as he did this, Sir John began muttering something in my direction, which I could not quite understand. At first, I thought it a prayer; yet potentially calamitous as was the situation, it did not seem to me that prayer was called for. But then did the magistrate explain.

"You are now deputized as a constable," said he to me. "Arrest whomever I tell you to arrest."

Shouting back to the two girls in the hackney to stay where they were until they were summoned, he felt about for my arm. When at last he found it, he instructed me to take him forward.

"Where to?" said I.

"Into the fray," said he rather dramatically.

Indeed, the battle had begun, so to speak, for Mr. Turbott was leading his men forward, waving his sword most ferociously. The rank of armed men moved forward behind him; and behind them, not quite so bold, came the unarmed group.

We marched through this latter group on our way across the road. They seemed more than willing to clear a way for us. We were just approaching the forward rank when I happened to notice one of the upstairs windows move. And, being unlatched, the window was then pushed open; it hit the wall of the house with a big BANG! Whereupon Turbott and all those with him threw themselves flat upon the ground, hoping to make smaller targets of themselves, for they supposed that they were being shot at. The woman responsible for that great noise stuck her head out the open window and, seeing a number of armed men in the front yard, let out a lusty scream.

Sir John did not miss a step. We picked our way through the prone figures as Turbott began shouting slogans and battle cries at his men as he urged them onto their feet that they might storm the door.

"Come along, Jeremy," said Sir John, "right up to the door, if you please."

"As you will, Sir John."

When we reached it, he instructed me to give a good, loud knock upon it, which I did in a most commanding manner. Almost immediately, the door came open a crack—no more than two or three inches. Then, from inside, a female voice, fearful and in a mere whisper:

"Who are you?"

"Madame, I am Sir John Fielding of the Bow Street Court, and I have a need to question you and others in the house on a criminal matter."

"But who are those men with guns out there in the yard?"

"Though it be difficult, I urge you to pay them no attention. They will cause no trouble so long as I am here. But doubtless you would find it easier to answer my questions without them looking on? May we discuss these matters inside?"

After a moment's hesitation, she said, "Well, all right."

Then did the door open sufficient to allow us to pass inside, single file.

The woman with whom Sir John had spoken closed the door after us. I knew that she must be the one called Mother Jeffers, for Elizabeth had remarked upon her ugliness, and, truth to tell, I had never seen a woman uglier than this one before us. She had a large, misshapen nose with a wart upon its end. Her upper jaw overhung her lower in such a way that she seemed to have no chin at all. But she had a very sweet voice, the sort which seemed to go not at all with her most unfortunate appearance.

"What matter does this concern?" she asked Sir John.

"'Twould be easier, Madame, if I were to bring you together with the complainant that these matters be thrashed out between you. Would it be well with you if I were to bring her in?"

"I suppose so," she said, "but I've water on for tea. Perhaps we could talk in the kitchen?"

"Of course. Jeremy, would you fetch Elizabeth and Clarissa from the coach? And if Mr. Turbott should insist upon coming along, you may tell him that he, and only he, may enter. He must leave his brigade outside—and that is on my explicit orders."

And so I took my leave and made straight for our hackney. I hurried the two girls out of the coach and bade them follow me. Just as our little group was starting for the house, the driver called down from his seat.

"Say, lad, I see guns and suchlike carried by some. Will there be shooting?"

"Oh no sir," said I. "Not a chance of it, I'm sure." A lie, of course.

"Well, that's good, 'cause if I hear any shots, I shall be out of here quicker than it takes to tell. Tell the blind gentleman that, will you?"

I promised I would, then hurried Elizabeth and Clarissa to the front door. But alas, before reaching it, we were intercepted by Mr. Turbott, who left the group with whom he had been arguing but a moment before.

"Where are you taking her?" he demanded.

"Taking who?"

"As if you didn't know who I meant! Taking Elizabeth, of course."

"Sir John requested her presence," said I. "He wishes to put accuser and accused together that they may thrash things out—so he said."

"Oh? He did, did he? Well, there's no need for that. Once we get inside, we'll have them all pleading with us to listen to their stories. We'll get the truth out of them!"

"Sir John asked me to tell you that you and you alone may enter—and none of the rest. Any who try to follow you inside will be arrested. I may add, sir, that if you make so bold as to urge and abet any else to enter then you, too, will be arrested."

"On what charge?"

"Oh, home invasion would do. And one thing more. You must leave your sword outside. Do you accept the terms?"

To which he replied with a sigh so deep it might well have been a growl. And then: "Yes."

When I turned back to the two girls after the brief negotiation, I found Clarissa all a-giggle and Elizabeth appearing most concerned.

We were admitted by one scarce older than myself, pretty enough and plump. She curtsied near as well as Elizabeth herself, then led us down a hall to the kitchen. On the way, Clarissa whispered into my ear.

"I thought you quite wonderful with that man, Turbott," said she. "Wouldn't give an inch, would you?"

It was not the sort of question that called for a response—a statement, rather. Yet as I glanced at her at that moment, I saw something in her eyes that I had never before seen: Clarissa seemed truly admiring of me. It was as if in the past few minutes I had grown near a foot in her estimation. I had never been given such a look before. It was the sort that one had to live up to.

Just then we did hear something that must have disturbed

Turbott and Elizabeth. From the kitchen came the sound of laughter—Sir John's booming baritone and, mingled with it, a light soprano; the latter was surely that of Mother Jeffers. Yet, if we heard them, they also heard us, and the laughter halted soon as ever it had begun.

Ugly though she may have been, Mother Jeffers proved an adequate hostess. She had only to nod at the pot of tea and the cups surrounding it, and the girl who had opened the door to us set about serving up the promised tea. In another minute or two, there was tea and buttered bread before us all.

"Now," said Sir John, "we meet here that accuser and accused might have the opportunity to confront each the other direct, to defend themselves, if need be, to make the other prove her innocence."

He stopped at that point to clear his throat. It was in the nature of punctuation. He wanted it made clear that, beyond this point, he was speaking ex officio. He began:

"Elizabeth Hooker, here on my left, has given it to me that on the evening of Easter Sunday, two young men, promising to see her home, set off instead for this place, where they might show her to you, Mrs. Jeffers, and get for their trouble some amount of money from you."

"What were their names?" asked Mother Jeffers.

"Dick and Bobby," said Elizabeth.

"I must think upon that," said the old woman, "but just now I can think of nine or more I know by those names. You have only the first names?"

"I am near certain that is the case," said Sir John, "but let us move on, shall we? You were, as she has given it, sitting in this very kitchen when the two brought her to you." Then did Sir John turn to Elizabeth and ask her most direct, "Is this the woman who spoke to you and asked if you were willing to join her company?"

"Is this the woman? Yes, indeed it is. This is the one who asked me, would I join them."

"Are you sure?"

"How could I forget a face such as hers?"

"If you will pardon me," said Sir John, "it seems to me that what you just said was unnecessarily rude."

"So be it," said Elizabeth.

"And you, Mrs. Jeffers, what defense have you against this accusation?"

"I have none," said she almost proudly.

"None?"

"I have never seen this girl before in my life," said she.

There matters seemed to hang. It was not so much the denial as the manner in which it was given which put things at a halt. It was so coldly complete that I, for one, felt that there was nothing more to say. Yet impeded though he was, Sir John pressed on.

"May I, then," said he, "take Mistress Hooker through your house and visit such of it as she remembers? Note that I ask your permission in this, for you would be within your rights to demand that you see a search warrant before allowing us the run of your house."

"I understand," said she. "But yes, you have my permission to go anywhere within this house." And then, emphasizing each word, she said: "*I have nothing to hide.*"

"Thank you."

"My daughter will show you round."

And with that, the girl who had spied us from the floor above showed us the way, and we followed her on a room-by-room tour of the entire house. That she was the daughter of Mother Jeffers surprised me—and I'm sure others, as well—but that was not the only surprise that awaited us.

We had visited every room but one and routed two women out of their beds. Elizabeth would search all for her stolen frock; we then started up the narrow stairway to the garret room. There it was that Elizabeth had spent all the time of her imprisonment. She had described it well enough so that I had a fair idea of its look. Once inside, however, we found this garret room was altogether different from the one she had described. Where she had told of sleeping on a pile of straw with naught but a thin blanket to keep her warm, what we saw was a comfortable-looking bed with a comforter that would, it seemed, have kept anyone warm. There was a chair and a table, curtained windows which were held by latches alone. And, in one corner, a wardrobe.

"They've changed it all," said Elizabeth. "They've changed it completely!"

"Nothing has been altered," said Mrs. Jeffers's daughter. "And I should know, for this is my room here."

Elizabeth gave her a killing look, then hastened to the wardrobe.

"This proves she lies, and I alone tell the truth," said she, "for here—look! This is mine! This is the frock taken from me when I arrived at this place."

She held it up proudly, but it was obvious to me, as it was also to Clarissa, that the frock had been made for one much more corpulent than Elizabeth—indeed, it had been made for Jeffers's daughter.

"I shall not fight you for it," said she, "for my mother would not have that. But it should be plain to all who see you with it now that it was not made for you."

The matter of the dress, as well as much else, was held in abeyance—undecided till we reached Bow Street. Sir John took with us Mother Jeffers and gave Elizabeth in exchange. ("Well rid of her!" said Clarissa, who had soured completely on her old friend.) I confess, reader, that I slept through our entire return journey, rocking back and forth, bouncing up and down, just as Elizabeth had done on the voyage out. According to Clarissa, Jeffers was quite entertaining, though she declared it pained her to leave her daughter in the house. Sir John did not say that he was officially detaining her; he said simply that he had further questions for her to answer in his office in Bow Street. He wished to ask them after he had held his court session. Again, all this was reported to me later by Clarissa, for I was of a sudden so exhausted that I heard nothing, said nothing, and was totally unable to recall anything of the drive to Bow Street. The night I had spent, awake on the road in the post coach, had at last caught up with me.

Upon our arrival, Sir John ordered me upstairs and to my bed. 'Twas not me who carried out his orders, however. Rather 'twas Clarissa who, both guiding and supporting me, got me upstairs and into my bed.

. . .

And it was she, too, who woke me, five or six hours on. I heard her footsteps on the stairs moments before she appeared, and so I was at least sitting up in bed when she appeared in the doorway.

"You're much in demand," said she.

Still half-asleep, I grunted a reply of some sort, then rose to my feet and staggered to the wash basin, poured a bit of water into it, and splashed water upon my face. Only then did I feel I could communicate.

"By whom am I wanted?"

"First by Mr. Patley, who must see you before he goes out this evening to make his rounds. Second, by all the rest of us who respectfully request your presence at the dinner table, and third, by Sir John who, after dinner, wishes to have your report on the trip to Newmarket." She looked at me closely to make sure that I was fully awake and would not collapse into bed the moment she left. "There," said she. "I can trust you to rise, can't I?"

"You can trust me. Where's Mr. Patley?"

"Downstairs, waiting by the door to Bow Street."

Satisfied at last, she left as I hurriedly ran a comb through my hair and descended to meet Mr. Patley. He was there, in the dark, waiting for me just at the door.

"Ah there you are," said he. "I've news for you. Bad news, I fear—but it's important."

"Let me hear it, by all means."

"Well, it's this way. As you may know, Mr. Bailey covered for me whilst we was in Newmarket. He made the circuit for me, talked to all my snitches, and so on. But he wasn't actually on hand when it happened."

"*What* happened? What have you to tell?"

"It was last night whilst we was on the road back. Who should come walking into the King's Favorite around eleven o'clock at night but Alice Plummer. She comes up behind one of the local drinkers, Walter Hogg by name, and she says, 'Walter, I've got something for you.' Then, quick as anything, she whips out a razor and, just as quick, she cuts his throat from ear to ear. It all happened so fast that those at the table could do naught but gape. Nor could they do more when she then took that selfsame razor and cuts her own throat with it. All this in less time than it takes to tell. Mr. Bailey said that when he got there just a little time later, there were two dead and more blood on the table and floor than he would have supposed that two bodies could hold."

There he stopped. I knew not what to say to him.

"I just thought you ought to know," said Patley. And, having spoken his piece, he opened the door and disappeared into the night.

TEN

*In which I hear a
startling confession
from an odd source*

❄❄❄

The news that I had heard from Mr. Patley was such that during dinner I had constantly to hold myself in check lest I take it upon myself to tell all or part of it to Sir John. We had long been in unspoken agreement not to discuss matters of the court at the table. Generally, he thought it best that Lady Fielding not hear of such matters, for she was easily distressed and would worry for his safety. I, on the other hand, had lately become more and more open with Clarissa. Still, much of that was between us two, and I trusted her not to repeat it. In any case, I held my tongue all through dinner, but soon as ever I had finished the washing up afterward, I hied myself up to see Sir John in the darkened room he called his study.

"Jeremy? Is it you?"

"Indeed it is, sir. And though it be a sorry tale, I've come to tell you of all that came to pass in Newmarket."

Which I did, more or less, though I admit that I held back a bit. I said nothing of the good fortune Mr. Patley and I had had in wagering what we had on Pegasus and Mr. Deuteronomy to win. Sir John must have guessed that something was missing from the story I told, for at about the time I had done with Newmarket, he stopped me with a question or two that were directly to the point.

"What I do not quite understand," said he, having heard me through, "is why, when Alice Plummer was in hand, you and Patley did not simply take her immediately to the nearest post coach and bring her here to London that I might question her."

"Uh, yes, well, had we done that, Sir John, we should have missed the King's Plate race."

"Ah!" said he, as if he had made a considerable discovery.

"We felt the least we could do for Deuteronomy Plummer was to see how he and Pegasus fared in the big race. After all, he had given us the tip that had enabled us to find her."

"Oh yes, of course, I recall well enough—the stable and the fellow named Stephen, all of that."

"Yes sir."

"But you stayed for the race, did you? Then tell me, how did it come out? That is, who won? Charade was the favorite, as I believe I heard from Mr. Baker. Was Charade the winner?"

"Uh, no sir, Pegasus was the winner."

(I had the distinct feeling that Sir John was once again toying with me.)

"You don't say so," said he. "Truly? How nice for Mr. Deuteronomy, winning such an important race on a horse running his first race."

"Second."

"All right, second. All the same, quite an accomplishment, eh? You didn't happen to have something wagered on Pegasus, did you?"

"Oh, a little something, a few shillings, not much more."

"Hmm, interesting."

And that, reader, was the extent of his comments. He left it all hanging in the air, for then I told him of what I had just learned from Mr. Patley. Sir John was most truly disturbed by the news.

"Good God," said he, cursing in dismay, "was that Alice Plummer who was involved in that nasty attack in Bedford Street? Mr. Bailey told me about it in his report this morning, yet at the time he knew only the name of the man. Walter Hogg, wasn't it?"

"It was, and when I heard that, I understood what earlier had eluded me. You'll recall, sir, that when Katy Tiddle was dying she called for water so insistently that I ran out and brought some to her and, I then thought, missed her dying words. Well, 'twas not so at all. She named her murderer to me—not *water,* you see, but *Walter.*"

"And how did you come to this conclusion?"

"From what Patley and I were told by Alice Plummer. She said that she had entrusted her daughter Maggie to a man named Walter at Katy Tiddle's urging. He had promised to find her a home with a couple who were unable to conceive."

"But how did she learn what had become of her daughter?"

"That, I fear, she learned from me," said I.

"Oh, Jeremy," said he, truly mourning what he had just heard. "One of the most important rules in interrogation is never to let the one you are questioning know just how much *you* know. She acted on your information. You do understand, don't you?"

At that I sighed. "Yes sir, I do understand."

"Now if this fellow Walter Hogg was acting as an agent for another, as we both suspect, then we have lost our chance to get the name of that other. Truly, you should have brought her straight to me whilst she was in your hands."

"Yes sir, you're right, I know. If only . . ."

"Ah yes, 'if only'—that covers a multitude of sins, does it not?" He was then silent for a time, brooding upon the news that he had got from me. Then did he say, "This is specially painful to me, for I confess that I reached a complete impasse with the one they call Mother Jeffers."

"I did notice that the strongroom was empty," I ventured timidly.

"What could I do? I could not hold her for further questioning on the evidence we had, much less could I pass her on for trial in Old Bailey."

"Then you do not believe the testimony of Elizabeth Hooker, sir?"

"Indeed I do not. Do you? Clarissa told me of that awful muddle in the garret room in which Elizabeth claimed to have been held prisoner. 'It's all been changed,' said she. Well, it could not have been changed so much in so little time, as I understood it from Clarissa. Do you agree with her?"

"Oh, indeed I do, sir. And there was also the matter of the frock which Elizabeth claimed as her own. It would have been much too large for her, and would have fit the daughter quite well. So you believe Mrs. Jeffers when she says that she had never before seen the girl?"

"I did not say that."

"What then?"

"In all truth, Jeremy, I do not believe either one."

. . .

Again, it was Constable Patley who had brought the word to me. Whilst on his rounds, he had encountered Mr. Deuteronomy who announced to him that he had just returned from Newmarket and would be happy to receive me at any time — "but the earlier the better." We both knew, of course, what he would be happy to receive.

"He wrote down where to find him. Let's see now, I've got it here somewhere." And, so saying, he began going through his pockets.

"Save yourself the trouble," said I. "I believe I know the place. Would it be up above the Haymarket Coffee House?"

"So it is, so it is. Hurry along, lad, and bring the lally. I'll take you there safe."

I had already divided it into two separate bags, both of which were stowed beneath my bed. I grabbed them, gave the smaller to Clarissa, who had let Mr. Patley into the kitchen and had summoned me.

"Be careful," said she. "Don't do battle for it, Jeremy, for when all is said and done, 'tis only money."

With that caution, she opened the door and sent us on our way. Yet, thinking ahead, I remembered that I, in a sense, did yet owe Mr. Deuteronomy a pistol — the one which I had taken from Katy Tiddle. And so I did stop off for it and got no argument in the matter from Mr. Baker.

"You brought it in," said he, "so it's yours to take back."

"Good," said I. "I'll not be bringing it again."

"As you wish. Just remember that it's loaded."

And so at last we headed out, Mr. Patley and I, moving swiftly through the city streets. Though it was not late, there were not many about. We kept our silence through most of the journey, and only toward the end did I speak up.

"Mr. Patley, when you saw Deuteronomy, did you tell him about his sister, Alice?"

"I did, yes, Jeremy."

"Well, thank goodness. I would not want that burden upon me."

"Indeed, I can understand that. But, truth to tell, lad, he took it right well. Almost too well, it seemed to me, like it really didn't matter to him much at all. He's a strange sort, ain't he? She was his sister, after all."

I had no response handy for that, and so I simply held my tongue. Ahead of us were the lights of the Haymarket. There seemed always to be a crowd thereabouts, as indeed there was that evening. They were women, mostly, prostitutes and the like, though a few seemed to be moving swiftly through the crowd as if on their way to some destination. To what that might be I had no notion.

We went direct to the coffee house, which was there on the far side of the square. Still open it was. And I realized, to my surprise, that often as I had been there, I had never been there after dark.

"Ever been up there?" Mr. Patley asked.

"To Deuteronomy's rooms? No, I never have. Do you see the way up?"

Both of us studied the façade of the building, but try as we might, we saw no way up—until we ventured down the left side and discovered a sort of side entrance to the upper floor.

"Well, I guess that's it," said Patley. "Go on up there, rap upon the door, and if he comes to open it, give me a wave."

I did it just so. And when Mr. Deuteronomy appeared, I gave to Mr. Patley, at the foot of the stairs, a great wave. He called his farewell to me and departed.

"Your partner down there?" Deuteronomy asked.

"He was. He thought it would be a bit safer for me, considering what I was carrying, if he were along."

Having said that, I passed to him the cloth bag, heavy with banknotes which I had been guarding since the day before. Then did I make a movement toward the stairs.

"Wait," said he. "Come inside. I've someone wants to talk with you."

Curious, I followed him down the hall to the second door, the one toward the rear. He opened it and waved me inside. There I found Mr. Bennett awaiting me. I had not seen him since those early-morning exercise sessions wherein Deuteronomy put Pegasus through his paces. Bennett, the trainer, would observe and make a few suggestions and would answer the questions I put to him. And though he always seemed guarded and somewhat ill at ease, I liked the man well enough. (Strange it was to perceive how long ago and far away all this did seem to me at that moment.)

"Mr. Bennett," said I politely, "how happy I am to greet you in London. I hope that you had a good journey here from Newmarket."

He seemed even more ill at ease than I remembered. His eyes shifted to Deuteronomy and then back to me two or three times in as many seconds. He rose and touched hands with me—one could hardly call it more than that—and returned quickly to his chair. Tense and strained, he wanted little to do with such amenities.

"You work for Sir John Fielding, don't you? At the Bow Street Court?"

"Why, yes I do."

"Well," said he, "I've got a confession to make. Only it ain't just mine, not even mostly mine, as you'll see. But I know the facts, 'cause I was involved in it, so I'm the only one can tell it. Besides, Deuteronomy here says I got to."

I settled into a chair nearby, and Mr. Deuteronomy sat down in another. We prepared to listen to his tale. I know not how many times he had heard it, but I, hearing it for the first time, sat quite transfixed by what he told. This is what I heard:

"Now I'm a fairly simple man, truth be told," he began. "I come here from the country—out of Wiltshire, as it was. I didn't know much, but I knew horses. Otherwise I'd never have got to work at Lord Lamford's, or maybe just as a porter, or whatever. It was mainly Deuteronomy Plummer here, who got me the job. He knew he needed help managing this string of horses, and most of those sent out from the big house didn't know a thing about them and were frightened of them.

"So we worked on them together for over a year. He'd ride the horses each Sunday in races round London and exercise them and do whatever need be done. The stable boys and me fed them, kept them well and happy. And if that had been all there was to the job, we'd have been just as happy as any could be. But we had Lord Lamford to contend with, too. First, there was his 'suggestions,' as he called them, which were really orders, and they could come any time of the day or night. Right away it was drop anything you might happen to be tending to and do whatever little thing he might happen to want you to do. That dueling pistol I took into Griffin's in London was a good example. We were doing trials, Mr. Deuteronomy and I, out in the little course we'd set up in the west pasture, preparing Pegasus for racing. Anyway, Lord Lamford had to have that pistol fixed, no matter what, and it couldn't wait. He knew I didn't know my way round London, but he sent me out with it."

I had listened in silence up to that moment, but when he mentioned the pistol I recalled that I had one of the two in question in my pocket at that very moment. I fetched it forth and handed it over to him, taking care to caution that it was loaded. He laid it down carefully upon a small table next to his chair.

"I guess you know what happened to this one, the one that didn't need no work done on it. I loaned it to Katy Tiddle, and there it sat with her. Might never have got it back, if she hadn't got herself murdered.

"But anyway, that wasn't the worst of it with Lord Lamford. The worst was his personal habits, his 'amusements,' as he called them. There never was a Lady Lamford, but I don't know that he would have been any different if there had been a wife, because in my opinion the man wasn't right in his head. Maybe one of those mad doctors they got at Bedlam could have done something with him—but prob'ly not."

"Tell me about his 'amusements,'" said I to him.

At that, he sighed. "Well, I might as well get to it, for that's what this is all about. I'd been there near a year when I started to hear rumors and little hints from the big-house staff about him—how he liked them young and didn't care how much he had to pay, and so on. But I didn't really understand what they meant by young until one day this little girl—couldn't have been more than five or six—must've escaped from where they kept her locked up and come down to see the 'horsies.' I could tell by the way she talked that she was from London. Then this old bat, the housekeeper, she comes down and slaps her good and proper and tells her that Lord Lamford is going to be very unhappy with her. And so on. She told her that if she ever did this again, she couldn't be his queen anymore. I could never quite figure out what he did when he was through with them. There must have been—oh, I don't know how many in the time I was there. The truth is, I didn't want to know. I looked the other way.

"But Lord Lamford must have had some idea how I felt about him. Maybe I was a little careless and spoke out in front of one of them in the big house, and the word was passed on. Or maybe I wore the wrong sort of expression too often when I looked upon him, for truth to tell, the man disgusted me something horrible.

"Anyway, he seemed determined to bring me into it, and he did it the worst way he could—by making me part of his crime from first to last. About a month ago he come out from the house at the end of the day just to tell me he had a request of me—a 'request' was even stronger than a 'suggestion.' It meant, if you didn't do it, and do it right, you might as well just leave and not come back. He told me to ride to Bermondsey and go halfway cross London Bridge. There I'd meet a fella named Hogg who had something for me to bring back to the big house. That's how he put it.

"Well, I did just like he said, and there at the midpoint in London Bridge, I come across the man named Hogg sheltering against the cold and holding on to the hand of a little girl. I thought she was about five or six, but later on I found out she was all of eight years."

"She always was small for her age," put in Mr. Deuteronomy, thus confirming what I had suspected.

Bennett nodded. "That's right, Deuteronomy," said he. "Just like I told you, it was Maggie, your niece." Then did he return to his tale: "This fella didn't say more than four or five words, just 'Here's what you came for.' Then he lifted her up to me, and I held her close against the cold, 'cause by now 'twas after dark, and I feared she might catch a chill. She was quite the charmer, she was. She said she'd never been up top a horse before. And I told her I took care of the horses, and she wanted to know all about that, and so that was just about all we talked about all the way back to the big house."

At this point, Mr. Bennett stopped. He breathed deeply a time or two, as if to gain control of himself, then did he set his jaw before continuing. "The next part," said he, "is hard to tell." Yet he managed, by stopping from time to time, wiping his tears before they became a problem, and clearing his throat as necessary.

"So we got there to the big house," he resumed. "I carried her to the door, and the housekeeper came and took her from me. I heard no more of her or from her for quite some time, two weeks at least. But then at night I began to hear weeping; just the sort of tears to break you heart. Then there was nothing more until, toward the end, there was some screaming. Deuteronomy here didn't hear none of it because it was always at night that the tears and the screams came, and by that time he was back here in the Haymarket. There was this one night it got terrible bad, just before Easter. But then it stopped, and somehow or other that seemed even worse.

"They sent somebody down for me, and right at the door I was met by the housekeeper, and she takes me upstairs. She unlocks the door, and she takes me inside what seemed like a child's room, a— what is it they call it? —a nursery. There was toys, dolls and such, all over it. The bed didn't seem to have nobody in it, just blankets and a pillow. Only then, the housekeeper lifted up the pillow, and there was Maggie, the little girl I picked up on London Bridge. Dead. 'Who done this?' I asked the housekeeper. And she gave me a kind of smirk, and she says, 'Who do you think?' She took a blanket and wrapped the body in it, even covered her face up. Then she presents it to me. 'Here,' says she. 'Lord Lamford wants you to dispose of this.' I'd no choice but to take it from her. I went back to the stable, saddled up a horse, and took the trail to the river. There's a place upriver with a shallow bank. I threw Maggie's body into the Thames right there, and kept the blanket, as I was told to do."

Having said his piece, Mr. Bennett halted. He pulled from his pocket a kerchief and blew his nose loudly upon it.

"When we came up with that ticket for the pistol at Griffin's," said Deuteronomy to me, "I was naturally pretty curious, because I could remember the very day that Bennett was sent off with it. As he said, we were just starting to train Pegasus for racing."

"Did you confront him with it immediately?"

"No, I started to work on him, though. It wasn't till the journey back from Newmarket that he started to see things my way. I told him to talk to you—tell you the story—then you could sort of prepare the way for him with Sir John."

"I ask him, could I trust you, and he said he'd trusted you with all his winnings," said Mr. Bennett to me. "I don't know what laws I've broken, but I know I must have broken some, but what I did in getting rid of the body ain't nothing compared to what Lord Lamford did in killing that child. But what I done has been on my conscience something terrible."

"When did you begin to suppose that the little girl you picked up on London Bridge was Mr. Deuteronomy's niece?" I asked.

"Well, he told the tale of Maggie disappearing and then his sister going off somewhere, and I began to wonder because the times matched up pretty fair. And then Deuteronomy showed me the dueling pistol I'd left off for repair and said the woman who had the mate to it—Katy Tiddle—lived in a room next to his sister and Maggie. But now Sir John Fielding had it and considered it property to do with the investigation of Katy's murder." Then he wailed: "Oh, how did I ever manage to get in with that drunken whore?"

Bennett was so disturbed by the rhetorical challenge he had offered himself that I thought it likely that he might break into tears once again. Though he did not, I thought it wise to get him to Sir John immediately.

"I fear your confession will be useless unless you make it direct to Sir John. Why not come with me now? He would, I'm sure, listen to you, no matter what the hour."

"Alas, I cannot. I think it likely that I might not return from such a trip. If I'm to go to Newgate, I shall need all my money to bribe the guards. I'll go back and gather together what I can and return on the morrow soon as ever I can."

"Must we do it so?" I asked. "I can virtually guaranty that you would not be sent to Newgate, but rather to the Fleet." I saw that made little impression upon him. I could not persuade him to go with me to Bow Street, and so I did urge him to come in the morning, if at all possible, all to no avail. He repeated that he would come soon as he could. He stood, bade me goodbye, and, pocketing the pistol, made for the door. Deuteronomy bounced out of his chair and accompanied Bennett to the door. There they exchanged a few words and Bennett left.

"Well, what did you think of that?" Mr. Deuteronomy asked me.

"Why, I believed him. Did you not?"

"I've known him for two years, and I've yet to hear a lie pass his lips."

"When did you hear this from him?"

" 'Course I suspected ever since I saw that pistol, but it was just last night on the drive back from Newmarket that he told me all. He's been carrying a terrible burden for over a month."

"I can see that," said I. "He seems a man haunted by guilt."

And so did I return to Bow Street, quite bursting to tell Sir John of what I had just heard from Bennett. Yet upon my arrival, I discovered that it was far later than I had supposed. Past midnight it was, and not a soul awake in our upper floors of the court. I had not heart to wake anyone to tell them, though, I confess, the thought did cross my mind.

Next morning, I was up at my usual early hour. I set the fire and lit it and waited a bit impatiently for Sir John to appear. He arrived last of all. As he sat down, I told him eagerly that last night I had heard news that would materially affect the prosecution of the Maggie Plummer case. He took that in his stride and suggested we talk about it just as soon as he had given adequate attention to his breakfast. He was not to be hurried. When at last he had finished, I sought to persuade him to go upstairs to his study that we might talk freely and without interruption. (That remark earned me a look of great annoyance from Clarissa.) Yet he thought it proper to hold our talk in his chambers. There we should find peace and quiet aplenty, said he, and be on hand should Mr. Marsden, his clerk, require anything of him. You will not be astonished, reader, to learn that we headed directly to Sir John's chambers.

I had barely begun to relate Mr. Bennett's speech when a series of familiar sounds announced the arrival of William Murray, Earl of Mansfield, the Lord Chief Justice. First was there the slamming of the door to Bow Street, which was followed by the sound of Lord Mansfield's heels clicking along the corridor, and then, last of all, Mr. Marsden's vain attempt to persuade the visitor to allow the clerk to announce him to Sir John. Lord Mansfield would have none of it, of course, for in the next instant, he fair exploded through the door and into the magistrate's chambers.

We awaited him upon our feet: I, respectfully ready to surrender my chair to him, and Sir John already offering his hand. Lord

Mansfield accepted Sir John's hand and gave it a wiggle, but he declined my offer of a chair. He would remain standing (so, naturally, Sir John and I had also to remain upon our feet).

"This won't take long," said he.

"What then?" said Sir John. "How may we serve you m'lord?" There was an unmistakable touch of irony in that. Lord Mansfield ignored it.

"I have stopped here on my way to Old Bailey to ask why in the world you did not return an indictment against that woman, Mother Jeffers? She is, as I understand it, naught but a madam, a keeper of bawds in a house out in Clerkenwell. Is this correct?"

"Oh, no doubt," said Sir John. "She did not deny that in so many words to me."

"Then why did you not indict her?"

"Because, Lord Mansfield, that was not the complaint against her."

"Well, what was the complaint?"

"I suppose that 'unlawful imprisonment' would have covered it."

"Then why did you not charge her with it and pass her on to me?"

"Because, Lord Mansfield, I did not believe the complainant. She is a girl of no more than fifteen or sixteen, pregnant, two-faced, and caught in a number of lies in the course of a tour through that bawdy house in Clerkenwell. In fact, there is some doubt as to whether she had ever been through that place before her visit yesterday."

"You seem terribly certain, Sir John."

"Well, I am not, for I give no greater credence to Mrs. Jeffers than I do to Elizabeth Hooker. The old woman claims never to have seen the girl before. Well, I do not believe her. There is something — a great deal, perhaps — that she has held back. In such a circumstance, how could I bind over anyone for trial? No indeed, the only proper course to follow is to delay, allow things to cool off a bit, and investigate further."

"Well and good," said Lord Mansfield, "and in theory I agree with you. Nevertheless, you know as well as I that I must consider other factors besides the law — not above the law, simply along with it. Among those factors is public opinion. I have heard from a few individuals on this matter of Mistress Hooker already. If I were to allow you to follow the course you propose — and mind you, sir, in many ways I think it the best one—I have good reason to believe that I would hear from many more.

"Therefore," he continued, all but shaking a finger in the air, "I have decided to relieve you of responsibility in this matter and present it to Mr. Saunders Welch. It has been pointed out to me that he, as magistrate for outer London, has some claim upon the case anyway, for the crime, if crime it be, was committed in Clerkenwell. You were called in, as I understand, because of some previous acquaintance of one of your staff with the girl in question. Is that correct?"

"More or less."

"Then you can see the sense of this. I shall represent it so."

"Not on my account, I hope."

"Of course not. And let me assure you, Mr. Welch has made no overtures to me in this, nor has he made any sort of claim upon the case. I have, in fact, not spoken with him on this at all."

"Well, then," said Sir John, "I am relieved of a burden."

"Good. Do think of it so."

Then, having spoken thus, the Lord Chief Justice said his goodbye to Sir John, and departed—click, click, clicking away down the hall, leaving as he had come.

"Close the door, Jeremy."

I did as Sir John said and we resumed the chairs we had held till the coming of Lord Mansfield.

"So," said he to me, "what thought you of that?"

"I thought it a terrible mistake—on Lord Mansfield's part, of course. But at least Saunders Welch did not go behind your back to solicit the case."

"Oh? You think not? Well . . ." He shrugged. "Perhaps it was just as the Chief Justice said, though if Welch got wind of this, he'd be off in pursuit of it like a hound. That's my view of it."

"Why do you say that, sir?"

"I say it because I believe it to be so. And why not? I've been hearing for about a year that he secretly covets a seat in Parliament and would run in a trice if ever a suitable seat came open. That man is a political animal, no doubt of it. He is hot after whatever will bring him notice."

"But is it not so with all men?"

At that he pulled a sour face. "Not so with me. Comical, when you think of it, eh? To have a case taken away because you insist on following proper legal procedure."

There he let it rest. The visit of the Lord Chief Justice had so sullied the atmosphere that I thought that the present moment might be an even more propitious time to deliver to Sir John the news of my previous evening's conversation with Mr. Bennett. He might then have something to cheer him.

And so I told the magistrate just what I had heard from Bennett, and though I made no mention of the reason that brought me to Mr. Deuteronomy's quarters for my meeting with Bennett, my report to Sir John was as full as otherwise could be. I told him of Bennett's tears, his self-acknowledged guilt in the matter, and his plain-spoken accusation of Lord Lamford in the death of little Maggie Plummer.

As for Sir John, he listened even at the beginning more carefully than I had known him to do before. By the time I told him of Bennett's summons to the "big house," he did hang upon my every word. To the extent that it was possible, I quoted Bennett exact. Yet I tried also to give some sense of my own reaction to the words of the man. Sir John was quite overcome.

"Ah," said he, "if only these poor, ruined eyes of mine permitted to weep, I would drown us both in a river of tears. What a sad, sad story you've told me." He paused briefly. "And what an evil sort is this Lord Lamford! I have never met the man, have you?"

"Yes," said I, "and I can honestly say that I detested him right from the start."

"All England will detest him when he is brought to trial. He will be hated as none other before him, I should hope." The thought of it seemed to give him pleasure. "But tell me again," said he, "why was it he declined to return with you here to Bow Street? I did not at first understand."

"'Twas because he feared that he shared some part of the blame and would surely be sentenced to a term in Newgate."

"Considering that he had disposed of the little girl's body, he was right in that."

"I tried to persuade him, but it was useless. He said that if he were to go to prison, he would need all the money he had to bribe the guards."

"Pathetic, is it not, that a man must prepare for a term in prison by gathering together all the ready cash he has that he may make his situation tolerable?"

"Indeed so," said I. " 'Tis said that they have prices set for all 'courtesies.' For instance, removing manacles and chains, a single shilling, et cetera."

"Disgraceful," said he. "I fear that one day there will be a great retribution to be paid. When did this fellow Bennett say that he was coming by?"

"He didn't say, actually. Though I encouraged him to name a time, he would not. I asked him to come in the morning, yet he would not even allow himself to be committed to that. I believe he feels that he must sneak away, and Lord Lamford keeps him rather tightly under his thumb."

"Then I shall keep you close here at Bow Street through the day. Bring him to me soon as ever he appears."

He was as good as his word. During that morning and most of the afternoon, we two kept busy answering letters and filing reports. It is the sort of work which collects, piles up, and ultimately may bury us completely if we do not, from time to time, dedicate a single day to disposing of it. This was that day.

Mr. Marsden was present on that day, no better but no worse than he had been on most other days that month. And so, in addition to dictating, Sir John conducted his usual court session at noon. Because there were no serious cases to be tried (that is to say, none to pass on to the Felony Court at Old Bailey), it was a fairly short session. And afterward, Sir John and I attacked what remained to be done to that now-dwindling pile of letters.

Then, at some point—let us say, when there were but two or three letters more to be answered—Sir John heaved a great sigh and asked how many more there were till we were done.

"Not many," said I, "a few, no more."

"Well, let us answer them, and then I would have you visit that fellow with the biblical name—what is it?"

"Deuteronomy," I suggested.

"Yes, of course, Mr. Deuteronomy Plummer. I suggest you visit him and ask if anything has gone amiss with your friend Mr. Bennett. I must admit that I have a rather bad feeling about him."

"Something tangible?"

"No, I wish it were, but it's simply an uneasiness I have."

And that was the way we managed it. Having done all that could be done that day, I parted from him, promising to return for dinner by seven o'clock at the very latest.

"No matter what, I want you back by then. Is that understood?" And that is all he would say about it.

What, I wondered, could be so terribly important that I should be told so sternly to be back at seven for dinner? Were we to have some special guest? Was something secret planned? Such questions as these troubled me all the way to Haymarket—and would today, as well, if I were to find myself in a similar situation, for I am one of those who dislikes surprises. Perhaps this is because I, more than most, had suffered at life's vagaries. At bottom, I suppose, I was even then a rather settled sort.

Having arrived in Haymarket, I went direct to the coffee house and jog-trotted up the stairs to the upper floor. I banged mightily upon the door and waited. There was no response. Twice more I repeated this, with the same result. I put my ear to the door but heard nothing. Well, there was still much time before it would be seven, and so I took myself down the stairs to the coffee house, and there did I spend the better part of an hour, reading and sipping that most hearty of blends. It did move me to further action and sent me up to the top of the stairs once again to knock upon the door. Yet again and again did I knock, to no avail. But then a sudden thought came to me. I had in my pocket a pad of paper, which I had lately taken to carrying about, as well as a pencil. Putting the two to use, I wrote out a note to Mr. Deuteronomy. In it, I said that we had waited for Mr. Bennett at Bow Street, and then I had come to Haymarket in search of Mr. Deuteronomy. Though I had waited, I had missed him, too. "I shall come early tomorrow to discover what has happened," I wrote. "Sir John is worried, and I, as well."

Having written that, I felt that I had done all I could under these awkward circumstances. It was now certainly time to return to Bow Street. I folded the note and slipped it under the door so that it was just visible from the outside. I saw that the street lamps were now lit, and only a bit of light could be seen in the west. It was now well past six and time to hurry home.

Coming in as I did, I spied Mr. Donnelly—doctor, surgeon, medical examiner for Westminster, and friend to us all. He was just entering Sir John's chambers at the end of the hall, and that (I told myself) must mean that there is to be some special guest of honor. He was always present at such occasions, lending his own wit and good humor to the dinner conversation. Upon entering the kitchen, I saw that Clarissa, rather than Molly, was serving as cook this evening. That gave me a bit of a surprise, for though she had often cooked dinner before, and had proven her worth again and again, she had never done so for one of Sir John's guest-of-honor affairs. I wondered where Molly was and what she was about. Clarissa looked up at me and smiled.

"Ah, it's you, Jeremy. Quickly with you now, get upstairs and change into your best. This is a grand occasion."

"But what—*What* is the occasion?"

"Oh, I'm sure you can guess. Go, go, go! Out of the kitchen, if you please."

Thus was I driven out and up the stairs where I did hastily change into my better suit of clothes (I had but two)—really quite ordinary-looking; yet the shirt, recently washed and crisply clean, seemed to work a sort of magic upon the attendant parts. I was indeed ready to present myself to whoever was to be the guest of honor.

When I descended into the kitchen, I did so with as much grace and dignity as I could muster. Therefore, I was somewhat taken aback when, no sooner had I made my appearance than I was given a great platter containing ribs of beef by Clarissa and told to bring them to the dining-room table.

"You must carve them, as well," she did call after me.

Was this why I had dressed myself so handsomely? Was I to be a mere server? Yet Clarissa, who was herself excellently decked out in her finest, and prettier than I had ever before seen her, followed me closely with the Yorkshire pudding. The sauce, as she pointed out, was already on the table.

But where was the guest of honor? As I carved the lovely beef, I kept throwing anxious glances at the door, wondering what personage might come through it and excite us one and all. Then, however, did I note that there were but six places set at the table. Where would he sit?

Finally, as I sat down beside Clarissa, it came to me at last that there would be no others at the table, and that the guests of honor were already with us, sitting across from us, touching fingers upon the table, beaming smiles, each at the other. Mr. Gabriel Donnelly and the widow Molly Sarton were about to announce their engagement. Yet, it seemed, they would have to wait a bit.

Sir John called down to his lady: "Kate, my dear, what is proper form here? Do we toast them before or after we eat? I know how it's *usually* done, but are there special rules for this special occasion?"

"None that I know of, Jack. Do it as you like."

"Well then, I always think that toasts are best drunk on a full belly, and so I say to you all, fill your bellies!"

There was laughter round the table at that as we fell to the dinner—and what a dinner it was! Could this truly have been cooked by Clarissa? Though of course it could, for had I not always said that she had only to put that considerable mind of hers to cooking and she would soon be the best cook in all of England? Perhaps she was not yet quite so good as all that. Nevertheless, as we cut into our meat, and the juice ran forth, we must each have had the thought that we had never eaten better before. Thus the table fell silent as all continued to eat, and, of all compliments paid to a cook, that sort of silence is the most profound.

There were seconds asked for and quickly consumed. Clarissa's Yorkshire pudding was near as much in demand as the roast of beef. Many is the trip I made round the table with bottles of claret in hand. It was quite the finest and most festive meal we had ever eaten. Our bellies were full. It was now time for toasts to be offered. I made sure that all glasses were filled. Sir John rose and raised his glass.

"I shall not make this a long oration, though the Good Lord knows that I could. There is so much to tell of Gabriel Donnelly that I'm quite sure that I could fill the rest of the evening with it. It was in 1768 that we met, and immediately we did, we found a basis for friendship, and it was as a friend that I rejoiced when, but a year ago, he came to me and declared his interest in Molly Sarton, who had come to us from her home in Deal where she had been recently widowed. She agreed to fill in for us as cook for a time — we never thought for a moment that we could hold on long to one as talented and experienced as she. In any case, her time with us has not been wasted, for here in Bow Street she met Mr. Donnelly, and that has led to a most favorable situation for both. They are here to announce their engagement, and we are here to celebrate it."

Then did we raise our glasses and, standing, drink a toast to the two of them. As we resumed our seats, Mr. Donnelly remained upon his feet and, looking slowly round the table at each of us, he smiled and began his own brief oration.

"I bless the day that I met Sir John Fielding, and I have any number of good reasons for doing so. First of all, I met in him one of the brightest and deepest minds in London. And through him I met the second-brightest and second-deepest mind in London — " He paused, and then, with a grand gesture — "Clarissa Roundtree!"

The entire table exploded in laughter at that — and I louder and longer than all the rest. I had, just prior, fixed a rather complacent look upon my face, one I thought suitable for accepting a grand compliment. It must indeed have been comical to see my face drop so quickly.

"And oh yes," continued Mr. Donnelly, "it was by my friendship with Sir John that I met my lovely wife-to-be, Molly. I was not along on that fateful trip to Deal. I have often wished that I had been, for I would likely have met Albert Sarton, a man whose measure I hope to live up to. Marriage, any marriage, is a journey into the unknown. Partners often need all the help they can get. Yet from all that I have heard from Molly about Mr. Sarton, I think we may well have him as our guide and helper in the years to come. And so, all, I propose a toast. Ladies and gentlemen, to the memory of Albert Sarton."

There was, round the table, a chorus of "Hear, hear"s. We drank, and Mr. Donnelly turned to Molly before seating himself.

"Will you have something to say?" he asked.

"I will," said she, "but I shall make it short."

"As long as you like, my dear."

"In our time it does not often happen to a woman that she falls in love. They write poems about it and romances—and I'm sure you'll add to the number, Clarissa. But still, it does not happen often, as in our hearts we all know. Yet I, of all women, have been doubly blessed, for I thought my world had ended when Albert died, but no, God has given me a second love, as strong or stronger than the first. I can only thank God and his blessed angel, Gabriel. And God bless you all—and thank you a hundred times over. I offer a toast to you all, my family."

We drank the toast, such as it was, seated ourselves once again, and then, of a sudden, was the table all abuzz with their plans. It was a complicated matter for two Catholics to marry in a Protestant country—so complicated, indeed, that they had decided to do all that needed to be done in Ireland: the bride-to-be would meet his family; banns would be posted; and they would at last be married. The entire process would take some weeks, of course, but they felt they had little choice in the matter. They would leave for Dublin in two days' time.

On and on we talked, for it was a joyous occasion. Sir John sent me off to the kitchen for a bottle of the French brandy. He and Mr. Donnelly each had a taste of it; yet I, knowing that I would be out early in search of Mr. Deuteronomy, declined respectfully. I explained to Sir John.

"You were unable to see him?"

"Yes sir, I waited for over an hour without result, and then left him a note promising to be back very early in the morning."

"No one could have done more," said Sir John. "Wait for him all day, if need be. And don't forget, you're still my deputy in this matter. Arm yourself before you go."

"Yes sir," said I.

"What, pray tell, is this about?" Mr. Donnelly inquired.

"A matter which Jeremy will clear up in no time. I have every confidence in him."

ELEVEN

*In which it is fate
that dispenses
final justice*

Mr. Deuteronomy had kept silent ever since we had left Bermond-sey, utterly exhausted by his effort to tell all. In truth, the nature of what it was he had to tell must also have weighed heavily upon him.

He had been awake and waiting for me when I tramped up the stairs to the floor above the Haymarket Coffee House. Nor had I arrived late: I was certain, in fact, that I should have to waken him, for it was just a bit past five-thirty when I made myself known. He opened the door so swiftly when I did that it seemed to me that he must have been holding the handle when my knock came.

"Right on time," said he to me.

"If not early."

"Well, let's not argue about it. Come along with me to the stable. I've much to tell you."

But he would not be telling it immediately. He led me round the corner to Burnaby's in Market Street, and there he ordered up a wagon and a team of two.

"What will we be needing the wagon for?" I asked.

"You'll find out soon as we get under way."

I contented myself with that, though it was not much of an answer, for in truth the night ostler, a young lad no older than I, worked so swiftly that it was but a few minutes till all was ready. We were soon moving right along in a westerly direction, following the river. It was not yet six. There were few hackneys to be seen along the way, nor were there many dray wagons. It was simply too early. The hooves of the horses echoed hollowly through the streets of the dark city. I waited for Mr. Deuteronomy to begin. It was not long before he did.

"Most of this I got from the stable boys, so I can't vouch for it exactly, but when I got there yesterday morning, it was all just about as they said, so I'm inclined to believe them, in all the details."

"About what?" I was growing impatient with him.

"I'd appreciate it if you'd let me tell it my way."

"All right, as you will then."

"Anyway," said Deuteronomy, "it was late, getting on toward midnight, when Bennett came back from my place. It shouldn't have taken him that long, so it's plain he stopped off somewhere between here and there, most likely for a little Dutch courage, if I know my man Bennett.

"Now, you know how the stable and the sleeping quarters are laid out, the one is attached to the other, so there's really only a wall between them. So what the stable boys heard through that wall was Bennett coming home. He made a good deal of noise, the way he always does when he's had too much to drink, and this time he was heard by Lord Lamford, who came out to talk to him.

"This was unusual, very unusual. The master seldom bothered himself with what went on in the stable, and never, so far as I know, with what went on there late at night. And so, it seems to me that he must have been up and waiting on Bennett. He must have had something special to talk to him about. And I think I know what it was."

"And what was that?" I asked.

"I'll tell you later."

"Tell me now."

"Oh, all right, Lord Lamford wants to have his picture painted with Pegasus."

I was properly puzzled by this. "And Bennett paints pictures?" That seemed unlikely.

"No, 'course not! He—" Mr. Deuteronomy fumed a bit as he sought the right words. "Let me come back to it. It makes more sense that way."

I sighed. "Do it your way." The man was quite impossible.

"As I was saying—and it don't matter much what brought Lamford down to the stable—the point is, he came down, and right away the two of them started arguing. Not like he *came* to argue, understand, but they fell to it just minutes after he arrived. All this is according to the two stable boys who got wakened by it all."

"What were the two of them—Lord Lamford and Bennett—arguing about?" I asked.

"The stable boys said they couldn't tell. It was just the sound of their angry voices till they heard their master yell loud and plain at Bennett, 'You dare to judge me?' And it couldn't have been much later that they heard the shot."

"The shot?"

"That's what I said, ain't it?" He looked at me fiercely.

"You mean he . . ." Confused, I began again. "Who was it was shot?"

"Bennett," said he. "Shot dead, right through the head. But that ain't the question."

"What *is* the question?"

"The question is, who pulled the trigger? The pistol—which was the same one you gave to him night before last—was the weapon that killed him. 'Twas found in his hand. Lord Lamford admits to being there, and he says the two of them was arguing about Pegasus—whether 'twould be possible for Lamford to sit astride Pegasus to have his picture painted."

"Why would he want to do that?"

"Oh, he's got some mad notion that he should be painted with his proudest possession, which is what Pegasus is now that he won the King's Plate in Newmarket."

"But how did that lead to Bennett taking his life?"

"Lord Lamford's pretty vague on that, but the damndest thing is, he can be just as vague as he wants to be because nobody actually saw him shoot Bennett. And besides, that magistrate they got out here would sooner die than disagree with Lamford."

"We're headed so far out from London?"

He nodded. "So far indeed."

"And the local magistrate calls it suicide?"

"That he does."

"Well, didn't the stable boys tell him about that shout, 'You dare to judge me?'"

"Yes, I thought I had to say something about that myself," said Deuteronomy. "But the magistrate wouldn't hear of it. You know what he said? 'The bullet was in his head, and the pistol was in his hand. What could be simpler?'"

"And that was where it ended?" I asked.

"No, not really. I pushed a little more, and I got from him Lord Lamford's account of the so-called suicide. He said that according to him, Bennett got nastier and more personal, and that was when Lamford said, 'Who are you to judge me?' Bennett backed away from him then, and pulled out the pistol. He pointed it as if he meant to kill Lamford with it. Then, as if changing his mind of a sudden, he put the barrel of the gun to his temple and pulled the trigger. When I asked the magistrate if he accepted that, he looked at me as if I were a troublesome fellow and said to me that I seemed to be implying that there was some irregularity involving Lord Lamford. 'Is that your game?' he asked. 'The very idea!'"

Somewhat bewildered by all that I had heard, I spent some minutes trying to master it, looking at it this way and that, questioning what I had earlier assumed to be so. All this as the horses plodded along. Thus was I occupied as we crossed London Bridge and headed off down Tooley Street into Bermondsey. We both kept silent for a long while. At last, Mr. Deuteronomy spoke up.

"'Course you and I know," said he, "that it wasn't that way at all. We heard what poor old Bennett had to say about his master. The way I see it, he must have handed over the pistol to Lord Lamford. Then, somehow or other, with all that Dutch courage in him, he must have got carried away and accused him of all that he told you about night before last."

"Yes," said I, "that's the way it seems. How much farther is this farm of Lord Lamford's, anyway?"

"It's still a piece on from here—around Deptford it is."

"Well, I'm sorry to tell you this, but I may not be able to do much more than shake my head and go tsk-tsk-tsk when we get there."

"Well, how's that happen? Ain't you a Bow Street Runner? You do investigating and the like, don't you?"

"I'm Sir John's assistant and a deputized constable, but Sir John's power as magistrate only goes so far."

"What do you mean by that?"

"I mean, each magistrate has his own jurisdiction."

"What's that mean?"

"Each magistrate has his own territory. For instance, Sir John just had a case taken away from him because the crime in question was committed outside his jurisdiction, his territory, which is the City of London and the City of Westminster."

"You mean if you and me went before him, and we both swore as to the story we heard from poor old Bennett, Lamford couldn't be tried on the basis of that?"

"No, probably not."

"Why?"

"Why? Well . . . because it would be merely hearsay evidence. That's hearsay, as in we heard him say it, but he didn't live to say it himself."

"Well, what's wrong with that, just so long as we swear to it and tell the truth?"

"You've just put your finger upon it," said I, "for *we* would tell the truth, but another might swear the same oath and tell nothing but lies."

"Like Lord Lamford."

"Exactly."

"Why, that ain't fair, is it? I thought the law was supposed to be fair."

"Usually it is fair, but the law is made by man, and all that's made by man can be improved upon."

Deuteronomy chewed upon that for a bit. Then did his eyes narrow as he declared: "Well, by God, I intend to improve on it some."

I didn't ask Deuteronomy Plummer how he might go about that. I really didn't want to know.

By the time we reached the horse farm, I had learned from him that since Lord Lamford knew my face, I was to keep as far away as I was able. It was just as well he didn't see me at all, said Deuteronomy. Therefore, I was to remain in the barn to interrogate the two stable boys and stay inside just as long as Lamford was about.

When I protested that I would not willingly hang about in a barn eight hours or more, Mr. Deuteronomy assured me that there would be no such lengthy wait ahead for me.

"I cannot suppose," said he, "that Lord Lamford will be with us for more than a couple of hours."

"But he may well see me from a distance. Are you prepared to account for my presence, should he ask?"

"Oh, that's all taken care of," he assured me. "I told him you were Bennett's brother and had come to claim the body and cart it away."

Thus was it set, and all was ready for me as we entered by the dirt track which led off the main road. It had taken a good hour to get there, yet it was still quite early, owing to our departure time. The place was quite as I had expected, though I will say that Bennett's description of the manse as the "big house" did it little justice. Oh, it was indeed big, yet it was also comparatively new and far more stylish in design and execution than one would expect so far out in the country. As for the rest of it — the outbuildings, et cetera — they were no better and no worse than one might happen to see anywhere in the realm. The stable was not ramshackled, nor did it lean to any extent. Still, the fact that under its broad roof were housed the stable boys and, until night before last, Bennett as well, made for a larger structure than one might have looked for here. There were, after all, only six horses a-gamboling in the meadow.

Mr. Deuteronomy caught me studying them at a distance, shielding my eyes from the morning sun.

"Don't look for Pegasus out there on the green. Lord Lamford decreed that he must wait in the stable till Lamford has arrived with the painter fellow."

"What's his name?"

"Who? The painter?" Deuteronomy frowned in his effort to remember. "Reynolds, I think — something-something Reynolds."

"Sir Joshua?"

"That's it!" said he, brightening. "Why? Do you know him?"

"I met with him once. I don't recall that I was introduced to him, though. He's terribly good, you know."

"He better be, for what he's charging. Two hundred guineas to paint a picture. Could you suppose such a thing?"

"That's fifty guineas more than he was set to charge Sir John."

"Lord Lamford told me to help him set up. What's that mean, exactly?"

"Oh, I don't know, just do as you're told."

He smiled rather bitterly at that. "I've got pretty good at that. Had a lot of experience doing what I'm told." Then, more to himself than to me: "Not for long, though."

As Mr. Deuteronomy had warned me beforehand, the two stable boys had little more to say than what they had already said to the local magistrate. They had been wakened by angry voices the other side of the wall. About the only words they understood for certain had been, they agreed, spoken by Lord Lamford: "You dare to judge me?"

Quite frankly, I was surprised that the two had gone that far, for their master had evidently had some difficulty explaining to the local magistrate just on what matter it was Mr. Bennett had dared to judge him. After he had tried twice ("I'd had a bit to drink, after all, and . . ."), the magistrate had dismissed it as "probably of no importance, anyway."

All this was told me by the two of them who were from the same village in Kent, as they loaded Bennett's body into the wagon for the trip back into the city. They covered him over with a horse blanket and made a pillow of straw for his head.

"He was a good sort," said one of the boys, the one who had introduced himself to me as Amos. "Taught us all we know about horses."

"Well," said the other, "Mr. Deuteronomy taught us some, too. He's going to look after us."

"So he says," said Amos with the modicum of doubt which that implies.

"One thing I'll say for Deuteronomy," I put in, remembering him back in Newmarket, "if he said it, you can be sure that he means it."

Then, as if summoned by our words, he appeared in the door to the stable and called me over to him.

"Get anything from those two?" he asked me.

"Just what you had already told me."

He nodded at that and whispered, "They're good lads, though not the brightest. But Jeremy, tell me, do you know anything about these painter fellas?"

"Not much, but what is it you wish to know?"

"Well, he's just out there drawing pictures of the horses, quick little line things."

"Sketches."

"I guess that's what they call them. Shouldn't he be painting, instead of that?"

"No, they don't just start in laying on the paint right away, they have to work up to it. Last thing he'll do is draw a kind of big picture of the picture he'll paint—and then he'll start painting."

"Well, now he's sent me off to bring out Pegasus. Says he wants to meet him."

"That seems reasonable, doesn't it?"

Mr. Deuteronomy considered that for a long moment. "I s'pose it does. You wouldn't want to paint a picture of a man without meeting him first, would you? Horses are a lot more like people than you'd ever guess."

"Come to think of it," said I, "Pegasus and I have never been properly introduced."

"It ain't necessary. He knows you—likes you, too."

"He does?" I chuckled. "When did he tell you that?"

"Oh, some time ago, back in Newmarket. He thinks you're very polite. Horses admire that in people. It's a rare quality, after all."

I laughed at that a bit uncertainly, unsure whether or not he wished to be taken in earnest. He gave no indication of which it might be as he excused himself and made for the stalls toward the far end of the stable.

When he brought forth Pegasus, I half-expected to see the animal agitated, or at least frisky, having been shut up so long whilst his fellows were free to skip about and frolic over the meadow. But no, the horse moved in a dignified, almost stately fashion. It could hardly be said that Deuteronomy *led* Pegasus, yet there was a lead-rope dangling from the bridle, and the jockey had a loose hold upon it. Yet, at the same time, he whispered into his ear. Pegasus bowed his mighty head that he might catch every word and once or twice did whinny in response. It was almost in the nature of a conversation between the two, man and beast. Particularly noteworthy was the fact that the stable boys paid them no attention whatever. They seemed so well-accustomed to such occurrences that they were of no interest to them.

I went direct to a window in the stable which promised the best view of the meeting of artist and horse. Sir Joshua Reynolds hung back a little as if shy or slightly fearful. I hoped Pegasus would take it for politeness, for Sir Joshua seemed to want in the worst way to be accepted by the horse. The artist turned to Mr. Deuteronomy and said something quite unintelligible to me, with a wall and a windowpane between us. Deuteronomy certainly understood, however, for he smiled, and nodded, and said something in response. Only then did Sir Joshua dip into the deep pocket of his rather elegant coat and come up with an apple. He extended it carefully to Pegasus, holding it loosely in his palm, and, with a single bob of his head, the horse took the apple from his hand. Sir Joshua did then laugh in delight as Pegasus began nosing about the pocket from which the apple had come in hopes that there might be another inside it. This was cause for great merriment among us all.

The three of us within the stable were drawn irresistibly to the door, where the view was undeniably the best. At least, in my case, this proved to be a mistake, for I had hoped to stay out of Lord Lamford's sight for the length of this visit. Yet here he came, rounding the path from the big house, emerging from the stand of trees, which had hidden him until that moment. He waddled as he walked, like some great fat goose.

"Here now, to work with you," he shouted. "Get that horse saddled. And you there, whoever you are, go to the house and get a stepladder." As this last came from him, he raised his arm and pointed direct at me.

What was I to do? I could not turn my back upon him, much as I would have liked to do just that. Nor could I have explained to him that I was neither servant nor employee, and I had no obligation to obey his orders. I had no wish to call attention to myself, for I was there under false pretenses. And so, having no choice in the matter, I simply put my head down and ran for the house. I was some distance from him when we passed. I chanced a quick glance and found him staring fixedly at me. Turning sharply away, I continued to run, listening fearfully for him to call me back. But no call came. Though I had probably looked familiar to Lord Lamford, he had not recognized me.

Blustering into the kitchen by way of the back door, I announced to the cook that the master was greatly in need of a stepladder—and that was all it took. One was hustled into my hands by a wan-looking kitchen slavey, a girl of little more than twelve by the look of her.

Though the cook paid me no heed, the girl blinked and asked me in a puzzled manner, "Who're you?"

"Just helping out," said I. Then, thanking her, I took my leave and hurried back toward the stable. Did I say that I "hurried"? Well, let it stand that I went as fast as I could whilst hauling an object as cumbersome as a stepladder.

Burdened as I was, I felt the danger of discovery even more than before. Yet luck was with me, for I stopped at the stand of trees and, peering through them, I saw that Lord Lamford had taken Sir Joshua off for a stroll of the grounds and, with his back to me, was pointing this way and that at the six horses as they flashed by at play. I moved forward and deposited the stepladder at approximately the same spot where Deuteronomy, Sir Joshua, and Pegasus had stood but minutes before. Then did I run for the stable.

Inside, Amos and his mate were just finishing all that needed be done to prepare Pegasus for the honor to be bestowed upon him. (After all, how many horses manage to have their portraits painted?) He was properly saddled, bridled, combed and curried, and otherwise prepared for his appointment with Sir Joshua. Mr. Deuteronomy took no part in all this, for he was once more busy whispering messages of a secret sort into the horse's ear. Pegasus listened closely, head bowed, except once when, I swear, he did nod his head in understanding to Deuteronomy.

"Hey in there," came Lord Lamford's shout from outside, "are you not ready yet? Bring out the animal, if you please, and let us start. I've not got all day, you know."

Then did Mr. Deuteronomy a most peculiar thing: he laughed—something between a giggle and a cackle it was. And so, gathering it from deep within him, he bellowed forth a most compliant and polite response.

"We are ready, my lord, and Pegasus the most ready of us all."

At the mention of his name, the horse beat his front hooves upon the rough boards of the stable's floor. Laughing again as he had before, Mr. Deuteronomy grabbed up the reins, and, with Pegasus beside him, he jog-trotted out and into the light. Then did the two boys scramble to the window through which I had earlier watched. I wondered why till I took a spot which they had made for me: In my absence, as I had watched the preparation of Pegasus, someone had set up Sir Joshua's kit—yet set it up, I was sure, so that the better view was through the window; no doubt this had something to do with the movement of the sun and the consequent shifting of the light.

I sensed the rising excitement in the two boys, and I wondered what they might know that I did not.

"What's going to happen?" I asked them. "What goes on?"

"We don't know," Amos declared. "But by God something will. That horse out there will do anything Mr. Deuteronomy says, and Deuteronomy's been talking to him the whole day long and part of yesterday."

Outside, I saw that Deuteronomy had led Pegasus to a point opposite that which Sir Joshua had claimed as his own.

"Who moved things around?" I asked.

"Oh, that was Deuteronomy, whilst you was in the big house. Didn't take but a minute."

"Oh, my God, will you just look at that," the nameless lad marveled. "Lord Lamford's actually going to try to mount Pegasus. Look, he's moving the stepladder up close."

"I wondered what that was for," said I, "yet I never really gave it much thought."

"He's tried it once or twice before."

"But never with a stepladder."

Lord Lamford had pushed it so close to Pegasus that its top rung (or step) pressed into the horse's ribs.

"Oh, Pegasus don't like that at all."

"Foolish thing to do. Lamford's going to be sorry. Just you wait."

"You see," said Amos to me, "Pegasus won't let anyone ride him but Deuteronomy—not even Mr. Bennett when he was alive."

"And he *liked* Mr. Bennett."

"Just imagine how he's going to feel about it when someone as big and fat as Lamford tries to crawl up on top of him."

"Well, quiet down, you two," said I to my informants, "because it certainly looks as if he's going to allow him to remain up on top of him this time."

And indeed it did. Lord Lamford had inserted his boots into the dangling stirrups. He now shifted his great weight in the saddle and called out something to Mr. Deuteronomy.

It is rather difficult to describe the appearance of the nobleman upon that horse, for he certainly did not appear noble upon it. The way that he overflowed the small racing saddle made him look quite like a huge bear perched tentatively upon a small pony. Yet, still, the horse held his ground, his four hooves planted solidly beneath him.

Deuteronomy came over, no doubt in response to Lord Lamford's call. An order was given. Deuteronomy collected the stepladder and backed away quite some distance. And then, as I was wondering why he had gone so far, the answer came in a series of powerful leaps—four in all. On the second of them, Lord Lamford lost his hold upon the stirrups. The third unseated him and landed him flat upon his back. The fourth leap seemed to be executed simply for the grand sport of it. For his part, Lord Lamford found no pleasure whatever in his grotesque position. He struggled to right himself and regain his feet. Shouting for help, he demanded a hand up.

All this we heard easily from our place at the window. Yet I hoped for the sake of the stable boys that they could not be heard by Lord Lamford, for they were laughing quite rudely at the plight of their master. Another shout was added to the cacophony in and outside the stable. Having tossed the stepladder aside, Mr. Deuteronomy came forward, calling the horse by name, attempting (I assumed) to calm him. Pegasus seemed quite calm. He studied Deuteronomy as he backed off a bit. Then did Deuteronomy shout the horse's name for a second time and a third, and clapped his hands together, just as Pegasus cantered forward, as if still at play. As he reached the flailing form of Lord Lamford, the horse reared and, a moment later, brought his front hooves crashing down upon Lamford.

A howl of pain was heard. The boys, who had at last stopped laughing, ran to the door and then outside. Yet, for the time being, I kept my place at the window and saw the entire exercise repeated: Pegasus ran back a bit, then cantered forward to rise once again and come down most brutally with his hooves upon the body. Lamford no longer moved. If there were cries for help, I heard them not. I went to the door just in time to hear the horse's hooves beat down once again upon him. And then, a fourth time—the most frightening of all, for I was that much nearer and could see the damage wreaked by Pegasus upon that disgusting man. Oh, he was dead right enough. His broken limbs were thrown about in astonishing angles. Joints were added. Worst of all was the head, which had been quite flattened, and the worst of the worst was the face—a hideous pulp of flesh, brain, and blood.

"That may be quite the oddest story I have ever heard," said Sir John with a sigh. "Forgive me for asking—and I mean it as no sign of doubt—but did it all happen just as you said?"

"It did, sir, just as I told it to you."

"And Deuteronomy Plummer simply jumped into Pegasus's saddle and rode away?"

"Well, not quite so casually as all that, perhaps. He asked me to return the wagon and the team to the stable—Burnaby's in Market Street—and to Sir Joshua Reynolds he gave assurances that he was simply taking the horse away to shoot him. It seemed to satisfy Sir Joshua, though he was so eager to get away that I believe he would have been satisfied by whatever he was told."

"I must speak to him about this," said Sir John. "Oh, and the stable boys—you said he'd made certain promises to them."

"Well, implied certain things, anyway. Just before he mounted up, he took them aside and seemed to be giving them instructions of some sort. I believe they have a meeting arranged."

"But you didn't hear where it was to be, or when?"

"No sir, I did not."

He let forth another deep sigh. "You know, Jeremy, I put no credence in tales of the great understanding of some animals."

"Of horses, for example?"

"Right to the point, yes. If Pegasus had perhaps been a dog, a trained wolf, something of that sort, I do believe I might be able to accept the facts that you have given me. I might be able to take them as you do."

"And how do you believe I take them?"

"Gullibly, in a word. You seem to accept it that Deuteronomy instructed Pegasus to kill Lord Lamford, and is therefore responsible for his death."

"Well, I have already quoted to you what I heard from Deuteronomy in Newmarket: that Pegasus is the smartest horse he ever knew. That was his claim, and so he proved in winning the King's Plate in Newmarket."

"Oh? Did he?" said Sir John in his argumentative fashion. "I thought what he proved was that he was the fastest horse on the track that day."

"But sir, I saw Deuteronomy barking out orders to him, and Pegasus followed those orders in a manner most exact."

"Do you think he was the *only* jockey that day barking out orders—as you put it? 'Faster, faster!' They must all have said that one time or another."

"No doubt, but—"

"And did you not hear from both Mr. Bennett and this very morning from the stable boys that Pegasus never allowed any other but Deuteronomy climb upon his back?"

"Yes, but still, if you had only seen the two of them—Deuteronomy and Pegasus—in the stable together, you would have sworn that they were planning something." As soon as the words were out of my mouth, I realized my faux pas.

"Unfortunately," he responded coolly, "I was denied that on two counts. First of all, I was not there. Secondly, even if I had been there, I could not have *seen* any such thing for reasons you know only too well. But further, Jeremy, even if I had been there and been able to watch the human and the equine conspirators at work, I would nevertheless have denied them responsibility for what followed. Why? Simply because a man cannot communicate to a horse in the manner you have described—not with any reasonable expectation that his instructions would be followed. Because it is *not* reasonable, simply that—and nothing more. Do you not understand that?"

Thus our conversation on this matter paused where it usually ended. This, as it happened, was the third time we had had the discussion. The first followed my visit to Mr. Donnelly to drop off the body of Mr. Bennett. (Over his protests, of course, for he was to leave with his bride-to-be for Ireland the next day.) I ran into Number 4 Bow Street and blurted out to Sir John that Lord Lamford had been killed—and little more.

"Murdered?" he had asked.

"Perhaps," said I. "I shall give you all the details soon as ever I return."

And that I did less than an hour later, seated in his chambers, telling a much longer version of the same story, including many details. At that point, he seemed satisfied. Finally, after dinner that evening, he requested my presence in his "study" to talk a bit more of the case of Lord Lamford: "Some information has come in from Mr. Donnelly that fills out the picture a bit more completely." The "new information" of which he spoke was that in the opinion of Mr. Donnelly, which he had freely expressed in his report, Mr. Bennett had almost certainly been murdered. The wound was in the back of his head, which made a suicide physically possible but highly unlikely. Then did he ask me to go through the entire story once again, for he had caught some hint earlier that I actually believed Deuteronomy Plummer to be in some sense responsible for the death of Lord Lamford. And so have I included here the lively talk we then had on these matters of the culpability of humans who act through the agency of animals. Yet there was, as I recall, a bit more to the matter; for having talked through it thus far, he added a sort of coda, as I sat puzzling through what already had been said.

"Jeremy, let me ask you something. What is the purpose of the statements that you have made supporting the notion that Pegasus killed Lord Lamford on the instructions of Mr. Deuteronomy? What result do you seek? Do you wish me to bind him for trial at Old Bailey? The charge: murder. The weapon: a three-year-old stallion."

Even to speak of such a thing did chill me. "Oh no, sir. I would not wish that at all."

"I mention it in this way because your intention is still to be a barrister, is it not?"

"Oh yes sir, most emphatically so."

"You must remember then that the job of pleading is by and large a game of wits. You must win over the judge and the jury,

which is hard enough in itself, but to give the prosecution something to work with—that would surely be quite mad, don't you
think so?"

"Yes, I see what you mean."

"Why, a good lawyer for the prosecution could work wonders
with a jury if he had something like your theory to go on. Intellectual speculation in its proper place is one thing, yet its proper place
is not the courtroom, nor is it a good subject for discussion with a
magistrate, such as myself. Lucky for you I put no faith in such the-
ories of communication between humans and animals. Why, I
would sooner credit Divine Intervention in this case. Yes, Divine
Intervention might work very well indeed. Such a pity that such a
fine animal as Pegasus must be destroyed."

"Must he be?"

"So says the law."

I let that stand without comment. Thinking that he had said
about all he wished to say, I made ready to take my leave of him. Yet
before I did, a thought did occur to me.

"I wonder, Sir John," said I, "if there have been any further developments in the matter of Elizabeth Hooker."

"Ah, yes, indeed there have been," said he. "If Saunders Welch
is given a push by the Lord Chief Justice, there is no magistrate can
match him for swift justice."

"Why? What has he done?"

"Mr. Bailey informed me when he came in that he had just
heard that Welch had called a special session of his court, had his
constables bring in Mother Jeffers, and based solely upon the testimony offered by Elizabeth Hooker, had bound Jeffers for trial in
Felony Court."

"On what charge?"

"The only one possible—wrongful imprisonment."

"Can she be convicted?"

"I don't know. Perhaps. I will say, however, that in his haste to
please Lord Mansfield, Mr. Welch has put a burden upon the prosecution much greater than usual. Whoever it is appears for the
Crown must build his case from scratch—and he will have little
time to do it."

"Why so little time, Sir John?"

"Because the trial has been set for Monday next," said he.

"Monday next? Why, that is but four days hence!"

"So it is."

"But why such dispatch? This is no matter of state. No insult has been thrown at the King. What is the great engine that drives this with such urgency?"

"Ah, you have it right, Jeremy. This indeed is no matter of state. And certainly no insult of any sort has been offered. What then is the great engine? It is known quite prosaically as Public Opinion."

Well have I learned the power lodged in those two words. Though the public's opinion may be right or wrong, it is seldom that much can be said against it once it is formed. How then is it formed? Why, most often by those who write pamphlets on such subjects as fall before the public's view. The purpose of these pamphlets, in fact, is to form the opinion of the public. That is why those who write them take on such airs, and why it is said up and down Grub Street by such as these that *they* are the true rulers of England.

True enough, there are occasions, and many of them, when the writers of pamphlets have done good works, supporting this or that cause which needed and deserved support. In other instances, the pamphlets had attacked that which richly deserved it and brought the light of opinion upon that which many would have liked to keep hid. These are, in this way, battles of the pamphlets, wherein pamphleteers on either side of a question will rage and contradict each the other through their pamphlets, fighting to form public opinion.

Nevertheless, the weakness of the pamphlet as a means of public discussion lies precisely in that. A pamphlet presents only one side of a question, argues only for innocence or for guilt. I have seldom (not to say never) read one which presented a balanced, detailed picture of any situation, or admitted that there was something to be said for both sides. Pamphlets tend, by their very nature, to be splenetic, rather than intellectual.

The only place one may expect to find both sides of a question presented with a degree of fairness is in a court of law. That is what first attracted me to the law, and what, in spite of occasional disappointments, has kept me at it for a good many years. It would, however, be altogether vain to pretend that the law is uninfluenced by public opinion. On the contrary, it is indeed often a factor in ways that Sir John suggested. Public opinion will often bring a matter to trial with unseemly haste—that is, before one side or the other, or indeed both sides, are ready for the trial. And beyond that, public opinion may put undue pressure upon members of a jury, making those who must ultimately decide a case fearful of voting yea or nay in contradiction to the popular cause.

Pamphleteers had first discovered Elizabeth Hooker when she disappeared. They brought her a sort of fame. They declared her the most beautiful and clever, the sweetest-natured, and above all, the most innocent of all maidens. How could such a one be stolen bodily from the streets of London? Was ours then a city so unsafe, populated by criminals, kidnappers, and the like? Et cetera. And then, when Elizabeth returned, telling her tale of abduction and imprisonment, word came to the writers of pamphlets, and they flocked to her, interviewing her (some did not even bother to do that), accepting her every word as truth and fabricating those she did not supply. Her captor, Mother Jeffers, looked every bit the wicked witch. Her imprisonment was like that of Rapunzel. Her escape from her tower was like unto that of a princess in some fairy tale set in the dim long-ago.

In all, some six or seven pamphlets appeared before and during the trial. Each of them extolled the innocence of Elizabeth Hooker and denounced the guilt of Mother Jeffers. Had the pamphlets any great effect? They certainly did much to form public opinion in the matter. There was a great crowd that assembled in Covent Garden in her behalf the very evening of her return. And, on the eve of the trial, there was a torchlight parade from the Garden to Old Bailey in which the marchers carried signs bearing legends such as "Punish the old whore!" and "God bless the innocence of our dear Liz." It was an altogether impressive showing and some eloquent speeches were made. But did all this influence the outcome of the trial? You must read the next chapter if you wish to discover that.

TWELVE

*In which a death is
discovered and an end
is brought to all*

We thought it odd when Mr. Marsden failed to appear next morn—
odd, that is, because he sent no word by the landlord's lad, whose
responsibility it was to carry word to us when Sir John's clerk felt
unable to put in his usual day of work.

Mr. Marsden's malady was a puzzle to us all. We had been assured that his was not a case of consumption. Still, his dry cough,
which could, of a sudden, explode into a racking, rasping spasm,
was sometimes quite frightening and little different to us who heard
it from that of the nasty illness which had half the population of
London spitting blood upon the street.

Once I had asked him how he felt on those days when he was
too ill to report for work. He answered me straightaway.

"Jeremy," said he, "it's the awfullest feeling you could ever
imagine."

"Oh?" said I, "can you describe it?"

"It's like I can't get enough air into my lungs, like they just won't
fill up, and I'm chokin' to death right there in my room. A man can't
work when he feels himself in such a state, I'm sure you'd agree."

"Certainly he cannot."

He remained silent for a moment, reflecting. And then: "As jobs
go, you know, this is a pretty easy one," said he.

"But an important one," I responded.

"Oh, I'll grant you that—specially with Sir John being blind
and all. But you're used to writing letters for him and all kinds of

other things. You'll be able to do this job of mine better than I ever could."

What an odd thing for him to say! Was he thinking ahead to retirement—or . . . what? Yet I did not immediately ask him to explain, and he never gave me a later opportunity.

All this I rolled over again in my mind as I made my way to Mr. Marsden's dwelling place in Long Acre. What I learned there saddened me no end.

When Mr. Marsden failed to respond to the landlord's knock upon the door, the latter had let himself in with his key and found the clerk dead in his bed. His body was cold to the touch; there was no sign of breathing, nor of a heartbeat. Nevertheless, out of respect for one who had been a longtime resident, he sent for a doctor who lived nearby. The medico was still present and was filling out the papers which declared Marsden officially dead. I introduced myself and asked what he was listing as the cause of death.

"A stoppage of the heart," said he.

"Indeed?" said I. "He had for some time been troubled by a difficulty of some sort in the lungs and had been under a physician's care."

"Which physician is that?"

"Mr. Donnelly."

"*Mr.* Donnelly, is it? Then he is but a surgeon."

"Not so," said I. "He is a graduate of the University of Vienna."

He shrugged. "You may have him come and look at him, if you like."

"Impossible, I fear. This very morning he and his bride-to-be departed for Ireland."

"Then be satisfied with what I have put down here, for if this Marsden fellow's heart had not stopped, he would, I assure you, be with us still today."

When I returned to Bow Street, having made arrangements with the embalmer in Long Acre, I passed the sad news on to Sir John. He said I had done right in selecting a plain, board coffin to bury him in. ("Little would it matter to him if we were to put his remains in some grander box," said Sir John.) Mr. Marsden would be buried out of St. Paul's, Covent Garden, in the same churchyard where Margaret Mary Plummer, Deuteronomy's niece, had been laid to rest. A collection would be taken among the Bow Street Runners, all of whom knew him, to defray the costs of burial.

"I shall contribute something," said I.

"As you will," said Sir John, "but if there is a need, by custom it would fall to me to supply the deficiency."

"How so?"

"My annual stipend."

"Ah yes, of course—noblesse oblige."

He grinned in amusement. "Something of the sort. But Jeremy?"

"Yes sir?"

"It will fall to you today—and until I can find a permanent replacement—to work as Mr. Marsden's replacement. I fear we've used up a good bit of the morning in this painful business. You must get on with the interviews of the prisoners and the disputants. I know not how many there are, but . . ."

"Of course, Sir John." I rose and started to the door.

"Just one more thing, lad. What was it like, Mr. Marsden's living quarters, I mean. Had he a good life, do you suppose?"

What an odd question, I thought, and what a difficult one to answer. "Why, I know not quite what to say, Sir John. Though it was but a single room, it was a large one—not lavishly furnished but comfortable. There was wood for a good fire. What more does one need?"

"Well, yes, I suppose, but . . . did he have many books about?"

"Two or three law books, as I recall—all of them rather old."

"When he first came to me," said Sir John, "he wanted to be a lawyer."

"The rest were all penny-dreadfuls—a great stack of them."

"Oh dear," said he with a sigh.

"And oh yes, there were a great many pipes about. He had quite a collection, so he did."

"He was a great one for his pipes, was he not? I daresay that they were well kept, too."

"Oh very. And another odd thing: When you entered the room, the first thing you noted was the smell of tobacco smoke. It seemed quite pervasive."

That seemed to satisfy Sir John. "Then perhaps 'twas not such a bad life, after all—a bit of dinner, a bottle of ale, and a pipe or two afterward. Ah, but he was alone. I could never live so."

. . .

As a consequence of Mr. Marsden's death, I missed most of the trial of Mother Jeffers. We buried him upon the Monday the trial commenced. It continued through Tuesday and Wednesday, which made it quite a long session in court for those days. The length of the trial came as a result of Jeffers's choice of counsel. She was wise enough (and wealthy enough) to have her solicitor engage William Ogden, to my mind the finest barrister in London, to plead her case. He was young, he was energetic, and his method was to throw out a net and bring in as many witnesses as possible. Then, having attacked the character—and therefore the testimony of Elizabeth Hooker—he launched a final assault in his summing-up before the jury.

Louis Edgington, for the prosecution, had little more to work with than Elizabeth's story of her abduction and imprisonment. She told it at great length, having embroidered it considerably since last I had heard it told. A couple of character witnesses were called, including her employer, Mr. Turbott, the silversmith. Perhaps Mr. Edgington thought this to be sufficient, what with mass meetings and torchlight parades in her behalf. Or perhaps he, a veteran of the courts, had simply grown lazy.

In any case, Mr. Ogden assailed the testimony of each of them in cross-examination and spent most of the time quite rightly jabbing and cutting away at the story of Elizabeth Hooker. Though she was less believable by the time he had done with her, it could not be said that he had destroyed her testimony. The most deeply wounding shot of all was the last. William Ogden had turned his back upon her and walked away, as if to his seat. But, of a sudden, he turned and confronted her.

"Mistress Hooker," said he, "I have one last question for you, and it is this: Are you pregnant?"

She was quite taken aback, unable for a while even to speak. Since this question was asked at the end of the first day of the trial, I was able to be present and can attest to her confusion.

After sputtering and stuttering for some moments, she managed at last to declare her denial: "Why . . . why, no. I mean, I certainly . . . NO!"

Mr. Edgington jumped to his feet, obviously intending to object. But, thinking better of it, he looked around him and sheepishly resumed his seat. His difficulty was that if he were to object to the question and get it stricken from the record, he would also lose her response which, no matter how faltering, was certainly categorical. Nevertheless, Mr. Ogden had scored a point with the jury.

As it happened, it was but the first of many points, for, once on the offense, he was virtually unstoppable. First, he brought Kathleen Quigley to the witness box, and he took her at length through the tale of the Easter dinner, the late departure of the two girls, and their separation in Covent Garden. Yet he went deeper with her than I had done, and got from her that though the two shared a bed in a small room down in the servants' quarters of the Turbott residence and shop, there were often difficulties.

"Was Elizabeth a good bed partner?" Mr. Ogden put it to her.

"No sir, she weren't," said Kathleen. "She would oft sneak out the bed, dress herself, and let herself out with a duplicate key she'd got hold of."

"Did she offer you any account of her whereabouts during these secret expeditions of hers?"

"No, not at first, but though she could go on less sleep than I ever could, eventually her hours began to take a toll in her work. She'd be dozing at her washing up and all. And so one day I just up and asked her where she went. 'Oh, Kathleen,' she says to me, 'there's a whole other world out there at night. It's ever so much more fun than this one. Mostly, I go with my guide, my own special friend. He shows me round, wherever. And sometimes, I admit, we make mischief together.'"

"And that was all she said?"

"All that I can remember about that."

"Your witness, Mr. Edgington."

Truth be told, Mr. Edgington knew not quite what to do with her in cross-examination. So overwhelmed was he by what he had just heard from her that all he could manage were one or two perfunctory questions. The first, as I recall, was whether or not anyone else had noted Elizabeth's nocturnal ramblings. Kathleen Quigley said that perhaps they had, but 'twas only to the cook she had ever mentioned it.

"And what was her response?" asked Mr. Edgington.

"She said to me, 'That's as may be, but what you say will get no farther than me.' 'Why not?' says I. 'Because,' said she. " 'Twould do no good, and would only get you and me both into trouble.'"

Was there another question? I believe there was not, for I have a strong impression that he refused to pursue this further for fear of where it might lead.

Next did Mr. Ogden call one Sally Ward, who referred to herself as a "hostess" at the Rose Tavern. She, it seemed, had seen Elizabeth Hooker at the Rose and in the company of two young men. "They were having a grand time," said she. "Stayed to all hours, they did." Mr. Edgington's questions seemed intended only to get the "hostess" to admit that she was a prostitute. Her responses were such as to make it clear that she was not.

A short parade of witnesses for the defense followed. Virginia Jeffers, the daughter, told of the inspection of her room, the taking of her frock, et cetera. The room was much different when it was viewed by Elizabeth. "But," said she, "months back it had looked a bit more in that way Elizabeth had described."

That, of course, was interesting, yet Edgington had no questions to put to her in cross-examination; nor had he questions for Joan Simonson, a "resident" of the house, absent at the time of the search. She attested, in response to Mr. Ogden, that she had never seen the girl known as Elizabeth Hooker until she had given her testimony the day before in court.

And on, at last, to Mother Jeffers. Hers was perhaps the shortest time spent in the witness box of all those called to testify. Mr. Ogden had but two questions he wished answered. The first was to give an account of her business.

"Would you describe the house that you own and operate as a brothel?"

"No, I would not," said she.

"How then would you describe it?"

"As a lodging house, an inn. I rent out rooms to travelers."

"To travelers only?"

"Well, I cannot be certain, but that is indeed how they strike me."

That brought a rumble of deep laughter from those in the courtroom. Had it continued, the judge, a Sir Hubert Timmons, would likely have cleared the courtroom. The second question to be settled was Mother Jeffers's relation to Elizabeth Hooker. How did she answer that?

"I had never seen that girl until she was brought to me in the company of Sir John Fielding and the Mr. Turbott who testified here yesterday."

"Never seen her?" Mr. Ogden pretended great shock at her response.

"Absolutely not."

"Your witness, Mr. Edgington."

The prosecution had at least thought out his questions in advance, but Mr. Ogden had thought them out, too. And, having done so, he had prepared her well when they came.

"This house of yours," said Mr. Edgington, "how was it you described it?"

"As a lodging house, an inn for travelers."

"An inn, you say? Do you serve meals?"

"We do. I do most of the cooking myself."

"How nice," said Mr. Edgington. "But tell me more of those who stay at your inn. For instance, how do you know that they are travelers?"

"Well, they seldom stay more than a single night."

There was a sudden explosion of laughter. Even Mr. Edgington unbent sufficiently to smile at that.

"But occasionally they do stay longer," added Mother Jeffers, apparently embarrassed by all the commotion and wishing to put an end to it.

"Are these travelers mostly men and women?"

She looked at him oddly. "Well, what else could they be?" More laughter.

"Oh, what I meant to say was, do they appear in couples? A man and a woman, that sort of thing."

"Ah, well, that's the usual, I suppose, but there are others, you know—men and men, and even women and women, occasionally."

And then, with great dramatic emphasis, Mr. Edgington demanded to know: "Just what do you believe they do in those rooms of yours, Mrs. Jeffers?"

She drew herself erect and said to him quite indignantly, "Why, sir, I would not presume to guess. Would you have me spy upon my guests? That would be sinfully improper."

Again—and actually for the last time during the trial—there was sudden merriment at her response. "Sinfully improper" was the phrase which seemed to amuse most. Even Sir Hubert Timmons, the judge, joined in, and so it was quite some time before proceedings might continue. And when they did, it was evident that Mr. Edgington had been bested by the woman in the witness box. He briefly attempted to bring her to account for her refusal to identify Elizabeth Hooker and to describe their relations.

"You say," said he, "that you had never seen Mistress Hooker until her appearance with Sir John Fielding and her employer, Mr. Turbott, on the nineteenth day of this month. Is that correct?"

"That is correct, yes."

"Then how do you account for the fact that Elizabeth Hooker found in your daughter's closet the very frock that you took from her upon her arrival at your . . . your . . . house?"

"I know of no such frock," declared Mother Jeffers. "I know only of one taken unlawfully from my daughter by that girl. Mistress Hooker claimed it as her own. It fitted my daughter, and here is the dressmaker's bill to prove it is hers. You have seen her and you have seen Mistress Hooker, and thus you know that the same dress could not have fitted both. I challenge them to show it to us now."

"Bring forth the frock that we may see it now," cried Mr. Edgington.

There was an awkward pause. And then a small voice was heard from behind the attorney for the prosecution. "It is . . . unavailable."

Mr. Edgington whirled about angrily. "Unavailable? What does that *mean*?"

"It has disappeared, sir," came the voice again. "Probably stolen."

Mother Jeffers said naught, yet the look of withering contempt which she showed her interrogator was far more eloquent. It was, in any case, far too much for Mr. Edgington. He turned away in disgust.

"I have done with her," said he as he strode back to his seat.

Thus did the prosecution of Mrs. Jeffers come crashing down. I mean no disrespect to Mr. Edgington, for he was in his prime as good as any barrister at the bar, but his failure in this instance proved once again the importance of proper preparation. There was but one more chance for him to win back the jury, and that would come on the morrow with his final speech in summary of the case for the prosecution.

In just such a way did the support of public opinion begin to ebb from Elizabeth Hooker. It was physically perceptible how the talk upon the street in front of Old Bailey quietened down as word came out to them of developments inside the vast court building. The crowd began to shrink. By the morning of the third day of the trial, there were few there before the great doors. Where over a hundred had gathered on the first day, there were now less than ten.

Inside, Mr. Edgington attempted to do with oratory what he had failed to do during the previous two days of questioning. In truth, all that he managed to accomplish was to retell the pitiful tale of abduction and incarceration which Elizabeth had recounted a couple of days before. He left nothing out; in fact, he added a few flourishes of his own, all intended to wring sympathy from the twelve stolid faces in the jury box. His performance was indeed impressive, yet it was, in spite of all, a performance. When he raised a hand to brush away the tears, his fingers remained dry. Yet had he told the same tale to them at the beginning and then polled the members of the jury, he would have had an immediate conviction.

Mr. William Ogden, on the other hand, said little in defense of his client. Rather, his device was to attack her accuser—and attack and attack yet again.

"Gentlemen, behold a liar," said he to the jurymen, waving his hand in the direction of Elizabeth Hooker, who sat in the front row. "I do not believe that I have encountered such a complete liar in all my years at the bar." (Which, indeed, at the time were not so many.) He went on to cite the many statements made by Elizabeth and the ways that they had been contradicted by others who had appeared as witnesses—Kathleen Quigley, Virginia Jeffers, Sally Ward, Joan Simonson, and, of course, the most forceful contradiction of all, from Mother Jeffers. Nor did Mr. Ogden hesitate to remind them of what was the most embarrassing moment of all for Louis Edgington: the discovery that the frock in Virginia Jeffers's wardrobe claimed by Elizabeth as her own had vanished.

All in all, it was a most instructive trial for one such as myself who hoped to make a career in the law. So far as I could see, William Ogden had not made a single mistake, whereas Louis Edgington had made many; and, as Sir John had put it to me, one can learn as much from another's mistakes as from his greatest triumphs. Sir Hubert Timmons must have thought as highly as I did regarding Mr. Ogden's ability to pull a case together in a short time, for he commented upon it and praised him for it in his summing-up to the jury. He stopped short of directing a verdict, yet it was clear that he felt that Mr. Ogden had made the case for acquittal. And it was acquittal voted by the jury. The only surprise was that their verdict was returned in less than fifteen minutes' time.

My account of the trial here, while no doubt accurate enough, was pieced together from the memories of William Ogden (whom I came to know quite well in later life), my own sketchy recollections, and other, incidental research. As I mentioned earlier, 'twas the death of Mr. Marsden which prevented me from spending more time at the Old Bailey during the trial. It meant that I would serve as Sir John's court clerk for an indeterminate length of time (which, in the event, proved a very long time indeed). It also meant that I, along with all the rest at Bow Street, would attend Mr. Marsden's funeral at nearby St. Paul's, Covent Garden. Following the graveside service, as the Runners hurried off along their separate ways, Sir John took me aside and asked if I might return with him to Bow Street.

"Certainly," said I. "Was there something special . . . ?"

"As it happens, there is," said he. "I know you wish to get on to the Old Bailey—but this shouldn't take long." Saying no more about it, he started off at a brisk pace through the field of gravestones, swinging his walking stick in wide arcs before him. 'Twas all I could do to keep up.

There was a single letter upon Sir John's desk. For whom it was intended I could only guess, for it was placed so that the address and addressee were invisible to me. Nevertheless, I could plainly see that the seal which it bore was that of Sir John's himself. Perhaps, I thought, it is a letter he wishes me to deliver. However, I soon found out that in this case Sir John was the deliverer.

"This is the usual time for attending to such matters," said he.

"If you will pardon me, sir," said I, "what sort of matters do you mean?"

"Oh, the reading of wills, that sort of thing." He felt around the top of the desk until his fingers touched the letter. When they did, he pushed it across the desk toward me. "Open it," said he. "I know the contents. I am in fact witness to them. That scrawl below Mr. Marsden's signature is mine, as you, I'm sure, will recognize."

And, below that familiar scrawl, was this note: "Witnessed and signed to on this date, the 25ᵗʰ day of April, 1774."

"Less than a week ago," said I.

"Yes, Mr. Marsden knew that he had not long to live, and he came to me and asked if I might help him a bit in the wording of the will and then witness his signature. I agreed, of course, and what you have before you is the result of that unequal collaboration. 'Unequal,' I say, because all the thoughts and intentions expressed here are his own. Read it, if you will, Jeremy, and read it aloud."

"All right, sir," said I. After clearing my throat, I began: "I, Jonathan Partridge Marsden, being of sound mind, et cetera—"

"That 'et cetera' was mine," said Sir John, interrupting. "Neither of us could think what it was followed 'sound mind.' That's the important phrase, anyway. But continue, lad. I shouldn't interject in such a way. Forgive me."

"As you say." After again clearing my throat, ". . . sound mind, et cetera, do hereby declare this to be my last will and testament."

We went on in just such a way—I reading ahead, and he interrupting after every sentence or two (it seemed) with comments of his own and explanations. (Just as if any were needed.) The burden of it was that after Mr. Marsden's possessions had been sold by his landlord, all the rest in money and coin was to go to me. His approximate wealth he estimated at a little more than thirty pounds— and most of it was mine. This did quite astonish me.

"It should have been more, I know," Mr. Marsden had written, "but I was never very good at holding on to money, and I've enjoyed myself a fair amount. I have left twenty pounds in the hands of Sir

John. There should be ten more coming from the sale of furniture, clothing, et cetera. It is the custom, I am told, to split the proceeds of the sale with him who does the selling—in this case, my landlord. He has been made aware of my wishes and has agreed to them."

At this point, Sir John interrupted and assured me that he had the twenty pounds locked away and that I might have it whenever I wished. "As for the sale of his goods and furniture," he added, "that is scheduled to proceed Saturday next. You may or may not attend, as you see fit."

Then came a brief section which to me was most interesting of all. Sir John told me that in its intention, it had all come from Mr. Marsden. "My only part in it," said he, "was to approve what was said and in a few places suggest more forceful wording that it might resist challenge from some distant and unknown relative."

Having heard this much, I hastened to read the remainder, for I was deeply curious. I cleared my throat, lowered my voice half an octave or so, and began reading:

"I never married and therefore have I no legitimate children. As for the other sort, there are none known and none likely. Indeed, I have no known kin, having come to London as a babe with my parents so many years back. I have no recollection of my parents' home, which was said to be Bristol. I have no ties to that city, nor do I know of any aunt, uncle, or cousin living there, or anywhere else on this earth.

"For this reason, and for a few others which shall be made plain, I have chosen to pass on my little fortune to Jeremy Proctor. He is, as I am, an orphan. He was in his thirteenth year when I first came to know him, and so I have seen him grow in mind and body into the sort of lad I should be proud to call a son. This small amount which I leave him may in some way help him along in the career which he has chosen for himself in the law. If that be so, then I am grateful, particularly in that it was once my chosen career, as well. Godspeed to him in pursuit of that which I was never able to achieve.

"Thus do I give this as my wish and mine alone. May Jeremy Proctor prosper in life, then shall I rest ever easy into eternity."

Below that he had signed his full name with a grand flourish. It occurred to me then that I had never known that his middle name was Partridge. Was it a family name? His mother's, perhaps? There were so many things I had not known about Mr. Marsden. I found myself wishing greatly that I had known him better, that I had taken more time with him instead of rushing round the great city on errands of varying importance. Then did I think upon my only visit to his room in Long Acre — the sense of solitude I perceived there, the coldness, the stale smell. Only then did I discover that I was weeping.

I had not seen Mr. Deuteronomy Plummer since that day upon which Pegasus dealt so cruelly with Lord Lamford. Nor, in a sense, did I expect to. I had not quite believed Deuteronomy when he rode away upon the horse, declaring that he would see to destroying Pegasus. Nor, apparently, did Sir John, for after a day or two, I was sent by Sir John to the Hay Market Coffee House to inquire after horse and rider.

Just to be sure, I rapped loudly upon the door above the coffee house, waited, and rapped again even more loudly than before. I called out his name a couple of times. Getting no response, I trudged down the stairs and, entering the place, I sought out the chief and was directed by one of the servers to a man in the rear of the establishment. He sat at a desk, tallying sums. When I impatiently sought to draw him away from his figures, he held up a hand to silence me. But a moment or two later, when he had reached the sum at the bottom of the column, he smiled and gave me his attention.

"How can I serve you, young sir?"

I explained that I had been sent by Sir John Fielding of the Bow Street Court to inquire after Deuteronomy Plummer.

"Ah yes, Mr. Deuteronomy," said he with a smile.

"Has he been seen by you?"

"Seen? Yes, oh yes, and I bade farewell to him, as well."

"Then he is gone? Did he say where to?"

"No, but if your name happens to be Jeremy Proctor, I have a letter for you."

"That is indeed my name. May I see the letter?"

"Not quite so fast, young sir. He said that Jeremy Proctor would know the odds that were paid on Pegasus to win this year's

King's Plate race at Newmarket." He ended that with a look sharp enough to stop any pretender.

"Pegasus paid bettors—and there were not many—at the rate of thirty to one."

"Excellent," said he, "and here"—he opened the top drawer of the desk—"you have your letter." He presented it to me.

Wasting no time, I tore it open rather roughly and took off a corner of it as I did. Still, I had done no real damage to the body of the message, for it was short and quickly read:

"My dear Jeremy," he greeted me, and then continued: "I have decided that Pegasus deserves far better than to be destroyed for killing that great, fat lump of midden, Lamford, and so we have gone off where we cannot be easily found. Don't bother to search for us, for Britain is a large island—and we may not even be here. Little good has come of this whole nasty experience. Yet I am glad to have had the chance to meet you and Sir John. Tell him that, and bless you both." It was then signed, "Your friend, Deuteronomy."

During all of this, Clarissa had attended to all of my tales from the trial of Mrs. Jeffers and rejoiced with me when William Ogden's masterly defense of the woman brought a not-guilty verdict from the jury for his client. She was particularly interested in my explanation of why the barrister had put to Elizabeth that curious question, "Are you pregnant?"

"Do you suppose he knew that she was?" Clarissa asked.

"I don't think so," said I, "though it's possible. Yet when such questions are asked, it is often the case that even if denied, and even when the jury is told by the judge to disregard, the idea has nevertheless been planted in the minds of the jurymen that this might be so: she *might* be pregnant, in which case her testimony is compromised in their eyes."

Her eyes narrowed as she gave thought to what I had just said. "Hmmm," said she, perhaps in imitation of Sir John, "interesting."

And indeed I thought her interest quite interesting—specially when, a week or two later, she rose to her feet and addressed the three of us who remained at the dinner table.

"I have an announcement to make," said she, as all eyes turned toward her. "I am pregnant."

No three words could have caused a greater stir among the three who heard it. After a moment's stunned silence, in which we did naught but gawk in amaze, we let forth a confused babble of comment, complaint, and questions.

"Oh, Clarissa," said Lady Fielding, "it cannot be! Tell us it is not so."

"What are you saying?" I wailed.

"My dear girl," said Sir John, "surely there's some mistake!"

But, tight-lipped and erect, she gave no hint that any mistake had been made.

"Who is the father of your child?" Sir John demanded, turning in my direction. "I must have it from you!"

"Well, it's certainly not my son, Tom! She's not near big enough for that. How far along are you, Clarissa?" Then Lady F., too, turned to me.

(It seemed, reader, that I stood accused without so much as an opportunity to defend myself. Surely you understand that I would not skip over such an event with no mention whatever. In short, reader, I knew I could not be the father of Clarissa's coming event for the obvious reason. Though we had come close on a couple of occasions, one or the other of us two had shied at the last moment. Would she—could she—have found a lover bolder than I? Then what a wanton she was!)

Thrusting out her jaw, Lady Fielding stared at me in a manner most severe. "Jeremy," said she, "I am shocked. In truth, I had thought better of you."

"But," said I, "but . . . but—"

"You've disappointed me, lad," said Sir John in a deep and sorrowful tone. "Alas, I have little more to say to you than that."

Clasping her hands, Lady Fielding raised her eyes most dramatically, as if to the heavens above.

"I admit," said she, "that I had thought that perhaps someday in the distant future, you, Jeremy, and you, Clarissa, might marry. I had even hoped as much, for after all, you have so much in common. But this . . . now . . . why, you are both children. There is so much that you lack."

At that, my pride prompted me to rebel. I would not allow her to dismiss me, nor for that matter, dismiss Clarissa, as a proper candidate for marriage. I knew well that children of the gentry and the nobility married even younger when money or land was concerned. And whatever had passed between Clarissa and her secret lover was something that would be settled between her and me. So I, too, rose and, standing cross the table from my intended, responded to Lady Fielding.

"You say that there is much that we lack," said I to her. "What is it that you mean by that? What do we lack?"

"What indeed! You lack all. You have no experience of life."

"I daresay that, between us, Clarissa and I have greater experience of life than any others our age who are not locked away in Newgate, or not actively engaged in lives of crime or —" gesturing across the table —"harlotry."

"Be careful, young man, you had best not suggest such things with regard to her. Show a little respect."

"*Respect?* I have naught but respect for her. She can at this moment cook near as well as Annie. You remarked but minutes ago on the excellent quality of the meal just eaten. She is intelligent, clever, able to do sums with the best. From the very beginning she proved invaluable to you as your secretary. You have often said you could not do without her there at the Magdalene Home. And she —"

"Enough!" said Lady Fielding, interrupting with a wave of her hand. "Let us talk plain, Jeremy. And the plain truth is that you simply have not money enough to keep her — much less her *and* a child."

I was ready for that and expecting it. Yet as I opened my mouth to respond, Clarissa leaped in, so to speak, and spoke in my defense.

"Ah, Lady Fielding," said she, "so he would have said himself — and did, less than a month ago. He reasoned with me. When I brought marriage up to him, he argued just as you have and said he would not have money enough to marry until he had years of practice as a barrister behind him."

"Exactly!" shouted Lady Fielding.

"But since he spoke thus, two things have happened," Clarissa continued. "First, a fortunate wager made by him at Newmarket brought him one hundred fifty-one pounds and thirteen shillings. Do I have the amount correct, Jeremy?"

"To the shilling," said I.

"A hundred and . . . Jack, what do you know of this?" said she to Sir John.

A sigh. "It seems to be true."

"In addition," Clarissa went on, "we discovered after Mr. Marsden had died that he left behind a will. In it, he left a sum of twenty pounds to Jeremy and the likelihood that five more will be coming to him when Mr. Marsden's possessions are sold. Not near so impressive as his winnings at Newmarket but it brings the total close to two hundred pounds, you see. Many marry with far less."

Lady Fielding turned once again to Sir John. "Jack?"

"True, Kate."

It was her turn to sigh. "Clarissa, you know that I want only good for you, but, truly, two hundred pounds may seem a great deal, but it isn't. We must marry you off, however. That much is certain."

"Ah," said Clarissa, "but I have a plan, and it should cost no more to execute than what is presently spent." She explained that she and I would marry and occupy the large bedroom at the end of the hall, which she had shared first with Annie and then with Molly. Clarissa would continue to cook and, in exchange, would be given board and room for herself and for me. (This was essentially the present arrangement.) But I would assume all responsibilities which had previously been Mr. Marsden's, and for that would be paid his salary.

"But what about the baby?" Lady Fielding wailed.

"Ah yes, the baby. When he or she arrives, we shall have prepared Jeremy's old room atop all the rest for him. Now, how does that sound?"

"Rather complicated," said Lady F. "Will you be working no more at the Magdalene Home?"

"I'll work there as needed."

"Well . . . what do you think, Jack?"

"It does seem fair, don't you think, Kate? After all, Jeremy does deserve something if he is to do old Marsden's job."

"But he's only a boy. To pay him the same seems wrong. Mr. Marsden worked for years as your clerk."

"Still, he does the job better than Mr. Marsden ever did."

"Oh." She said nothing more for a time. "Well," said she at last, "let the banns be published then. We may as well do this right. Clarissa, when do you think the baby . . . ?"

"Not for quite some time."

"That's good. There's something rather vulgar about those weddings where the bride is in her eighth or ninth month. If you'll excuse me now, I'll go upstairs. I've a lot to plan for."

We sat down and watched her go, saying not a word one to the other. Sir John listened carefully to his wife's footsteps ascending the stairs and waited till he heard the door to their bedroom close. Then did he lean forward.

"It went perfectly," he whispered to us. "And by the bye, if you need more ammunition, just ask her when *she* was first married." He paused for emphasis. "Just past her sixteenth birthday, as I understand it." Then did he wave his good evening and himself start for the stairs.

I was much confused by his behavior. He had at first seemed darkly disapproving of me. But now his manner was secretive, even (one might say) conspiratorial. I was equally confused by Clarissa. She grasped both my hands in hers of a sudden and squeezed them for all she was worth.

"Oh, Jeremy," said she, "you were quite wonderful. You stood up to her so beautifully. How was it you put it? 'Respect? I have naught but respect for her'—and then setting out to name my achievements. I fear I blushed as never before, but none seemed to notice."

"That is all well and good, Clarissa," said I. "But you must now account to me for your condition. I mean how did you . . . that is to say, we never . . . tell me then, who is the father?"

She then gave me a puzzled look that ended in laughter.

"You goose," she whispered, "there is no father. My 'condition,' as you put it, is what it has always been."

"Then you're *not* pregnant?"

"Shh, no, of course not."

"Oh, I'm so glad." And truly, reader, I was glad. I felt as if a great weight had been lifted from me.

Clarissa said naught for a short space of time. And then: "Jeremy, you've no idea how proud I am of you and your praise of me when you did not even know that I was lying."

"Well, I was not completely convinced—just, well, alarmed. But I thought that whatever happened, we would work it out between us. We always will, you know."

"Oh, Jeremy, I'll make a good wife for you. You may be sure of it. Sir John says so himself. He was in on this right from the start. It was his idea to keep you in the dark."

"It was? But why?"

"He thought that you would react more emphatically—and you certainly did react in just such a way. It was all done, you see, to deal with Lady Fielding."

"I don't quite understand," said I.

"Well, you said yourself that Mr. Ogden had asked Elizabeth a question of that sort to plant in the minds of the jurymen that indeed she might be pregnant. I wished to plant in the mind of Lady F that though I may not now be pregnant, I might soon be so, if we two remained living under the same roof and within easy kissing distance."

Whereupon, having spoken thus, she jumped up, ran round the table, and kissed me soundly upon the lips.

"And when will you tell Lady Fielding of your mistake?" I asked.

"Oh, eventually," said she, "eventually."

Now, having all but ended this tale, I offer but two post scripts. The first, relating in a manner to what I have just written, concerns Elizabeth Hooker.

Seven months or a bit less after denying to Mr. Ogden that she was pregnant, she delivered a healthy eight-pound baby boy. Though efforts were made to keep the birth secret, it was not long before the matter was made known to the public by word of mouth. It also became known to the law, and Elizabeth was brought to trial on the charge of perjury. It was all handled very quickly. She might claim—and indeed she did—that she had simply been mistaken in most of what she had said from the witness box—but to be two months pregnant and nevertheless be ignorant of it was more than this jury chose to believe. She was sentenced to five years transportation to the colony of Connecticut, where she was taken into the home of a Methodist minister and worked her time as a servant. Her child was adopted into the Turbott family. Her former employer thus had the son he had long hoped for.

Finally, my second post script is little but a rumor. I heard from Mr. Patley that far up in Yorkshire someone very like Mr. Deuteronomy by description had founded a stud farm. He was happy up there in the north. Pegasus, it was said, was even happier.